THE
Sitter

ROBERT FOWLER

CHAPTER ONE

Tuscany, January 1943

Isolina felt the blanket being eased back, allowing the chilled night air to caress her exposed skin. The rickety wooden bed rocked gently under the strain of another body. Isolina kept her eyes closed: the day had been long and, given the circumstances, she wanted nothing more than to sleep, for tomorrow, like a spoilt child, would take all her attention.

A hand brushed her bare shoulder, and an arm lay heavy across her chest. Yet, her eyes stubbornly refused to open. Outside, the wind grew angry. She focused on the wind and pictured the landscape being battered: the tall chestnut and beech trees bending with the wind's formidable power as it swept over slopping hills and through the fields of wheat, down between the rows of olive vines. Her mind's eye followed its progress across the rich, rustic patchwork quilt that was the Tuscan countryside, before sleep slowly drew her back into its clutches.

'Mamma ...'

How long had she slept? Seconds? She did not respond immediately, knowing the night would be prolonged if she did. Tiredness held her in a firm grip, unwilling to relinquish its dominance.

'Mamma.' Again the voice, soft and melodious, sweet, and yet ... annoying. 'Mamma.' Unless answered, the voice would not go away.

'Sofia ... what is it?' She spoke against the potent pull of sleep.

'Mamma ... the wind woke me and I felt frightened.'

Isolina's hand now rested upon her daughter's thick locks of hair, but her eyes remained shut.

'Come hold me ... go back to sleep.'

'I cannot ... everything is too real.'

Isolina's fingers moved between her daughter's curls.

'What is this nightmare?' she asked in a whisper.

'I saw Papa.'

Isolina felt her own body tense, and the muscles in her neck became taut. 'Go on, Sofia ... tell me.'

'He came back, he was outside my window calling up to me to let him in. He told me he was cold and wet, and that he had walked for a week to be with us.' Sofia's arm drew her mother in.

'Papa is dead, Sofia ... you know that,' Isolina spoke in a whisper.

'Yes, but ... but what if they were wrong?'

'His cousin identified the body, Sofia ... there has been no mistake, child.'

Isolina's hand sought out her daughter's face through the darkness, finally touching her moist skin. She kissed her daughter's cheeks; they tasted of salt. 'Sofia, listen to me.' She pulled the girl closer. 'Papa died two years ago. If ... if a mistake had been made, do you not think he would have returned to see you by now?'

Outside, the wind grew fiercer. Inside, her daughter's sobs similarly intensified.

Sofia's body stilled in time.

'Did Papa love me?'

Isolina held her breath; the blackness in the room concealed her daughter's pain. She found this worrying as Sofia had never talked about her father like this before; never asked such questions.

'Yes, very much …'

'And you, Mamma?'

Isolina bit her bottom lip and felt her chest constrict. 'Yes, Papa was good to me.'

'And did you love him?'

Isolina pulled Sofia's head towards her. Not even the gloom could disguise her uncomfortable response. She was rescued by a loud crash from outside, making both mother and daughter flinch.

'The barn doors,' Isolina whispered, certain she had closed them. But this was not the time to share her concerns. The doors slammed together with another thud.

'I must have left them unlocked,' Isolina lied, while pulling back the warm covers.

'I am certain you –'

'It would not be the first time,' her mother interrupted.

She swung her feet onto the floor, feeling the dampness of the wood. Seeking warmth, she placed one foot upon the other, before standing.

'Don't go, Mamma,' Sofia begged from the darkness.

Isolina disguised her answer with a smile. 'It will only take me a moment to secure the doors … we will not sleep with all that noise otherwise.' She stretched her arm out until her fingers touched the fabric of her coat. 'I will be back and we can cuddle up to sleep.' Sofia remained silent as Isolina draped the coat across her shoulders and felt for her shoes, before making her way towards the stairs.

'Mamma, what if ... what if you find ... someone there?'

'Nonsense, child, who would be out on a night like this?' Isolina stopped at the bottom of the staircase and looked back over her shoulder before removing a loose floorboard with her fingernails. She reached inside the cavity and wrapped her fingers around the butt of a gun. Isolina stood and glanced back through the gloom before continuing to the front door.

~ ~ ~ ~

What had started as a stiff breeze was now a full-blown gale. She pulled the coat tight across her chest as her hair was blown in several directions. She felt for the box of matches in her coat pocket. Above, the clouds obscured an almost full moon.

She moved swiftly towards the barn, touching the handle of the gun for reassurance. A noise from the thicket behind her caused her to spin around and withdraw the gun in a single movement. She waited for whatever it was to show itself, her arm outstretched and shaking with the weight of the weapon. Nothing moved except the wind. Feeling foolish, she replaced the gun in her coat pocket while removing strands of hair from her mouth and eyes. Ahead, she saw the unlocked barn doors swaying in the wind. She reached them just as another large gust arrived, forcing her to use her body to keep them from slamming together. Again, she felt certain

6

she had locked them earlier. A deep anxiety began to grow within her.

She let the doors gently come together but remained outside, listening closely for any sounds from within. Maybe the strength of the wind had dislodged the handle? She dismissed that theory instantly: she was searching for answers created out of fear. That meant only one thing: someone or something had got inside, and could still be there. She removed the gun from her pocket and gripped the handle firmly.

She eased back one of the doors, to be met by a solid wall of darkness. She looked back up at the moon, hoping the clouds would clear enough to brighten the night. Taking a deep breath, she stepped inside and stood silent, moistening her lips with her tongue. The wind sounded melodic as it passed through the wooden structure, while outside, branches creaked and leaves rattled in the gale.

She saw it just as her eyes adjusted to the darkness. A human form lay sprawled across the floor, motionless. Isolina placed the gun on an old wooden table and fished out the box of matches. Grabbing one of the nearby rusty lanterns, she struck a match. Moments later, a flickering yellow flame lit up the barn. As if on cue, in that instance, the door behind her creaked. Isolina reached for the gun ... Sofia screamed.

'Sofia,' Isolina gasped, 'what are you doing here?'

'I was scared ... sorry ...'

Isolina pulled her daughter close. It was only then that the girl saw the body on the floor.

'Mamma ...' she gasped.

'Shh ... I know.'

'Is ...?'

'I do not know,' Isolina whispered, loosening her grip. 'Wait here.'

'Mamma …' there was pleading in Sofia's voice.

Isolina placed a finger across her lips. A dozen steps later, she stood over the motionless figure. It was only then that she realised she did not have the gun. She knelt by the man. He was young and, to her relief, his skin felt warm and his pulse strong. She wiped her brow, knowing this was only the beginning of their problems.

'Bring over the lantern, Sofia.' Her eyes assessed the man, noticing the odd angle of his right leg.

'Mamma –'

'Now, Sofia, please.'

The girl reluctantly brought the lantern to her mother. Holding it aloft, Isolina let the light spread over the man. He wore no uniform. Instead, a thick, dark brown coat covered a lighter brown suit. His white shirt was tieless and his shoes were caked in mud. He had almost certainly come across the fields.

She inspected the leg further. It was, as she suspected, broken just above the ankle. Just as she gently placed a hand on it, the barn was filled with a piercing scream. Sofia threw herself at her mother, adding her own shrill cry.

'Mamma … Mamma.'

'I am sorry,' Isolina whispered, looking at the man.

He clamped his hands to his face and let out another muffled cry. As the pain subsided, he finally managed to speak, but not in Italian.

'Sofia, go and fetch my bag, please.'

'But Mamma … what if –'

'Sofia, do as I say.'

The girl ran off into the shadows.

'I am a nurse and I may have some morphine … but you will need proper medical care.'

'No … please.' The man suddenly switched to fluent Italian. 'I am English.'

Isolina stared at him through the gloom; this changed everything. As Sofia returned with the bag, Isolina turned and smiled at her, hoping to calm her.

'There is nothing to worry about, Sofia, I promise.' She placed her hand on her daughter's cheek before kissing it. 'I love you. I would never let anything harm you.' She then stared down at the stranger and shivered.

CHAPTER TWO

Isolina opened her eyes, although tiredness tried to force them shut again. She focused on the sleeping girl next to her, but her thoughts returned to the night just gone, and the Englishman in the barn. She had used her last shot of morphine to ease his pain, but knew it was only a temporary measure. He needed specialist help to set his leg, which meant seeking out Simon.

She carefully slipped from beneath the covers, attempting not to wake her daughter in the process. It had been a traumatic night for the young girl, and sleep would hopefully help ease her anxiety. Isolina looked down but resisted the urge to kiss her. Placing her coat over her shoulders, she moved swiftly towards the staircase, glancing back at her daughter before descending.

On reaching the bottom step, she looked down to where the gun lay hidden. She decided against taking it: there was something harmless about the stranger. Isolina stepped out to a grey, chilly Tuscan morning. She took a deep breath and headed towards the barn.

As she walked, she did up the buttons on her coat while surveying last night's storm damage. Vines in the nearest field lay on the ground, while broken branches surrounded a large chestnut tree. A fencepost lay at right angles, and several slates were missing from the roof of the house. She stopped as she reached the two large, rotting wooden doors. The rusting hinges squealed as she pulled them open and gazed inside.

She pulled one door back a little further. The sound of a bird scampering across the roof made her heart race. Otherwise, only silence greeted her. Isolina pulled one of the doors to, whilst leaving the other partially open, allowing enough watery daylight into the gloomy interior. The rich, overpowering smell of damp hay wafted to her nostrils. The man was still covered in the blanket Sofia had fetched last night, and had not moved.

She felt pride in her daughter. They had had to work quickly, while the morphine was at its most effective, to place a splint on the broken bone. She had straightened his leg, knowing that it went against everything she had been taught, but needs must. With the aid of two cut-down broom handles, part of a fencepost and strips of linen, they finally managed to achieve their goal.

The Englishman had screamed and used words that meant nothing to her. Looking into her daughter's eyes, she'd seen the anxiety, yet she observed Sofia doing everything that was asked of her. Every touch brought a louder cry, until tears flowed from both the Englishman and her daughter. Sofia could not bear to look at him, choosing instead to stare into the darkness, while the noise of the wind helped to muffle his cries.

Isolina approached the man and knelt beside him, and took her first long look at his face. He was young, twenty-five, no more. It was a boyish, attractive face, soft and welcoming, unlike the harsh faces of many around the village.

Tiny bristles grew in isolated clusters, thicker around his chin than anywhere else. His brown hair resembled a bowl of spaghetti. She smiled: he was unkempt, like a young schoolboy. Suddenly his eyes opened: hazel eyes; somehow, she had known they would be. He took a deep breath and arched his back as a spasm of pain attacked his leg. Letting out a cry, tears of agony left those hazel eyes. She resisted the urge to wipe them away.

He stared at her. 'Morphine,' he pleaded.

'No … I have no more … sorry.'

His Italian was excellent; his voice seemed younger than his years.

'Please … the pain.'

'You must listen to me …' She leant forward and felt the warmth of his breath. 'What is your name?'

'Will telling you my name get rid of the pain in my leg?'

'No …'

'Then why ask?' Another tear ran down his cheek.

'Let me fetch you some water.'

'Morphine.'

'Water – but I need to call you something, so please give me your name. Lie if you want to, but allow me to call you something.'

'Richard … Richard Mason. There, happy now?' He tried to stifle another scream and turned his face away from her to spit into the dust. He clenched his jaw and looked back up at her.

'Richard, you must be seen by a doctor. I can only do so much for you. I am just a nurse.'

He moved his hand from under the blanket and grabbed her wrist. 'No doctor,' he whispered, his eyes wild, beads of sweat forming on his face. '*No doctor!*'

Isolina remained calm. 'That's fine with me … but I must move you.'

'Move me?'

'Yes, I cannot have a spy dying on my farm. They would think I had something to do with you. If you want to die so much, do it off my land.'

He continued to stare at her face, holding her wrist. Finally, he released it.

'How foolish men can be,' she spoke in a whisper. 'If not treated, there is a chance you will get gangrene … blood poisoning … and you will die, Mr Mason. It's as simple as that. Whatever you have come here to do, you will not get the chance to do it.'

He winced before speaking, 'Can the doctor be trusted?'

'First ask yourself: do you trust me?'

'Yes.'

'Good, so you have a brain after all.'

Richard Mason smiled through gritted teeth.

Isolina returned with a cup of cold water. 'I am sorry about the pain, but I will go and get the doctor. Then we will begin the process of healing you, but you will have to endure it a little longer, I'm afraid.'

'I understand.'

'While I am gone, these barn doors will remain closed … no one will come here.'

'How can you be certain?'

'I can't … you just have to trust.' She smiled at him before walking away.

'What is *your* name?' Mason shouted across the barn.

'Isolina.'

'*Isolina*,' he whispered, 'very beautiful …'

She turned and slipped between the doors without answering him.

~ ~ ~ ~

'Mamma.' Sofia stood at the bottom of the stairs. 'It's cold.'

'Then put some clothes on, child.'

'Where have you been? To see …?'

'Yes … now listen to me, Sofia.' She moved across the room and wrapped her arms around her daughter. 'No school this morning …'

Sofia smiled.

'But you can go after lunch.'

'But … do I –'

'Yes, you do. Now, do not leave the house while I am gone.'

'Where are you going?'

'To get Simon. Please listen: do not go near the barn and do not leave the house. I will be as quick as I can – promise me you will do as I ask?'

Sofia nodded reluctantly. 'Will he live?' she asked.

'Yes, I think so.'

'Good.'

CHAPTER THREE

Tuscany in January painted a rural setting in soft pastel colours. An idyllic countryside canvas that looked better when painted in watercolour and not oil. This morning, a misty greyness hung low, but the land remained easy on the eye. It was unspoiled and tranquil, except for the roads that were full of deep potholes. Isolina Donatelli sat upright, head forward, as if she were short-sighted. She hated driving, hated the grinding noise that leapt from the engine. She whispered obscenities as another wheel fell into another deep cavity. She feared this road and this car more than any Blackshirt or Nazi soldier.

Her gaze fell on the petrol gauge. She tapped the glass but quickly returned her hand to the steering wheel. The joints of her fingers ached from gripping the wheel with such intensity. She did not judge the petrol gauge by litres, but by the number of journeys to and from the village. She knew there wasn't enough petrol to get to Florence, and that annoyed her.

Isolina prayed that Simon had not left early today, and she was soon calmed when she saw his car. As usual, it was parked a good distance from the curb. She smiled: his poor eyesight would cause an accident one day. She parked opposite, glad that her journey was over for now.

Her heart skipped a beat as fingers tapped against the window. She switched off the engine just as Luca Tucci's face appeared. He was unshaven and his bloodshot eyes stared back at her. As always, a cigarette protruded from between his lips; the tip grew bright red as he drew on it. He turned and walked away from the car. Isolina got out and briefly glanced across to the doctor's house before following the young man.

'Morning, Luca, early for you.'

'Yes …' He took in another lungful of smoke before dropping the stub to the ground. 'I hear some children have arrived at Fino's.'

'Yes, from Genoa. Sent by the Red Cross.'

'Perhaps when you visit them, you might take a moment to see another.'

Isolina took a deep breath. *Please, God, not another complication*, she thought.

'Who am I to see, Luca?'

'A friend.'

'An anti-Fascist like yourself, Luca, I suspect.'

'Perhaps.' Luca withdrew another cigarette, lit it, and blew the smoke skyward.

'Do not involve me in your war, Luca.'

'You *are* involved … all of Italy is, Isolina. Turin and Genoa have been bombed; it has begun, and soon the war will be on our own doorstep.'

Isolina thought about the Englishman in her barn. Yes, the war was getting closer, much closer than the young man in front of her knew.

He blew another cloud of smoke into the morning air. 'Tunisia will fall soon, then Sicily will be invaded by the Allies … Rome will be next –'

'Yes, Luca, I understand,' Isolina interrupted. She turned upon hearing the doctor's front door open and close.

Simon stood buttoning up his coat as she walked towards him, still speaking to Luca, but not directly. 'I will be at Fino's at two.'

Luca dipped his head in acknowledgment and walked away, hunched against the early morning chill.

'Isolina,' smiled Dr Simon Stein, scrutinising her. 'To what do I owe this pleasure?'

'I need to speak to you.'

'Why do I feel a drop in temperature when I have just put my coat on?'

Isolina returned the old man's smile; he had a dry sense of humour, even in these trying times.

'I awoke last night to find I had an unwanted guest in my barn.'

'I gather this guest has two and not four legs.'

'One and a half, to be precise.'

The doctor gave her an odd look.

'A break above the ankle.'

'Uh. I see ... is he ...? I guess it is a man. Is he a native of Tuscany, or –'

Isolina filled in the gap, 'He is English ... and not in uniform.'

'I understand. Your car or mine?'

~ ~ ~ ~

Isolina drove back to the farm with Simon. He sat in the passenger seat, gripping the door handle, all colour drained from his face.

'Is he at death's door, Isolina?'

'No, but he is in much pain.'

'Then … why are we risking our own lives?'

'Pardon?'

'Our speed, child … I am seventy, and, if possible, I would like to see seventy-one. There is nothing I can do about the Germans, but I am sure you could cut your speed.'

'Sorry.' Isolina gently raised her foot from the accelerator and began to laugh. 'I am sorry, Simon … really.'

'I thought we were being pursued by bandits.' He smiled but his hand remained on the door handle. 'I would like to have talked about your guest, but it might be best if you concentrate fully on your driving.' They looked at each other and grinned.

Sofia greeted them with a smile and waited patiently for the engine to cease growling.

'Morning, Sofia,' said the doctor, emerging from the car. 'Your beauty grows with each day.'

Isolina looked at him. 'Flattery, doctor?'

'I find a little helps … our patient …'

'Follow me … Sofia, make some coffee please. It's under the floorboard at the end of my bed.'

'So, you don't just keep guns under the floorboards.'

'Sofia!' Isolina's look was firm, with no trace of a smile.

Simon Stein glanced from the girl to mother, loath to immerse himself in a family spat. Isolina composed herself and looked at the doctor.

'Do you want me to bring the coffee into the barn?' Sofia asked.

'Leave it to heat, we won't need it straightaway.'

'Mamma,' Sofia called out, 'sorry!'

Isolina turned to stare at her daughter before continuing towards the barn.

'Children,' the doctor muttered before quickening his pace to keep up with Isolina.

Inside the barn, they stood in silence. Isolina kept both doors partially open to let in what little light the overcast sky allowed, but the inside remained gloomy. Both took a moment to adjust to their surroundings before the doctor approached what looked like a pile of clothing. He looked down as the man opened his eyes.

Damp from sweat, the man's hair stuck to his face, which was colourless and full of discomfort. The doctor knelt and pulled back the blanket before reaching into his bag for a pair of scissors. Holding the blanket to one side, he cut the strings that held the make-shift splint in place.

'You have done well, Isolina. The ties are a good distance away from the fracture.' He nodded his head in approval. 'And not too tight … perfect.'

'I had a good teacher.'

'That you did …' he whispered, smiling. Addressing Richard, he continued, 'No open wound. How very lucky you are, young man.'

The Englishman said nothing, but his eyes never left the doctor's face.

'I am going to give you a shot of morphine, then we will go to work. Nevertheless, you may feel a little pain … and it may not be pleasant.'

Richard Mason had been listening to the doctor. 'You are not Italian,' he stated, wincing as another surge of pain engulfed him.

'Uh … you can detect it, can you?' Simon Stein held the syringe up into the half-light. 'Frankfurt, if you must know … a small village –' He did not get the chance to finish.

'You're German ...' Mason looked up at Isolina with anger in his eyes. 'You double-crossed me, bitch ... why?'

Simon found a vein and injected.

'You have not been double-crossed ... and refrain from using such words. Yes, I am a German.' Simon Stein looked into Mason's eyes. 'I am a German Jew. I live here because my life in Frankfurt was a living hell ... I am a Jew and, to other Germans, I am the scum of the earth. Soon, I will have to leave here ... my second home, a place I have grown fond of, like its people.' He looked up at Isolina, then back at the Englishman. 'Soon they will come for me, not because I am the enemy like you, but because I am a Jew. So, rest assured, it is me they will take first ... not you.'

Richard Mason felt the pain subside, but shame quickly took its place. He watched the old man as he worked away at his leg. Simon was also talking to the woman. They were both working towards one aim: to save his leg. Yet, it was his soul that needed saving at that moment. A restless sleep finally gave him some respite from his humiliation.

They went about their work over the next hour, putting together a crude supporting splint using torn sheets, string and more wood. Finally, with the job done, they left the barn. Outside, Isolina accepted a cigarette from Simon and inhaled deeply; it tasted good. She only smoked when things were chaotic, like now. The doctor lit his own and drew in the smoke before turning to face her.

'Be careful ... these are dangerous times for Italy. It is changing and we are living at a turning point in history and, so often at times such as these, it is the innocent that suffer.'

'Why my barn?' asked Isolina.

'It is what it is. Soon we will not know who the enemy is. They will come in many disguises ... like they did in the thirties in my country. Who is the enemy? The Nazis ... the Fascists ... the Vatican ... even your neighbours, maybe ... Luca Tucci, who I saw you talking to this morning.'

'Not Luca, Simon ...'

'Why, child, why not him? Right now, you are useful to him. Did he ask you for a favour this morning? Yes, I thought so, your face cannot lie. You are useful to him now ... but, one day, you will become expendable.'

A shiver ran up Isolina's spine.

'Why did you not tell Luca about your British spy?'

'I – I just thought it would be for the best.'

'Best for whom? Him?' Simon turned to face the barn. 'Or best for you?'

Isolina dropped her cigarette and put it out.

'You were right to say nothing, Isolina,' said the doctor, stamping out his own. 'It is best you tell no one yet, not until he is mobile again, which may take six or seven weeks at least I'm afraid.'

'That long?'

Simon Stein walked towards the small picket fence that overlooked where the valley fell away.

'What a wonderful view. Whoever's God made this should be thanked – mine, yours, who cares. It was made with love and I just pray war will not come and turn such beauty into a wasteland.'

'Do you know they are rounding up Jews in Florence?' Isolina asked.

'Yes, I have been told that. But you, what has Luca asked of you?'

'To see a friend.'

'No doubt he carries an injury.'

'More than likely.'

'Strange … the more we try to stay out of this war, the stronger it pulls us in.' The old man stared out over the hillside, across fields of brown and beige and down through straight rows of Cyprus trees. A church steeple could be seen in the distance, nestling between hills. To Simon, it felt like a dream, and yet, it felt like he was looking at this humbling scene for the last time.

'And, so it begins again … I left Germany in 1933, ten years ago now.' He reached for his cigarettes; Isolina politely declined a second. 'Hitler had come to power and the war against the Jews had begun. Did you know he blamed the loss of the First World War on us, a mere five hundred thousand people in a county of forty-two million? Can you imagine that? Yet, the people believed him and one per cent of the nation took the blame.' Simon Stein laughed and shifted his gaze from the splendour laid out before him.

'I came to Italy to make another life: Mussolini himself, as well as the people, held a different view. Did you know that the Jews helped Mussolini to power?' He turned to Isolina and wagged his finger. 'I bet you did not know that, child. I read an article in a paper once that said: in Italy, there is absolutely no difference between a Jew and a non-Jew, in every field from religion to politics … Il Duce himself, Mussolini, said that.'

'Where will you go, Simon?'

'I have a cousin in Canada … but –' His eyes sparkled with unshed tears.

Isolina felt his pain and looked away. 'You must think about going soon,' she said, placing a hand upon his shoulder. 'As you said, things are changing fast, and one Englishman is not enough. We'll need a whole army of them.'

Simon smiled.

Sofia was just leaving the house holding two cups of coffee, when a cry emanated from inside the barn. Simon and Isolina rushed past and ran into the barn. The Englishman was sitting up, awake and reaching for his jacket, which had brought on another bout of pain.

'Let me do that,' Isolina said walking across to him.

'What have you done?' Richard asked Simon.

'Saved your life … and your leg.' Simon Stein stood behind Isolina. 'It was a good break, luckily for you.'

'A *good* break?' Richard Mason whispered with some sarcasm.

'Yes, otherwise you would have needed surgery, something I could not do, and you'd be at greater risk than you are now. So, yes, a good break.'

'How long before I can be on my way?' the Englishman asked.

'Six to eight weeks.'

'I don't want to be here for six days, let alone six weeks.'

Stein placed the cigarette back between his lips.

'Could you spare one?' asked Mason.

The doctor smiled and held out the pack to the young man. Mason rested his head back and enjoyed the pleasure it gave him: it was his first in three days and was just what he needed. He looked up at the old man and blew out a cloud of smoke.

'I'm sorry.'

'Sorry?'

'For what I said … I'm grateful to you, sir, I meant no disrespect.'

'I feel your apology is directed at the wrong person. It is this woman who you really owe your life to.'

Mason looked up into the face of Isolina Donatelli, making him draw breath sharply: the woman was simply quite stunning.

'He is right, let me first thank *you* … I hope you have it in you to forgive a stupid Englishman. It is not an excuse, but I was cold, tired and in pain … as well as scared. But I should not have said what I did. I am sorry.'

'Apology accepted,' she smiled. Her jet-black hair rested in curls on her shoulders.

A stab of pain hit Mason. 'Can you give me anything?'

'Yes, but not yet. I will leave a little here for Isolina to administer when the pain is bad. In time, the pain will lessen. Do not put any weight on it, any weight at all – understand? Stupidity, not the Nazis, will be your downfall if so.'

'Is one for me?' Mason asked.

The doctor and Isolina looked puzzled until they followed Mason's stare. Sofia stood in the doorway with two cups of coffee.

'Yes,' said Isolina. 'Would you like something to eat?'

'That would be very nice … thank you.'

'And you, Simon?'

'This coffee will do.'

Isolina moved towards the doorway, where a transfixed Sofia gawked at the Englishman. Isolina smiled: the man was very handsome. She took the mugs and handed them to the men before seizing her daughter's arm to leave the barn.

A concerned Simon Stein observed and followed. But now another worry troubled him: the car ride home.

CHAPTER FOUR

Leaving Sofia to keep Simon company while he had his coffee, she filled a large bowl with her homemade vegetable soup for the Englishman, and placed a sizeable piece of moist bread next to it. Richard Mason greeted her with a welcoming smile, but his face exhibited a great deal of pain as he attempted to sit upright.

'Here.' She gently placed the wooden tray across his lap.

'Thank you,' he said, hastily tearing off a chunk of bread.

She watched him fill his mouth; she had not realised the extent of his hunger.

'Sorry,' he said, dragging his hand across his mouth, 'I have not eaten for best part of three days … and this is the best soup I have ever tasted.'

'Do not worry,' Isolina replied, 'Italian women enjoy watching people eat what they have cooked.'

Mason ran more bread around the bowl and Isolina used the silence to speak.

'You will be alone soon, and I will secure the doors … no one will come, of that I am certain.' She leant against a wooden upright. 'When I come back, I will bring you fresh clothing and soap to wash.'

'Please don't go to too much trouble, you have done enough already.' He spoke as he swallowed the last of the soup.

'It is no trouble.'

Richard Mason looked at the woman, his eyes following the ridge of her cheeks, the high bone structure set below her eyes that promoted her beauty. Suddenly, he became aware of the silence around him.

'Sorry ... but you are so ...' He stopped.

'I am so?'

'Attractive ...' He felt his face turn crimson. 'Sorry, I was brought up to be truthful at all times ... my mother's influence I'm afraid.'

'Then it must be difficult being a spy.'

He laughed and looked away.

'Can I ask ...?' He looked back at her.

'Go on,' she said.

'How old are you?'

'Didn't your mother never teach you not to ask a woman her age?'

'Sorry ... I'm saying that word a lot, so it seems.'

Isolina smiled. 'I must be going now.' On her way to the wooden doors, she stopped. 'Uh – nearly forgot.' She picked up a bottle with a large neck and walked back to where the Englishman lay. 'Here.' She handed it to him. 'We will be gone for several hours,' she told him as she returned to the doors. 'Thirty-seven,' she said, closing the doors behind her.

Mason heard the noise of a chain, and allowed a smile to slowly surface.

~ ~ ~ ~

Isolina drove slowly back to the village and dropped off the doctor first. Sofia climbed into the front seat and, five minutes later, kissed her mother's cheeks before hopping out of the car. Isolina cast a worried glance at the petrol gauge – although, the young Englishman in her barn was a far greater concern. Simon and Luca were right: no one, not even the children at Sassa's, would remain untouched by this war.

Fino's wife, Sassa, greeted her with arms wide open, theatrical as usual and a little overwhelming. Sixty-three-year-old Swedish Sassa was an eccentric with a larger-than-life character, and a heart of gold. She and Fino lived in a large villa set in its own grounds, surrounded by woodland, farmland and hills. The main villa had nine bedrooms and sat next to three large outbuildings, as well as stables. Two of the outbuildings had been converted into dormitories, while the other was to become a small clinic.

Fino Zotti was a self-made millionaire in his late sixties. He had made his money during the twenties and thirties, before selling his business interests. He had the enthusiasm of a much younger man, and his love for Sassa was unquestionable. He had married her twenty-five years before, after both had lost their original partners. Countless times, Isolina had seen them strolling hand in hand, much like a young couple in love. It was rumoured that they had lost a child in pregnancy and were unable to have more children.

Isolina often caught Fino staring at his wife, his eyes full of sadness, and felt certain the loss of that child weighed heavily on them, even now. Maybe it was the reason Sassa loved children so much. She lavished so much love on them, including Sofia, whom she spoilt, much to Isolina's annoyance. And the chance to take in a dozen evacuees from Genoa could not be passed up.

'Isolina, you look tired,' Sassa said as the two approached each other. She stopped suddenly and backed away a little to get a better look of her. 'Yes … very tired.'

'A bad night?'

'Just one?' Sassa placed an arm around her waist.

Isolina smiled: the woman missed nothing.

'Come, let me show you the children … Rosa,' Sassa turned to a woman in a maid's uniform who was collecting cups from a table, 'coffee please. Bring it to where the children are.'

'Si, signora.'

The children sat either side of a long trestle table with half-full bowls of warm soup in front of them. Italian refugees … what next? Isolina stared at the bewildered, dirt-stained faces and smiled. She received nothing in the way of a response; instead they remained stony-faced and seated, some on the knee of one of Sassa's staff. Their ages ranged from four to six.

'Some have lived below ground for two months, not seeing daylight in all that time. In fact, some only emerged yesterday.' Sassa placed a hand on a child's head. 'They tell me the British have been bombing day and night.'

'They are so thin, Sassa.'

'Yes … there can't have been much to eat down there. Some of them have lost their parents,' she whispered, 'but the children do not know this.' Sassa's eyes glazed over. 'Look at me … how silly.'

'Poor things,' whispered Isolina.

'Most were dehydrated and we have given them plenty of water, but I need you to look at the boils and sores some have acquired.'

'Yes, let me begin.'

'Your coffee?'

'It can wait, these children cannot.' Isolina placed her bag on the table as a blue-eyed girl came over and stared at her. Isolina smiled, but she was still unable to prise out any response. She crouched and stared directly into eyes that radiated fear. How could this be – barely on this earth for five minutes and already fearful of those around her?

'What is your name, little one?'

The girl remained silent. Isolina licked her thumb and wiped away dirt stains from an almost unblemished cheek. It reminded her to take soap and water to the Englishman.

'Are we to play a game?' Isolina placed her face close to the child's. 'Your name is … Michaela?' Nothing. 'Then I will try one more. Let me see … what about Sofia?' Nothing. Isolina abandoned the game and gently took hold of the child. She was undernourished and her legs were covered in boils and cuts. Thick dirt sat between her toes, and her clothes smelt of dried urine. The room's hushed silence was suddenly disturbed by a large metal pot crashing to the tiled floor. It sent the children into fits of panic, screaming and crying as the explosion of noise reverberated around the walls. The young girl buried her head in Isolina's chest and her tiny fingers gripped her coat.

'Shhh, little one, you are safe here.' Isolina stroked the girl's blonde hair.

'Mamma … Mamma, I want my Mamma.' It began with one child, but soon, all were shouting and screaming for mothers, fathers, brothers, or any other absent family members. Isolina swallowed the giant lump that had risen into her throat.

'Here – your coffee.' Sassa placed a cup next to her. 'Heart-breaking, is it not?'

The child would not release her grip and continued sobbing, soaking Isolina's coat with her tears.

'They have no idea what is going on, what this is all about,' Sassa said while resting a hand on the girl's head. 'This is supposed to be the best time of their life. What will these children remember of it and what will become of this world. There must be rooms full of children just like this all over Europe, children who will never know what being a child is like. To feel loved, to run and play with friends without fear … to be children, just children. And all because of a few crazy men.'

Sassa went across to a stack of toys and began to distribute them. Slowly the cries quietened, the tears slowed, and the children began to play.

'Bedtime will be the next major problem, I fear,' Sassa said, standing.

Isolina moved from one child to another, smiling, hoping for some response. Instead, she received despairing looks.

'Tomorrow, you will have coffee first. I have thrown away two today – but thank you, Isolina, thank you from the bottom of my heart. Here …' she handed her a banknote.

'No, not today … today was –'

'Your petrol, not your time, Isolina. Please take it.'

~ ~ ~

She walked slowly towards her mud-stained car, expecting to see Luca next to it. It was already two o'clock; she would wait five minutes and then go back to see to the Englishman. Tired, she lost the fight to keep her eyes open. Ten minutes later, she awoke, feeling just as tired. She had waited long enough, and switched on the engine. The car began to make its way down the long muddy drive, when, without warning, Luca appeared out of nowhere, forcing her to brake hard. With the car now at a standstill and the engine ticking over, Isolina rested her head on the steering wheel. He stood staring at her through the front windscreen, smoking.

Isolina laid her head back, breathing a sigh of relief. The passenger door opened and he got in.

'Drive.'

'Are you crazy, Luca ... what if I had not –'

'Drive. We are late.'

She drove, uncertain of where they were going. He remained silent, only issuing instructions every now and then. Suddenly, he ordered her to turn right, up a dirt track. She navigated it with difficulty, with the car bouncing and sinking into deep ruts.

'Stop!' shouted Luca, without warning. 'We go on foot from here, bring your bag.'

'But my car ...'

'Look around ... who the hell is going to steal it?'

Luca seemed agitated, but she followed him like he asked. The wood became denser before they reached a small clearing. Luca whistled like a bird and a like response came from behind her. A moment later, a man appeared, carrying a shotgun over his shoulder.

'Luca.'

'Enzo.'

The two hugged.

'Come.'

'How is he?'

Enzo, the man carrying the shotgun, looked at Isolina, not answering Luca's question. They moved deeper into the woods. Isolina was desperate to ask where they were going, but knew that she would not receive an answer. Finally, they reached what looked like some sort of camp. Smoke drifted up from the remains of a fire and a rusty kettle hung from a tripod. Sheeting was spread between trees and over bushes to form shelters. It was a crude attempt made by people who were uncertain of what they were doing. She shivered, feeling the cold. The stove at Sassa's house had warmed her, but here, she felt the harsh Tuscan winter burrow under her clothing.

'Here,' said Enzo, the shotgun was now in his hands. He pointed towards a man lying under a sheeted canopy, covered from head to foot in dirty blankets. She thought of the Englishman.

'His name is Tino ... he has a wound and a fever.'

Isolina knelt and pulled back one of the filthy blankets. The man tried to conjure up a smile, but failed. After removing the crudely wrapped bandages, she saw just how badly infected the wound was.

'A bullet passed through his side, and he has become feverish these past few days,' muttered Enzo, a lump of cheese entering his mouth.

'I'm not surprised – everything in contact with the wound is filthy. What do you expect?'

'I expect you to help him.' Enzo leant forward and placed his face close to hers. 'Do you understand?'

He stood, replacing the cheese with a cigarette. She opened her bag. 'Start the fire,' she ordered.

'Why?'

'Just do as I say.'

'Aldo, do it.' Enzo ordered.

She set about cleaning the wound as best she could, throwing the old bandages onto the newly built fire, followed by the man's clothes.

'He will freeze to death,' shouted a man.

'He has more chance of dying from blood poisoning. If you are his friends, you will find him some clean clothes.' She did not look up but continued to work on the man's injury. She would do her best, the rest was down to luck.

A new bandage covered the wound and another was left for later.

'Burn every bandage you use, best to be on the safe side. Give him these tonight.' She held out three small white pills. 'They will make him sleep, that is what will help him. Rest, and lots of water … not wine.'

'We will do as you say,' said Enzo, placing the shotgun down.

'Yes, thank you.'

A voice came from behind her, a voice she instantly recognised. It was one she had not heard for quite some time. She turned in its direction.

'Hello, Isolina.'

'Silvano.' Isolina felt the breath leave her lungs. The tall man smiled and drew on his cigarette before flicking it away. It had been almost seven years since she had last laid eyes on him. He had lost some weight in that time, but still had his chiselled good looks, the Roman nose, and that smile that had snared her first time.

'How have you been?' he asked, walking towards her.

She wondered if he was going to sweep her into his arms, but that was just self-delusion.

'Fine.'

'I heard about you're ... Fausto ... My condolences.'

Isolina felt her eyes moisten but not for a dead husband – no, they were tears founded in anger, betrayal, deceit and lies.

'Do not say things you do not mean, Silvano. I thought you might have changed by now, but it seems a leopard does not change his spots.' She picked up her bag. 'Come, Luca.'

'Stay, Luca, I will walk her back to the car.'

'Please yourself.' Isolina strode away from the group with purpose.

'Isolina,' Silvano shouted.

'What?' she replied, her voice full of irritation.

'It is this way.' He stood pointing in the opposite direction.

Red-faced, she heard sniggers coming from those sat around the fire. She did not respond.

'Take that smirk off your face,' she whispered, walking by his side, 'It does not suit you.'

It was a full minute before either of them spoke again.

'Thank you for coming, I know you had work to do with the children Sassa has taken in,' Silvano said.

'Believe me, if I had been given a choice I ... How long have you been here?'

'Two months.'

'Why here, Silvano? Why here ...?'

'In war, you have no say on when or where ... I'm sorry.'

Silvano smiled and removed a pack of cigarettes from his top pocket. 'Here,' he offered her one, 'do you still have the odd one?'

She refused, then cursed herself for doing so. The smoke drifted across her face, making her all the more irritable. The chilly north wind, the Tramontana, swept across the exposed uplands.

'What happened to him?' Isolina wished she had not asked.

'We were out the other night looking ...'

'Looking?'

'For a British man who had been dropped.'

She stopped and turned to face him. How attractive he still was ... *Bastard*. 'For what reason?'

'To help us ...'

'Us?'

'The Partisans, so we will be ready for when they invade Italy.' He sucked on his cigarette. 'Our job will be to hinder the German retreat and to tackle the Fascist bastards that have ruined our county, along with their Nazi masters.'

'No more, you have told me too much, I do not want to get involved.'

'You will have your part to play in this too, Isolina, it will not go around you, or over or under your house.'

'So everyone tells me.'

She now had one thought in her head: was the man Silvano was looking for in her barn? Surely not.

'Tell me, did you find him?' Isolina prayed they had.

Silvano gave her a strange look. 'No, we found just his radio set under some bushes, it was untouched ... We have it with us now, but not the knowledge to use it.'

'Maybe *they* have him.' Isolina knew she was clutching at straws.

'No.'

'How can you be certain?'

'That Blackshirt, Bernardo Forni, would be screaming out his success from the top of the Duomo.'

Suddenly, Isolina saw Florence: the green façade, the golden doors – and a loving arm wrapped around her waist. The hotel ... the Arno ... and the moment she wanted it to swallow her up.

'I see.'

'Do you?'

She began to walk away. *Tell him*, she said to herself ... *Tell him you have the Englishman.* But she said nothing.

They reached her car.

'You know your way back?' he asked.

'Yes. I'm fine, don't worry.'

'I do.'

Isolina looked into his blue eyes and was as captivated as she'd been the first time. 'How is Nicia? I hear you and –'

'It is over. Three years ago now ... our marriage was never going to work after –'

'I'm sorry,' she interrupted.

'You were the honest one, Isolina, be so now.'

'I did not hate Nicia. I did not know her.'

'We both knew what we wanted.'

'Don't fool yourself, Silvano.' She needed to be gone. The dam was beginning to crumble and she was determined not to give him that satisfaction. She walked around the car and threw the bag inside before climbing in herself. Silvano stood silent. She started the engine and put the car into reverse. The noise of gears grinding together echoed through the wood. She cursed under her breath as she struggled to bring it into forward gear. Unable to resist, she quickly glanced up – he had not moved. Once around the first bend, she brought the car to a halt, unable to see through the waterfall of tears.

CHAPTER FIVE

Mason's leg felt as if it had been placed inside a pot of boiling water, the pain was unbearable. Part of him wished they had cut it off. Having drunk almost all the water, he'd brought on more problems. He had stared at the bottle for almost an hour, before finally, with his bladder at bursting point, he had filled it. He lay back, grateful and contented, with the bottle of yellow liquid next to him. Exhausted, he closed his eyes, but moments later, a nagging, anxious thought forced them open again. 'The bloody radio!' he said aloud, and instantly began to go over the events of the night he landed.

He had practised falling on coconut mats at least a hundred times, from both balloons and, finally, planes. Not once did he pick up an injury, not a scratch, but now look at him. And, to add insult to injury, God knows where in Tuscany he had ended up. It had started so well, being dropped in the correct location, a mile from the rendezvous zone.

Richard Mason closed his eyes and recalled the moment his legs came into contact with the ground. He knew then that something was wrong. As he tried to stand, the pain hit him like a train and he collapsed. He had lain in total darkness for hours, trying to figure out how he was going to move with a radio set strapped to his back. He found a sturdy branch with a convenient 'Y' shape to it, and adjusted its length with his knife.

With the aid of this self-made crutch to keep him upright, he clasped the radio and lifted it. Just two hops later, he knew it wasn't going to work, so he decided to hide the set under some thick bushes. He then set off in, what he hoped was, the direction of the rendezvous. Less than a mile later, he detected movement up ahead. It was too soon to have come across his welcoming committee; these were Italian or German troops.

He lay flat for an hour. The dampness slowly soaked into his clothes and the smell of moist earth wafted up his nostrils. The pain in his leg increased; he clenched his teeth and felt for his cigarettes. *Shit.* The pack was missing. He quickly felt for the cash and was relieved to find it was still there. For an hour, he lay watching shadows. What if the welcoming Partisans came looking for him? They would walk straight into this group, whoever they were. The intense pain made it hard to think clearly, and soon after, he passed out.

He awoke to the sound of gunshots. Startled, he fumbled for his gun, only to find that it, too, was missing. Suddenly, he heard voices close by, while more gunshots exploded in the darkness. Screams followed; it sounded as if a man was hurt. He began to panic: he was too close to the action. Using the cover of darkness to retreat, he got to his feet with the aid of his crutch and moved as fast as he could in the opposite direction to the gunfire.

It was ten minutes before the shooting stopped. Now, the only sound was his own breathing. His heart pounded and sweat soaked into his already damp clothing. He was cold and disorientated. Reaching into his pocket, he almost laughed out loud: the compass, like almost everything else, was gone.

He needed to make a decision: which way? With his choice made, he began walking. The leg was a painful dead weight and he had to stifle a cry with every other stride. Suddenly, he stumbled in the darkness and found himself plummeting downhill; it was as if his feet had been swept from under him. He hollered in pain with each rotation of his body, past caring who heard, before finally being swallowed up in darkness and agony.

It was still dark when he regained consciousness. With effort, he looked around in the half-light. Shivering, he wrapped his coat tight around his body. His head ached, and the pain in his leg was excruciating. He looked up and saw that he had fallen down a steep hill. He smiled grimly to himself: it had all gone so bloody wrong. He looked down at his leg and saw the damage. Moments later he passed out again.

A strong wind woke him some time later; it was getting stronger and the sky was black and starless. He needed to find cover. He dragged and hopped himself across a field for what must have been two hours, stopping when exhaustion and the pain got the better of him. Finally, he spotted a farmhouse with an inviting barn beside it. Using all his remaining strength, he managed to crawl inside before losing consciousness.

~ ~ ~ ~

He must have dozed off again. Opening his eyes he saw her, sitting cross-legged across from him: the face of an angel.

Had he died? If she were a statue standing in the centre of Florence, they would flock in their thousands to see it.

'You're awake … would you like some water? It's fresh, I changed it myself,' she smiled.

'Yes … I thought you were at school.'

'Our teacher's mother lives in Genoa. Someone came to tell her that the house in which she lived had been bombed.'

'How awful,' he said, sipping from the cup she'd handed him.

'Yes … but it meant I could come home early. I know Mamma did not want me to come here, but I thought I should see how you were.'

'I am fine. Please don't get into trouble on my account.'

'I won't. She will not be back for at least an hour, so I will sit and keep you company.'

Richard Mason smiled. 'Thank you.'

'Are you married? You have no ring. How old are you? Where do you live?'

'Woah … hold on … you're going too fast for me.'

'Sorry, it's just that … you know different things and …'

Richard Mason held up his hand. 'Can you do me a favour? Do you know if your mother has any cigarettes in the house?'

Sofia instantly produced one from her coat pocket, along with a box of matches. A knowing grin leapt onto her lips.

'Resourceful girl,' he whispered.

She handed him both. 'Yes, I am.'

Richard Mason lit his cigarette, staring at her. Strangely, she made him feel uncomfortable. Although just a child, she had the body and face of an older woman.

'How old are you?' he asked.

'You have not answered any of my questions.'

'No, I haven't, have I. No … Twenty-five … London. Happy now?'

Sofia smiled and Mason saw her mother within the folds of her face.

'Fourteen, but I am fifteen in September.'

'Young.'

'No I am not. I have had a boyfriend before.'

'Oh.'

'Yes. Carlo Sergi. We held hands all the way to the village once. He is almost nineteen.'

'Isn't that a little old for you?' Mason held a mouthful of smoke inside his lungs before continuing, 'What did your mother say?'

Sofia looked away. 'She does not like him, but that is because he is a Blackshirt, a supporter of Mussolini and the Fascists. Mamma calls him a fanatic.'

'So, what did she think about you and him holding hands?'

'Please don't tell her, it was months ago,' she pleaded.

Sofia brought herself upright and Richard felt his breath become shallow. Her skin was like porcelain, unblemished, and if her lips belonged to a woman, they would demand to be kissed. Her jet-black hair curled into ringlets and lay neatly on her shoulders.

'No … it can be our secret.'

Sofia's face brightened. 'Thank you.'

Mason felt his eyes begin to close. He fought against it but, for a moment, lost. When he reopened them, she was still staring at him.

'Has anyone ever drawn you?' he asked.

She looked confused. 'No, why would they?'

'Because people enjoy painting and drawing beautiful things.' The moment those words were out, he knew he had made a mistake. Sofia's face flushed and she looked away. After an awkward minute, he felt the need to break the silence.

'I learnt Italian when I stayed in Florence. I was an art student … my parents are rich you see. I was seventeen, almost eighteen, and I stayed three years.'

'So, you draw and paint?'

'Yes, but –'

'And you want to draw me?' Her eyes lit up.

'Hold on – I have nothing to draw or paint with, no charcoal or oils, no canvas or paper. But, yes, it would be nice to sketch your face one day.'

Sofia stood suddenly. 'I should be going now.'

'Fine.'

'Do not tell my mother I came here … she worries.' She moved towards the doors before pausing. 'So, you think I am beautiful?' she asked, turning to face him.

Richard Mason looked up, before making the mistake of smiling.

Sofia took that as a yes.

~ ~ ~ ~

Isolina unlocked the chain with the key that was hidden under the stone. He was upright but asleep, his back resting against a wooden post. She walked across to him and put her bag down, then knelt and lifted the blanket to inspect the splint. It was doing its job. A foul odour met her senses; his body could do with a wash. She returned to the house and placed a pan of water on the stove.

'Mamma, you're home.' Sofia appeared at the top of the stairs. She had lain on her bed after leaving the Englishman, and had fallen asleep thinking of everything he had said. 'What are you doing?'

'I am heating some water so the Englishman can have a wash.'

'Would you like me to help?'

'No,' came the sharp reply.

Sofia's face dropped.

'You can get the ham out, I think we deserve a treat tonight.'

Sofia put on her best sulky smile and left.

She placed the steaming bowl of water next to him. A clean cloth floated on top. She unwrapped a small bar of lemon-scented soap before unbuttoning his coat and shirt, knowing this was going to be a difficult task. His eyes opened as she was about to ease the coat off over his shoulders.

'Let me,' he whispered, breathing in her fragrance.

Isolina watched him remove his coat, shirt and vest. She saw the pain it brought him. Squeezing out the excess water from the cloth, she placed it on his chest and felt his body stiffen.

'Are you all right?'

'It's hot.'

'Sorry.'

'Don't be.'

She moved the cloth across his body, under his neck and pulled him forward to clean his back. His body reflected his young age, but his firm muscles were that of a man. His chest was free of hair, which made her smile.

45

The barn was silent; not even the birds played on the roof. The silence gave her the opportunity to think about Silvano; she even imagined it was Silvano's body she was washing, and she drifted into a trance.

Isolina continued to wash him in silence, when Mason whispered, 'I'm sorry to put you to so much trouble.'

'What?' She returned to reality. 'Sorry?'

'I said I'm sorry for putting you through this … that was all. I could tell you were elsewhere, did something happen this morning?'

'No.'

Mason closed his eyes and enjoyed the feel of her touch.

She got him to remove his trousers and pants as best he could, turning her back as he did. The trousers had to be cut off the injured leg and she picked up his underpants, making his face flush. His socks came off next and, just like the young girl she'd seen earlier, he, too, had dirt between his toes. When she finished bathing his limbs and upper body, she handed him the cloth.

'You can do down there.'

'Of course …'

As he washed under the blanket, Isolina laid out fresh clothing, including underpants and a vest. It took an age to dress him because of the pain.

'These clothes?' he enquired through gritted teeth.

'My husband's,' she said quickly.

'Your husband's?'

'He is dead, he has no more use for them, so don't worry. He will not come to claim them back.' She smiled, feeling guilty about teasing him.

'I'm sorry.'

'For what?'

'Your loss.'

This was the second time today that someone had said sorry about her husband. Why? She was glad he was dead.

'Are you okay?' On hearing his voice, she realised she had been daydreaming again. The shock of seeing Silvano after all this time had disturbed her. She was angry with him and herself.

She smiled at Mason. 'Yes, I'm fine … How do you feel now?'

'Much better, even with the pain.'

'Good. I will get some food now, you must be hungry … do you eat ham?'

'Yes.'

'Then that will be dinner.'

She began scooping up his clothes into her arms.

'Wait!' Mason suddenly said. 'Bring me my coat, please.'

He took it from her and removed his knife, before proceeding to cut the lining. He removed three envelopes; two he placed aside, the other he opened.

'Here.' He held out several Italian bank notes. 'Please take it.'

'No, I do not want your money.'

'It is not mine … it is the British government's.'

'I cannot.'

'Please.'

'No.'

'Please.'

'I will take enough for petrol.' She took just one note.

He knew it would be fruitless to argue, so he slipped the notes back inside the envelope.

'I am in your debt,' Richard Mason said, adding the envelope to the others.

Isolina smiled and left. Why did she not tell him about Silvano? About the Partisans who were just seven miles from here? She walked across the yard and met Sofia coming the other way. Maybe it was the same reason she had never told Sofia the truth about her father: *fear*.

CHAPTER SIX

It rained on the first day of February, so hard the roads flooded. The sky became a solid block of grey with the sun concealed somewhere behind its misty cloak. With her coat draped across her shoulders, Isolina ran to the barn with a wooden tray in her hands. She had left Sofia gazing dreamily into a mirror. She feared that a boy was on the scene and prayed it was not Carlo Sergi.

'Morning,' she announced on entering the barn's gloomy interior.

'Good morning,' Richard Mason answered, straightening his collar. 'Could you possibly get me a razor at some point … I presume your husband shaved?'

'No … he had a beard, a very long beard.'

'Oh.'

Isolina laughed. 'Yes, of course. Sorry, it was a joke … but your face would suit a beard, I think.'

'It itches too much and seems to grow in some places and not others.'

'You are still very young,' she said placing the tray onto his lap and stepping back. 'I fear my daughter has her eyes on a boy, which concerns me.' Isolina leant against a post with her arms folded. 'She has sat in front of the mirror brushing her hair all morning.' Although she spoke with a smile on her lips, concern laced her voice.

Mason swallowed a piece of bread. 'I have a confession to make … I do not think a boy is the trigger.'

'Oh?'

'It might be me.'

'You?'

'Something I said …'

'You'd better explain.'

Richard Mason told her of their conversation several weeks ago, and how she had reacted to it. Isolina listened but said nothing.

'I see. So she came to see you when I had told her not to.'

'Look, she is young and inquisitive … weren't we all at that age?'

'At that age, I obeyed my mother when she told me not to do something.'

'I understand … but these are strange times in your county.'

'Do not make excuses for her, Mr Mason. But, if you are correct, and I hope you are, then I am happy.'

'Are you going to tell her I told you?'

Isolina walked to the doorway and looked out at the falling rain, not that she needed to observe it, for the noise coming from the roof told its own story.

'No … not this time, Mr Mason, but I cannot have her disobeying me. She is almost fifteen, and my job as a mother is to protect her.' She took a deep breath, still looking out. 'And protecting her in the middle of a war is almost impossible.'

'I understand.'

'No, Mr Mason, you do not, but it is not your fault. Until you have a son or daughter to care for, you will never fully understand how a parent feels. I will tell you now, I will do anything to protect Sofia, and I mean anything.'

He swallowed a mouthful of coffee and felt it scald his throat. Isolina then checked his leg. "*All good*," she mumbled under her breath, then stood, holding the tray with an empty plate and cup on it.

'We will be gone for most of the day, Mr Mason. I will bring you some books I have found, some cigarettes and matches. I will empty your bottle before I go ... is there anything else you need?'

'No, I am very grateful.'

Isolina remained for a moment. 'So, you paint, Mr Mason. What do you specialise in? Landscapes? Buildings?'

'Portraits.'

'Portraits?'

'Yes, of beautiful women such as yourself.'

'Have you not caused enough problems with your flattery, Mr Mason?' Isolina smiled.

'Let me paint you.'

'Paint me? No, I am not the type ... I move about too much.' She grinned. 'And I do not consider myself beautiful ... not at thirty-seven. Maybe at fourteen my head might have been turned ... but not now.'

'I will keep asking.'

'And I will keep refusing.'

'What about Sofia, you won't deny her the chance?'

'Maybe ... anyway, you have no equipment, Mr Mason. Let me think about it.'

Mason watched her walk away, staring at the rhythmic swing of her hips. The woman had it all; if only she would let him draw her naked. He heard the chain being tightened around the wooden doors. He rested his head back and imagined the finished drawing.

~ ~ ~ ~

'If you do that again, I will make you walk.'

Sofia had stuck her head in front of the rear-view mirror for the umpteenth time.

'Sorry.'

Isolina fought back a smile before returning her focus on the wet road. Every mother thinks their child is beautiful, but in Sofia's case, far too many people had commented on her looks. People like Carlo Sergi. The boy was a Fascist fanatic, obsessed with Mussolini, consumed by the thought of power, just like his father Vito, who was high on the Fascist Council. And, just like his father, Carlo was a bully.

Isolina had seen Sofia walking hand in hand with Carlo, a sight that had terrified her. She had come home early that day and had driven to the top field. Neither of them had seen her, they were too engrossed in each other. She had decided not to say anything to Sofia, knowing how the young behaved when scolded: Sofia would have gone further against her wishes. Isolina seemed to be accumulating secrets: Sofia and Carlo, the Englishman, and now Silvano. Keeping silent was becoming a habit with her of late.

'Goodbye, Mamma,' Sofia said, getting out of the car. Isolina watched her daughter run to the building without looking back. How sensible was Sofia? Still a child who crept into her mother's bed for comfort, scared of thunder and lightning. She desperately wanted the baby she had held in her arms to remain a child a little longer.

She headed towards Sassa's, with the faces of Carlo Sergi, the Englishman and Silvano all competing for space inside her head. She slowed to a crawl as the wipers struggled to keep the screen clear. Through the beads of rain, she saw herself and Silvano walking hand in hand in Florence, just as Sofia and Carlo had done. The rain had fallen in torrents that afternoon, too, but it had gone unnoticed by them. A wheel sank into another pothole causing Isolina to wake from her dream about that day a lifetime ago.

~ ~ ~ ~

Sassa placed a coffee and a dry towel in front of her. They were gathered in the clinic, awaiting the arrival of more refugees from Turin. The other evacuees were being cared for by Sassa's maids in another room. Fino warmed his hands on the giant stove at the back of the room. Next to him stood Father Mariano, holding a coffee. He was the local priest, God's Fascist representative here on Earth, as some called him. His boss, Father Remo, visited the village occasionally and clearly despised the man.

Two more of Sassa's recruits sat drinking coffee. Eva Pinto and Rosalba Calvi were hardly friends, they just about tolerated each other. Both were trying to impress Sassa, who was considered an angel in Tuscany.

'Twelve more children are to join us soon,' Sassa announced, 'all from Turin. Those coming today are older than those from Genoa. Eight-, ten- and twelve-year-olds, I am led to believe … they should be here any moment. Isolina, we need to assess them, so I will bring them in here first, before introducing them to the children from Genoa.'

'Do you want me to give them a medical examination, Sassa?'

'We shaved four of the children yesterday,' Rosalba interrupted.

'Yes.' It was Isolina who answered. 'They had lice, it was the only thing to do to stop it spreading.'

'And have we contained it?' Rosalba queried, looking slightly concerned.

'Hopefully.'

'Hopefully?'

'If not, we shave the rest,' Isolina said, staring at the older woman.

The frosty atmosphere was thawed by Fino. 'We could have collected the lice and added them to a risotto.'

'*Fino*,' Sassa admonished, giving him one of her stares, 'keep your sick humour to yourself.' But Sassa could not contain the straight face and a grin surfaced on her lips.

Father Mariano, still holding his coffee, crossed himself. 'I fear everything of beauty will be destroyed soon. Rome first, Venice, then here, Florence. It feels like the end of Italy.'

Eva Pinto gave him a look of contempt. 'Then we have brought it upon ourselves ... but we can stop it.'

'How?' asked the priest.

'Let the king abdicate, seize the Fascist leaders, form a liberal government headed by Bonomi, and seek an armistice with the Allies ... it is that simple.' Eva finished and placed a cigarette between her lips whilst staring around the room. The priest, Isolina and Rosalba all stared back at her.

'What?' the woman said, blowing smoke towards the ceiling. 'So, shoot me.'

'You speak like a traitor, Eva,' Rosalba finally spoke. 'We must show unity … revive the spirit of national unity. We must stand up to the British and American invaders.'

Eva held up her hand. 'Was it not Hitler who invaded lands that were not his? Was it not our renowned leader, Il Duce, who held onto his coat-tails while the rest of Italy told him how great he was when things were going well? Now, it's all falling apart and the Italian people have finally opened their eyes and seen him for what he is: a bully and a murderer.'

Except for a cup being placed down, there was silence in the room.

'You speak with passion, Eva,' said Fino.

'I speak as a mother who has not heard from her son since he went to Greece.'

'To fight for his country, Eva,' Father Mariano added. 'You should speak about him with pride in your voice.'

'You, a man of God, Father …' Eva rose from her chair, stubbing out her cigarette in anger. 'You tell me I must be proud of him. He is my son. I was proud of him the day they pulled him from my womb … Pride … you speak of pride … how can we feel pride? What have the Greeks done to us? Why is my son, Angelo, in a place he does not want to be, fighting an enemy he has no argument with? Do not speak of pride to me.'

'Eva, sit.' Sassa walked across to the trembling woman.

'All we are saying,' began Rosalba, 'is that we should be proud of our troops.'

'I agree,' Father Mariano added.

'What do you know, priest …' Eva pulled herself away from Sassa. 'How many children have you? NONE. Do not tell me what is in a mother's heart, priest … I tell you now, and I do not care who hears me … I pray that the British and American troops sweep up Italy and so ends this war, and so that I may be reunited with my son. I want to be rid of all the vermin that has crawled out of the gutter these past few years … and I will do all I can to help, at whatever cost.'

'If you speak as you do, it could well cost you your life,' said the priest.

'Yes, priest … Like Jesus died for us … have you forgotten?'

'I have not forgotten.' The priest looked at the woman with scorn.

'If he were here now, Father, he would *not* be a Fascist.'

Isolina sat listening, and, for the first time, felt a genuine fear about this war, which had crept up suddenly on them. She accepted another coffee from Sassa, smiled, and thought about Sofia again, wondering how she would keep her safe. Italy was losing the war, she had seen it in those innocent children's faces. The war was now on her doorstep and, when it came, which it surely would, it would pit Italian against Italian, father against son, brother against brother, family against family. It would wrench the heart and soul from the country, its people and its way of life.

'Fascist, Christian, Nazi or Jew,' Sassa broke a thoughtful silence, 'my only concern is for the innocent: those children in the other building, and the ones on their way here now.' She ran her fingers through her unkempt hair. 'All we can do is feed, shelter and love them … But even I know that is not enough.' Moisture filled her eyes. Fino went across and placed an arm around her.

'I will take photographs of the children and send them to their mothers. Unlike poor Eva, these children's mothers will see they are being cared for and loved.' She placed both hands flat on the table and stared around the room. 'I do not care where you place your allegiances, my only concern here is for the children. Give these unfortunate children as much love as you can, as much as you can spare, please.' Sassa drew breath. 'I hear motor cars … They are here.'

Sassa and Fino left the room. Eva followed, deep in thought about her lost son. The priest cleared his throat and spoke to Isolina.

'I saw you with the doctor yesterday, I hope nothing is wrong. Sofia is well?'

'She is very well, thank you.' Isolina thought it strange that a simple everyday conversation had an underlying fear attached to it. A sign of the times. It told you all you needed to know about Italy under the Fascist government.

'Has he been contacted by the authorities?' Rosalba Calvi asked. 'Or is it just those in Florence?'

'Contacted?'

'He is a Jew, is he not?'

Isolina truly despised the woman. 'Is that a good reason to remove the man from our country … a good man?' She fought hard to control her anger.

'Mussolini is moving them to places like Yugoslavia, where they will be well cared for. I hear some might go to parts of France we control.'

'I don't understand,' Isolina said.

'Understand? What is there to understand?'

'Why they have to leave at all.' Frustration made her voice rise.

Rosalba stood; Father Mariano was a step behind.

'Because he's a Jew, Isolina. Simple as that.'

She turned her back and disappeared through the door.

Twelve girls were brought to Isolina for examination. The youngest was seven, the oldest twelve. All kept close to each other.

'This is our nurse, Isolina Donatelli.' Sassa placed a hand on Isolina's shoulder. 'She will take a look at you … there is nothing to worry about.' One of Sassa's maids entered the room carrying a pair of clippers. Sassa quickly placed her herself in front of her, not wanting to alarm the children.

Sassa watched as Isolina saw each child in turn, displaying such genuine tenderness that the children warmed to her instantly. One, Nella, became her shadow after her own examination had finished, following Isolina around closely. Five of the children needed their heads shaved. One became concerned – not so much about the loss of her hair – but that people might think she was a boy.

Isolina picked up fragments of information from each child about the conditions in Turin. The Allies had bombed the factories the children's parents worked in, something that made the children anxious. They all displayed good manners, despite Rosalba's warning about the kind of children that came from places like Turin. The oldest, Anna, was almost thirteen. She was a sweet-faced girl, despite her head being shaved. Anna came and stood with Isolina as she packed away her bag.

'When will this be over?' she asked.

'I hope soon … but who can tell.' Isolina placed a hand on the girl's shoulder and smiled apologetically.

'My brother has been sent to Sicily to fight.'

Isolina looked at the girl. 'How old is he?'

'Sixteen … almost.'

'Sixteen? How can he be in the army, Anna?'

'Our local Fascist council rounded him up, along with many of his friends.'

'Did your father or mother not object, and the other parents?'

'Yes, they did, and they were jailed for doing so. By the time they were released, the boys were gone.'

Isolina could not believe what she had just heard. She drew the young girl to her and felt her jagged bones through her thin dress. 'I think you look very nice with your new hairstyle ... very elegant.'

The girl gave a warm smile. Suddenly, Isolina found herself wiping tears from her cheeks.

'Why do you cry?' Anna asked.

'Because ... because it is so unfair.'

~ ~ ~ ~

Richard Mason threw the book in frustration. He felt helpless, along with every other emotion of inadequacy that came with being incapacitated. He had spent a considerable length of time trying to find ways he could become mobile again, although he knew the consequences. So, if he could not get to the Partisans, maybe they could come here? He would need to recruit Isolina to the cause, but would she be a willing participant?

Look at how she had stuck her neck out for him. Deep in thought, he reached inside his pocket, only to realise he had smoked all three cigarettes. Irritated, he sat with his eyes closed – what else was there to do but think? She was a nurse, and if he were a Partisan in the hills, that is the kind of friend he would like to have with him. Maybe she could help him find his radio set. The problem was, how would he approach the subject. How could he get close to her. After all, she was a very attractive woman. His hand moved to his pocket again … shit.

CHAPTER SEVEN

Sofia had gone to the barn twice, only to find the chain locked and the key gone. For three days, she had refrained from bringing up the subject of the missing key, knowing it would awaken her mother's suspicions. So, she behaved like the perfect daughter and bided her time. She thought about the Englishman constantly: not even Carlo Sergi had told her she was beautiful, but what would he know? He was just a boy; the Englishman was a man.

She had told no one, not even her best friend, Marta. Although, on several occasions, she had almost let it slip. Sofia imagined him painting her. Imagined him looking up to tell her how lovely she was, and how much he wanted to kiss her. At school, on a dusty bookshelf, she had found an old book about artists. In it were hundreds of sketches, plus several photos showing artists at work with their models. Maybe she could be *his* model.

Only one thing bothered her: in most of the pictures, the women were naked. For Sofia, this was a major concern – not the nudity itself but, what if her body disappointed him? Sofia took every opportunity to inspect her breasts, unable to make up her mind. Her eyes flashed from the pages to her own nakedness. She studied the details intricately: her breasts pointed directly forward, while those on some women sagged. Others were fuller, elongated; some were more generous and less rounded, not solid like hers. Sofia felt disheartened.

But there were other things on her mind. A tense atmosphere had developed at school: teachers looked solemn and parents spoke in low whispers. Places like Tunisia and Tripolitania were mentioned frequently, and she would hear people say: '*This* is where they have got us,' ... referring to the Fascists. She could not remember people speaking so openly before. But that was not all: some spoke about the king abdicating, the removal of Mussolini and an armistice with the Allies.

Many maintained their support for continuing the war, for standing shoulder to shoulder with their German brothers. They spoke of braving the heavy bombing, just like those in London had done, and everyone seemed suspicious of the person next to them. And it was not solely confined to the adult population. In her class, there were those who had high-ranking party members as parents, who worshipped Mussolini. But many also whispered obscenities about him, the Fascist and the Germans in general. Her mother told her never to speak about such things. She had warned Sofia many times to keep her views to herself, and that is what she had done, which left just one huge problem ... were her breasts too small?

~ ~ ~ ~

Richard Mason wanted to engage Isolina in conversation each night, but the woman looked and sounded exhausted.

Instead, he found himself staring at her like a painter studying his model. Running his eyes over her body, he closely examined the texture of her skin and the small folds of loose flesh, features that enhanced her beauty. The thin lines around her eyes and the smudge of darkness below them, symbolised the complexity and severity of the life she led. The contours of her facial bones formed the foundation of her overall beauty. All this detail was only visible to someone taught to appreciate such splendour.

He wondered what Isolina had looked like at fourteen. Like Sofia? It made him think about the father, who was seldom mentioned. Sofia, when she visited with her mother, just sat and stared at him, saying very little. He wondered if she was the key to Isolina – could he get *her* to talk. But he had not been alone with her since that day she had come home early.

Her father must have been a handsome man. To make someone as perfect as Sofia needed the correct ingredients. Richard Mason found himself laughing out loud – the stupid things you thought of when you were bored. From the little snippets he'd gathered from Isolina, the war seemed to have ground to a halt. It sounded like Mussolini was still clinging to power, and little had been done to oust the Fascists. As for the Italian nation, there was continued apathy of the highest order. They criticised, but did nothing about it.

These people stared defeat in the face, yet they did nothing to speed up the process of victory. The sooner the Allies arrived, the better. It was the reason he was here: to help organise this mutiny, this uprising; to arm them. Instead, he sat on his arse doing bugger all. All that was needed was for someone to light the touch paper and this region would go up in flames. Florence would fall in a matter days, although, all the reports suggested it would be the Communists who would benefit.

These past weeks had been tedious, to say the least. He needed to get in touch with the Partisans, and if it meant taking risks and trusting Isolina, then so be it. It might mean placing her in danger, which worried him – more than he'd expected. This was war. Heavy consequences were likely, not just for Isolina, but also for her daughter. Would Isolina be willing to take that chance? No, she would never knowingly agree to any of it. But she was his only chance of re-entering the war, even if that meant using the innocent … which he would reluctantly do.

~ ~ ~

'It's mild … but it is St. Vitus' dance,' said Simon Stein.

'You are certain?' Isolina asked.

'Yes …' He went to the sink and began to wash his hands.

'What is that?' Eva queried, looking down on the pale-faced girl.

'Put simply, it's Chorea in a mild form.' The doctor lit a cigarette. 'See the blotches?'

'Why does she keep moving her arms?'

'It is a symptom. She will need plenty of bed rest, Sassa.' Simon looked tired. 'Two or three weeks, I cannot be certain … maybe more. I'm sorry, I wish I could be more helpful.'

'Is there nothing else we can do?' Sassa said, picking up a cloth.

'Rest, rest and more rest … and a little love.'

'We have love in abundance here, doctor,' the Swedish woman said, smiling, 'if only that was enough to solve all our problems.'

'I will sit with her.' Eva brought a chair closer to the bed.

'Come, doctor, have a coffee before you go,' Sassa offered.

Isolina followed them outside. The rain had stopped, but the sky remained dirty grey in colour. Isolina suddenly felt very tired. Her joints ached, and all she wanted to do was go home and sleep.

Sassa had marched ahead and was almost at the door to her house. She did nothing at a leisurely pace, or so it seemed.

'Look at her, she puts us to shame, Simon. How can I say I am tired when I see her doing everything she does?'

'It is no crime to admit you are tired, Isolina. If you were to sleep an hour longer in the morning, no one would question you.'

'I care little for what people think, Simon. It is what I think of myself and, as long as Sassa keeps going, so will I.'

Simon Stein placed an arm around Isolina's waist and held her back. Sassa was already inside the house. 'How is our patient?'

'Fine, he just sits there. I check on him daily.'

'Good.'

'I can tell he is restless. It's obvious that he is bored. Although, I did give him some books ... I picked one up the other day, one he had thrown across the floor.'

'Have you found out anything about him?'

'He was an art student in Florence for three years, it is the reason he speaks Italian so well.'

'I meant, what is he doing here?'

Isolina smiled. 'Sorry – he is supposed to be organising the Partisan.'

'I see. So, instead, he sits in your barn doing nothing. I can understand his frustration.'

'Yes.'

'Look, stop by my house in the week. I have a pair of crutches he can use when the time is right. Let us get him up and about as soon as possible.'

'I will do that. Have you thought any more about Canada?'

'Yes. I have decided Tuscany suits me better … I have no longing for Canada or my cousin, whom I have said no more than a dozen words to in ten years. I am old, Isolina, and, like you, I feel tired, but it is a different tired, I am tired in here.' Simon placed a finger on his temple. 'I think I will take my chances here. And I hope I can get your young Englishman up and about so he can help end this war.'

'Simon!' Sassa's voice came from somewhere within the house. 'Your coffee will get cold.'

Simon and Isolina looked at each other and smiled as they made their way inside.

'Oh, by the way,' Isolina said as they neared the house, 'I think Sofia is in love with him.'

She continued into the house, leaving Simon in her wake, the smile on his face long gone.

~ ~ ~ ~

Isolina's decision to visit her aunt and cousin in Florence was not a spur of the moment one. She'd been thinking about it for the past six months. Aunt Savina, her mother's younger sister, had had her cousin, Fabia, late in life, at forty-two. The birth had been a difficult one, but Fabia had turned out to be a beautiful healthy child.

In 1926, after her mother had died, Isolina had gone to stay with Savina and her husband, Cleto, and had not been back for over a year. She had begun her nursing training at the Florence hospital in the Piazza Santa Maria Nuova, about the same time Savina found out she was pregnant. Savina had given up any hope of having a child and, coming as it did so soon after the death of her sister, it had filled her with guilt.

It was a distressing time for Isolina. She'd had to leave her grieving father alone at home to go to Florence to fulfil a promise made to her dying mother: to fulfil her dream of becoming a nurse. Her mother had placed a rosary in her hand and made her promise that, whatever happened, she had to realise that dream.

Savina and Isolina had supported each other during this difficult time. Isolina returned home for a couple of days once a month to see her heartbroken father. Baby Fabia arrived weighing seven pounds. Her arrival seemed to ease their pain and, even today, Fabia was considered a special child. Both Savina and Cleto wanted to call her Dona after Isolina's mother, but Isolina talked them out of doing so, telling them that the baby must have her own identity, and so the child was christened Fabia Dona Grosseto.

It was just over an hour's journey to Florence, a drive she hated. By the time she reached the outskirts of the city, her fingers ached from the intensity of her grip. Florence brought back memories of her mother, as well as Silvano, for this was where they had met for the first time. His image flooded into her mind as familiar sights came into view.

Savina greeted her with enthusiasm and lots of tears.

'You will squeeze the life out of me,' said Isolina, her head resting on her aunt's shoulder.

'I miss you, Isolina ... I see so little of you ...' Her aunt released her niece and stood back to see her better. 'You remind me so much of Dona ...' Again, the tears flowed.

'Come ... coffee? Why no Sofia?'

'She is at school and I am only here for a few hours.'

'School? Things must be normal in the countryside, then. Here, in Florence, we sit and wait to be bombed.'

'They will not bomb Florence, Savina,' Isolina said, removing her coat in the hallway. 'It will be like Rome, an *open* city.'

Savina moved around the kitchen slowly. Now nearing her sixtieth birthday, she had put on some weight. Isolina breathed in the aroma of home cooking.

'Where is Fabia?' she asked.

A momentary shadow crossed Savina's face and she quickly turned away, opening several cupboard doors, searching for some hidden utensil. A stalling tactic, thought Isolina.

'What is it, Savina? What has happened?'

'Nothing has happened,' said Savina looking up, 'nothing has happened ... yet.'

Savina lifted the coffee pot with an unsteady hand, but Isolina forced her to put it down on the table.

'Sit,' she ordered.

The older woman obeyed without protest while Isolina poured out two cups.

'Tell me.'

Savina reached for a cigarette. Isolina watched and waited, allowing the woman time to compose herself.

'Fabia is mixing with the anti-Fascists, mainly Communists. I do not see her, Isolina, she is out almost every night … she delivers leaflets, I have seen them … I found them under her bed. Yes, I have stooped that low, Isolina … going through her things when she is out.'

'What do these leaflets say?'

'They call for the end of Fascism, for Mussolini to be replaced, for the masses to rise up, take control and support the Allies when they invade.'

Isolina looked down at her coffee. How many mothers today were filled with concern for their children? How many tried desperately to shield them from this war, which seemed to be gaining momentum by the day? Like Fabia, Sofia was growing older and had her own mind, her own way of living. Isolina knew that a protective motherly instinct would, sooner or later, be rejected by these girls. She understood how Savina felt, but she also knew the hopelessness of what she desired.

'Will you talk to her?' Savina asked, her hand now covering Isolina's.

'If you think it will do any good.'

~ ~ ~

Fabia was a sweet-looking girl, attractive without being beautiful. Her nose was long and thin, the centre of attention on an elongated face. Her real beauty was her smile.

'Isolina, how lovely to see you.' Fabia stood hugging her cousin in the hallway. 'Why did you not tell us you were coming? I would have waited in for you.'

'I did not know myself until I was on the road.'

'And no Sofia?'

'No, I am not staying long, I need to get back before she returns from school. I want to go to the shops … come with me?'

'Yes … but I am meeting someone at three.'

'I will be well on my way home by then, Fabia.'

'Then that's fine … yes, I will come.'

Fabia went off to change while Isolina and Savina had another coffee. Savina spoke about how nervous people were in Florence, and the scarcity of goods in the shops. She lowered her voice and talked with disdain about the Fascist secret police and their leader, Mario Carita.

'They are everywhere,' she said, 'in the bars and the cafés … they do not hide in the shadows anymore. Instead, they openly watch and intimidate people.' She lit another cigarette.

'I fear for Sofia in all this. I try to think as a fourteen-year-old would, living in the middle of a war … a war we are losing by all accounts.'

'You say *we*, Isolina, but both you and I, like so many Italians, never wanted to be part of this.'

Isolina smiled: Savina spoke just like Simon. 'As much as I try to distance myself and Sofia from it, the more it seems to draw me closer.'

'What do you mean, surely the countryside is less affected by all this?'

Isolina thought about the Englishman in her barn, Luca and Silvano, and the Partisans in the hills, who were ready to start fighting at the drop of a hat.

'No – even in the tranquil setting of our small community …'

Savina made the sign of the cross then sipped her coffee.

~ ~ ~ ~

Florence seemed quiet today, or maybe this was normal for Florence these days. A thin, grey covering of cloud hung above the city. The roads were damp and Isolina wondered if it had rained, or whether the street cleaners were still doing their job. Fabia linked arms with her. Savina had remained at home, cooking lunch. The city felt strange to Isolina; smiles and pleasant greetings seemed sparse, while many refused to make eye contact.

People pulled their hats down and their collars up. Hunched in their overcoats, they moved briskly through the streets. The shops reflected the remoteness she saw in people's faces, window displays were meagre, dull and unadorned. The sun would have had little effect upon the city below; no amount of sunlight would remove the gloom from the narrow streets that wound through the city. German soldiers replaced the tourists, armed not with rifles but cameras; an army of sightseers dressed in field grey. The city had been endorsed by the Führer himself, hence its popularity.

Isolina went in search of dress material. Sofia's fifteenth birthday was coming up, and only in Florence would she find a good variety of fabrics. Fabia enthusiastically helped, advising Isolina on which patterns to buy. Isolina also bought cigarettes for herself and the Englishman. Finally, she asked Fabia where they could purchase paper and pencils, which brought a surprised look from the young girl.

'It is for Sofia, a school project she is working on.'

'I see,' answered Fabia. 'I know where we can go.'

Isolina hoped she had enough money. As it turned out, she had plenty. The man in the shop was so desperate to make a sale, he offered her a discount before she had asked. He reduced everything she touched, including eight large sheets of drawing paper, a small box of charcoal sticks, several pencils and a small sketch book.

Finished, they set out to find somewhere to have a coffee. For almost three years, this had been Isolina's home, and she had come to love it. Now, though, it seemed to have disguised itself beneath a gloomy spectre of insecurity. Not that it had changed visually; it was this wonderful city's ambiance that had altered. As though it had lost its very soul.

They walked alongside the River Arno, where a boat with eight rowers glided past mid-stream, silently cutting through the water towards the Ponte Vecchio Bridge. They strolled past the Uffizi Gallery, past the statue of David and into the vastness of the Piazza della Signoria, where she had first met Silvano. She was back there again, aged twenty, a student nurse still coming to terms with the death of her mother, and now living in this large and beautiful city. She saw him with his bandaged finger, eating an apple. She had stood still at that moment, wondering whether to lose herself in the crowd, but it was too late, he had seen her and, with the apple clamped between his teeth, he waved.

'Isolina ...'

Fabia's voice echoed around in her head as 1926 faded into the distance. She found herself staring into the young girl's face.

'Sorry ... I was just remembering the last time I was here.'

'Let us go in there.' Fabia pointed to an almost deserted café.

They ordered two coffees and decided to sit outside as it was not cold and the rain had stopped. Fabia sat staring across the piazza. Isolina wondered how she was going to approach the subject, but it was Fabia who broke the silence.

'What is happening in the hills, Isolina?'

'Happening? ... What do you mean?'

'The Partisans ... is there a growing movement? Are they organised?' Fabia kept her voice low while her eyes shifted in all directions.

Isolina took a sip of her coffee, which tasted bitter.

'I know nothing of those things, Fabia.'

'You have no contact with the war?'

'I am helping to look after evacuees from Turin and Genoa on a large farm close to me.'

'Yes, I heard the Allies have begun bombing ... it is a good sign.'

'Not for the children ... and certainly not for their parents.'

'Casualties of war,' Fabia stated.

Isolina sat back, not recognising the young girl who sat across from her.

'Surely they are the innocent party in all this ... you speak so –'

'Unsympathetically? Maybe I do ...'

'No ... it is more ... callous ... almost brutal, how you see things ... so black and white.'

'And for you it is grey, with neither side winning the argument. The problem is, sooner or later, Isolina, you will have to take sides. All of Italy will have to decide which side it will be.'

'I did not see this the last time I visited, Fabia.'

'I did not know then.'

'Know ... know what?'

'That the Fascists murdered my father.'

Cleto died in 1935. He had been an outspoken critic of the Fascist state and Mussolini. Many admired Cleto, but, equally, many thought him a fool to air his views so openly. Each time Mussolini visited Florence, he was arrested, and only released after Il Duce left. Cleto had died in a road accident, a head-on crash with a van carrying bricks. Isolina remembered crying at the news, and recalled holding onto Fabia's hand the day of the funeral. Fabia was nine.

'He died in a road accident, Fabia.'

'That is what they told Mamma ... but people know different.'

'People?'

'People I see now, those who have a voice that will be heard soon, when everything crumbles and we finally rid ourselves of Fascism and Mussolini.'

'I have never heard you speak this way, Fabia ... And how do you know what you have been told is true?'

'Because Mamma told me ... just not in so many words ...'

'What does that mean?'

'Those who knew, told me. And when I confronted her ... she did not deny it, instead she cried. I knew it was the truth then.'

'If that is true, Fabia, you cannot blame her for wanting to protect you.'

'I do not want protecting, Isolina.'

'What do you want, then?'

'*Revenge.*'

Isolina looked into the girl's eyes: they were merciless. Fabia placed her small, soft hand on Isolina's and tried to force a smile.

'The country talks but does nothing ... so it is up to us.'

'*Us*, again ...'

'The Gappist, those of us that want to see an end to Fascism. Isolina, I have found my patriotism, you need to seek out your own.'

~ ~ ~ ~

Isolina drove home slowly. She had eaten with Savina before Fabia had left for her appointment. They had talked about the past, but nothing else. How simple life had been back then, or had it been naïvety, the natural ability *not* to see what you know is there … the way we hide under the covers as a child when danger closes in.

But Fabia was not a child anymore, she was a woman, albeit she was only seventeen. But she saw Italy differently to others. To people like her, Fascism was the real enemy within. Mussolini's charisma had fooled a generation, but now they were seeing through him. His vision of *peace and order* had been exposed as just another smoke screen. As the Italian army invaded Ethiopia, she remembered seeing schoolchildren being forced to wear uniforms, and teachers wearing black shirts. Everyone had to read books that stressed Fascist ideals. Her father could not find work, simply because he did not possess a party membership card.

The road ahead became wet as the grey clouds above began spilling their contents. The patter of raindrops on the metal roof slowly increased to a crescendo, until the grinding sound of the engine disappeared totally. She suddenly felt scared – but was her fear for Fabia, or her own daughter? Was she concerned with the Englishman's presence? Or was it the simple fact that she could now see where all this was leading and her real anxiety was for the future, her future and Sofia's? All over Italy, lives were about to change, and none of it could be avoided. So, she drove, looking through a rain-soaked windscreen; the clouds wept for the future.

CHAPTER EIGHT

Isolina decided to stash the paper and charcoal safely away. She had not told Sofia of her trip to Florence, thus adding more secrets to her already growing collection. There was a further complication two weeks later when she found the Englishman's breakfast untouched and his forehead coated in sweat. He lay shivering, asking for his mother. Isolina fetched Simon. The Englishman had inconveniently caught the 'flu.

Sofia was banned from entering the barn. Isolina chose to nurse him herself, taking the risk of contracting the illness. It also meant she could put off telling him about Silvano and the group of Partisans in the hills. Instead, she would do what she did best and nurse him back to health.

Sassa and Fino had problems of their own. Four British POWs had been taken to the farm by the local Carabinieri. The Italian officer had offered them a rifle, but Fino had declined, insisting they would not try to escape. Meanwhile, the war, still many miles away, had stuttered to a halt. The Allies continued to bomb Turin and Genoa, but talk of an invasion had become a rumour.

There was a gradual decline in letters for the children, and now, two weeks had passed without news of their loved ones. Forlorn faces and tears were a daily sight at the farm now. Sassa read out old letters from the parents of the youngest, leaving out the more disturbing accounts of the war. The contents painted a depressing picture of life back home, one of destruction, death, hunger and illness, which had Sassa continually wiping tears away. These details were not shared with the children.

The British prisoners greeted Isolina with smiles each time she visited. She found them polite, and one, a Sergeant Foster, always ran to open her door before carrying her bag into the clinic. All of them played with the children, although, only Foster spoke Italian. Two others, Carter and Edwards, built a sturdy set of shelving for Sassa. Like Richard Mason, Isolina thought they looked quite young – only Sergeant Foster looked like a man old enough to be fighting a war. The others looked like schoolboys.

All had photographs of their loved ones. Foster showed Isolina a photograph of his wife and daughter; he had not yet held the child. The others were all single, although Edwards, at nineteen, was engaged to a girl from up north – Foster had to explain what that meant. Carter revealed a photo of his mother. He was the youngest. The creased photo shook in his hand before Isolina realised he was crying.

~ ~ ~ ~

At Sassa's, Anna always hovered close to Isolina. She had made up her mind to become a nurse, so she sat and observed everything Isolina did. She carried Isolina's bag with pride, handing her bandages, scissors and pots of cream when asked. The girl was a natural, thought Isolina, not squeamish, and stayed calm, even when young Carter severed a finger.

Sofia, however, remained withdrawn, constantly enquiring after the Englishman. Isolina noticed that, when the fever was at its height, Sofia almost became tearful. Her concern for her daughter grew; she missed the girl who had once climbed under her covers and snuggled up to her. Isolina felt the need to know that she was still protecting her child – because that was what Sofia still was to her, a helpless child. But everything was changing, and that included her little girl.

Savina was not alone in agonising over her daughter. Isolina, too, was struggling to slow time down. Although, she felt that she and Sofia were drifting apart. The feeling of not being able to comfort her child burnt a hole in Isolina's stomach. If the mother was the safety net below the trapeze wire, the worry now was: would she be strong enough to break the fall?

When the Englishman was well, she would tell him about Silvano. It was a promise she made to herself. But first, he needed to regain his strength. He had not eaten solids in almost three weeks, and was weak. He slept for most of the day and, with almost no strength, he would not be going anywhere fast. That meant she would have the Partisans come here, which would cause further worry.

She tried to push the trip to Florence to the back of her mind, but it still evoked memories of those days spent with Silvano. Back then, he was a young Architecture student, with dreams of designing and building a home in the Tuscan hills one day, where he would eventually live with his wife and four children. Isolina recalled lying alone in bed at her aunt's, dreaming of what it would be like to have children and live with this handsome young man (who had not even given the slightest hint that it was *she* who he planned to marry).

But first he had to make his fortune, how else could his dream become a reality. For Silvano, it would mean going away, first to Rome and, possibly, later to Paris, to study. His parents were comfortably wealthy and, as he was their only child, they lavished everything on him. She remembered the last day she had spent with him and why she had returned home.

Her father had been badly injured in a road accident and left paralysed down one side. As much as she wanted to remain with Silvano, this was her father, and she had a duty as a daughter. She remembered staring into Silvano's eyes the day she had to depart, and the tears he brushed away. His parting words had been so tender, revealing the depth of his feeling towards her; feelings that had only strengthened the short time they'd known each other.

Had he used the word love? She could not remember. She remembered little of that moment, other than staring into those brown eyes and knowing *she* was in love. She saw it now through a haze, for nothing about that day was clear anymore: no plans were made, no promises to write; they parted with just a kiss, their first intimate moment.

CHAPTER NINE

Richard Mason finally swallowed the meat he had been chewing for the past five minutes. He waited to see if it remained in his stomach. To his delight, it did, so he forked more into his mouth, eating just enough to kill the hunger pains. He looked up every now and again, to watch her sewing on the wooden stool. He felt better, having finally emerged from a never-ending nightmare. He placed the plate down and Isolina chose that moment to look up.

'That was nice ... made a change.'

'A change from my soup?' she retorted with a smile.

'Your soup is the best I have ever tasted, but you *can* have enough of a good thing ... it became a little –'

'I understand,' she interrupted, before biting through the cotton thread. 'There,' she whispered, holding up a brown sock.

'I cannot tell you how much I feel indebted to you, Isolina ... first my leg and then looking after me when I was ill ... I don't think I could ever repay you.'

'I ask for no payment.'

'You are a saint.'

'Saints are without sin.'

'And you have sinned?' He smiled.

'I mean ... I am not perfect ... do not make me out to be something I am not.'

'That might be how you see yourself ... I see a different person.' He reached for his cigarettes and lit one.

'I managed to get you some paper and pencils,' Isolina told him. She felt uncomfortable whenever she spoke about herself and was glad to change topic. From the doorway, she heard footsteps.

'Oh, Mamma,' Sofia ran and embraced her.

'Nosey child,' Isolina laughed.

'When?' Sofia looked at Mason.

'Not yet,' Isolina answered. 'Our guest is not quite ready ... another week.'

'Oh, but –'

'A week, Sofia ... or nothing.'

Mason cleared his throat. 'Sofia, your mother is right, I still feel weak. I need to hold my pencil steady if I want to capture you.'

Sofia's face lit up. 'Yes ... yes ... sorry ... I can wait.'

'Good. Now let us go so Mr Mason can get some sleep.'

Isolina placed an arm around her daughter, before remembering to go back for the plate. As she bent down beside him, she whispered a thank you.

~ ~ ~ ~

It was ten days before Isolina handed over the paper, more than eight weeks since the splint had gone on. The primitive manipulation meant Richard's leg had taken longer than expected to heal. Simon had visited one evening and recommended another two weeks before they could confidently remove the splint. Mason would need to use crutches for a further three weeks, possibly more. Simon did not want his leg bearing much of his weight for a while. Without an X-ray, there was no way of knowing if the healing process had been successful. At first, Mason was downhearted, but his spirits lifted when Isolina produced a pair of crutches.

Sofia walked around the house holding a hairbrush. Her mood had dampened just once, when she discovered a spot on her chin. Isolina had warned her not to speak a word of the portrait painting at school, knowing how young girls enjoyed bragging. It was a strange time; Isolina almost forgot they were in the middle of a war. It was only when at Sassa's that she was reminded. Away from the calm tranquillity of the Tuscan hills, a war was raging across Europe. People were dying, losing loved ones, and the conflict was coming their way.

~ ~ ~ ~

Richard Mason made himself comfortable. It felt good to be holding a piece of charcoal between his fingers again. Clipped to a wooden board was a sheet of white paper, maybe not the quality he was used to, but it would serve its purpose.

Sofia ran into the barn, breathless. It was a late, warm spring afternoon, and she had run all the way from school wearing a smile that stretched from ear to ear.

'What would you like me to wear?' she asked.

He smiled. 'I am doing your portrait, Sofia ... what you have on is fine.'

'No, wait, I will be back.'

With that she was gone, returning several minutes later wearing a white blouse and a red and white check skirt.

'Will this do?' She spun around.

'Yes …' He smiled. 'You look nice.'

'Just nice?'

'Elegant, then … will that do?'

'Do I look fourteen? Be honest.'

'Sixteen … yes, sixteen … But, Sofia, as I said, I am drawing your face, not the rest of you.'

She did not hear him.

Mason made her sit on the small wooden stool. Sofia immediately produced her hairbrush and began to pull it through her hair. On her head she wore a yellow *Alice* band, which in fact gave her the look of a young child. He watched her fuss as the brush became stuck in the thickness of her hair. With each downward pull, she began to remove her curls, the very feature that gave her hair its character.

'Stop,' he suddenly said. 'Come here, Sofia, and give me that damn brush. Now kneel down here beside me so I can reach.'

She did as he asked. He reached up and removed the yellow band and threw it across the room, along with the brush. Next, he picked up his glass of water and sprinkled it over her hair. He reached up, gripped fistfuls of her hair and squeezed it into the palm of his hand, moving from one section to another, before sitting back and staring at her.

Sofia wanted to cry at first. With each grasp of her hair, she felt her eyes fill with moisture – but then another sensation began to overcome her. As his fingers slipped through her hair, a feeling of calm descended on her, forcing her to close her eyes. Could this be how love felt?

'There … that's better,' he whispered.

Sofia struggled desperately to hold onto that feeling, to store the memory of his touch, to be retrieved at a moment's notice. She did not move, although she felt breathless. Something had caught alight in the pit of her stomach. She opened her eyes and stared into his, wondering if this was the moment they would kiss. She felt ready … she had imagined what it would be like … and she waited.

'Sofia, go back to the stool, please, and *do not* touch your hair.'

She woke with a start, the dream over; pieces of it lay all around her, shattered. She stood and almost floated to the stool. Mason inhaled: the girl was exquisite. Her beauty jumped out at him like no other woman before. Not only did that inspire him, but it also made him feel uncomfortable. Her hair looked as it did that first night he saw her: untidy, yet natural. It hung in masses of damp curls, resting on her shoulder and spilling down her back. She had the sweet face of an innocent child, yet the look of a sensual woman.

'Come here again, please.' He knew he had to be careful, he was close to overstepping the mark, and yet, for this portrait, he wanted it perfect.

She knelt next to him without complaint. He undid the second button of her blouse, and found himself mesmerised by the fullness of her lips and the tiny indentation below her nose. He took a deep breath and quickly turned her collar inward to expose her neck.

'Go back.' He felt the dryness in his throat but had no water left to moisten it. He picked up a piece of charcoal and tried to compose himself. His hand trembled, so he swapped the charcoal for a pencil.

'How long will it take?' she asked.

'Today, I am going to do some rough sketches, three or four small ones maybe. So try not to move.'

He drew several lines. As his confidence grew, he replaced the pencil with the charcoal stick. Looking up, he stared at her face whilst lightly gripping the charcoal between his fingers, studying every detail. The structure of her face enthralled him. He allowed the charcoal to hover above the paper, focusing hard on every minuscule aspect. Finally, the hand dropped and the charcoal smudged the virgin white sheet below. The lines, at first, had no meaning, no configuration, they were just random shapes on a piece of paper – then, suddenly, he was drawing perfection, something he had rarely achieved before.

It was almost an hour before he spoke. Four sketches covered the paper, each one a different exhibition of the same face. His attention to detail was a result of stopping and exploring her face, for as long as five minutes at times, until the image became tattooed on his memory. He felt drained, yet was unable to stop. He had drawn two sketches in pencil and two in charcoal. One day he would paint her in oil.

'We will stop soon, Sofia … your mother will be home and she is a busy woman.' His gaze moved constantly from the paper to her face as he spoke.

'Yes … the children at Sassa's take up a lot of her time.'

'Tell me about Sassa,' he asked.

Mason put the finishing touches to his drawings as Sofia spoke. She spoke about the evacuees as he continued, half listening, until she said something that made him stop. Sofia had mentioned a man named Luca Tucci … It was not the name so much; more what Sofia said afterwards.

'Simon said Mamma met with Luca.'

'What is wrong with Luca?'

'They say he is a Partisan ... an anti-Fascist ... a fighter from the hills. He is nasty to me, pokes his tongue out.'

'Why would your mother be talking to him?'

'Someone they know is probably injured ... I don't know really ... Anyway, I hate Luca, he keeps making ugly faces.'

She giggled like the young girl she was, not the woman who adorned the sheets of paper he held. He asked more questions, which Sofia happily answered. She told him the boy had met with Isolina on several occasions. Now, why would that be, he thought?

'Sofia – home!' Isolina stood in the doorway. Sofia turned her head to face her. 'And do your blouse up, and take your collar out.' Isolina moved swiftly towards the girl, her face serious, her eyes flitting towards the Englishman, who sat holding a piece of charcoal between his fingers.

Sofia's face reddened and her eyes filled with tears as she ran from the barn.

'Well, Mr Mason, I hope you are happy with yourself.'

'Me? I have just been sitting here sketching your daughter ... I think it is you who have upset her.'

'You expect me to be happy ... to find my fourteen-year-old daughter half naked in front of a man?'

Richard Mason began to laugh.

'You find that amusing?'

'No ... I just think you're overreacting. I just wanted her neck free.'

'I thought it was her face you wanted to draw?'

'It is.'

'So where will it stop ... at her breasts?'

Isolina stood shaking. She turned and began walking towards the open doorway.

'Have you seen Luca Tucci today?' Mason shouted from where he sat.

Isolina froze to the spot.

She reached into her pocket and removed her cigarettes. She faced the doorway, looking out towards the hills, knowing he was staring at her. She lit the cigarette and blew out a cloud of smoke, which the wind seized and lifted skyward.

'What is it to you?' Her voice hardly carried.

'I hear he is Partisan.'

'My daughter told you that?' Isolina sucked in another mouthful of smoke.

'Then tell me it is not true.'

'It is hearsay … this is a small community …' Isolina looked out at the darkening sky and the fields in the distance.

'Not a good answer, Isolina.'

'I am not in your army, Mr Mason … if that is your name. I never asked you to come here. I did not need you to bring me another problem. I have enough problems of my own. So, do not speak to me like that … I am desperately trying to protect my daughter, to keep her safe in this crazy world; all I want to do is be left alone without all these demands placed upon me.' She stopped speaking abruptly.

'So, they ask you to help, do they?' As much as he hated doing it, he had to force the issue.

Isolina remained silent.

'What demands have they made recently?' Mason put the drawings down; Sofia's face stared up at him. 'How close are they?'

Isolina dropped the cigarette to the floor and stamped on it.

'They have your radio set.' She did not look at him. Mason was like an erupting volcano. 'All this fucking time … and you never said a bloody word … I could have been sending vital messages from here, broken leg or not. I could have been doing something useful instead of just lying here drinking bowls of bloody soup.' His face was crimson with anger.

Isolina did not respond.

'If you did not want to tell me, then why not tell them?'

She saw Silvano in her head. 'You were in no fit state.'

'Bollocks!'

'I don't want your war here.'

'You have no bloody choice, Isolina. It is coming whether you like it or not. The rest of the world did not want this bloody war either, but they had to face up to it, and so should you. By not helping me, you are extending it.'

'Me?'

'Yes … we can speed up the end to this war … all we need is the rest of you to help instead of sitting on your arses doing bugger all. You moan and moan, yet you do nothing about it.'

Isolina thought of Fabia; had she not said something similar?

'Believe it or not, Isolina, I'm on your side. I, too, want this bloody war to end … before I get my head shot off … so I can return to the life I had before that bloody madman started all this.'

Mason leant his head back against the post, closing his eyes as he realised what he had said and how he had said it, wishing it hadn't come out so harshly. He thought about the hours she had sat with him, cooked for him, washed him and helped save his leg – the list went on and on. How ungrateful he sounded!

'Sorry, Isolina, I did not mean that. I was angry … not with you but with myself.'

'I understand.'

'No, you don't … I owe you my life. Without you, I would be lying out there somewhere … At least now I can begin to do what I came here for … Without your help that would not have been possible … And, as for Sofia, I would never lay a hand on her.' He wanted to stand, to cross the floor and take her in his arms. Instead, he took out a cigarette and lit it. Isolina came back into the barn and sat on the wooden stool, but did not speak.

'I understand how you feel about the war being brought here,' Mason began. 'As soon as I can move, I will make contact with this Luca fellow and go into the hills. I promise I will not bring this war to your doorstep.'

'It is already here, Mr Mason … and you did not bring it. It is everywhere in Italy. I see it in the faces of all those children, I saw it in my aunt's face, heard it in my cousin's words, and those of the people I saw in Florence. I see it in Simon's face too … It is here, I know that, I am not blind … I'm just scared, Mr Mason, scared for my daughter.'

Mason remained silent.

'May I?' Isolina gazed at the sheet of paper next to him.

'Yes … yes. Be my guest, they are just rough drawings, so don't think …' He stopped speaking as she knelt down to pick them up.

Isolina instantly saw the talent in the young man's hands: in all four sketches, he had captured her daughter perfectly: cleverly portraying the child interwoven with the woman.

She saw Sofia in a different light, and it almost revealed what she refused to accept. In her efforts to protect her, she had not noticed that Sofia was changing, and with that change came the next stage, the one in which Isolina would lose her.

'You have a fine talent, Mr Mason … these are very good.'

'You sound surprised.' He smiled.

'Do I? I'm sorry, I did not mean to … it's just …' She looked away and composed herself. 'May I have this when it's finished?'

'You will have the portrait … the full size one.'

'That is fine, but I feel that these will mean more to me … They have captured something a photograph could never do.'

'And what is that, Isolina?'

'Life … These sketches go below the surface … I do not expect you to understand what a mother sees in her child, but you have revealed it in these. You might be young, Mr Mason, but you are not without empathy.'

He smiled as she returned the drawings. Then he reached across to her and, as her face turned towards his, he lightly kissed her lips. She pulled away and stood silent. There was no emotion in either her face or voice. 'I will tell Luca you are here. I will allow them to visit you. They can bring the radio set here if that is what you want …'

Mason opened his mouth to speak, but Isolina held up her hand.

'Is that all right with you, Mr Mason?'

'Will you call me Richard? And yes, it is my real name.'

'Is that fine with you, Mr Mason?' she asked again.

'Yes, it's perfect with me … Isolina.'

He sounded crushed and looked tired. His face had an embarrassed look about it.

'I am tired. I need my bed … Are you all right? Do you need anything before I go?'

'No …'

'Then I will see you in the morning.'

He watched her go. It had been an instant reaction, no thought had gone into it. But he was shocked at his boldness. He wondered what had made him do such a thing – especially after being so bloody ungrateful to her. He now had the information he needed, even if he had been deceitful in getting it – although, of course, there had been no alternative. However, he regretted dragging Sofia into his little scheme, and deceiving her with his questions. He shuddered to think just how far he was prepared to go to win this bloody war. It was only later that he remembered the kiss.

CHAPTER TEN

Isolina took a detour on her way to Sassa's, and came across Luca sitting on a collapsed wall opposite Gavino's bar. He watched as she brought the car to a shuddering halt. The morning had a chill woven into it, a chill that kissed her cheeks as she climbed from the front seat and began walking across to where Luca remained seated, sucking hard on what was left of his cigarette.

'Buongiorno,' he mumbled.

'I need to see Silvano, Luca.'

His face became roused; the early morning drowsiness left it. He threw the butt to the ground, where it lay smouldering.

'Why?' he asked.

His voice had a cockiness about it that irritated her.

'That is between us … myself and Silvano, Luca.' She spoke with irritation in her voice.

He smiled, seemingly pleased that he had disturbed her normal calm. Eventually, he got to his feet and stretched his back and arms, his eyes never leaving her. He strode past her in silence, opened the passenger door and got in. Isolina stood for a moment, composing herself, before joining him.

They drove in almost total silence, broken only by Luca's occasional directions. Although the route they took was different, she sensed that they were returning to the same place as before. She would let Luca play his silly game. Twenty minutes later, they parked in the same spot and began walking through the undergrowth, where a familiar face met them. Unlike Luca, the man had a welcoming smile and expressed his thanks to her for fixing his wound: despite several minor ailments, he felt on top of the world. Isolina smiled but only half listened, preparing herself mentally for the moment she set eyes on Silvano again.

He stood talking to an older man; next to them stood a wireless balanced on a tree stump. The other man was shrugging his shoulders when he caught sight of her. Silvano turned to see what had transfixed the man.

'Isolina.' He greeted her with a warm yet puzzled smile. 'Why are you …?'

'Can we talk somewhere?' she asked, cutting him off mid-sentence.

'Yes, of course, follow me.'

He made his way past two small, pathetic-looking tents and then beyond another just as pitiful.

'All that education, Silvano … to produce this.' She winced as she heard her own hostile words. That invisible wound was still so raw, making her insensitive, tactless and cruel. She took an instant dislike to herself.

He just grinned. When she was younger, her tongue sometimes got the better of her, but he would never interrupt. He would just stare at her and smile, just like he was doing now.

'Until we get that damn radio working, this place will remain as it is.' His smile grew broader: her tongue could be as sharp as a knife, but he loved her passion. 'It is the best we can do. Most of the men return to family and friends overnight, but the deserters remain up here. I hope that answer satisfies you … So, tell me, why have you come?'

'It seems to solve your problem.'

His eyes met hers, waiting for her to enlighten him.

'Your radio operator is sleeping in my barn.'

'What?'

'His name is Richard Mason and he has a broken leg.'

Silvano tried to absorb what she was telling him.

'How long has he been with you?'

'Is that important?'

'Yes, it is … How long, Isolina?'

'Almost eight weeks.'

'Eight weeks!' The men spread around the camp looked up.

Isolina remained silent. She wanted to look away but, all she could do was stare into his face. There had not been so many lines upon it back then, although, she, too, must have aged. She could still make out the enthusiastic boy; he sat just below the surface of the man. Could he see the girl? The life she had lived had made her advance towards old age swifter. The girl was gone … Only the woman stood before him remained.

'Why did you not say anything when Luca brought you here last?'

'I had my reasons,' she replied, knowing the answer was a weak one.

'And what might they be?'

'My daughter … my home … my life … my choice?' She was talking too fast, and not thinking about what she was saying.

'No harm would have come to you … or your daughter … or your home, for that matter. I would have made certain. Why could you not trust me?'

Isolina stared into his eyes. 'I once would have trusted you with my life … but you let me down. Why would you not do so again?'

'I never let you down, Isolina. I was –'

'Enough, Silvano … what do you want to do about the Englishman? I want to go now.'

Now it was Silvano who became silent. His eyes moved from her face to the hillside in the distance. He thought about that villa, diminishing dreams, and the sadness of it all.

'Can I come and meet him?'

'It is why I am here.'

'Just that?'

'Yes … Nothing else.' She felt her chest tighten. 'Well?'

'How is his leg?'

'He will need to remain with me for another week or two, maybe more.'

'I see.'

'You can bring the radio set to the barn, it will give him something to do.'

'Will tomorrow be convenient for you?'

'Yes.'

'And your daughter, will she be all right with this?'

'She will be fine.'

Silvano stood for a moment looking at her. It made Isolina feel awkward, when he had always made her feel calm.

'Your daughter,' Silvano suddenly said, 'remind me of her name.'

'Sofia.'

His stare became intense. 'One of the names in our game.' He smiled.

Isolina thought about that game, naming their imaginary four children. When they could not agree, she'd told him they would have to have a fifth. She had a picture in her head of the two of them laughing together, the city of Florence in the background.

'Tomorrow then.' Her voice was just a whisper. 'Luca knows where I live,' she said, turning away.

'Isolina.' Silvano's voice was soft and touched with concern. 'I'm sorry.'

She did not look back, she desperately needed to get away, tears were filling her eyes and she was finding it hard to breathe.

'Luca, take me back.' Her words sounded strained.

'Until tomorrow,' Silvano said.

His voice echoed around her head.

~ ~ ~ ~

'Sofia, I have done your neck. There is no need to pull your blouse aside.'

'But I thought … look, my mother is not here, it is not a problem.'

Sofia had entered the barn dressed in a white blouse that was laced under her neck. Mason was certain it was her mother's, he could even smell her perfume on it. She carried a bowl of water and stood waiting for him to prepare her. On her face was a mischievous smile, which made the Englishman all the more unnerved. He looked away as she slowly untied the lace strings.

'Please do it back up.'

'This is my mother's doing.' She was becoming angry.

'It is nothing to do with your mother, Sofia … It is me who asks … and seeing as you are my model, you should obey.'

Sofia's face lit up all at once. 'Yes, I am, I am your model … of course …' A moment later she was doing it up.

'Good,' said Mason staring at his charcoal-stained fingers. He imagined Sofia's mother before him; he would not have asked her to do the blouse up – quite the opposite. He had decided on two more sketches.

'Have you ever been in love?' Sofia suddenly asked.

'I don't think I have … No.'

'But you must know, surely.'

He smiled, reached down and took a cigarette from the pack. He studied the side of her face where the light touched it, creating small shadows below her high cheekbones.

'It is not that simple.'

'All adults say that … but it is simple to me, you are either in love or you are not.'

Mason did not answer. He felt uncomfortable being drawn into this conversation with a fourteen-year-old. He rested the charcoal tip on the paper and slowly ran it downward, and then, with the tip of his finger, smudged it. For the next half hour, he worked in silence.

'When I held hands with Carlo Sergi …'

'The Fascist?'

'Yes … I felt nothing … except how clammy his hands were.'

He laughed. 'His clammy hands.'

'I know *yours* would not have been.'

The smile left his face instantly; things were getting out of hand.

'That is it for today, Sofia. I feel tired.'

'Can't we –'

'Remember what I told you about questioning the artist. I am tired and cannot concentrate.' He laid the board down and stretched his arms. Sofia sat studying his face.

'Do you not miss your father?' asked Mason. The question was a foolish one, only asked to deflect the course of the previous conversation.

'No … not really.'

He was surprised by the answer.

'Does that sound bad? It's just … well, I should do … shouldn't I? Sometimes I feel so …'

'Guilty?'

'Yes … Yes, that is how I feel.'

She seemed to brighten up, to Mason's relief.

'So, why don't …' Now it was he who was searching for words.

'My father was a hated man, a devout Fascist that moved in high circles. He met Mussolini when he came to Florence and worked for the party, and in the corporations set up by the party. It was how we came to live here.'

'You did not always, then?'

'No, it belonged to a Socialist Party member.'

'And he sold it to your father?'

Sofia looked away. 'I'd better go and replace this blouse before Mamma returns. You were right: it is hers.'

With that, she left the barn. Mason lit a cigarette. It seemed that every family had its fair share of skeletons.

~ ~ ~ ~

The sound of a car woke Isolina. Through a haze, she looked at the clock; it was 7.45 a.m. She swung her legs from under the covers and sat for a moment, shivering. Although, it was not really that cold. Perhaps tiredness had brought on a chill. Leaning forward, she grabbed her coat and stood. Still in her nightdress, she pulled it on as Sofia entered the room.

'It's all right,' Isolina smiled, 'they are friends of the Englishman.'

'What do they want?'

'They need help to repair a wireless set.'

Sofia gave her a strange look. 'A wireless set?'

'Come here.'

Her daughter walked slowly towards her. Isolina drew her close, feeling her warmth.

'They are Partisans, Sofia. The Englishman has come to help them. It is the reason he is here – unless you think he came all this way to draw you ...' Isolina smiled.

Sofia returned it. 'Of course not. But ...'

Isolina rocked her, then kissed her forehead before placing a finger under her chin, lifting her head up. 'Stay here please, Sofia, I must go down. Nothing will happen to me or you, and you must never speak of what you see.' Isolina began to tie the belt around her waist.

'Mamma,' Sofia whispered. 'He asked me about Papa.'

Isolina stopped. 'Who?'

'Richard.'

'What did you say?'

'Nothing ... what do I know?' Sofia looked down at her feet.

Isolina said nothing for a moment; there was no time now. In fact, there had never been any time.

'One day, Sofia … one day …'

'When will that day be, Mamma?'

'Soon.'

Isolina turned and made her way downstairs and outside.

Silvano leant against the car, smoking. Behind him Luca blew out a cloud of smoke. Luca had noticed the curtain move when they arrived, and had caught a glimpse of Sofia pulling it back. Without thinking he stuck out his tongue and smiled, watching as the curtain was hastily closed. He did that every time he saw her – why? Well, maybe because she liked the Fascist bastard Carlo Sergi, or maybe because she was becoming more beautiful each time he saw her.

A man sat hunched behind the wheel of a rusty green van, uninterested in what was going on around him. Isolina walked towards them, still securing the belt of her coat. Silvano studied her.

'Buongiorno,' he greeted her.

'You came early.'

'Yes … is it not convenient?'

She stared into his face. 'No … Come,' she made her way towards the barn.

'Luca, the radio set.'

Richard Mason was sitting up. He had already dressed and shaved that morning. He cursed his leg under his breath as he looked up to see three people standing in the open doorway. Mason watched as Isolina held her ground, allowing the tall man to advance with his arm outstretched. Mason took hold of it and felt the solid grip tighten around his own.

'Parla Italiano?' said the Partisan.

'Si,' Mason replied.

'Good – my English is very rusty.'

Luca came forward holding the wireless set. 'Bring it here, Luca.' The boy put it down gently next to the Englishman and stepped back, removing a cigarette.

Isolina wondered if she should leave: the less she knew the better. Instead, she found herself rooted to the spot, leaning against the barn door.

'Is it damaged at all?'

'I have no way of knowing,' replied Silvano. 'We have not been able to get the damn thing to work.'

Mason smiled; he did not feel quite so useless now. 'Have you the aerial?'

'Here.' Luca stepped forward shyly.

Mason now ignored everyone around him. He lifted the wooden lid, revealing a cream metal panel full of knobs, buttons and switches.

'Crystals?'

Luca stepped forward and handed the man four.

'They are important?' asked Silvano.

'Yes. Without these, we cannot make contact with those who can help us. Can your boy take the aerial to the highest point of the barn?'

'Yes. Luca …'

Luca climbed a short, fixed ladder, which took him to half way. With the help of several bales of hay, he managed to stretch up and place the ten-foot aerial in the eves. Mason had fixed the other end into the wireless set. With the aerial sorted, he plugged the transmitter into place, took hold of the headphones and placed them over his ears. Silvano and Luca watched as he turned the knobs and flicked dials. Two lights suddenly glowed in the gloom. Mason continued without saying a word. It was a full ten minutes before he removed his headset and leant back against the post.

'We are operational.' He grinned.

'That's it?'

'Yes … that simple … unless you're a complete idiot.' Mason gave him a smile of superiority – he might be an invalid, but he knew how to work a damn radio set, and that gave him power over these people.

'Leave the aerial where it is … I would not ask if we were in France, but it seems Tuscany has not been found by the war yet, so no one will come looking for it.'

'So, it is safe?'

'For the time being,' Mason answered. 'But as soon as I can get mobile I will leave here and come with you. I have explained what has happened, but they will need to check. I have given them my call signs. For all they know, we could be Germans working the set, but I am sure when they have checked everything, all will be fine.'

'I will send Luca here every day.'

'Not necessary … every other day will do for now.'

'How long before you can walk?'

'You will have to ask my private nurse over there.'

Isolina came forwards from the shadows and stopped next to Silvano.

'Later in the week … Simon will come then and check his leg again, just to be on the safe side.'

'There, you have your answer …' Mason struggled for a name.

'Silvano.'

'Silvano … I am Richard Mason, SOE.'

Silvano smiled, and then his eye caught something on the ground; he bent down and picked up a sheet of paper.

'Your work?' he asked Mason.

'Yes.'

'My daughter.' Isolina spoke.

Silvano's smile broadened, 'Really? Is she shy, for she has removed herself from the page.' He handed it to Isolina.

It was Isolina's face that covered the sheet of paper. He had sketched her in different emotional states, from every angle possible. A smiling Isolina. A sad Isolina. A tearful Isolina. Every inch of the paper had her image on it. Anger rose inside her and she felt her face burn like it was on fire. For some reason, she felt she had been violated. He had exploited her kindness. She looked at Silvano and saw the beginnings of a smile. She allowed the sheet of paper to slip from her fingers and float towards the floor; before it had come to rest, she had left the barn.

CHAPTER ELEVEN

Richard Mason spent each day doggedly walking up and down the barn floor. The crutches dug into his armpits, making them sore and tender. But only when the pain became too much did he stop. He had asked Isolina if there was anything she could do to relieve the soreness, but she had hardly spoken to him since the day Silvano had visited. He made several attempts to bring up the subject, but the words he used had been clumsy.

She spoke about the weather, what he wanted for dinner and whether his leg was painful. She also passed on messages from Silvano, but she never looked at any of the drawings of Sofia. He let it wash over him. He did wonder about one thing – the look this Silvano had given her that morning. Was it one of dislike or of attachment? He smiled, wondering if the tall Italian thought they were lovers, then he placed his head back on the wooden post and blew out a cloud of smoke. Now, that would be nice, he thought.

Mason met with Silvano four times over two weeks. The news Mason shared was good for the men's morale, but Silvano was more interested in getting guns and explosives. Mason spoke of Rommel's retreat in Africa and Mussolini's visit to see Hitler in Bavaria, but the most interesting news of all was that Germany would not come to Italy's aid if attacked: they would offer no military help, although Mussolini repeated that the Axis still held with Germany.

'When Tunisia falls, they will invade Sardinia,' Mason said, sitting down on the wooden stool, exhausted.

'That is good news for Sardinia … but what happens to us? The planes drop leaflets, but little else. Sooner or later, I want to join this war.'

'Patience, Silvano.'

'I have been patient for almost a year now and my patience is beginning to run thin.'

Richard Mason stared at the man and decided that he did not like him. Why? He wasn't sure. Perhaps it was something to do with Isolina, who, he was certain, had not warmed to him either. That pleased him. He looked up to find the Italian was still staring at him. 'There is a rumour circulating of an intended invasion of the Tuscan coast, which would mean the Italian defence lines would be the Tuscan Apennines. That would place us right in the middle; and then, Silvano, you will get your war.'

'But that is just a rumour.'

'No one is going to give away their intentions.'

'So, we sit and do nothing?'

'What else is there to do? The war has still not reached us as yet.' He studied the Italian before smiling. 'You will get your chance to shoot Germans … and Fascist Italians, sooner or later.'

Silvano stared at the Englishman. 'Do not judge me, Englishman. I am glad of your help but do not try to see into my mind. This country is in pain right now, but it will heal itself one day.'

Mason said nothing for a moment. 'I have never known such a divided country, Fascists, Communists, Socialists, all out to gain power. Democracy has vanished into thin air, yet, here I am, risking my life – and for what? You curse Mussolini, yet you do nothing about him – not you but the rest of your people; you bellyache and bellyache, but sit on your arses doing nothing but talk … which it seems you are good at.' He grinned, then removed a cigarette from his top pocket, glad he had said what he had. Now Silvano knew where he stood.

There was silence again, but the atmosphere inside the barn was thick with hostility. Silvano placed a cigarette between his lips, his eyes catlike as he stared at Mason. He set fire to the tobacco and blew out a cloud of smoke.

'Send Luca if there is any more news.' Silvano turned and walked from the barn, leaving Mason smiling on his stool.

~ ~ ~ ~

Fino and Sassa listened to the Italian officer; they had no intention of turning down his request, even if it had been possible. The stable building behind the house was almost empty, it would not take long to clear out what was left inside and whitewash the walls. Planned well, it could house forty to fifty men.

'How many men did you say, Captain?' Fino asked.

'No more than thirty.'

'And where are they from?' added Sassa.

'The camp at Laterina, near Arezzo.'

'We will need time to ready the stables, Captain.'

'Yes … yes, of course.' The Italian officer adjusted his cap. The dark smudges under his eyes emphasised how tired he was. 'I will send a truck with wood, nails and some paint; and six strong men.'

The stable would be perfect to house the prisoners: just one door in and out, no windows – all he would need to do was secure the door and roof.

'Coffee, Captain?'

'That would be most welcome.'

They walked back slowly to the main house. The day was warm and the children played outside on the lawn. Isolina sat with Anna, wrapping clean bandages; the captain smiled at them as he walked past. Carter and Edwards came out of the clinic carrying a large wooden box.

'Good morning,' said the Italian in good English.

They both nodded as they struggled past.

'You speak good English, Captain,' Sassa said.

'I should do, I married an English girl fourteen years ago. We live … or used to, in a place called St Albans.'

'These must be hard times for you both.'

'Yes.'

'Is she with you?'

'No, thank God … She loves this county as she does me; to see it now would break her heart.'

'This is a crazy war.'

'Yes,' replied the Captain, whose eyes had misted over.

~ ~ ~ ~

Sofia walked quickly towards home. Richard Mason's time now seemed split between her and his radio set, meaning her portrait was taking forever. Inside, she felt the anticipation of his fingers travelling through her hair, and it made her breathe in a lungful of air and close her eyes. Opening her eyes, she found herself looking straight into the face of a boy.

'Sofia.'

Carlo Sergi stood in front of her, along with his friend Alfeo Sita, a puny, pale-looking boy, whom she despised.

'Carlo ... Alfeo ...'

'How have you been?'

Sofia wanted to walk on, but, out of politeness, answered his question. 'I am fine.'

'And your mother ...' Carlo seemed nervous, 'where is she today?'

'With Sassa.'

'And the Englishman ...'

Sofia froze on the spot – how did he know about the Englishman? Her mouth became dry and her heart began to beat a little faster.

'Englishman? What Englishman?'

'Those at Sassa's.' He gave her a strange look.

Sofia felt the relief spread through her body. 'Yes ... the prisoners of war.'

'Who did you think I meant?'

'I was not certain they were English.'

'Well, they are, and there are more on the way my father said, a lorry-load.'

'More?'

'Yes, we capture more every day. Most surrender, they have no stomach for the fight. They throw up their hands at the sight of an Italian with a rifle pointed at them ... But, after Grosseto, we should just shoot them all.'

'Grosseto?' Sofia asked.

'You have not heard of the massacre at the amusement park?'

'No.'

'They machine-gunned the tents where the children were playing on the merry-go-rounds. Even running to the parish priest for protection did not save them: they swooped again, shooting at everything they saw. They even bombed the nearby hospital, to prevent the injured from being treated there. They were left with nothing, no swabs, bandages or medicines.'

'Were any of them children?'

'Yes, there were many who died: women and children … I will bring you a copy of the newspaper my father received, it will make you sick.'

'No, I do not wish to see it.'

'They tell so many lies about the Germans … although, now we see the Americans as the barbarians.' Carlo stopped talking and stared at Sofia, she really was turning into a beauty. His eyes removed every stitch of clothing from her body. 'My father spoke about your father the other night. He told me he was a good Fascist, loyal, a credit to Mussolini and Italy. It is such a pity what happened to him.'

Sofia stared at the boy. 'And what did your father tell you?'

'That he was murdered … on the train, somewhere between here and Rome.'

Sofia felt nauseous. She had heard the same overall story, but she had been told he had died in a bomb blast, a simple case of wrong place, wrong time. She had watched him leave for the last time from her upstairs window. Her mother was to drive him to the station. Isolina had looked up briefly, smiled and waved. Sofia could still see the bruise on her cheek and the cut on her lip.

Her father had not spoken to her that morning as he had still been annoyed with her over something that had happened at school. She and little Aaron Bak, the Jewish boy, had been playing together since they were six. She had never argued with her father before – fear had always got the better of her – but, on this occasion, she had demanded to know the reason why she was being prevented from playing with him. This was the first time he had raised a hand to her. Only her mother's intervention averted the threat.

She had gone to bed in tears, but a storm had begun downstairs. Her parents screamed at each other, but it was unusual to hear her mother raise her voice to him, for his voice alone always dominated their house. Even from her bedroom, she had heard flesh striking flesh violently, which was followed by silence. No more raised voices, just the ticking of the clock and Sofia's breathing. She crept to the top of the stairs and saw her mother standing with her back to her, before she turned to reveal the blood stain on her dress.

Sofia had remained hidden, embarrassed by what she had seen. How strange it was to feel that emotion. Should she not have been ashamed of her father? She had never spoken to her mother about that night, or really mourned her father's passing like a daughter should have. She also never saw Aaron Bak again.

'You and your father are like old women … you listen to all the gossip.'

Carlo smiled. 'Sofia, one day you will come running to me for help.'

'I would never do such a thing.'

'Today, you say that … you have your mother to protect you … but, one day, she will not be around to do so, and you will become the perfect Fascist mother and give birth to an army of fighting boys ... Just how many children will we have, Sofia? Five, six?' He began to laugh.

Sofia felt her face turn crimson. She turned and ran, knowing it was the worst thing she could have done. She could still hear their laughter coming from behind her.

~ ~ ~ ~

'I have never seen so much food.' Sassa was staring at the contents of a POW's Red Cross parcel. 'Butter, marmalade, cocoa, tinned meat ... soap ...' She looked up at Isolina, who showed little interest. 'Is something the matter, Isolina?'

'No ... no, not really ... Sofia seems quieter these past few days, and she has not gone to the barn.'

'Is that not a good thing, in light of what you have told me?'

'Maybe ... but I feel there is something else.'

'She is fourteen ... today's problem is forgotten tomorrow, like an argument with a good friend.'

'Yes.'

'Bring her here, Isolina, the change of scenery will do her good. She can come and see the new Tuscan prison.' Sassa laughed out loud. 'The stables are cosy and clean, a little primitive perhaps, but nevertheless habitable, and far better than those at the other camp, so Captain Adams informs me.'

Sassa had taken in twenty-seven prisoners yesterday. She stood and looked towards the distant hills, which were shrouded in mist, while the morning sun burnt a hole through the haze.

'The children ... are they well?' she asked. 'Anna?'

Isolina suddenly came back to life. 'Yes … Anna is my star pupil.'

'She adores you, Isolina.'

'She misses her parents … whom she will hopefully see soon.'

'I think there will always be a place in her heart for you.' Sassa's face suddenly became dark. 'Father Mariano came yesterday with some chilling news.'

'What did he say?'

'Some disturbing news about Grosseto.'

Sassa explained about the lives lost and the carnage left behind by the Allied bombing.

Isolina's face lost its colour. 'Surely that is not possible.'

'The women in the village are barricading their doors, it seems … to keep out the enemy we have in our stables.'

'I cannot believe it, Sassa.'

'I find it hard to swallow myself … but they have photographs to support their claim … pictures of dead women and children laid out in a line.'

'No more,' said Isolina.

'The Fascists will use this to arouse hatred in the Italian people towards the British and Americans, while the anti-Fascists will say it was Fascism that brought all this on us. It is a never-ending circle of hate and fear … I do not know where it is going to end.'

~ ~ ~ ~

Richard Mason stood staring at Silvano as the sun set on another uneventful day.

'London thinks there are three quarters of a million Germans in Italy already, spread around the country … The

Germans are worried about something … maybe the Axis breaking?'

'It means they will not need to invade … since they are already here,' the Italian added.

'Bravo, Silvano … Now, the good news … They want to make a drop of weapons in roughly two weeks. Your long wait, it seems, is over.'

Silvano's face lit up.

'I told them what we needed,' Mason went on.

'Without consulting me?' Silvano felt his neck muscles tighten.

'Look, old boy, I've been doing this for two years now, let me tell you what I have asked for before you pee your pants.'

Silvano's hand formed a fist, but it remained hidden. He listened to Mason tell him about the consignment, and yet his anger increased despite the list being more than he could have hoped for. It was the sheer sight of the Englishman that irritated him now.

'Another thing …' Mason cleared his throat. 'Carlo Sergi – do you know him?'

'Not the boy so much as his father, a Fascist, who craves nothing but power and money. Surrounds himself with armed men twenty-four hours a day. Why do you ask?'

'It seems the boy is going around telling people about an American raid on a place called Grosseto … have you heard about it.'

'No … why?'

'The Zotti's' place has been turned into a prison camp.'

'I know.'

'Carlo's stories are arousing passion in Fascist circles … It's making them hot under the collar, shall we say. With temperatures running high, anything could happen.'

'Are you asking me to keep an eye on the place?'

'What a grand idea, Silvano … we will make a soldier of you yet.'

CHAPTER TWELVE

Simon Stein looked up as Isolina approached. Sitting outside Sassa's door, he had just finished his coffee. The aging doctor felt his joints protest against his decision to stand and greet the woman, as was his custom.

'Buongiorno.'

Isolina smiled, but it was a weary attempt. She had woken this morning with a feeling of suffocation. During the night, she had found it hard to breath. A sense of panic had wrapped tightly around her chest, squeezing the oxygen from her lungs. When sleep had been possible, she recalled, fragments of dreams had penetrated her slumbers: Silvano's smile; Carlo Sergi holding Sofia's hand, and the Englishman sketching her daughter's naked body.

'You look well, Simon.'

'You lie so well.'

Isolina's smile grew. 'Why are there so many people here?'

'They have come to see Fino. It seems the young men from the surrounding farms have been called to the colours – not that he can do very much.'

'None are Fascist.'

'Quite so, but they have been given promises of safety,

frequent leave and all have been asked to join the militia, not the army.'

'But they must know that Fino cannot do anything to help.'

'It seems the promises did not work; all of them have refused. Now they want to hear what Fino thinks the young boys should do.' Simon removed a cigarette from the packet. 'Do you know, Isolina, what day it is today?'

'I have no idea.'

'It is the third anniversary of Italy's entry into the war.'

Isolina did not answer; she would certainly not celebrate the fact. A woman dressed in black approached, a farmer's wife. Next to her walked a boy of no more than sixteen, wearing baggy dirt-stained trousers and a grubby white shirt, both far too large for him.

'I do not know what to do, doctor,' the woman stated as she approached Simon. Her face was lined from the harsh farming life she had led in the hills. 'He is my youngest ... My husband is bedridden, my oldest boy somewhere in Greece, my daughter has gone to Milan ... he is all I have to help keep the farm running ... and now ...' The woman broke down in tears. The boy placed a thin arm around his mother, and rested his head on her shoulder.

'Mamma, do not cry. I am not going anywhere, they will understand, I am certain.'

Isolina and the doctor glanced at each other. If Vito Sergi had anything to do with it, there would be no such understanding. Mother and son wept side by side, and Isolina's nightmares of last night became a harsh reality of the morning. With each passing day, Tuscany becomes further touched by the war, she thought. She gazed at

Simon, looked at the mother with her boy, and felt the panic of last night return.

~ ~ ~ ~

Mason heard the sound of a car engine. He reached for his jacket and removed the revolver, before ducking back into the shadows. Sofia had gone back to the house just as her session was about to start, and had left the barn unlocked. Four shadows now approached the open doorway. He swallowed the small amount of saliva inside his mouth, clicked back the safety catch, and waited in silence.

'Mason,' Silvano called out from just inside the doorway. Mason, with one crutch fixed under his arm, hopped out from the darkness. 'Why have you brought an army with you? I'm not sure Montgomery has this many men?' His voice was filled with sarcasm.

'What?' Silvano said, not fully understanding the Englishman's humour.

'Never mind,' Mason said, replacing the gun. 'By the way, thank you for the gun … not as good as the one I lost, but it will do.'

'Why was the door left unlocked? You have the radio set here?'

'You're worried about the radio … and there I was thinking your concern was for my wellbeing.' Mason grinned.

His eyes travelled across the faces of those who had entered his domain, his stare lingering on the last of them, a woman. He drew himself upright and stared a little longer. She was about his age, pretty in a boyish sort of way. Her hair was a mass of tight curls pulled back, but her lips were harsh; he wondered if her smile might soften her stern face. Her eyes met his stare, eyes that were full of determination. Could this be Silvano's woman? Suddenly those stern lips parted and she spoke.

'Do you want me to get on my knees and suck your cock?' Her voice had a huskiness about it.

'No,' Mason said, taken by surprise. He almost laughed out loud.

'Then why do you stare at me like I was some common whore?'

'I am sorry, I am an artist, maybe I was –'

She interrupted him. 'Removing my clothes? Put them back on. Unlike a lot of Italian women, I am not about to thank you with my body, you need to earn my respect first.' Now she smiled, it had the required effect of softening her face.

The others in the barn began to laugh, including Silvano. Mason smiled, too; all he could do was to accept defeat with dignity.

'There is to be no drop,' he suddenly said. In a flash, all the smiles disappeared. 'Things are going on, bigger things,'

'Things … what things?' Silvano asked, annoyed at the smug look on the Englishman's face.

'I can't say.'

'Can't or won't?'

Mason desperately wanted a cigarette … what he was telling these Partisans was all he had been told himself, and although he did not like the tall Italian, he could sympathise with his frustration.

'I really do not know … If I did, I would tell you.'

One of Silvano's men lit up a cigarette, almost compelling Mason to ask if he could have one.

'So, what next?' prompted the woman.

'We wait.'

She shrugged her shoulders. 'And that is it?'

'Yes.'

'We will do as you say, but we won't wait forever … Come, Ambra, unless you want your portrait painted – I think you have made an impression.'

The young woman smiled, just as Sofia returned holding a packet of cigarettes.

'Sorry – should I go?'

'No,' said Mason catching sight of the packet.

'Sorry … I could not find them.' Sofia addressed Mason but stared at Silvano and the woman next to him. She wondered where Luca was.

'This is Isolina's daughter,' Mason informed the group of visitors.

Silvano stepped forward and smiled. 'A pleasure,' he said, unable to take his eyes from her face; it was like staring into her mother's face, which he had done long ago. Daughter and mother were so alike, almost every feature comparable.

'I knew your mother … before you.'

'A long time ago then?'

'Yes … many years.'

'What is your name?'

'Silvano.'

'Strange, I have never heard her speak of you …'

Silvano smiled. 'Maybe I was not so important … who knows – but you are blessed with her looks, so I apologise if I stared at you. It is just that you look so alike. When I first knew her, she was only several years older than you are today.'

Mason coughed. 'Sofia, may I have a cigarette?'

'Sorry.' Sofia glanced at Silvano again before walking across to give Mason the packet.

'Look, Silvano, leave it a week or so, then come and see me. I am certain that whatever it is, it will be of benefit to us all.'

'Let us hope so.' Silvano said, before looking again in Sofia's direction. 'Pleased to have met you, remember me to your mother.'

'I will.'

As all four began to leave, Richard Mason shouted out, 'Goodbye, Ambra ... and yes, one day, I would love to draw you naked.' He laughed.

'Maybe one day, Englishman ... maybe,' she returned, not looking back.

Mason laughed again. Sofia glared at him before following the others outside.

'Wait, Sofia ... We have not finished for today.'

'Maybe Ambra can stand in for me.'

Mason's smile broadened; jealousy was such a female emotion.

~ ~ ~ ~

Overhead flew six German planes. Southbound. Isolina watched as they disappeared across the valley and beyond the hills. This had gone on all morning: something was happening somewhere. She was waiting for Sofia. It was Anna's birthday and Sassa had laid on a party and Father Remo was going to conduct a mass. Isolina went and sat inside the car, gazing at the house and the barn as she waited. Both Mason and his wireless set were in the hills. Three men, including Luca, had come to collect him at dawn.

Two weeks had passed since Sofia asked: '*Who is Silvano?*' *She had said it innocently, and why not, it was all before she had been born, in another life, when Isolina had been another person, not the Isolina of now.*

'Yes, I remember him.'

'Why have you never talked about him, never mentioned his name?'

'Why would I? I have met many people in my life, Sofia, and have never needed to tell you their names, or anything about them for that matter. They are just people you come across in life.'

'He said it was because he was not an important part of your life.'

Sitting here, she felt the pain of those words come back to haunt her, as if betraying an old friend. Suddenly the door opened and Sofia got in.

'Shall we go?'

~ ~ ~ ~

Sassa's greetings always embarrassed Sofia. They were so theatrical, filled with love and over-enthusiasm.

'Anna is waiting inside for you. She has driven us all mad this morning … constantly asking when you were coming.'

Isolina felt for her daughter's hand, hoping she did not feel left out. Simon Stein came up behind, smiling at Sassa. The woman was so full of energy – if only he possessed just some.

'Simon,' Isolina acknowledged him.

'Come,' said Sassa, placing her arm around Sofia's waist and advancing towards the house, where a tired Father Remo stood smoking by the door.

'I heard sounds in the distance this morning,' Isolina whispered, holding onto Simon's left arm. 'It sounded like bombing.'

'Most likely a naval bombardment on the Tuscan coast.'

Isolina said nothing and continued to walk. Father Remo stepped on his finished cigarette and smiled at the approaching party.

'A young girl inside is very much looking forward to seeing you.'

'Yes, I've been told.'

Twenty German planes chose that moment to fly overhead, on the same southbound path as the earlier ones.

'I wonder what's happening,' Simon said.

'All I hear in Florence is rumour,' Father Remo answered, 'most of it unbelievable. These are strange times. Times without faith, almost unbearable.'

'Each day my faith becomes more diluted,' Isolina said, looking towards the sky.

'Come, child,' said the priest, placing a hand on her shoulder, 'remain strong, for he will watch over us … of that I am certain. Now, let us go inside and place a smile on the face of these unfortunate children, let us bring some joy into their lives.'

Baskets of flowers, along with several smaller presents, had been given to Anna by the other children, all paid for by Fino and Sassa. Anna, her hair now growing back, cried with each gift received, especially the soap given by Isolina and Sofia. Father Remo then began the small Mass.

'The Lord is my light and my salvation, whom shall I fear? The Lord is the protector.' Father Remo stared at Isolina. 'Of my life, of whom shall I be afraid?'

Isolina heard no more, becoming lost in thought. The planes and the sound of bombs in the distance, disturbed her. It had brought the reality of war a step closer. It had crossed her mind to leave Tuscany, maybe take Sofia to Switzerland where it would be safe; Simon too. A door opened behind her and she turned to see Simon holding it open and beckoning her towards him.

'What is it, Simon?' she said in a whisper on reaching him.

His face had lost all its colour. 'The Allies have just landed in Sicily ... It has begun, Isolina.'

~ ~ ~ ~

Over the next ten days Sassa's radio became the focal point in the house. At various times of the day, Isolina found herself sitting with Fino and Sassa, huddled around the walnut-veneered wireless. It appeared the whole of Italy was being bombed: Genoa, Naples and Parma. Every broadcast on Radio London urged the Italian people to overthrow the Fascist regime.

'Turin has been bombed repeatedly.' The seamstress, Simona Piro, spoke while drinking her coffee. Simona had come to collect wheat as payment for work, with her fourteen-year-old daughter.

'Keep it away from the children,' Sassa urged in response, 'they have heard little or nothing over these past few weeks from home, and some of the older ones are beginning to worry.'

'I hear the Carabinieri Captain was here yesterday?' Simona Piro asked.

'Yes,' Sassa replied. 'He wanted to know who had told the Allied prisoners of the landings in Sicily.'

'They suspect one of my stablemen,' Fino stated, sitting in his leather chair and smoking his pipe.

A maid entered the room clutching a bundle of letters. Sassa took them all.

'Come, Isolina, let us see what news we have, and pray it is good ... Sorry, Simona, the wheat is outside the kitchen door.'

Fino watched Sassa with concern, knowing there would be little, if any, good news in the letters. He already felt despondent about his wife, and knew there would be nothing he could do. None of his wealth could make life better for her.

Sassa had already ripped open the first of the envelopes before they entered the study across from the radio room. Sassa began to pace, scrutinising the words on each sheet of paper. Some she read a second or third time, turning the page over to see if there was more on the other side. Her face reflected what she had read: anguish and distress mainly.

Isolina reluctantly opened one letter and began to read: tales of hardship and destruction. The Fiat works had been hit badly, as well as several churches. The houses of two children had been destroyed; only a miracle had saved the parents, and for that Isolina was grateful. Sassa suddenly held back a cry, making Isolina look up from her letter. One of the children had lost both parents, and her sixteen-year-old sister. Sassa slumped back into her chair, rivers of tears flowing down her cheeks. She looked across to Isolina, and, with her hand shaking, passed her the letter.

Isolina began to read. It was her turn to shed tears, tears that tumbled relentlessly down her cheeks. She found it hard to catch her breath, and still they fell, a monsoon of grief.

She knew already that it would fall to her to tell Anna. Fino entered the room to see both women crying; he did no more than stare in silence. He could think of nothing to say.

~ ~ ~ ~

'I have not seen you, Sofia. I would like to finish your portrait and it is your birthday soon. It would be nice to give it to you on that day.'

'You have not been here that much since you began to walk again.'

'I know, I've had to spend some time in the hills.'

'With her, I suppose?'

Mason tried hard not to smile. 'Who?' he asked.

'The woman, the one with that Silvano.'

'Sofia, this is silly, I have not seen her since that day.'

He had lied: he wanted to call a truce, irritated by the fourteen-year-old's childish behaviour. He saw the faint outline of a smile form on her lips.

Sofia crossed the floor to him. Her confident movement made him feel less confident of himself. She stopped, far too close for comfort. Today she wore a thin, check blouse, open around the neck, with her hair tied back.

'What?' he began to speak, but, before he knew what was happening, Sofia's lips were resting on his, and she was forcing her tongue deep into his mouth. Mason's first reaction was to pull away, but his attempt was weak. He returned the kiss before coming to his senses and pulling away.

'No!' He stepped back.

'But you kissed me back.'

He said nothing, his breathing hurried, his throat dry. Mason stared at the young girl and a feeling of shame descended on him. He was a man trained to kill, and yet he felt like a helpless child around this girl.

'You wanted me,' Sofia whispered.

Where had the young, shy girl gone? That sweet, innocent girl he had first set eyes upon? Sofia moved towards him again, her eyes bright, her lips tempting.

'No, Sofia! I do not want you … You are a child … What I did was wrong. It will not happen again.'

She stopped. Her eyes glazed over. Finally, a tear escaped and rolled down her cheek.

'Sofia,' he whispered, before making a second mistake and reaching out to her.

Now it was Sofia who backed away. She stared into his eyes, turned, and ran.

'Sofia …' Mason shouted as she disappeared out of the doors, passing a surprised-looking Silvano, who had just arrived.

'I see you have a way with women.' Silvano allowed himself a smile.

Mason stared at him for a moment. 'Fuck off.'

~ ~ ~ ~

Isolina sat with a silent Anna. Solitude had become her only company. Both Isolina's and Simon's attempts to talk to her had failed miserably.

'Time …' Simon whispered to Sassa, 'it's what she needs the most … Love and time. Her whole world has fallen apart. What has happened to her … someone older would find hard to deal with – you have to remember, she is a child.'

Anna freed herself from Isolina's embrace and walked towards the window. She stood looking towards the hills while Isolina remained seated, feeling helpless. She wondered if taking Anna home would help. Although, the Englishman visited the barn at times and Sofia had become almost unrecognisable, a girl who merely masqueraded as her daughter.

From overhead came the sound of aeroplanes. Moments later, Anna was out of the room and running down the hallway, out the front door and into the sunlight.

'Anna!' Isolina shouted in pursuit. 'Anna, stop …'

Sassa came out the study, while Fino ran down the staircase.

'What's happened?' he asked.

'It's Anna,' Sassa screamed.

The planes continued to make their way towards the hillside with Anna giving chase.

'ANNA!' Isolina shouted again. 'Please, stop.'

But Anna was in full flight now, desperate to keep up with the planes overhead, it seemed. It was the young English prisoner, Carter, who caught her.

'Hey, what's going on?' he said in English. 'Where you going, lass?' He smiled at the girl.

Anna fought to free herself just as Isolina arrived, breathless.

'Thank you.'

She held Anna, but the wild-eyed young girl stared straight at the young soldier.

'Murderer …' she screamed at him. 'We should have let you bleed to death when you cut your finger … *murderer* …'

Isolina fought to restrain her. 'Anna, stop this.'

Carter had no clue as to what the girl was saying. It was obvious she was upset, but he failed to understand why she vented her anger at him.

'English bastard,' Anna spat at the young soldier.

'Stop this, Anna.' Sassa had now arrived. 'Stop this, girl, this instant.'

'Bastard ... bastard ... bastard ...'

'Anna.'

'What is she saying?' Carter asked, his face full of concern.

Fino came to lead the young man away. 'It has nothing to do with you ... do not concern yourself.'

'Okay,' Carter mumbled, but continued to look back over his shoulder.

Isolina held Anna in her arms, hoping to calm her. The girl began to sob, burying herself in Isolina's chest.

'When will this end?' Sassa whispered.

'Maybe sooner than you think.' Fino had come back from the house.

'What is it?'

'Mussolini has fallen ... he has resigned ... last night, so it seems. The King has appointed Marshal Badoglio in his place.'

Isolina rocked Anna gently in her arms, while Sassa looked at the two of them.

'Is this the end ... or just the beginning?'

CHAPTER THIRTEEN

Isolina parked close to the footpath, with Sofia sat beside her. There was to be no school for the foreseeable future. Isolina had come to the village to see Mario Pinto, hoping he might spare some oil for the car: the grating noise inside the engine had become deafening. The village seemed quiet today, not that it was ever busy lately. These were awkward times, speculation being the order of the day. After twenty years, change impacted on the people here. Sassa reminded Isolina that martial law had been imposed: as well as a curfew at sunset, public meetings were also banned.

The talk on most people's lips was simply, *what has happened to Mussolini? And, what of the Germans' silence?* Mario sat as usual at his workbench, his hands stained permanently with oil. Nuts, bolts, washers and tools covered the work surface. He sat with his glasses perched agonisingly close to the end of his nose. He looked up as Isolina and Sofia entered.

'Buongiorno, Isolina,' he murmured, his eyes quickly returning to the work in front of him.

'I hope I am not disturbing you.'

'You are …' he said without looking at her. 'But you have a good reason … hopefully.'

Isolina could not keep the smile from her lips: the old man never changed, always appearing grumpy with his customers, who nonetheless remained loyal to him.

'I need some oil, Mario, the engine sounds dreadful.'

'I know. I heard it. My *wife* heard it ... and she has been dead for sixteen years.'

Sofia, already bored, turned her head to look outside. Carlo Sergi chose that moment to walk past with friends.

'Yes, I have some, Isolina ... if you can wait while I finish here.'

'I could do it my –'

'No, no, no ... wait, child.'

Lorenzo Ales, a newspaper held in front of him, came running into the workshop.

'Have you seen this?' He placed it under the old man's nose.

'Am I to get no peace today?' said Mario, puffing out his cheeks. The job he was working on lay hidden under the newspaper. 'Sorry, Isolina, Lorenzo here feels the need to inform me about more bad news ... for that is what keeps the man happy.'

Mario pushed his glasses back and began to read.

'It seems he was betrayed by his own men,' he said aloud.

'Poetic justice, I say,' Lorenzo added. 'See down there.' The man reached over and pointed his finger.

'I can see for myself, Lorenzo. Kindly allow me to do things in my own time.'

Lorenzo ignored the old man and turned to Isolina. 'There have been demonstrations all over Italy ... Milan, Bologna, and also in Florence.'

Isolina thought about Savina and Fabia.

'In Rome, they shot some Blackshirts,' Lorenzo spoke with enthusiasm. 'They destroyed busts and statues of Mussolini.'

'Badoglio's decreed that all public meetings will be dispersed by the police,' Mario said without looking up. 'He said that this is no moment to give way to impulsive demonstrations, the gravity of the hour ...' Mario looked up just then and stopped speaking.

'Go on, Mario, you seem passionate. Continue.'

It was the voice of Vito Sergi. Lorenzo, Isolina and Sofia turned and looked at the man. 'Go on,' Vito urged the old man.

Mario laid the paper down slowly. 'No, Vito, I have read enough.'

'Like in the old days, the papers print lie upon lie for the simple people to swallow.'

'These are all lies, Vito?' Mario smiled.

'Do you see people demonstrating here, old man?'

'No ... but that might have something to do with your thugs walking around carrying guns.'

'Are we not to protect ourselves? You have read yourself about Fascists being shot for no reason.'

'For no reason ...' Mario mumbled under his breath.

Lorenzo reached across and gathered his newspaper up. 'It says in here that it is forbidden to carry firearms.'

Vito laughed. 'And you, Lorenzo Ales ... the biggest coward of all – are you going to disarm us?'

Lorenzo could not meet his stare.

'I thought not ... Listen to me, the Germans will not allow a great leader such as ours to be treated this way.' He looked around the workshop. 'Today is a good day for Italian cowards ... enjoy it.' Vito turned, replaced the hat he had been holding across his chest, and dipped his head to Isolina and Sofia.

'It is you I came to see, Isolina. I noticed my car parked outside.'

'*Your* car? ... I think you will find it is *my* car.'

'Only by my generosity, and the high regard I held for your late husband, a great man.' He drew breath. 'A man you seemed to mourn for a short period ... if at all. How long did you wear black, Isolina ... a day, an hour, or the blink of an eye?'

'I mourn when and how I like, Vito.' Isolina stared at the man she despised more than any other.

Vito smiled. 'I touched a nerve I feel.'

Isolina thought about responding, but refrained.

'And Sofia ...' Vito looked at the young girl standing next to her mother. He lifted his hand and Sofia took a step back. 'Your husband and I had great plans for her and my boy, Carlo.'

'Well, some things were never meant to be, Vito.' Isolina had regained her composure, and took hold of Sofia's arm. 'Mario, could you give me the oil, please, I feel the need to leave.'

'Yes,' said Mario rising from his chair.

'I will allow you to keep the car for now.' Vito smiled as he spoke. 'I, myself, still mourn a good friend.'

Isolina was already outside in the watery sunlight, her body shaking with anger. From across the street, Carlo Sergi stared at them both, with the look of his father about him.

~ ~ ~ ~

Richard Mason folded his clothes, took the gun, and placed everything inside the bag. He gathered his sketches, glancing at them quickly, knowing his decision to leave was the correct one. Sofia's actions had made it impossible for him to remain here. Mason stared at her face, tempted even now to make alterations. But there was no need to improve on perfection.

How many times had he succumbed to temptation? He was weak, like most men, when confronted by beauty, fresh soft skin and the innocence of an angel. But it was not always his fault. He found it strange that, when he held a pencil or brush, it always seemed to arouse passion in a woman, some kind of animal sexuality. He was human. Was it his fault that he was unable to refuse what was being offered? He had lost count of the times he'd woken naked, stained with paint, and a beautiful, naked woman lying next to him.

But he had lost more than he had gained. Those he cherished most had left him. When he found love, he had tossed it back like a pebble into the sea. And it was love that he craved, not sex. He often though he was in love, but when temptation came, it swallowed him whole … and no one in love should surrender so easily.

He had not been able to speak with Sofia: either she was avoiding him, or it was a simple case of circumstances changing. At first, he feared she would say something to her mother; the evidence would be damning, and Isolina would always back her daughter. But that had not been the case: Isolina had remained pleasant to him.

He heard a car pull up outside as he tightened the bag straps. He had expected to walk across the country, and was looking forward to the exercise. But Sofia's face, when it appeared, told him something was wrong.

'Germans … two of them,' she whispered. 'Mother told me to come and warn you … You are to remain here.'

'What do they want?'

'Only one speaks Italian – I am not certain. He was being very polite. She has hung out the white sheet to warn those coming for you.'

Mason smiled. 'That is good. Go and stand in the doorway, Sofia, and tell me if they come this way.'

'What will you do?'

'Hide.'

'Not shoot them?'

'No.'

A strange conversation to have with a fourteen-year-old, Mason thought, a sign of the times.

'Sofia, I am sorry I hurt you,' he whispered. 'I did not mean to call you a child, you are not. I was wrong, although it was wrong to kiss you back.'

'But you did.'

'I know … but it was wrong of me,' he continued to whisper.

She took a step inside the barn, and Mason pressed his back against the door. He suddenly realised that the alarm he felt was not from the presence of the Germans, but how close Sofia was to him.

'Kiss me again,' Sofia said, looking straight into his eyes.

'No.' He almost laughed.

'You want to.'

'Sofia, there are two Germans in your house, does that not worry you?'

'Why would I worry when you are here?'

'Go back now.' His voice suddenly became stern. '*Now*, Sofia … Please.'

He stared at the girl, her lips within reach. Her unblemished olive skin summoning him, her eyes hypnotising and clear. He swallowed hard.

'Please …' he whispered.

Sofia was gone in a flash. Mason rested his head on the door and ran his fingers through his hair.

~ ~ ~ ~

Isolina turned off the main road, exchanging one dirt track for another. She drove past a group of six small cottages, past the local café, seed shop and garage and continued deep into rural Tuscany, Sofia silent next to her. The engine sounded quieter after adding Mario's oil, but it did emit a sickly scorched smell.

The car climbed the narrow county roads, which looked down on golden fields of ripening wheat. As they continued to ascend between rows of olive vines that fell away down the hillside, Cypress trees lined the road ahead and birds became airborne with the sound of Isolina's noisy engine. She drove with care, panicking occasionally when the car came too close to a sheer drop, until finally the home of the Stolfi family appeared.

The Stolfi family numbered nine in all. The father, Gianni, and his wife, Suzetta, their offspring, the oldest boy Vincenzo, Lucia his wife, his brother Dario and his wife Cristina, plus their son, Paolo. Finally, there was seventeen-year-old Fabrizio, and Mimi, the youngest at fifteen.

If this war had barely scratched the surface of rural Tuscany, then the Stolfi farm was in another world altogether. Only the eldest, Vincenzo, took any interest in it. His awareness of the world beyond the boundaries of his farm grew the more he learned about the conflict, and so the more drawn to it he became. But, to his father, it just meant it was becoming harder to transport their produce.

Like the rest of the family, Vincenzo could not read. It was not necessary, since he only needed his hands to plant and pick what grew. One sweated, washed, ate and slept – what purpose would reading play in rural life? Vincenzo took the wheat or olive oil to market, travelling to Lucca and Florence, amongst other places. There, he would buy newspapers, before waiting for either the Jewish doctor or Isolina to visit.

Isolina parked behind an abandoned hand cart. A single oak tree grew in the field adjacent, under which two mules chewed on grass, seemingly content. Isolina climbed out and removed her bag.

'Are you coming?'

Sofia sighed deeply, pulled an irritated face, and climbed from the car. The midday sun gave the day the feel of a furnace being opened, scalding their naked skin and sucking the moisture from it. The farmhouse sat at the base of a steep hillside where old olive trees gently swayed in the warm breeze that swept down from the higher slopes.

Groves of chestnuts robbed the farmhouse of a north-easterly view. The two-storey building was rendered with cement, which, in places, resembled festering sores, all painted in a washed-out pale green. Stone slabs covered the roof where the house had been extended. Suzetta came out to greet them wearing her stained white apron and a headscarf. In all her visits, Isolina had never once seen her hair loose.

'Buongiorno … Buongiorno …' the woman cried, quickening her pace with each step.

'Buongiorno,' Isolina smiled.

Suzetta wiped her hands, adding further stains to her apron before embracing them both. She gazed towards the bottom fields.

'The boys and their father will be back soon for some lunch … You will join us?'

This was not an invitation you turned down.

'Sofia, you look so beautiful.' Suzetta gripped her cheek between thumb and forefinger. Sofia forced a smile. 'You need to be married, child.'

'She is just fourteen, Suzetta,' said Isolina.

The woman placed a hand on Sofia's stomach. 'You can give your mother plenty of grandchildren … My Fabrizio will be here soon.' There was mischief in her smile.

As Suzetta walked back to the house, Sofia, with a face like thunder, turned to face her mother.

'*Don't …*' said Isolina.

The moment Isolina stepped inside the house, her senses were overcome by the smell of cooking: herbs and spices mixed with that of burning wood. Steam rose from saucepans on the wood-burning stove, each well-used and battered in places. Mimi was laying out bowls on a long wooden table that almost ran the length of the room. Her eyes widened as she saw Sofia.

'Sofia,' she screamed. 'Are they staying for dinner, Mamma?'

'Of course they are.'

'Where is Cristina?' asked Isolina laying her bag down.

'She is on her way,' Lucia responded, coming down the staircase.

'And, how are you?' asked her mother-in-law, stirring the saucepans with a long wooden spoon.

'I am fine.'

'It would not surprise me if you were with child … and not a moment too soon.'

Lucia looked at Isolina and shrugged.

'Are you not well?' Isolina asked.

'I felt tired, that is all.'

'Cooking for four hungry men, now *that's* what makes you tired,' shouted the old woman, continuing to stir each pot in turn.

Cristina appeared at the top of the stairs. The child she held was naked except for a pair of white pants, his head a mass of blonde curls.

'Put the child down, Cristina, he is two years, not two months.' Suzette's face had become stern. 'Let him go and play, run around, get dirty …'

Cristina's shin was bandaged to the knee, covering an infected cut which Simon Stein had attended to. Isolina had come to change the bandage.

'You should test her eyes while you're here, Isolina … she makes a habit of walking into things.'

Isolina, Lucia and Mimi smiled, while Sofia cursed under her breath. She tried to revive the feeling of *that* kiss.

'Where can I take Cristina, Suzetta?' asked Isolina.

'Use the table, they won't be here for another twenty minutes.'

'I have to remove the bandage, I do not want to do it where food is about to be eaten.'

'Please yourself. Go through to where they are building the new rooms.'

Isolina walked from the kitchen and into the building works. It was just a shell, the roof not fully covered. Various agricultural instruments lay about the floor: axes, scythes, boxes of hand-forged nails. Amongst the empty wine bottles were traces of animal droppings, and the shredded skin of a snake. Two chairs, covered in dried cement and dust, rested up against the wall. She brought them to the centre of the room.

'Cristina, come,' she shouted.

'Here, take Paolo, Sofia.'

Sofia's face showed alarm. Crestfallen, she took the child from Cristina and immediately felt the dampness in his pants. Then, seconds later, Paolo wiped his snot onto her blouse. Sofia wanted to put him down and walk the ten miles home, except that would be impossible in this heat. Isolina, who had witnessed it all, looked away, but not before her daughter saw the smile forming on her lips.

'Sit … place your leg on the other chair …' Isolina looked up. 'Take Paolo outside, Sofia.'

Sofia glared at her, before leaving the room holding the child.

'Wait for me, Sofia,' Mimi shouted.

Isolina knew that would be the final insult. Mimi was a lovely girl, but she could talk the hind legs off a donkey. Sofia would find herself bombarded with questions, on a day she was not in the mood to talk. The ride home will be fun, thought Isolina.

'I might go with Vincenzo to Florence soon.' Mimi sat on a half-built brick wall, her fingers feeling the fabric of Sofia's skirt. 'Maybe I could find a dress like this there.'

'It is a skirt,' Sofia said coldly.

The child wriggled in her arms, so she placed him down to play in the dirt.

'Where did you buy it?'

'My mother made it for me.' Sofia wondered how long her mother would be.

'Would she make me one?'

'Maybe, if you bought the material.'

'Did she also do your hair?'

Mimi touched hers, which hung limp and lifeless. Her clothes up against Sofia's looked like rags, and her shoes were worn and dirty – she was nothing like the girl sitting next to her.

'No, it was the Engl ...' Sofia suddenly stopped. 'No, I did it.'

'It's so beautiful ... like you, Sofia ... You must have a boyfriend?'

Sofia's first reaction was to say no, but she was in need of a little light relief, something to ease the boredom of being here.

'Yes, but it is a secret ... you must tell no one, Mimi.'

Mimi's eyes widened and she leant forward. '*Who?*'

'You must swear not to tell, Mimi, not even the priest must know.'

'I swear,' she said enthusiastically.

'Well, in that case ... His name is Richard.' Sofia smiled as his name passed her lips. 'He is twenty ... seven.'

'What are you saying ... he is a man and not a boy?'

'A man ... a real man ... and that is not all: he is a painter.'

'Fabrizio paints.'

'Not walls, silly ... girls like me.'

'He has painted you?'

'Yes.' Sofia drew in a deep breath. Suddenly she was enjoying the day. 'Naked!'

Mimi's face drained of colour. She now sat open-mouthed, while, unseen at her feet, little Paolo began eating the dirt.

'Sofia.' A boy's voice cut through the heat. 'Sofia.'

It was Mimi's youngest brother, Fabrizio. He wore black shorts and had his red shirt slung over his shoulder. He waved. He wore a knitted cap on top of masses of black curls.

'Fabrizio … wash, make a good impression … remove the sweat, brother.' The voice belonged to Vincenzo, the oldest, as he emerged from the wooded treeline. Behind him, Dario. Their father, came next.

The boy ran across to a wooden barrel, plunging his head inside, hat and all. Lifting it out, he spat a fountain of water into the warm air, before grinning at Sofia. Everyone laughed except Sofia, who just about forced a smile.

'My brother does not impress you, Sofia, I can tell. Maybe he is not as elegant as those closer to Florence or Lucca, but let him down gently. Fools have hearts that can be broken just as easily.' Vincenzo smiled at Sofia. She returned it, remembering the small crush she had once had on him.

'Sofia,' said a dripping Fabrizio, 'sit next to me at dinner.'

'Your mother, child …' Their father, Gianni, spoke next. 'She is attending to Cristina?'

'Yes,' Sofia answered.

Gianni splashed his face and body with water, before swallowing a mouthful.

'Go and see her, Dario,' his father shouted.

Dario was absorbed in throwing Paolo into the air. 'He's pissed his pants,' Dario shouted, and then to the child he said, 'What have you been putting into your *mouth*?'

They assembled around the table. Vincenzo broke off a handful of bread and looked at Isolina.

'What news of the war?' he asked, before dipping the bread into the bowl.

'Vincenzo,' said his mother firmly, 'can we leave the war alone while we sit around the dinner table?'

'Mamma,' he answered, 'we cannot ignore what is going on around us.'

'Did you know Mussolini has gone?' Instantly, Isolina wished she had kept silent.

'Gone? Gone where?' Fabrizio asked, but his eyes never left Sofia.

'He no longer rules Italy.'

'Will that mean the price of wheat will fall?' Gianni said, picking up a glass of red wine.

Vincenzo looked from his father to Isolina. 'Have the Fascists lost power, too?'

Isolina sipped the dry, bitter wine that burned her throat.

'No,' she answered, her throat on fire now. 'They have formed a new government. The king has appointed Marshal Badoglio, and he has taken control of the army ... But ...'

'What?' Vincenzo leant across the table.

'The war continues, Vincenzo.'

'How can this be?'

'No one knows. The Italian people cry out for peace, but it seems to fall on deaf ears.' Isolina reached for the pitcher of water, ignoring the small specks that floated inside.

'Your late husband was a Fascist.' Gianni spoke with his mouth full. 'I did not care for him ... untrustworthy.'

'Gianni!' his wife screamed. 'Isolina is our guest ... and there sits her daughter.' She made the sign of the cross.

The old man looked at his wife before he spoke again. 'He reminded me of a dog I once had when I was thirteen: a faithful dog, until, one day, I held my hand out and the animal sank his teeth into it.'

The rest of the table grew silent.

'What did you do, Papa?' asked Fabrizio.

'I got my gun and shot it dead, son, six times over, just to make certain.'

'Are you saying you would like to have shot my husband?'

'No ... No ... that is not what I am saying, but I found myself constantly on edge when around him. If I had let that dog live, I would have been forever on guard ... And that is not a way to live your life.'

'That is a stupid story, Gianni,' said his wife.

The man drained his glass, belched, and refilled it.

'What about the Germans?' Vincenzo asked.

'They have done nothing, said nothing. As long as the pact remains and the Axis stays in place ...'

The baby chose that moment to lean across Sofia and throw up on her skirt. The boys laughed. The women hid their faces, including Isolina. Sofia looked as if she was about to cry. Suzetta rose from the table.

'Come, child, let me clean you. Mimi, you come, too.'

Sofia's and Isolina's eyes met for a second: the young girl's were like daggers about to be thrown. All three women disappeared upstairs.

'Anyway,' said Gianni, 'none of this is our problem.'

'It is our problem, Father.'

'Mussolini did me no harm, the price of wheat rose and people like us – farmers and the like – well, he looked after us.'

'But he has gone.'

'And Isolina here has told us that nothing has changed.'

Cristina placed Paolo on her lap and Dario kissed his head, before whispering something into his wife's ear. She giggled like a young girl and blushed.

'I was paid a visit by two German soldiers the other day. They came to tell me they were doing manoeuvres and would be using my bottom field.'

'The one Dario and Vincenzo cleared last summer?'

'Yes.'

'I hope you told them to go elsewhere, Isolina.'

'Gianni, they were not asking.'

'No German has the right to do that. They are guests in our country.'

'Father, are you blind, the Germans do not see themselves as guests.' Vincenzo's voice grew louder.

Lucia placed a hand on her husband's shoulder. 'Calm, Vincenzo, please.'

He placed his hand on hers.

'I have a rifle and bullets and they will piss their pants if they come here.' The old man stated while swallowing another glass of wine.

Isolina and Vincenzo's eyes met for a moment. 'Are you going to Lucca or Florence soon, Vincenzo?' she asked.

'Yes – why?'

'Hold off, wait and see what happens.'

'And let our goods perish, Isolina?'

'Better than not having a son.'

The old man said nothing.

'Is there any other news?' Vincenzo asked.

'In the countryside, we hear little, but the papers are free to print what they like, which is good. Word of mouth is what we have been relying on, and too many mouths tell lies.'

'And the Partisans?'

'They are small in number, so I am told; they too wait. But, on my way here, I saw two trucks full of German troops.'

'They will not bother us, Isolina,' said the old man. He then bellowed for coffee.

~ ~ ~ ~

Richard Mason swallowed a mouthful of bread before resting his head on his bag. He pulled a crumpled pack of cigarettes from his top pocket, removed one, straightened it and lit it. Smoke escaped from his mouth and nose and floated up into the night sky. He gazed at the thousands of glistening stars and sighed with approval at what he saw.

'I thought the English prided themselves on manners.' Ambra's voice came from the darkness.

Mason smiled and reached into his pocket. He threw the packet in her direction, but continued to stare at the night sky. Moments later, a hand removed the cigarette from between his lips. The smell of smoke filled his nostrils before his own cigarette was replaced.

'Do you only draw beautiful women?'

He twisted his neck to look at her. The light from the fire flickered in her eyes, softening her face; she looked younger.

'No.'

'What else do you draw?'

Mason flicked his finished cigarette towards the bushes. 'Buildings, landscapes … chairs, flowers, trees …'

'Yes … yes … enough, you draw many things. But do you draw the war?'

Mason took a moment to think about the question. It was a good one. Why would he not? At this moment in time, the days were long-drawn-out; it was a thought. If he was honest, he missed Isolina. She had woken something inside him. It was not just her beauty, but her spirit. Strangely, it was not her looks that made him want to make love to her, more her self-assurance; she had an aura about her that sexually aroused him.

He thought about that kiss with Sofia and shuddered, remembering how he'd almost responded, how he had fought his weakness and only just conquered it.

'What do you mean?' he asked Ambra.

'Draw *us* ... those who will rid Italy of the Germans and Fascism.'

'You want to be immortalised?' He smiled.

She sucked on her cigarette. 'This is not a game we play here ...' Smoke escaped with each word that left her mouth. 'You seem to think we all want to be here ... doing this.'

'I don't know.'

'We all had other lives elsewhere, but our country was in turmoil. For twenty years, it has been run by a madman, a dictator, and the people have suffered. Mainly because those who made the rules did so for the benefit not of those they ruled over, but themselves. Every Fascist who had power, also acquired riches.'

'Bravo ...well spoken,' Mason said, not looking at her.

'Do not patronise me ...' She replaced the cigarette between her lips. 'Let me ask you,' Ambra continued, 'are you going to help us throw off Fascism ... for we have just done that, and yet, your Winston Churchill speaks of unconditional surrender, as if we will accept peace at any price.'

Mason sat up on his elbows. The flames from the fire were active, creating tiny shadows on her face.

'This war was imposed on us by the Germans … we cannot be held responsible as a people. Yet, I do not see that understanding from the Allies. I see us being used as a stepping-stone to Germany's destruction.'

'You want to see the back of the Germans?'

'You are not listening … Yes, we do, and we welcome your help, but treat us as equal partners. Not like uneducated peasants.'

'I did not feel we had.'

'Then, why do you smirk behind Silvano's back? You show him no respect, which makes me wonder: if and when the others arrive, will they do the same?'

With that, she walked away into the darkness.

Mason lay back and covered his legs with a blanket; he had begun to feel the chill the night brought. Ambra was far from uneducated, and spoke with passion. He thought about her words before falling asleep. Later, he became aware of another presence under the blanket. He opened his eyes to see Ambra's face staring down at him. Without speaking she reached down and undid his trousers. They made love in the dark.

CHAPTER FOURTEEN

'They get younger each time I see one,' Sassa said to Isolina, as she observed two young German officers walking towards them. A third man in civilian clothes accompanied them. They removed their caps and clicked their heels together in perfect unison.

'Ladies,' said the civilian, 'my name is Roberto. I am these gentlemen's interpreter.'

'Where are you from, Roberto?' asked Sassa.

'Milan, I have a bookshop there.'

Isolina looked at the two young Germans, both perfect Aryan specimens: blonde and blue-eyed.

'I have to tell you that they are here on manoeuvres and will be stationed here for some time, until the British land on the Tuscan coast. So, please do not be alarmed.'

'You do not alarm us,' Sassa answered. 'Would you and your ...' she hesitated '... friends have coffee with us?'

Roberto spoke to the Germans, who bowed and shook their heads.

'No, they cannot spare the time ... but thank you very much. They have informed the prison guards that all prisoners must remain inside the building.'

'Surely not,' Sassa gasped. 'They are harmless, and they

will cause no problems. The temperature has been reaching thirty-eight – plus they are helping to pick the fruit.'

The interpreter spoke with the two Germans.

'I am sorry, those are their orders, I am afraid.'

Two trucks came up the drive just then and turned into the adjacent field. Fino and Sergeant Foster were making their way across it as the troops disembarked. The soldiers stared at the British uniform, and one of them shouted across the field in good English.

'Where are you from?'

Foster looked towards them. 'Swindon,' he shouted.

'I worked for a month in Aylesbury ... in a tea house.'

Foster smiled. 'How nice it would be to be there now.'

'Earl Grey?'

'Of course, old boy ...'

'I wish it, too, Englishman.'

Then silence, until a German sergeant bellowed out orders, bringing them into line.

'What is all this about, Sassa?' Fino asked.

'It seems we are to have the pleasure of their company, at least until the Allies land.'

'And when might that be?'

'Who knows ... Why do you ask?'

'Because I don't want to attract the attention of the RAF, and I have a feeling they will.'

~ ~ ~ ~

Isolina fought with her daughter all morning as Sofia had wanted to remain at home against her wishes. Eight German divisions now filled the valley, including tanks and troop carriers. Almost every farm had been overrun. Each soldier who came into contact with Sofia let his gaze linger for too long, and that worried Isolina. On the road to Sassa's, she allowed herself a sideways glance at her daughter. Fifteen soon ... she wondered where the time had gone.

Suddenly, from further up the road, came an explosion. Smoke rose into a clear blue sky and through it flew two British planes. They began to bank before dropping out of sight. The sound of rapid fire followed and they reappeared. This time they flew directly at them. Isolina pushed open her door and ran around to Sofia's side, where her daughter sat transfixed. Isolina reached in and hauled her out.

Dragging Sofia into a ditch, she fell across her as the noise overhead increased. They were on their way back ... She covered her head with her hands and screwed up her eyes. Almost at once, the noise began to fade and the sky calmed. Isolina slowly got to her knees and pulled Sofia into an embrace.

'Are you all right?' Isolina asked, desperately trying to control her breathing.

'Yes.'

When they pulled up at Sassa's, the place resembled a battlefield. The main house and clinic were untouched, but part of the stables had taken a direct hit. The field housing the Germans had also been bombed: tents and casualties lay scattered across it.

'Isolina,' shouted Sassa. 'Thank God you're here. The Germans have their own medics ... can you go to the stables. I have sent Fino to get Simon.'

Isolina went back to the car to fetch her bag.

'What shall I do, Mamma?' Sofia stared around at the destruction.

'Come with me.'

The two set off towards the stables, where one wall had been blown out. Sergeant Foster knelt, administering a tourniquet to a young soldier.

'I can't stop the damn bleeding,' he said panicking.

'Higher.' Isolina reached down and moved it up the man's leg, instantly stemming the flow. Foster's face and uniform were smeared with the man's blood.

Sofia began to feel sick and sweat began to settle on her skin. The colour drained from her face. Finally, she vomited.

'Sofia.' Isolina knelt to help a man with a deep wound in his arm. 'Sofia,' she shouted again.

Sofia knelt, bent double. 'No ... No ... I cannot ...' She began to sob, looking down at her blood-stained hands. The world was now somersaulting around her.

'Sofia, stay calm ... Please ... stay calm, Sofia.'

Isolina could see that her daughter was in shock. Sofia's eyes moved from one bloody body to another. She began to run, needing to get as far away as she could, until she crashed into the returning Fino. She buried her head in his chest and began crying.

Isolina looked down at the man's arm, held on by a loose piece of skin. She needed to concentrate on the job at hand and began to remove the young soldier's jacket. 'It's going to be fine,' she said, glad he could not understand her Italian because it was never going to be *fine* again. Nothing in his life would be. She struggled with a bandage until another pair of hands joined hers. One held a pair of scissors and began to cut away at the material. Isolina looked up into Anna's eyes.

'Thank you,' she smiled.

Anna returned it.

Simon had worked non-stop for almost five hours, but despite his efforts, nine men lost their lives, while five needed hospital treatment. Several, in all probability, would not see another sunrise. Many would be scared for the rest of their lives, both mentally and physically. Isolina's hand shook as she lit up a cigarette.

Sassa poured Simon a brandy while Sofia lay fast asleep on the settee next to him. Anna slept with her head resting on Isolina's arm. The dead had already been buried, both German and British, and peace had finally come with the arrival of nightfall. Sassa switched on the radio as Fino refilled empty glasses. A deep eerie silence fell upon the room: countless shocking memories had been created that day, memories that even time would not be able to eradicate.

The war had finally reached their isolated community. Tuscany was no longer unknown to the outside world; its hiding place had finally been discovered. A voice on the radio proclaimed that Messina had fallen … The Sicilian campaign was over, and now the Allies would begin their invasion of the mainland. Sassa stood and turned the radio off. A continuing hush had greeted the news, because, with it, the hope for peace was banished.

~ ~ ~ ~

Isolina slowed the car down, having seen a cannon concealed in the bushes. She stopped at the makeshift barricade and removed both permits, ready to hand them to the very young Italian sentry who was strolling towards them. He lowered himself to see inside the car and allowed his eyes to linger on Sofia, who made a point of looking away.

'There is a German division further down the road,' the young soldier said. 'Be careful, they are becoming nervous.'

'Nervous of what?'

'There are strong rumours that an armistice is about to be signed.'

'Soon?'

'The next couple of days.'

'What will happen then?'

'I do not know … Me, I will go home to Rome to see my family. I will take this uniform off and burn it.' With that, he stepped away from the car and signalled for the barrier to be raised. Isolina smiled briefly and drove slowly through. The faces of the men told their own story: the dark hollowed eyes, the threadbare uniforms … the picture of a spirit that had been broken into a thousand pieces – their war looked over. And this heart-breaking scene would be repeated across Italy. Unable to control her emotions, tears flowed down her face.

Sofia glanced across at her mother before looking out of the window again. Without speaking, she placed a hand on her mother's knee and allowed it to rest there.

~ ~ ~ ~

Sassa was taking the children to pick blackberries, and invited Isolina and Sofia along. A peaceful, cloudless sky looked down upon the children. Cypress trees lined the pathway and, from their branches, swallows. The children laughed each time a rabbit raised its head above the grass, and a light breeze helped keep those below cool.

It had been ten days since the air raid, and yet the children remained a little tearful and subdued. It had been

Sassa's idea to go blackberry picking, to take them away from those memories. Anna took hold of Isolina's hand, much to the disapproval of Sofia. It had been a month since Sofia had seen Richard Mason. Hearing his name would heighten her interest, reminding her of that kiss, but memories were not enough now, she needed more than a memory.

The children seemed to enjoy their day out, filling four baskets full of blackberries. Sassa promised to make at least five large pies and the children cheered. For two hours, the children escaped the war: they laughed, ran and played in the fields. Free for the time being, free from the destruction and chaos that was coming their way.

Fino greeted them on their return with news that British and Canadian troops had landed in Reggio and Calabria, which meant the invasion of mainland Italy had begun. The Pope had called for peace and calm, which, like all his other appeals, would surely fall on deaf ears. Isolina saw Simon Stein's car parked outside the main house. Concerned, she strolled over.

'Simon, how good to see you.'

The doctor forced a smile, he seemed to have aged considerably these past six months.

'An entire garrison has deserted … they say to go and defend Calabria … But that is a lie: they see what is coming.'

'You feel the armistice will be signed?'

'Yes.'

'Soon?'

'My fear is what the Germans will do. They are here in force already. Just one word and Italy becomes another German occupied country, and I feel there will be retribution.'

~ ~ ~ ~

Silvano inspected the weapons that had been dropped the previous night. Twenty *Sten* guns and five revolvers, along with some ammunition and explosives.

'It is a start, but I wish there could have been more.'

'Don't be greedy, Silvano,' Mason said, breaking open a parcel of cigarettes. 'You're right, it is a start. And now that Sicily is over, and the mainland has been invaded, we can begin to give the Germans a few headaches.'

'The armistice … has it been signed? I would like to know that I have just one enemy.'

'They say any day now, but you of all people know that you fight two: the Fascists of your country also remain, Silvano. As unpleasant as it is, you *will* have to fight your fellow countrymen.'

'I do not need to be reminded of that.'

'But if the armistice is signed –' it was Luca who spoke '– then surely they will just disappear.'

'When the armistice is signed, the Germans will make their move. They will back the remaining Fascists, and I am certain there are many who still support Mussolini.'

'They should have shot the bastard,' said Luca.

Mason smiled. 'You had twenty years to get rid of that bastard. Three times, they say, you botched it, and so we find ourselves here today.'

Ambra came over with several drawings in her hand; her eyes met Mason's.

'They are good,' Ambra said, sitting down. 'Did you see them?' She looked at Silvano, who shook his head.

'Here.' She handed him several sheets. The drawings were of Partisans grouped around a burning fire. Silvano nodded. He had to admit they were good, very good in fact, but it stuck in his throat to admit it. He had been impressed by the sketches of Isolina, and, on several occasions, had almost asked to see them again.

'You have a talent … they are very good.' He handed the sheets back to Ambra. 'I envy you. I will see if I can find a large notebook, it will give you something to do while we wait for more instructions.'

Enzo smiled. 'Do one of Ambra's tits …' He burst out laughing, as did several others.

'I have already.'

Ambra looked up. Enzo and the rest stopped laughing. Mason sat back with a look of satisfaction on his face and lit up a cigarette. Ambra smiled, as did the rest, except Enzo, who stood and spat at the floor.

'Very funny, Englishman … just don't turn your back on me.'

Mason reached into his jacket pocket. Enzo took the rifle from his shoulder. Silvano stepped between the pair.

'Calm down … the enemy is down there somewhere, not around this fire.'

'I have no problem, Silvano,' Mason said, pulling a pencil from his jacket pocket. 'I am fine to just sit here and sketch.'

Enzo glared at him. Mason grinned back.

~ ~ ~ ~

Isolina pulled the string taut; it held. She stepped back to see if all the overhanging vines had been tightened. Originally, she was going to cut them, but Gianni had asked her not to. He had promised to send Vincenzo, but that was over a month ago. She shielded her eyes from the sun and looked in the direction of her house, hoping Sofia would appear. The distance between them remained as wide as ever. Their relationship had unravelled so fast, she had not seen it coming. Did the appearance of the Englishman have anything to do with it? The nightmare about her father?

Up to that point, their relationship had been special, built entirely on trust and nothing came between mother and daughter. Sofia's appearance in her bed the night the Englishman arrived was not unusual: she would often sneak under the covers. Could it just be this war? From the other side of the vines came a noise, and moments later, Richard Mason appeared.

'Buongiorno,' he whispered, smiling.

'What are you doing here?' she asked, looking nervously in the direction of the German camp.

'Don't worry, they are not looking for me … yet … they have other things to worry about now.'

'What do you mean?'

'Badoglio signed the armistice yesterday … We, meaning my county and yours, are not at war.'

Isolina tried to smile, but knew the implications of the signing.

'The Allies have landed south of Naples, but Rome is cut off. You and Sofia need to stay alert … We feel the Germans will occupy all the major towns and cities here in the north. These are going to be testing times.'

He spoke while looking deep into her eyes. In just a short time, her beauty had increased.

'Where is Sofia?'

'In the house.'

He was glad as her presence made him nervous.

'It is her birthday tomorrow,' Isolina said, wondering why he was here. 'Sassa is holding a party for her.'

'That's nice ... a little normality helps in times like these.' He stepped out into the blazing sun. 'Have you reconsidered my offer to draw you?'

'You have come all this way to ask me that?'

'Yes.' He smiled.

'Well, you should not have bothered. Your drawings of Sofia are lovely, let us leave it at that.'

'But I have rarely seen such beauty in a woman as I see in your face.'

'An old face ... a tired face.'

'A lovely face.'

'An ordinary face.' She smiled.

'How can you consider yourself ordinary?'

'There you go again ... Do you feel that if you tell me enough times that I am beautiful, I myself will believe it?'

'I say it because it is true.'

Mason reached up and touched her hair. To his surprise, she did not pull away. Isolina allowed his fingers to go deeper into her hair and, in doing so, she allowed the tension to depart, to be replaced by a feeling of calmness. She was shocked at how the gentle touch of a fellow human could bring so much comfort. For a few passing seconds, this war, with all its revulsion, was pushed to the back of her mind and she found her eyes closing.

Richard Mason's lips touched hers gently, awakening her from her dream. Her reaction was swift: she pulled back, staring at him with a look of horror on her face. Once again, he had taken advantage of her vulnerability.

'Do not do that again.'

'Each time I have … you do not seem to mind.'

'That is because your words take advantage of how I am feeling … You take advantage of situations, Mr Mason.'

'In what way?'

'You would have had to have lived in my shoes to know that. To have brought up a daughter during a war, sacrificing contentment and peace of mind to know your child is safe and well. So, when you say those words, when I feel the touch of a hand, it feels strange and I forget.'

'Forget what?'

'Forget how good it feels to be a woman.'

'Then be a woman, listen to what your heart is saying.' He took a step towards her.

'No.' She extended her arm. 'That will not happen again. You are a pleasant man … but you are far too young for me …'

'And that is all that is stopping you? It is such a small barrier … come.' He took hold of her hand before she could snatch it away. She felt his breath on her face, and in that second, she wanted him. Not the boy in front of her, for it could have been anyone. What she desired was that feeling of pleasure to flow through her veins again, to banish from her mind the war, her husband, Sofia and Silvano.

'No!' She turned away. 'Go, please … Just go.' She urged as tears left her eyes.

'I'm sorry … but I think –'

'Go …' She turned away, heard the rustle of the vines, and knew he had gone.

From the hillside high above, leaning against a tall chestnut tree, Sofia had watched it all play out below. What a fool she had been to think that someone like him would want her, a mere child, with no experience of men and all fingers and thumbs when it came to love. It hurt that he had chosen her mother over her. She understood now: her mother was jealous and wanted to keep them apart, wanted him all to herself. Sofia did not attempt to wipe away the tears that flowed down her cheeks. Inside, her anger grew.

~ ~ ~ ~

'Happy birthday, Sofia.' Simon Stein bent forward and kissed her. 'Fifteen is a special age.'

'Is it?' Sofia forced a smile.

On the other side of the room, Sassa stood next to Isolina. 'Such beauty.'

'Yes,' Isolina whispered. 'But it comes at a price.'

Sassa could tell that all was not well between mother and daughter. But now was not the time to pry.

'I told the British prisoners about the armistice, and that the new government has said they must be protected from any German attempt to seize them. The trouble is, I do not know how much longer the Italian guards will remain. Two have already deserted.'

'Could you not just let them go? Surely no one will say anything, and who would stop them?'

'Fino and I spoke to Foster about it. We told him it might be best to wait, to at least see if the next Allied landing is further north, then make their way across country.'

'Do you believe waiting is for the best?'

'I don't know what to think anymore.'

'What if you're wrong?'

'Then God forgive me ...'

'What of the children?' Isolina asked, continuing to stare across the room at Sofia.

'They cannot go yet,' Sassa smiled. 'They hugged and kissed me this morning … they cried out, "Peace has come … peace has come" … It breaks my heart, but it is worse where their families are. They will be safer remaining with us.'

~ ~ ~ ~

More guards deserted over the next few days. The stable doors now remained permanently open, allowing one or two of the prisoners to make a run for it. But, with more German troops flooding into the valley, some of the prisoners felt it was best to wait. Sassa and Fino began teaching them some basic Italian: "*Where are the Germans?*" "*I am English, can you help me?*" The last radio broadcast said that Badoglio was absent from the capital, and the frontier between France and Switzerland had been closed.

Fino had been called from the stables. Sassa watched as he stood talking to a man, presumably from the Partisans. His face grew increasingly glum. Finally, he patted the man's shoulder and began walking back.

'What is it, Fino?' she asked.

'Badoglio and the king have joined the Allies – we are now without a government, Sassa.'

Sassa looked towards the British prisoners. 'They must go, Fino …everyone knows they are here. The Germans will occupy the north in a matter of hours, not weeks, they must leave at once.'

Isolina walked outside to see Simon. He had a glass of wine in one hand and a cigarette in the other.

'How is Sofia?' he asked.

'I wish I knew.'

'Don't be hard on her, Isolina, the war dominates everything. It is all us adults talk about, and you know how young girls like to be the centre of attention.'

Isolina smiled, reached up and placed a hand on his arm. She noticed how his eyes looked bloodshot and he had lost a lot of weight.

'Come inside, Simon, let me get you another glass of wine.'

He said nothing at first, but, instead, looked towards the surrounding hills shrouded in mist. 'The terms of the armistice have been announced: Italian ships are to proceed to Allied ports, and airports are to be defended by Italian troops until Allied soldiers reach them.'

'Please come inside, Simon.'

'North of Rome is to be placed under German marshal law. Trains, telephones and the post are already under their control.'

Simon finished his wine and followed Isolina inside. She refilled his glass.

'What about Rome, Simon?'

'We surrendered to the Germans yesterday.' He took a large mouthful. 'Italian soldiers are being stripped of their uniforms as we speak, and they have surrendered their weapons. Some have fled into the hills … But that is not the worst of it, Isolina.' Simon Stein now swallowed the rest of the glass.

Isolina gave him a worried look. This was a troubled man, a scared man.

'What is it, Simon? Please tell me.'

'The rumour is ...' He stopped for a moment, as if needing to calm himself. 'German paratroopers have freed Mussolini.'

CHAPTER FIFTEEN

'It's like we are strangers.' Isolina placed the cup back on the table. 'She hardly speaks to me anymore.'

'Have you tried talking to *her*?' Sassa sat back into a high-backed leather chair.

'Only to moan … that she has not done this, or not done that …' Isolina drew breath. 'We end up being hostile to each other.' She stared into Sassa's eyes. 'Sometimes I feel I am talking with Fausto.'

Sassa said nothing at first, then leant forward. 'I had not realised things were so serious. Where is she now?'

'With Eva, sorting out warm clothes for the children. But there is one more thing.'

'Go on.'

'She asked me about him …'

'Why should that surprise you? After all, he is her father.'

'She dreamt about him not long ago, but I thought she had forgotten by now.'

Sassa walked to where Isolina sat and placed a hand on her shoulder, gently squeezing it.

'War brings things out of people, makes them think and speak in ways they would not normally do. It is true of us all, Isolina, and Sofia is no different. The secret is not to allow it to upset us, but to rise above it …'

'How?' Isolina interrupted.

'By holding onto something or someone you love, in fact, both really. Only so you don't get swept away in this tide of cruelty and hate. This war will destroy lives, but don't let it destroy yours.' Sassa looked out from the window across the courtyard, beyond the fields, and towards the hillside that surrounded her home. 'I hold onto this place and to Fino. Although, lately, I feel my grip weakening.'

Isolina stood. Sassa remained silent; a watery sunlight sneaked into the room unnoticed. There was a sudden chill in the air, yet, beyond the glass, September remained warm.

'Sergeant Foster has arrived, I see,' Sassa said as she continued to stare outside.

The British soldier was shown into the room. He stood erect, shoulders back, keeping his self-dignity, despite being shifted from one prison camp to another. He stood holding his threadbare cap between his fingers and waited for Sassa to speak.

'What have you decided?' she asked.

'The Germans must know about us by now.'

'They do, Sergeant.' Sassa poured the man a coffee, turned, and switched on the wireless.

'If we all leave at once –' The radio played Beethoven. '– They will suspect that you had a hand in it. It could put both you and Fino in danger and, almost certainly, you would be punished.'

Sassa handed him the cup and saucer. 'We are already under suspicion, as is most of Italy: the train drivers who slow down to allow people to escape; the farmers who feed soldiers and Partisans. We all know the risks, Sergeant Foster, and it is our choice to help.'

'With all due respect … you and Fino are not train drivers.' He lifted the cup to his mouth.

'So, what will you do?'

'Remain working in your fields, taking our kit with us. If the Germans come to collect us, then we will make our escape, thereby making it look as if it was a spur of the moment decision and that you and Fino had nothing to do with it.' He emptied the cup and placed it back on the saucer. 'Is it true about Mussolini?'

Sassa swallowed the lump that had formed in her throat before answering. 'Radio Rome has done nothing but crow about the raid by the paratroopers … on and on they go.'

'Is there any other news?'

'The Germans have issued orders saying all prisons of war must give themselves up and must not be given shelter or food. As for the war, Radio London has said the Germans have evacuated Sardinia, and there is fighting on Corsica between the Germans, Italian and French troops.'

Foster sighed and walked to the door, but, before leaving, he turned and stared at Sassa.

'It's coming this way Sassa … you know that.'

She smiled; his concern was touching. 'Yes, I do, Sergeant … I do.'

'Be careful, the world is very short now on good people … It can ill afford to lose someone like you.' He saluted, turned, and left.

~ ~ ~ ~

Roberto, the interpreter, pulled up outside Isolina's house and removed himself from the car slowly. He straightened himself, adjusted his suit and tie, and brushed down his trousers. He looked up before making his way to her door. After knocking three times, he turned and looked at the view, wishing he was back home, about to go fishing, a bottle of wine in his bag.

Sofia opened the door and caught the man by surprise. Isolina was walking down the stairs behind her.

'Buongiorno.' He lifted his hat.

Sofia took a step back.

'Are you alone?' Isolina asked, and found herself staring at the broken floorboard. 'What is it you want?'

'I have been requested to take you to Oberstleutnant Hoffmann.'

'Who?'

Roberto smiled. 'Your nursing skills, it seems, are required at his HQ. It is a quick, twenty-minute drive.'

'I see ... I suppose it would be silly to refuse.'

The man pulled a face.

'Fetch your coat, Sofia.'

'I am not going.'

'Fetch your coat, please.'

'We need to leave,' said Roberto standing in the entrance. 'He has a foul temper.'

Sofia had sat down with her arms folded in defiance.

'Then you stay in. Do not open the door to anyone ... do you hear me, Sofia?'

'Yes, I hear you.'

'But do you understand? Do not leave this house, Sofia.'

Isolina picked up her coat and walked towards the door, her eyes never leaving her daughter.

~ ~ ~ ~

Today, a bitter wind blew from the north. But for that, the day would have been a pleasant one. Isolina sat in the back seat with her black bag beside her. She stared out of the window at the passing countryside, wondering why she had been sent for, a nurse. If he was ill, then surely send for a doctor. Only, she remembered, the local doctor was Jewish. She smiled to herself.

Outside, all was peaceful. The car passed rows and rows of vines. Cypress trees divided fields, yet war was now just over the next hilltop. Nevertheless, some living in this idyllic setting had not witnessed its evil hand. They began to pass tanks parked at the roadside, trucks with depressed-looking troops staring out at the Tuscan countryside with ghost-like faces. The headquarters was merely a field consisting of eight wooden huts, barbed wire and dozens of military vehicles carrying yet more German troops, all with solemn faces. This was an army in retreat.

She was led to one of the larger huts, where a sentry stood outside smoking. Roberto spoke a few words in German before opening the door. Isolina walked into a sparse but sizeable room, which consisted of one filling cabinet, a stove and a wooden desk, behind which sat a large German officer. He had trouble vacating a high-backed leather chair and navigated around the desk somewhat awkwardly.

'Buongiorno,' he said in a broad German accent.

Isolina smiled nervously. The stove emitted an unbearable heat, making the officer's forehead glisten with sweat. He spoke to Roberto in a whisper.

'This is a very delicate matter,' Roberto began. 'Oberstleutnant Hoffmann has a problem that only you can solve, but you have to be discreet.'

'What is this problem, and would not a doctor be better?'

The interpreter smiled. The officer spoke again and the smile faded from Roberto's lips.

'He will show you … but I have to leave.'

'Leave? But how will I know what is?'

Roberto held his hand up. 'All will become clear.'

Turning back to the German, she watched in horror as he began to undo his trouser belt. Isolina took a step back, uncertain of her next move. The German then turned to face the desk, allowing his trousers to fall. The boil was the size of a small egg, and it brought an instant smile to Isolina's face, as much from relief as anything. She brought her bag over and placed it on the desk, before looking inside for her sharpest instrument.

~ ~ ~ ~

Sofia stood staring at the door handle. It turned first one way, then the other. Fortunately, it remained locked. Now a fist began to pound it with force, followed by harsh words spoken in German. She knew they wanted her to open it – except, how did they know she was in? Was it the reason they took her mother? No. She bit her bottom lip as the pounding resumed and a helmeted face peered through the downstairs window. She backed away upon seeing the shadow grow on the wall opposite. Sofia held her breath.

The door suddenly took a more violent beating and an argument ensued in German. What should she do? Then, without thinking, she was by the door and twisting the key. She swallowed, her mouth dry. The door was now unlocked and Sofia instantly knew she had made a mistake.

Both were young. They wore helmets and long brown coats, each with a rifle slung over their shoulder.

'Can I help you? My mother will be back in five or ten minutes, so if you would like to wait outside ...'

Both soldiers shrugged their shoulders and laughed. Sofia stood there, red-faced and scared. The taller of the two removed his helmet, revealing his cropped blonde hair. He placed the helmet on the table and rested his rifle against the wall, while his eyes searched the room.

He turned to Sofia suddenly. 'Vino?'

Sofia knew there were several bottles in the cabinet next to her. The other soldier tried to smile; he had kept his helmet and coat on. His friend, on the other hand, had removed his and draped it over the chair. Sofia reached into the cabinet and took out a bottle.

'Here ... vino bianco.'

'Uhh,' smiled the blonde one, and took it from her. She reached for a glass, but the boy was already drinking from the bottle.

'Amal ...' said the other.

Amal offered the bottle to his friend, who simply walked away.

'Erdmann.'

'No.'

Amal shrugged his shoulders and swallowed another mouthful. He continued his search of the property, until both began to argue all of a sudden. Whatever the language, an argument seems to have a certain tune to it. Sofia could tell that the one called Erdmann wanted to leave, while the other, who had almost finished the wine, disagreed.

'More ...' He held out the empty bottle. Without thinking, Sofia grabbed another from the cabinet, but he pushed past her and grabbed a bottle of brandy instead. Smiling, he showed it to his friend. Erdmann began to shout, putting Sofia on edge. The blonde boy looked at him and laughed; Erdmann walked away to stare out of the window. It seemed he had washed his hands of Amal, and that, for some reason, alarmed Sofia.

Amal sat on the chair and placed his boots on the table. Comfortable, he loosened his collar and stared at Sofia. He took large gulps of brandy, but never took his eyes from her. Sofia felt her heart beat a little faster and turned her stare to the floor, even glancing towards the loose floorboard at the bottom of the stairs. Don't be stupid, she told herself.

The blonde boy, Amal, stood up, and spoke to the other as he walked to the stairs. He stopped at the bottom and a grin leapt onto his lips.

'Come,' he said to her. 'Come.' He pointed up the staircase.

'I do not understand,' Sofia said, the blood turning cold in her veins.

She looked over to where the other soldier remained staring out of the window, bored with his friend's behaviour, so it seemed.

'Come!' Irritation had crept into his voice.

She slowly moved forward, stopping before reaching the steps. He reached up and played with her curls, just like Mason had. She could smell the brandy on his breath. He took another mouthful, wiped his lips with the back of his hand and ran a finger down her cheek. She flinched, taking a step back. In a flash, he took hold of her hair and pulled her towards him; the pain forced a scream from her mouth.

He gripped her arm and began to pull her upstairs. Step by step they got closer to the top, and with each step came another sickening surge of panic.

'Amal,' the other soldier shouted from downstairs. But he was ignored. They had reached the landing and Amal stared both ways before violently kicking open Isolina's bedroom door. His smile widened on seeing the large double bed. Sofia felt her legs become weak. This cannot be happening, she thought.

It was then she tried to wrench her arm away, screaming at the top of her voice. He seemed to be enjoying the struggle, taking another mouthful of brandy before putting the bottle down. With his hands now free, he threw Sofia down on the bed. She rolled onto her side in a desperate attempt to get away, but he was far too quick and jumped on top of her. The German was heavy, and held her face with both hands as he kissed it. He looked down at her with the face of a madman. He spoke to her in German before slapping her across the face. She gasped in shock: this time his tongue found its way into her mouth.

A hand clamp around her breast and tears filled her eyes. He squeezed both breasts, his touch violent. Feelings of terror, anger and nausea overwhelmed her. She felt her skirt being lifted and tried to pull it down, but he was too strong. She knew, now, that her underwear was exposed and she began to cry like a child.

It was not the noise of the gun being fired, but more the smell of gunpowder that brought silence to the room.

'Amal.'

Both heads turned and looked towards the doorway. Erdmann stood there pointing his rifle at them, with smoke drifting from the barrel.

'Erdmann,' said the blonde boy, removing himself from Sofia.

Sofia took the opportunity and leapt from the bed and stood on the opposite side of the room, her back pressed against the wall. With the soldiers distracted, she slowly she made her way towards the door. Erdmann backed away to allow Amal to leave the room, but kept his rifle aimed at the blonde boy's chest. They made their way downstairs, where Amal picked up his helmet and gripped his rifle by the neck before gathering up his coat. A lorry pulled up outside. She could hear more German voices. Erdmann shouted something and opened the door. Using his rifle, he pushed Amal out before glancing back at Sofia. His eyes attempted to apologise. Moments later, she ran to the door and locked it behind them, before falling to her knees, sobbing.

~ ~ ~ ~

'Remember: in three days' time.'

'I will.'

'Here's your note. Keep it with you at all times. Anyone who stops you will not bother you when they see his name on it, unless they want to see the Russian front again.' Roberto smiled. 'I will see you again.'

'Roberto,' Isolina placed a hand on the door. 'Working for the Germans – what will that mean after ... after the war ends?'

'You mean after they are defeated?' He smiled. 'I will have to leave Italy for a while, maybe for good. I have saved as much as I can. I might go to Switzerland, or maybe Paris, who knows. Look after yourself, Isolina, and trust no one.' With that, the car pulled away.

Isolina watched him leave before making her way to the house. The door was unlocked; surely Sofia had not disobeyed her? Right now, she could do without another argument. The smell of alcohol wafted up her nostrils – an empty bottle of wine sat on the table. Angry now, she placed her bag down and picked up the empty bottle. Sofia appeared at the top of the staircase.

'The door was unlocked, Sofia … where did you go?'

Sofia said nothing. No defence was offered, no defiant words. Instead, both stood staring at each other. It was then Sofia ran to her, missing every other step until she was in her mother's arms, sobbing.

'What is it?' Isolina whispered. The girl did not answer, just gripped her mother tighter. The smell of drink was not on Sofia. Isolina looked at the empty bottle again and felt a stab of fear as she eased Sofia away.

'Tell me.'

~ ~ ~ ~

Sassa handed Tommaso a glass of wine. She had not seen Fino's cousin like this before: his hand shook as he accepted the drink. He had managed to get out of Rome a week ago and made his way here, only to find that Fino had gone to Siena.

'The SS control the city,' he said as he sipped his wine. 'They ship Italian troops by the lorry-load to the station …

175

There, trains take them to concentration camps in Germany. I have seen terrified boys of no more than seventeen, even younger, taken from their homes, their mothers clinging to them, only letting go when a soldier threatens to shoot.'

'Surely they would not shoot an innocent boy?'

Tommaso swallowed another mouthful of wine. 'The war has not reached here as yet, Sassa, but when it does, you will not ask that question again. I have seen boys of fourteen shot because their fathers have refused to give themselves up.'

'No ...' Sassa gasped.

'The Germans take no notice of this new Fascist government. Badoglio's ministers are either in hiding or in prison. My car, like everyone else's, was requisitioned, but travelling by train is becoming impossible. So many arrive from Naples – terrified woman and children fleeing the bombing.' Tommaso closed his eyes and buried his face in his hands.

'Stay tonight. Fino should return tomorrow, although I cannot be certain ... as our phone line is down.'

He rested a hand on Sassa's arm and smiled. 'I will stay the night, Sassa, but I would like to be on my way early in the morning as I would like to get to Bologna by tomorrow evening to meet people there.'

'Be careful, Tommaso.'

'Is Simon still here?'

'Yes.'

'In the village?'

'Yes.' Sassa's face grew full of concern. 'Why do you ask?'

'Now the Germans govern Italy, being a Jew will be difficult if not dangerous. Young or old, it will not matter. In Rome, every Jew is being made to pay a tribute of fifty gold lire, whether you can afford it or not. If you can't, you are taken away; if you pay – well, maybe you won't.'

'That has not happened here.'

'It will, Sassa … As the Allies advance, Tuscany will be invaded by retreating German soldiers, and the more desperate they are, the more extreme they become in their methods. In Rome, Italians are starving, babies have no milk … I have left a nightmare behind … Hide what you have, bury it, put it where they cannot touch it, food valuables, anything of worth, or they will take the lot. It is behind me, Sassa, and soon it will reach Florence.' The man began to cry, making Sassa fold her arms around him. She, too, cried.

~ ~ ~ ~

Isolina was parked outside Simon's house, waiting to take him to Sassa's house. He had reluctantly agreed to her request, but only after the Germans had requisitioned his car. It was difficult for the doctor to get around since his legs were beginning to fail him. Sofia stepped from the car, her complexion pale; the girl had become a bag of nerves since the incident with the German soldiers. Slipping under her mother's covers was now a nightly ritual, yet this was not how Isolina had wanted it to happen.

Simon opened the door with a faint outline of a smile on his lips. Isolina stared at him, the lines on his face seeming deeper and longer than they were just a month ago. This was not the same man who had helped the Englishman recover.

'Go inside, Sofia,' said Isolina. 'I need to go and see if I can buy some salt from Alfonso.'

Simon accepted Sofia into his arms.

Isolina walked with her hands deep inside her coat pockets. She glanced across the street to where a radio played music and saw two German officers sitting outside Gino Vitti's bar. Vitti was a Fascist of the worst kind, a friend of Vito Sergi, who now sat drinking between the Germans. On the back wall between two large Italian flags hung a portrait of Mussolini.

The chill in the air had not put them off drinking outside. Isolina looked away, pushed open the door to Alfonso's shop and stepped inside. He was a small man with an oversized midriff, a double chin and rosy cheeks. He always wore a white shirt buttoned up under his chin, his trousers held up with a wide pair of braces. Today, he had on a grey cardigan. His wife of thirty years, Irene, sat knitting in the corner. Small like her husband, she wore black, as if in mourning, and her hair was pulled back into a neat bun. She looked up and nodded to Isolina before returning to her wool.

Cinzia Bria was inside, a widow at thirty. Cinzia hated all Fascists and vowed that she would dance naked on one of Vitti's tables if the day came when the Allies freed Italy from the Germans and Mussolini.

'Have they been to your place, Isolina?' Cinzia greeted Isolina with a question.

'Yes.'

'How dare they? Who gives them that right?'

'The uniform … the rifle …' Alfonso said, replacing a package in a drawer.

'Yes … yes … but by what authority?'

Alfonso laughed. 'What authority did they seek when they invaded Poland, Austria, France … do I need to go on? This Fascist government are just puppets, and when the time

comes, the Germans will cut their strings and let them fall.'
Alfonso stared across the street. 'There sits Vito Sergi licking
their arses again,' he mumbled.

'Alfonso!' It was his wife. 'Watch your mouth, we have
customers. We might not have anything to sell them, but
nevertheless, they are customers.'

'Yes, dear, sorry.' He bowed, a small smile surfacing on
his lips.

'Have you any salt?' Isolina asked.

'You know the answer to that, Isolina. I wish I had. I
could sell it ten times over, and at double the price … not
that I would … But no, I cannot get my hands on any at the
moment; maybe later in the week, but no promises.'

Isolina smiled and turned to go.

'I hear you helped the Partisans.' Cinzia caught her arm.
She moved her face closer to Isolina's ear. 'If there is anything
I can do … tell them to just ask.'

Isolina's heart began to pound. Who could have said
such a thing? Luca, perhaps … no, he would not have … so
who?

'I do not know who told you that, Cinzia, I have nothing
to do with any Partisans.'

'I understand.'

'No, Cinzia, I don't think you do.' Isolina went to the
door and opened it, allowing the sound of the radio to enter
the shop.

Cinzia followed Isolina out on to the street just as the
radio began playing the Fascist anthem, 'Giovinezza'. All the
men rose as one and began to sing in loud voices, all except
one man, who remained seated, drinking: Vanni Manzi, a
local farmer in his late fifties, who began to light his pipe.

'Stand!' shouted a man who sat behind him.

Vanni ignored him and continued to hold a match above the tobacco until it caught. He blew a defiant cloud of smoke into the air.

'Don't be a fool, Vanni,' said Vito. 'Stand like a true Italian.'

'I see no true Italians … just a bunch of thugs, whose time is running out fast.'

Vito smiled as the music played. 'You're a foolish man.'

'Better a fool than a lying, cheating rat.'

The music stopped. Isolina stepped from the shop's entrance, catching Vito's eye. Two men spat at Vanni's feet as they left the bar.

'Isolina – just the person I have been waiting to see.' Vito walked across the road towards her. 'I see you are still driving my car. I can't understand why, the Germans have made it quite clear that all vehicles are needed by them and that they should be given up at once.' A smile leapt to his face. 'Maybe I could take it now and deliver it myself to their HQ?'

'No, I do not think so, Vito.'

'Give me the key, Isolina, be a good woman.'

She took the paper the German officer had given her from her pocket and passed it to Vito, who slowly unfolded it.

'It is in German … what does it say?'

'That I can drive my car when and where I like.'

'Otto.' Vito shouted towards the bar.

One of the German offices stood and took a mouthful of his drink, before gently strolling across to where Vito and Isolina stood.

'Yes … how can I help?' he said in poor Italian.

'This … What is it?' Vito handed him the paper.

The German began mumbling the words under his breath. Suddenly, he looked up and removed his glasses, drawing himself upright.

'This paper has been signed by none other than Oberstleutnant Hoffmann. There is no question of that. I know his signature.'

'But what does it say?' Vito's voice was full of annoyance.

'That this woman has the right to keep and drive her car.'

'How?'

'A favour, perhaps.' The German looked at Isolina and smiled. 'He has very good taste.'

Isolina took the paper back.

'I never would have thought you, of all people, would have spread your legs for a German ... Welcome to our side.'

'Believe me, I am not on your side, Vito.' She turned and walked away.

Vito watched her hips swing. The bitch was an attractive woman, there was no doubting that, but the thought of her and this German did not make sense. There had to be another reason she carried that paper.

From the bar, a chair scraped the concrete as Vanni stood to leave. He stretched before setting off across the road. Isolina heard the sudden noise of an engine, the screech of tyres, the thud of something being hit. She turned as the car continued past her, leaving Vanni face down in the road. She ran across to him; Cinzia joined her. Isolina could see it was too late: the man was dead the moment he hit the road.

'Mother of Mary,' Cinzia made the sign of the cross.

Isolina closed the man's eyes and looked back towards the bar. No one had moved, and most sat with smiles on their faces. Isolina stood, walked slowly towards the bar, and addressed the German officer.

'You sit and do nothing? I suppose you did not see what happened.'

The man looked at her with a smirk on his face, saying nothing. Cinzia continued past Isolina and stopped in front of Vito Sergi and glared at him, then spat in his face. Two men rushed forward to grab her.

'No!' Vito shouted. 'The woman is upset, can't you see? She does not know what she is doing.'

'I know what I am doing. I hope to God the Allies get here soon, so I can see you strung up from the nearest lamppost.'

Vito Sergi began to laugh as Isolina watched. What have you done, Cinzia? she thought.

What have you *done*?

CHAPTER SIXTEEN

Sassa switched off the radio. She stood and walked to the window, lost in thought. The sound of children playing outside pulled her back to the present, just as a pretty young maid entered the room.

'Daniela,' Sassa greeted and returned the young girl's smile. 'Later, come to see me. We will begin to pack some boxes … And bring help with you,' she added as an afterthought.

Daniela left. Sassa returned to surveying the scene outside, waiting for the German commander. She looked at the small amount of post left on the table. So little had trickled through since the Germans had taken control, and the phone lines were taking too long to get restored. Certainly, the Germans had a hand in that as well, although they continued to blame the Allied bombing.

Being out of contact with friends and family worried her. Bad news was one thing, no news was quite another. The Germans were pouring into the north of Italy, and now this German officer was coming to see her. Maybe he was being polite, needing billets for his men – not that he needed to ask, he could just take them if he wished. But he wants to appear to be a good German, she thought, a decent German … She prayed that there were some left. But the more she met, the more her hopes faded.

The surrounding countryside was full of escaping prisoners: Italian, British, American and Polish. They came and she fed them, gave them clothes, shoes and money, but soon this would become too dangerous – not just for her, but for them, too. She missed Fino and wished he was here. She imagined his hand resting on her shoulder: only his presence made her feel safe. She feared for the children and for her staff, and she was concerned for Simon, who sat alone in the other room, silent most of the time, lost in thought. She hoped that happy memories filled his mind.

~ ~ ~ ~

'How many parcels is that, Sofia?'

'Ten … twelve,' she replied.

'Let's make this the last.'

'What about the gun?'

Isolina thought for a moment. 'Leave it where it is.'

Sofia did not reply, but picked up the two tightly-wrapped parcels.

'When you're finished burying them, cover the area with the bushes we cut earlier.'

Sofia picked up the shovel and left. The light was fading, it was late October, and both a cloudy sky and a fresh breeze greeted her: winter would soon be closing in. With the aroma of her mother's soup still in her nostrils, she made her way behind the barn. They had buried food, along with some personal belongings: valuables, like jewellery, that could be used later to bargain with. The Germans, it was rumoured, were stripping Italy bare: fields of food, livestock … They also ransacked people's property, empty or not, taking anything that might fetch a price later.

Sofia stopped in her tracks and stared at two empty holes when there should only have been one. The earth from one lay scattered around it: someone had worked furiously to uncover what they had buried. Sofia held her breath and allowed her eyes to explore the surrounding area.

She looked into the disturbed hole to see what remained. Then she refilled it with the parcels she carried, looking up with each shovelful of dirt, staying alert to any sound or movement. But nothing disturbed the calm, so she dragged the cut bushes across the disturbed earth. She picked up the shovel and began to make her way back to the house. Certain she heard a noise coming from within the barn, she stopped suddenly.

The Englishman had been gone for a while (even now, she could not bear to say his name). She waited to hear the sound again and stared at the chain on the ground. They had not bothered to lock the barn since his departure, since nothing of value was inside and it would soon be filled with German soldiers.

Sofia rested the shovel on the ground and walked towards the doors, giving a reassuring glance towards her house, briefly wondering whether she should alert her mother. Slowly, she eased one door back, making the rusty hinges protest loudly. The lamp and matches remained on the wooden bench by the doors. She sparked one into life, lit the lamp and held it up, allowing the glow to search out the darkest corners.

'Buongiorno,' she whispered. 'My name is Sofia … I live here with my mother.'

Slowly, she took a couple of steps inside, wondering whether it was bravery or stupidity. The lamp lit up the wooden stool where she had posed for Mason. It almost brought a smile to her face: it seemed a lifetime ago. Nothing stirred, so she walked back to the bench and placed the lamp down. As she was about to blow it out, someone sneezed. It came from the gantry where Luca had put the wireless aerial.

'Buongiorno,' she shouted up. 'I know you are up there … please come down.'

There was a long silence. 'I will sit here and wait then; and my mother will come to see what is keeping me.'

Silence.

It was several minutes before she heard a rustling from above. Stalks of hay floated down, and then a head appeared, silhouetted in the shadows. Sofia took a step back towards the open doorway, thoughts of the two Germans still fresh in her mind. Whoever the person was, now stood high above her, looking down. He was not much taller than herself: a boy, she thought. He began to descend the ladder.

Arriving on firm ground, he turned to face her. He was young, not much older than her.

'I am sorry about the food … please do not tell your mother … it is just that … that I …' His voice was soft, and Sofia wondered if he was about to cry. 'I have not eaten in two days, and I saw that woman …'

'My mother.'

'Yes … your mother, burying it … I only took one.'

'Not true: two have been taken, not one.'

He bowed his head and the light from the lamp shone on a tear as it travelled down the boy's cheek.

'Sorry,' he whispered.

'No, I am sorry,' Sofia said, suddenly overwhelmed with compassion.

'I still have one package … I will give it back …'

'No, it is all right.'

She studied him more closely. His clothes were filthy and torn in places, and he had on short black trousers with ground-in dirt staining his knees. His shirt was far too big for him. Under it, he wore a dirty grey oversized vest. He had turned-down socks, and his shoes looked like they were about to fall apart. He looked a sorry state.

'Where are you from?'

'A convent in Siena.'

'A convent … you're not lying again?'

'No … I am an orphan.'

She felt there was pain in his voice. 'How did you get here?'

'Walked … cart … but mostly I walked.'

'Why did you not remain at the convent?'

'Because they wanted to take me away.'

'Who?'

'The Germans … The nuns smuggled me out.'

'And where are you going?'

'To join the Americans and kill Germans.'

Sofia stifled a laugh. 'To kill the Germans?'

'Yes … please don't laugh.'

'I am not laughing … What is your name?'

'Gino.'

'Gino,' Sofia repeated under her breath.

'You remind me of one of the nuns,' Gino said.

'Thank you,' she smiled. 'But I am no saint, Gino … Come to the house with me and meet my mother … who is …'

'No … I must go.'

'Go? Go where? It is late. Gino, come with me.'

The boy bit his bottom lip while thinking it over; his eyes had large, dark pupils with long eyelashes.

'Well?'

'Yes.'

'Good.'

Sofia blew out the lamp and the two walked side by side towards the house in silence. Sofia pushed the door open.

'Mamma,' she shouted.

~ ~ ~ ~

'His name is Gino and he is fourteen, almost fifteen, if he is to be believed.'

Sassa placed her cup down. 'Where did he say he was from?' The coffee's bitterness made her pull a face. 'We must find someone with real coffee, Fino.' She stared at her husband, who pushed his glasses high up on his head.

'Sorry, Isolina.'

'Siena … a convent there.'

'And do you believe him?'

'I see no reason not to.'

Fino cleared his throat. 'How is Sofia now?'

The fear of what might have happened still haunted Isolina. 'Quiet.'

'Do you speak about it?' Fino stood and poured himself a glass of wine.

'No.'

'Maybe …' He sipped the red wine. 'Sometimes it is good to talk … so she can share her feelings. Maybe she is waiting for you to bring it up. It could be like cleansing the soul.'

'How is she around this Gino?' Sassa asked.

'He sits and stares at her,' Isolina smiled. 'Then, when he speaks, he trips on his words. I still think he is younger than he says.'

Fino laughed out loud. 'It is a place where I have been in my youth. I remember it well.'

'You old fool,' Sassa smiled as she teased him. 'Would you like him to come and stay here?'

'No, Sassa, he can stay with us.'

'They say, in Rome, they are taking boys of his age away by train, to who knows where. If you can't keep him with you, send him into the hills.'

A maid entered the room and handed Fino a letter.

'Are the children well?' Sassa asked Isolina, who had spent the past two hours checking each of them. A cold had spread like an epidemic through the dormitory, and Sassa was merely making certain that it did not turn to 'flu as there was a strong chance they would have to evacuate at any moment.

'Who is the letter from?'

'Alice, the English woman who came to Anna's birthday.'

'Uhh, I remember. She lives in Florence, does she not?'

'Yes, things are not good there, so it seems.'

Isolina's ears pricked up.

'There are trials to be held, special tribunals set up by the Fascist Republican government.'

'Fascist Republican nothing,' Sassa muttered under her breath.

'Can I continue?' Fino asked, a smile not far away. 'A friend of theirs has just arrived from Rome. Entire Jewish families have been deported. In Arezzo, if the young recruits failed to report, they arrested their wives and mothers, until they did.' Fino shook his head.

'What about Florence?' Isolina asked.

'You worry about your aunt.'

'Yes.'

'They seem to be arresting everyone,' Fino sighed. 'The prefect is a fanatic, ordering all employees to give a gift of a thousand lire to celebrate Ottobre.'

'How stupid.'

'They have formed an Italian SS, using the young thugs released from the reformatories. They walk around holding guns and threatening people.'

'I must go, Sassa,' Isolina suddenly said.

Fino put away the letter, whispering, 'Enough.'

'I have my car, and the letter allowing me to use it.'

'True,' said Fino. 'Do you have enough fuel?'

'I will see Hoffmann next week. Maybe he can find me some.'

'Winter is almost upon us, Isolina. Will you take Sofia?'

'No, would you look after her?'

'I would love too,' Sassa smiled.

'There is one other thing,' Fino stood and walked to the window. 'To the Allied planes, the only cars on the road are German, which will make you a target.'

~ ~ ~ ~

Vito Sergi and his son slowly emerged from his car. They had followed two Carabinieri vehicles, and now all three were parked outside Sassa's house. She walked out of her front door to confront him.

'What is the meaning of this, Vito?'

'We are merely here to make certain that all new Fascist Republican orders are obeyed.'

He stopped speaking just as a lorry full of German troops entered the grounds.

'Why are they here?'

'We went to some of the surrounding farms this morning, plus several homes in the villages, seeing as no one reported yesterday.'

'That does not answer my wife's question,' Fino stated while walking across the lawn.

Vito smiled. 'Well, Fino, seeing as it appears that these boys have miraculously disappeared, we would have to take their fathers, three of whom work here for you. As for the Germans, they are here simply to remove the Jew.'

Sassa looked at Fino.

'You have here a gardener called Orazio.'

A man in his late forties held up his hand. 'That is me.'

'Uhh, good. It seems your son failed to turn up yesterday … Is he ill?'

No answer.

'I thought not. Then, not only will you go to prison, but you will also lose your ration card and those of your family.'

The gardener spat to the ground.

'Don't make it worse, Orazio.'

Two Carabinieri came and took him by the arms to a waiting car.

A dozen German troops jumped from the lorry and made for the villa's entrance. Fino moved to block their route, but Sassa pulled him away: it would have been a futile gesture. Meanwhile, two more Carabinieri came across the lawn with another man between them, one of the olive pickers. Sassa and Fino looked on helplessly.

Simon Stein then emerged from the Villa. Frail and drawn, his stoop had become more noticeable.

'Simon,' Sassa called.

The doctor looked up and forced a smile as Fino moved closer. 'Simon, I am meeting the commander the day after tomorrow … I will bring up your case. I will do all I can to help, don't give up hope.'

'Give my love to Isolina and Sofia,' the doctor whispered.

Sassa began to cry and Fino placed an arm around her. Vito Sergi was about to walk to his car when he stopped.

'The Germans have their man … and I have two of mine. If I cannot find the third, I will take one at random, please get the message out.' He stood staring at the old couple for a few moments. 'I bid you good day … Come, Carlo, we will return tomorrow.'

~ ~ ~ ~

Isolina watched as the lorry made its way back down the valley. 'Go and fetch Gino, Sofia.'

'Are you certain they will not return?'

Isolina smiled. 'Yes.' She watched her daughter disappear into the woodland that led to the upper fields. She must thank Luca next time she saw him: it was his warning that gave them time to get Gino out of the house. Not that Luca knew anything about the boy. Isolina needed to get to Florence and the sooner the better. She was worried about Savina and Fabia. If things had got worse, maybe she could bring them back here. But that last conversation with Fabia still weighed heavy on her mind.

'Gino … Gino …' Sofia whispered. 'Where are you?'

A hand brushed her shoulder and she stifled a scream.

'You stupid boy.'

'What?'

'Creeping up on me like that. I should leave you here alone.'

The boy looked genuinely shocked at Sofia's reaction. 'I'm sorry, Sofia ... I did not –'

'Never mind now,' Sofia said, and began to make her way back.

'Where is your father?'

The question disturbed her. 'Dead,' she replied. 'Two years ago ... no almost three.'

'Do you miss him?'

She stopped and turned to face him. 'You ask too many questions.'

'Sorry ... but I have never had a mother ...or a father. I sometimes wonder what it is like.'

Sofia looked away; he had a face that made you want to apologise. 'The nuns ... surely they were good to you?'

'Some were ... and some not ... others ...'

'Others what?'

'Beat me.'

'Don't lie, Gino, women of God would not do such a thing.'

He said nothing at first and just walked slowly behind Sofia.

'That is what the mother superior said. Then she locked me in a small cupboard for three days and nights.'

Sofia began to laugh. 'You have a great imagination, Gino ... you should write books.' She continued to walk on. Overhead, a plane flew by, but it was too high to see who it belonged too.

'Even the good nuns were not as nice as your mother,' Gino suddenly said. 'I envy you, Sofia. Having such a kind, gentle woman as your mother must be a fine thing. I asked about your father because he, too, must have been a fine man.'

Sofia swallowed, hearing the sound of her mother being slapped: the cut lip, the purple bruise, the spots of blood. The Party, Mussolini, Hitler, those were the people he loved, not his wife and child. No! He was not a *fine* man ... he was a bastard.

'Let us get back,' she said.

'Have I said something wrong?'

'Look, Gino ... my father was a Fascist ... Let us leave it at that.'

The only Fascist he had ever met, he had hated. So, how could a woman such as Isolina Donatelli marry such a man, and then make a beautiful daughter like Sofia? He walked slowly behind her, trying to work it out, but could not come to any conclusions.

CHAPTER SEVENTEEN

Isolina glanced at the permit that lay on the seat next to her. Hoffmann had been grateful, pleased that he could finally sit again in comfort. He had had the permit typed while she sat in his office drinking a cup of real coffee. He signed it, then handed it over with a wide grin on his face, clicking his heels. Now she had an open road before her, although she remembered what Fino had said about being a target for the Allied planes.

The morning sky was an unbroken covering of slate grey, which stretched as far as the hilltops that lined the horizon, merging with a curtain of mist. The rain fell as a fine spray, coating everything in tiny droplets and distorting the view through her windscreen, the colours of the landscape seemingly running into one another. The road climbed steeply in places, revealing forested valleys and red-tiled roofs that punctuated the greens of the trees and the neutral browns of the land between.

Cypresses, erect like soldiers, divided fields of vines, olive trees and wheat. War had dissolved into the Tuscan countryside, but the tranquillity and beauty of the surrounding land remained untouched, for now. If only the sun would show itself, Isolina thought.

Everything changed as she approached Florence. Lines of German tanks sat resting on the roadside. Forlorn-looking soldiers, their uniforms soaked by the rain, sat around fires, smoking. On the opposite side of the road, a convoy of army trucks moved southward towards the fighting.

At the first checkpoint, a middle-aged German dressed in a heavy coat walked from the shelter of trees, looking far from happy about having to leave the warmth of his small log fire. By the time he reached Isolina, he was drenched from the fine Tuscan drizzle. His eyes stared back at her from below his coal-scuttle helmet as she wound down the window, allowing the cold moist air to invade the interior of the car.

'Papers,' he demanded, and held out a hand covered in a knitted, fingerless glove. 'Come on, come on.'

She handed over the permit Hoffman had given her, and waited. He coughed three times before spitting out a ball of phlegm, and then handed back the papers. Isolina knew what he had just read: that she was visiting sick relatives in Florence, and was his (Hoffmann's) personal nurse. She knew how that would be interpreted, but that did not bother her in the least if it got her into Florence.

She crossed three more checkpoints before reaching the outskirts of Florence, by which time the rain had eased. Civilian cars began to mingle with army vehicles, trucks, tanks and jeeps, and a constant stream of motorcycles. The streets began to narrow and the din of horns grew louder. It was then that her passenger door suddenly flew open. A gust of chilly air entered, along with Silvano.

'Silvano,' she gasped, almost hitting the back of the car in front.

'Careful.'

'What are you *doing*?'

'Getting out of the rain, and using you to get me into the city.'

'What?'

A horn sounded behind her, making Isolina realise she had stopped halfway across a junction. Now panic took root and she stalled the engine. She felt the blood rush to her face. The engine would not start; she wanted to scream to make it all disappear. Another horn sounded ... then another. Her eyes began to moisten.

'What is going on? *Move*.' A Carabinieri officer had walked over. 'You're holding up the whole of the German army.'

'Sorry,' Silvano spoke in a calm voice. 'Let me drive, darling,' he said, removing himself from the car. The horns continued to echo around the narrow side street. Isolina did not question his actions. Instead, she shifted into the seat vacated by him.

'Are you all right, Isolina?' He stared at her. 'Stay calm, we'll be out of here in a moment.'

She turned her head away from him, angry and embarrassed. Five minutes later, the sound of horns was absent and the road in front almost clear. The sun chose that moment to peek out.

'Where to?' he asked.

'You can stop here if you want.'

'Is this your destination?' He looked around.

'No ... it is where you get out.'

He smiled. Isolina looked out the window at the grey streets and the gloomy faces, before directing him to where Savina lived.

'What now?' she asked.

'A coffee, dry myself and these clothes …'

'You can't think you can come in with me.'

'One coffee … and let me explain …'

'No.'

He sighed, handed her the key and removed himself from the car. She emerged on the other side; both the morning chill and the rain were gone.

'Thank you, anyway,' he said, folding up the collar of his coat under his chin. Smiling, he turned away and began walking.

'Silvano,' she shouted.

He turned back, fighting to keep the smile from his lips.

'Come on.'

Savina's greeting was tempered with anxiety; she had not immediately noticed the tall man standing behind her niece.

'What's wrong?' Isolina asked. 'What has happened … is it Fabia?'

With eyes full of tears, her aunt struggled to speak. She gasped for air as the sobs came quicker. It took a further five minutes to calm her. Isolina searched through cupboards for the coffee pot, while Silvano leant against the door frame.

'This is a …' she paused '… friend of mine … Silvano.' Isolina looked at him, pleading with her eyes for him to reassure the woman.

'Pleased to meet you, I wish it was under different circumstances.' He remained where he was, feeling the dampness of his clothes begin to chill his skin.

'Now, tell me.' Isolina held her aunt's hand.

Savina spoke about how Florence had changed since the armistice, and she told them about the new Italian SS.

Groups of young teenage boys now roamed the streets with guns and whips, terrorising the population, urged on by the older Fascist men and supported by the Germans. Those caught out after curfew were beaten or thrown into jail. They also arrested people on vague unspecified charges, and what followed were brutal interrogations. These would sometimes last for days on end with their victims unable to admit to anything, simply because they had no knowledge of the crime in the first place.

'And into this, Fabia goes every day, every night, after curfew, before, whenever. She kisses me and smiles, but will not tell me where she is going or what she is doing. My fear grows with each day. She tells me not to worry, but how can I stop?' Savina broke down again.

Silvano coughed and Isolina looked at him. 'Can I get a towel for Silvano? Then I will make some coffee and we will talk, Savina, and let us see what we can do.' Isolina got up and lit a flame under a dented coffee pot.

She then fetched a towel and handed it to Silvano, before leading him into one of the bedrooms, where she lit a small paraffin heater.

'I will go back to see to her. Dry yourself and get warm. I will make coffee.'

Ten minutes later, they sat smoking and sipping the last of the *good* coffee.

'I will go and look for her, Savina,' Isolina said suddenly.

Savina's eyes lit up, but her hopes were soon extinguished by Silvano.

'That will be an impossible task,' his words unsympathetic.

Isolina looked first at him, then to her aunt. 'Why are you here? I don't remember you saying.'

Silvano sighed. He had annoyed Isolina with the truth, and in doing so, had robbed her aunt of any optimism. 'Can we talk?' He stared at Isolina. 'Please. In the other room.'

Isolina thought for a moment. 'Fine.'

'Tell me the reason you are here,' Isolina demanded as she looked out of the bedroom window. The sun was hidden behind thick, dark clouds again. 'You being here was not just a coincidence ... my car did not just happened to come by.'

'I needed to get into and move around the city.'

'Why?'

Silvano took out a cigarette and lit it. 'It is Partisan business.'

'You are a long way from the hills.'

'I am helping a friend.'

'But why do you need me?'

'You have that letter ... the one the German gave you.'

'How do you know?'

'Sassa ...'

Isolina smiled. 'Sassa ... you mean –'

'No! She had no idea, I went to pick up some clothing for the men in the hills and she just told me... It all seemed to fit into place.'

'So, what now?'

'I need to get to the Piazza Vittorio Emanuele.'

'Why?'

'All you need to do is get me close. If we are stopped I have papers that say I am your ... husband.' He looked away and drew on his cigarette, not wanting to see her reaction. 'Although, your letter should be enough. Then you can leave me there.'

'But why?'

'I am not going to tell you … the less you know the better.'

'So, I risk my neck, and you won't tell me what for?'

Silvano blew out a cloud of smoke. 'I will go by myself, then.' He began to walk away.

'Wait,' she whispered. 'Is it important? I will do this one thing … but …' She looked into his eyes. '*Ask* next time.'

'Yes … I'm sorry.'

'When do you want to go?'

He looked at his watch. 'One o'clock?'

'Fine.'

Florence seemed peaceful today, but the shop windows enticed no one in and the shelves remained bare. A woman typed at a desk, head down, with a cigarette burning in an ashtray. An old man sat staring at an empty wall. Maybe it was fear of what the future held now that the Germans were being driven back, that gave those here this look of foreboding as the Allies crept even closer.

Silvano had checked the bogus documents. He was Doctor Rico Donatelli, husband of the attractive woman who walked beside him, here to visit sick relatives. At every street corner, groups of Fascist youths stood smoking, guns tucked into their trousers, their eyes searching the faces of those who walked by. German soldiers sat playing cards in the back of parked trucks, more relaxed, smoking and laughing, while Carabinieri officers tried to make themselves less conspicuous, avoiding both the youths and the Germans. Suddenly, a man was dragged from the crowd and thrown to the ground.

'Did you think we had forgotten?' a young boy shouted.

The man got to his knees before a fist connected with the side of his head. Blood appeared from a cut above his eye and he held his sleeve against it. The man was around fifty, pale-looking and growing paler by the second.

'We saw you celebrating the fall of Il Duce ... We saw you lifting a glass of wine to toast his downfall ... Well, now he is back ... and so are we.'

A boot sunk into his ribcage while another drove into his spine. A heel came down firmly on the side of his face, which lay against the cobblestones. An occasional groan could be heard coming from his mouth.

Isolina looked up at Silvano, who discreetly placed a finger across his lips. So, we just stand and watch? she thought. Anger rose in her, and not just with the youths, but also with the crowd of onlookers, Silvano and herself included. A priest pushed his way past those staring at the unfortunate man.

'Stop this,' he shouted.

'Piss off, Father,' said one of the youths, a gun inside his oversized trousers.

The priest knelt by the man, took a handkerchief from his pocket and began to wipe away the blood from around his face.

'Leave him, I said.'

The priest ignored the boy. 'Is there a doctor here?'

Isolina took a step forward, making Silvano tighten his grip on her arm.

'Let go,' she whispered.

'Don't be stupid ... *please* ...' he whispered back. 'You can do nothing for him.'

'Leave him, priest, and go away,' a boy shouted, lighting up a cigarette.

'I will not.'

'Then I will charge you for hiding Jews in your church and in your home, which is an offence.'

The priest smiled at the boy. 'I knew your mother … If she were still alive …'

The boy drew the gun and pointed it at the priest. Those around them took a step back. The youth redirected his aim and shot the beaten man in the leg.

'Good shooting, Vico,' his friend laughed.

The priest looked at the boy. 'For the love of God, stop this.'

The boy stared back at the priest, smiled, then shot him in the foot. Silvano had seen enough and pulled Isolina away. She continued to look back as tears fell down her cheeks. Silvano needed to get her clear, fearing they would see where her sympathy lay.

'How can this be allowed?' she murmured when clear of the crowd. 'Why does no one help?'

'Because they are too scared, Isolina. Because they want to stay alive.'

'What has happened to us?'

'We woke up one day and realised that we were in hell.'

He stopped and removed his handkerchief. 'Here, wipe your face.'

She did as he asked. Staring down at her like this reminded him of another time. If only he could bring his lips to touch hers, to be lost for a few moments in her arms and not be here witnessing all they had.

'Papers.'

Silvano suddenly woke from his dream.

'Yes … sorry … here.'

He handed them to a tall German solider.

'You speak good Italian.' Silvano smiled, took out a cigarette and offered one to him.

'No … A doctor?'

'Yes, this is my wife … we are visiting –'

'Your papers.' He ignored Silvano and stared into Isolina's face. 'Are you well? You seem a little upset.'

'I am fine, I have not eaten this morning.' She forced a smile.

'You seem to have friends in high places,' he said, looking at the letter. 'You can both go.'

'Thank you.' With his arm around Isolina's waist, they walked away and turned down the first side street they came to.

'Are you all right?' he asked.

'How can anyone be all right with all this madness going on?' Her bottom lip began to quiver. 'Please – a cigarette.'

He handed her one and watched as her hand shook taking it. The German had seen that she was shaken too, and others would also see.

'Why would Fabia want to come out in all this …' Smoke left her mouth as she spoke. '… all this barbarity.'

'I do not know.' Silvano was only half listening, it was dangerous to linger too long. He felt guilty about abandoning her now, but Hoffmann's letter would keep her safe.

'Look, I can make it there by myself now. If you want to go and look for your cousin, by all means do so, but be careful, Isolina … be very careful.'

'I will come a little further.'

'You do not have to.'

'I know.'

Three more side streets brought them to the bank of the Arno.

'This is as far as you go, Isolina. Please don't argue.'

'I won't.'

'We have stood here before,' he said looking across the water.

The thought had already crossed her mind: it had been another of those special days. Breathing in the air, she could almost remember the aroma. If she closed her eyes, she might even feel the warmth of that summer's day. Too many memories, she thought.

'What are you going to do now?' he asked.

'Look for Fabia, not that I have that much hope … But she told me about several places she used to go to when I was here last. The least I can do for Savina is try.'

'I understand, but you have seen the city, it is not the same place we strolled hand in hand in all those years ago.'

Isolina's head was filled with a montage of images.

'Be careful, Isolina.'

'I will be fine.' She smiled. 'And no doubt you will want a lift back?'

'I know where to find you if I do.'

They parted.

Now alone, Isolina walked slowly in the opposite direction, past groups of soldiers leaning up against parked vehicles, smoking, each one looking apprehensive. More groups of Fascist youths congregated on street corners, standing aggressively, inviting trouble. She went out of her way to avoid them. The Carabinieri looked on, uninterested. One German soldier came over and tried to speak to her; she smiled politely and increased her speed.

She visited two bars Fabia frequented. In each, the waiters sat around idly without customers to serve. She went to a church, and then a shop that sold leather shoes. The girl who worked there was a friend of Fabia's, but she had not seen her today. Isolina strolled down the narrow cobbled streets that criss-crossed the city, hoping to catch a glimpse of Fabia. But it was futile. She leant back against the wall and lit a cigarette. Just then, Fabia appeared.

Isolina dropped the cigarette and went across the street, walking in the direction she herself had just come from. Her first thought was to shout, but she saw a group of youths on the opposite corner and felt that would be unwise, so she crossed the road in pursuit. It was then she realised that Fabia was not alone.

She walked side by side with a man. As Isolina gained ground, they crossed the road again, but a convoy of German lorries brought her to a halt. It was a full minute before she finally managed to cross the road herself, and by then she had lost sight of the pair. She continued to walk in the same direction, praying they had done so themselves. It seemed she had lost them, until Fabia suddenly reappeared further ahead.

Fabia came and went from her view: she was so much shorter than the man who towered over her. He looked to be in his late twenties, and she wondered if this was the secret Fabia was keeping from her mother. Maybe he was married and they were having an affair? Savina would be devastated to think that her daughter would do such a thing. Isolina continued to follow, her mind full of possibilities, and wondering how she was going to explain it all.

They were almost back to where she had left Silvano. She was now less than twenty meters away and gaining. Once again, she thought about calling. As they entered the Piazza

Vittorio Emanuele, she felt a hand grab her arm and pull her from the street.

'What the …? *Silvano* … What are you *doing*?' She tried to keep her eyes fixed on Fabia.

'What are you doing back here?' There was no smile on his face.

'Trying to catch up with Fabia … until you intervened.'

'Fabia?' His eyes stared down the street to where the couple had stopped outside a large café. 'That is your cousin?'

'Yes, what's wrong?'

'You have to trust me, Isolina. Stay close to me, say and do nothing, I beg you. Do not endanger those you love.'

'What are you talking about?'

'Not now … please.'

Silvano watched as two men stood and left a table free, as he knew they would. Smiling, Fabia and her escort replaced them. Isolina watched, too, noticing how full the café was with high-ranking German officers and Italian Fascists.

'What is this place?' Isolina whispered.

'The Café Paskowski: meeting place of Nazi officers, Fascists, and the head of the Italian secret police.'

'Why is Fabia here?'

Silvano ran his fingers through his hair, reached inside his coat and removed a pack of cigarettes. Fabia and the man now held hands across the table and kissed. Isolina could not believe what she was seeing. Standing next to her, Silvano lit up his cigarette and noticed a man staring at them from across the street. He pulled Isolina's head back and kissed her on the mouth, his eyes watching the man carefully. The man smiled and left.

'What are you doing?'

'We were being watched, Isolina.'

'What is happening, Silvano? And what has it to do with my cousin?'

'Your cousin works for the local resistance.'

'That cannot be so … She has only just turned eighteen and –'

Silvano placed a finger across her lips. 'Shh. So does that other man. He is not her lover, they are here for a reason: to plant a bomb.' Silvano let the words sink in. 'When they leave, there are four of us ready to aid their escape.'

Isolina's face drained of colour. '*Why?*' she whispered.

'She volunteered, I assume.'

'Why would she do such a thing?'

'You would have to ask her.' Isolina remembered their conversation: to seek revenge for the death of her father. Now it all began to make sense.

Nothing happened for twenty minutes except that the pair smiled, kissed and held hands across the table. They spoke and exchanged smiles with those around them, German and Blackshirt. Suddenly, Fabia stood and Isolina felt the panic take hold. 'Something's wrong,' she heard Silvano whisper. Fabia began to walk away at that point. Behind her, the man had been held back.

Isolina moved forward, opening her mouth to scream for Fabia to run, but Silvano's hand stifled the cry.

'Let go,' she said, struggling.

'This will not help her.'

'Bastard – let go.'

Silvano had no choice but to clamp his hand over Isolina's mouth, making sure no one was watching. Luckily, all eyes were watching the commotion outside the café.

Fabia, to Isolina's astonishment, swiftly walked back to them. A man broke free from the crowd and joined the melee, and was joined by another. Silvano knew who they were; people like himself, sent to help the couple escape. He looked on. They were brave, yes, but stupid, he thought. It would do no good.

Five minutes later, Fabia stood between two uniformed officers, while both rescuers lay beaten on the floor. There was no sign of her accomplice.

'Come, let's go.'

'Go! How can we go? How can we just leave her?'

'What is it you expect me to do?' Silvano grew angry, not so much with Isolina, but because of what he had just witnessed. He understood the reasons, but it had been a bad choice to use an eighteen-year-old girl, sheer madness. It made them look like fools.

Isolina sobbed all the way back to Savina's. Silvano's attempts to comfort her were dismissed. She repeatedly referred to him as a 'bastard coward'. Savina opened the door and Isolina fell into her arms.

'What is it? What has happened?' She looked up into Silvano's face.

'Take her in, Savina, and keep her here. I will return later. Do not allow her to leave … not if she means anything to you.'

Savina nodded and closed the door behind him.

It had been three hours since Silvano had left. Savina lay on the couch crying, while Isolina sat up at the table with tear-stained cheeks. Both women had drunk several glasses of wine, and Isolina had tried to explain as best she could everything as it had unfolded. She could not explain Fabia's reluctance to keep going, certain that if she had gone down the next street, the crowds would have swallowed her up.

Savina went over all the conversations with her daughter. What had she missed? She could make no sense of it. How could a mother not know or detect something so big about her own daughter? How could she not see any signs, or not ask questions for fear of the answers. She had kissed her goodbye this morning – had the embrace been stronger, the squeeze that little bit tighter? Perhaps. She began to sob. Isolina walked across and rested her head on her shoulder.

Silvano returned looking stressed, his hair untidy and his shirt open at the collar.

'We must go, Isolina.'

'Go? Go where? We can't leave Savina and we can't leave Fabia.'

Silvano looked at the distraught woman. She had aged.

'Savina. People will come and look after you, people who know Fabia – they have promised me this.'

The woman said nothing.

'And we do nothing?'

'What do you suggest? There is nothing we *can* do … not at this moment in time.'

'I see a bunch of cowards … you being the biggest.'

Silvano felt her words find their mark, like the sting of a whip, and it took his breath away. But this was not the time or place to defend either himself or the other brave men who were trying to save Italy.

'She has been taken to the headquarters of the secret police.' He addressed Savina. 'The place is a fortress and it would take an army to get her out. All we can do is wait for the right moment. I will give you my promise that I will not forget … We will return, she is a brave woman. They told me she is strong, and that is good also.'

'Kind words … You call her a woman, but to me, she is still a child, a child who is alone, and it will break my heart to think of her like that. Missing me, alone, scared, and I unable to do a thing to help her. Do you know what that is like … do you?'

Silvano struggled to meet her eye. Instead, he walked across and placed his arms around her shoulders. She laid her head on his chest and sobbed. Silvano looked towards Isolina, but she turned her head away.

CHAPTER EIGHTEEN

It was dark when they left. Silvano drove. Beside him, Isolina stared into the darkness. Her letter retained its power: at none of the checkpoints did they ask to see Silvano's identification. He offered her a cigarette, but she waved it away and leant her head on the cold glass.

'What will happen now?' she whispered.

'To Fabia?'

'Yes … Who else would I be talking about?' She spoke with annoyance in her voice. 'What will they do with her?'

'I suspect … I …'

'Don't lie, Silvano, I want to know the truth. Do not think I'm stupid.'

He took his time answering, trying to think of what to say and how to say it. There was no way round it, only the truth would do … He took in a lungful of smoke and held it … Yes, he thought, only the truth.

'They will question her,' he breathed out. 'Torture her, if the past is anything to go by.' He glanced across and saw Isolina's reflection in the window, saw the tears cascading down her cheeks. He cursed his callousness, but what else could he say? To lie would only make things worse.

'Isolina,' he whispered.

'Go on … I want to know.'

'First the Italian SS will have her … They will then pass her on to the Nazis.' He took a deep breath before continuing. 'They will keep her in a cell, alone, with just water and stale bread … Isolina –' He turned to face her.

'GO ON!' she screamed.

'Then the rest is up to her. If she wants to live, she will survive it, all the horror and all the pain …' He struggled now. 'She knew this might happen, Isolina, gambling with her life, I mean. Eighteen was just a number. She was well aware of the risks and she is not a young girl anymore, but a woman. Your cousin is very brave. So many people have respect for her … including me.'

'Respect! A man's word … Men always have *respect* for the dead or dying. You call her brave, I call her selfish… If she could see what she has done to her mother! If only all sons and daughters would think first about their actions.' Isolina's tears became a torrent as she looked into the darkness outside.

'This is war … the rules change.'

'Don't speak to me like I am a fool, Silvano.'

'I am not.' He tried to soften his voice. 'It's just that thousands of Italians are risking their lives to help free our country. Did nothing you saw earlier not open your eyes to what is going on? A priest being shot, a man beaten in the middle of the street in broad daylight … and would you like to know what happened to those two brave men who went to your cousin's assistance?' He stared at her. 'Both shot in the back of the head an hour later.' Silvano had not realised he had been shouting until he stopped. Now, only the sound of the engine could be heard.

The fate of the two men had shocked Isolina, Silvano saw that, but it was not what he wanted. When he left this morning, he had no idea that this girl had anything to do with Isolina, but now that this had happened, it complicated everything. Seeing her after all this time had awakened what he thought had died, a long time ago …

How pathetic … He was in love with a woman who hated everything about him.

~ ~ ~ ~

Father Remo swallowed the brandy Fino had given him, and stared from the window onto a countryside dusted with white powder. The first significant snow of winter had fallen, and there would be more to come. God's giant hand had sprinkled icing sugar over the trees and rooftops, and yet had left enough green and red on the landscape to let you know that Tuscany still lay underneath.

'Beautiful,' he whispered under his breath.

'What was it like in Lucca?' Fino asked.

'No different to anywhere else in Italy,' the priest answered, as he continued to stare at the landscape.

'They have arrested six nuns at the convent; the Cardinal sent me to see what I could do.'

'Why were they arrested?'

'Sheltering Jews.'

'I see.'

Father Remo had a tired look about him. His face was gaunter and his cheekbones were like razors under his skin. The man reflected a starving nation. He swallowed a mouthful of spirit, which burnt the back of his throat, a sensation that reminded him that he was still alive in this country of corpses.

'They took the adults ... the nuns hid the children ...' He stopped as if he had forgotten what he was about to say.

Fino took a deep breath, knowing the priest was here to ask for a favour – this was not just a visit to see an old friend to check on his welfare.

'Father,' he began, 'you have come here to ask me if I can take the children ... am I right?' He stood, picked up the bottle of brandy and walked across to Father Remo, pouring a small amount into his empty glass.

'Am I that obvious, Fino?'

'No,' Fino hesitated, 'but desperate people have a way of behaving ... and that alerts friends to a problem.'

'This war is making us all desperate.'

'They took Simon from this very room, and now the countryside is awash with escaping prisoners, returning Italian soldiers, Jews... Not a day goes by when someone does not ask us to help.' Fino sat behind his desk, cradling his brandy glass. 'And we have to say no, not because it is not safe for us, but simply because it is far from safe for them.'

'I understand.'

'We have the children to think about. What happens to them if we are taken? We give them food, clothing, sometimes money ... We try to find alternative accommodation, but everything we do is a risk. The other farmers are risking everything to help. With each passing week, the punishment for helping these people increases in its brutality, yet those in these hills, nevertheless, continue to get help.'

'I know, Fino ... I know. But I had to ask.'

'Now you have asked, let us speak no more of it … and not in front of Sassa. If she had her way, she would take in everyone who came knocking at our door … Her heart is big, but there are times when I feel as if it could explode … I will risk a lot, but not the woman I love.'

Father Remo walked slowly across to where Fino sat, placed a hand on his shoulder and lightly squeezed it.

'What news, Father, have you?' Fino cleared his throat, wiping the moisture from his eyes. 'The radio is off air … has been for several days.'

The priest went back to the window. 'Florence is a city in turmoil. Jew-hunting is the new Fascist pastime. In Lucca, too, I saw a column of very young recruits being marched to the station. They looked so scared … and so very young. They will not make good soldiers.'

'Those that come here offer us valuables … family heirlooms from the mothers who want us to hide their boys from being called up … I see so many tears … Put them all together and it would drown us all.'

Father Remo dropped to his knees, clasping his hands together. 'Let us pray, Fino.'

'I will leave you alone, Father,' said Fino as he walked towards the door.

'Let us pray together.'

Fino looked across the room at him. 'I stopped communicating with God six months ago … I fear he has also fled Italy.'

He closed the door quietly behind him.

~ ~ ~ ~

The wheels spun, but the car was going nowhere. Isolina thumped down on the steering wheel with the palms of her hands, cursing under her breath.

'What now?' asked Sofia, surveying the vast frozen fields all around her.

'I do not know, Sofia,' an irritated Isolina answered. 'Let me think.'

'I could get out and push.' Gino spoke from his hiding place in the back seat.

'No, Gino.' Isolina regretted being sharp with him, and her decision to bring him just added to the panic running through her veins. He had no papers, so they would say he was from Sassa's farm ... or an evacuee ... except, boys of his age were being called up and packed off to Germany. Outside, the land looked bleak and the sky looked about ready to drop another load. It was then she noticed the lorry.

It drew up alongside. Inside, were two German soldiers in their forties. The nearest one looked down and opened his window. Smiling, he asked, in reasonably good Italian, if they were in difficulty.

'Yes ... We are stuck.'

The soldier pushed open the truck door and, with a little difficulty, stepped down onto the snow-covered road. He blew white mist into his hands and rubbed them together. He wore a long thick army coat that was buttoned up to his chin. The driver shouted something in German and the other man smiled, answering him in his own language.

'May I try?' he asked.

Isolina looked at Sofia, who in turn looked back at Gino.

'Yes ... yes,' she said, removing herself from the car.

The German sat behind the wheel and looked across at Sofia, smiling. 'Let's see what we can do.'

He switched on the engine and rested his foot lightly on the accelerator. The car rocked back and forth and the noise of the engine increased. Isolina wondered if he knew what he was doing, for she had done the same thing for the past twenty minutes. The engine continued to scream in defiance, exhaust poured from the rear, but the wheels would not grip. The other German shouted again from his cab.

'Well, I don't think she wants to move.' He was looking over his shoulder at Gino. 'What do you think … stuck?'

Gino smiled, his eyes searched out Sofia's face for reassurance. To his relief, she, too, was smiling.

'Nothing for it …' The German got out and began speaking to his mate. The lorry moved thirty metres further down the road, and then backed up to the car.

'We will have to pull you free.'

The other man jumped into the back of the lorry, emerging with a thick coil of rope, which he secured to the car.

'Lucky you were passing,' said Isolina, stamping her feet in the snow.

'We have been in the woods,' he said as he fixed the rope to Isolina's car. 'We got ourselves some Christmas trees, and a few logs.'

Christmas, Isolina thought: it had gone from her mind, although, it was less than two weeks away. There had been too much to think about lately … Fabia for one; Sofia … not that it would feel like Christmas.

'Do you need to be out on the road when the weather is this poor?'

'I am a nurse on my way to see the evacuated children.'

'At the farm of the Swedish woman?'

'Yes, Sassa ... you know her?'

His face suddenly lost its welcoming glow. 'I have been there once ... to remove a man.'

Isolina instantly thought of Simon. 'You took away the doctor.'

'For my sins ... yes, we did.'

The other German shouted from the cab and lit up a cigarette, releasing a cloud of smoke through the window. The soldier got back into Isolina's car and signalled to the lorry. It revved up and the rope became taut. The lorry edged forward, the rope straining as if it might snap. With it, the car began to move, too, slowly at first, then both the lorry and the car were sixty metres down the road. The man in the lorry jumped down, smiling, and untied the rope.

'Thank you,' said Isolina, now standing by the car.

'It is nothing ... and, anyway, it is Christmas ... well, almost.'

'Thank you, anyway,' Isolina smiled.

'Look,' said the German, 'we have cut down five trees, why don't you take one to the children? We could easily tie it to your roof.'

'No, you have done enough, don't go to any trouble.'

'It is no trouble ... like I said, it is almost Christmas and those children are without parents. We all miss loved ones at this time of the year, and it will make me feel better.'

He shouted to his friend, who stood smoking: he held up his arm in acknowledgment. It was then that Isolina saw them, six in all. Partisans.

Moments later, both German soldiers had their backs against the lorry, with their hands raised above their heads and a look of fear on their faces. A woman with short, dark hair arrived, holding a rifle across her chest.

'Shall we shoot them now?' said one of the Partisans, spitting on the ground.

At which point Richard Mason emerged from behind the truck with a smile on his lips.

'No, Enzo, you fucking animal.'

'Don't call me names, Englishman, let us shoot the bastards and be gone – let's see what's in the lorry.' Richard Mason stared into Isolina's face. Could it be possible that she had grown even more beautiful?

'Christmas trees,' said Isolina.

'What?'

'In the lorry … Christmas trees.'

Mason grinned. 'Different,' he muttered to no one in particular.

'Shall I check?' asked the woman, staring at Isolina. 'Enzo's a fool, but he is right, we should shoot them.'

Isolina's stomach tightened. 'Surely that is not necessary.'

Mason took a small notepad and pencil from his inside pocket and began to sketch the two Germans, who stared at each other, uncertain as to what was happening.

'I see,' Isolina spoke in a whisper. 'You draw the victims before killing them … Does death need to be captured on paper? Is it not unpleasant enough for you?'

'Just trees.' The woman had returned. 'Let's get going, Mason. She's right: just trees.'

'Patience, Ambra, what is the rush? … Let me think.'

'What is there to think about? I do not want to be here when a lorry-load of Germans arrive.'

'They won't.'

'How can you be certain?' interrupted Enzo, who stared at the soldiers like a lion stalking its prey.

'Take the lorry, Mason, but spare their lives.'

'Why?'

'Because they will do you no harm,' Isolina continued. 'They are old soldiers weary of this war. They, too, want it to end so they can go home. They are victims as much as we all are.'

Someone began to clap and they all looked around to see Ambra, a large smile on her face.

'It's the woman in your drawings ... Now I know how she knew your name.'

Isolina looked at Mason with irritation. He just shrugged his shoulders.

'It is a good sketch, Isolina. As an artist, I like to show off my best work.'

'They know your name, they must die,' the woman added.

Enzo spat on the ground.

'Bastard, Richard.'

Mason watched Sofia come walking towards him.

'Sofia,' he smiled.

'Another.' The woman laughed. 'A whole brothel.'

'Shut up, Ambra. It is nothing of the sort. These people saved my life.'

'Does that not mean anything?' Sofia said, standing next to her mother.

Mason drew breath, pulled out his cigarettes and lit one. The gentle breeze of earlier had become a stiff wind, lowering the temperature further. What would be gained by shooting these men? Only reprisals against the farmers, maybe, and for what? Christmas trees. They did not need the lorry, at least not yet – but Ambra was right, they had heard his name and that was not good. It would create interest that an Englishman was with the Partisans. He drew in the smoke and held it in his lungs.

'Go, Isolina,' he said.

'No,' she replied, pulling Sofia to her. 'These men will stay silent.'

'Nothing will happen to these men … You have my word.'

'What?' It was Enzo, his face full of hate. 'If they know an Englishman is here, they will swarm all over us.'

'Do you not think I know that?'

As Mason spoke, Enzo lifted his rifle and prepared to fire.

'Stop, Enzo!' Mason held his revolver at arm's length. 'I will shoot.'

Silence. Nothing moved. A bird cried out from the snow-dusted trees. Both Germans had closed their eyes.

'I said, put it down … I mean it.'

Enzo's eyes moved from the Germans to Mason and from the Germans back to the barrel of Mason's gun. He swept his tongue across his top lip, tasting the tobacco that stained it. He wanted a drink and another cigarette as he felt the bitter wind begin to sting his exposed fingers.

Mason, too, felt the weight of the gun grow heavier; each muscle cried out in pain, forcing his arm to drop just a little. He clenched his jaw. Enzo finally lowered the rifle, but Mason continued to point the revolver.

'Mason,' Ambra whispered. '*Mason!*'

Mason slowly lowered his arm. The pain stabbed at his muscles.

Enzo walked away, smoking, just as the Italian-speaking German asked if he could relieve himself. Mason nodded.

'We are even now, Isolina. Never ask me to …'

'To what?'

'Never mind … Take the keys from the lorry, they can walk back.'

Both Germans returned after relieving themselves. 'Take a tree,' one said to Isolina. 'Please.'

'What is he talking about?' asked Mason.

'Could two of your men tie a Christmas tree to the roof of my car?'

'Anything else?' he laughed.

~ ~ ~ ~

The man stood shivering by the open fire, a young boy by his side. Both gazed around the grand room in silence. Cold and exhaustion had taken its toll. The door opened and Sassa, dressed in a pink floral dress, entered. On her feet she wore black wellington boots.

'I have been making a snowman with the children, apologies for my strange attire. You wished to see me.'

She held her hands up to the flames of the fire. Neither of her visitors was dressed for this time of year, more like a stroll on a late-spring day. With shoes that leaked, the boys looked old and shabby. The soles had been held on with some tape and string. Their coats were thin and, while the man wore no jumper, the boy wore two.

'Yes.' The man bowed to Sassa before searching his pockets and withdrawing a small object, which he held in the palm of his hand. 'We are trying to get to Naples, where my family live.'

Sassa turned away from the gold ring that rested in the palm of his hand. 'That would mean going through German lines. You would be foolish to do such a thing.' She looked at the small boy. 'You are Jewish, are you not?'

'Christian converts … 1934.'

'That will mean nothing to a Nazi or Fascist.'

'Yes, I know … please, take this.'

'For what?'

'Food and clothing, and the use of your cart for as far as it can take us.'

Sassa looked at the man, sensing he was not the boy's father: too old. The boy, for his part remained silent. He was so pale, he would not be able to walk more than a kilometre right now.

'Put the ring away, you will need that later. I will give you some warm clothing and food. If you insist on undertaking this journey, I will get my man to take you as far as the lower side roads beyond the village. But, for the sake of the boy, my advice would be not to. The chances of getting through the German lines are slim.'

The old man smiled, reached out and took hold of Sassa's hand. 'God bless you,' he whispered.

'Do not thank me.'

'Your kindness.'

'If I was being kind, I would have locked you in one of my rooms and prevented you from this madness, for the sake of your … the boy.'

'My grandson.'

Sassa smiled at the boy and placed her hand on his head, running her fingers through his hair.

'Wait here.'

She left the room. Outside, she suddenly felt the need to rest her back against the wall.

'Signora?'

A maid, concern etched across her face, came scurrying down the hallway.

'I'm all right,' Sassa forced a smile. 'I want you to go down to the kitchen and prepare two warm meals. I am going to my room. Tell Maria to join me there.'

The maid hurried away, allowing Sassa to compose herself. Slowly, she walked back to her bedroom, unable to shift the pair from her mind. She was sending them to their death. If they did not die of exposure, they would end up in a German concentration camp somewhere.

On reaching her room, she moved to the wardrobe and knelt. Somewhere here she had a pair of Fino's boots, and the soles had only just been repaired. Why these two? Did they just represent what was happening in this sad country? Did looking at them remind her of the uncertainty of it all? She looked around the room and allowed her eyes to settle on a picture of her and Fino on their honeymoon. Will they have any of this soon? A home, their possessions, even life itself? What was going on around them was out of their control. Soon, they would be caught between the advancing and retreating armies and, if life seemed bad now, it would not get much better then.

Sassa picked up the photo and ran her thumb across it. She replaced it softly, needing to find that pair of shoes for the boy.

~ ~ ~ ~

They brought the refugee children in four separate carts. Fino himself drove one. He sat proud and upright like the young man he once was. Christmas Eve was always a special time, a time to think about others, for children to be excited and for adults to reflect. The war had moved a step closer to the Tuscan countryside. Some, here in this beautiful corner of Italy, had turned a blind eye to what was happening in the rest of the country. But burying their heads in the sand was not an option for Sassa and Fino.

The constant trickle of people coming and going kept the war real. Seeing people escaping was a constant reminder of what was happening elsewhere. The stories of human brutality, suffering and injustice were endless. She had come to think of the evacuees as family. She often received letters from the parents, begging them to keep their child, with tales of the misery of life at home without food or shelter, as well as the constant bombing by the Allies.

Tonight, there was a clear sky overhead, and a moon that sat in pride of place. Around it shone a thousand stars. Below it, the ground had a frozen crust, which crunched under the shoes and boots of those attending Mass. The moonlight made the frozen snow sparkle. The setting was tranquil: peace had found a place to rest, however short-lived that pause might be.

The children's excitement had grown throughout the day, and this journey through the seasonal landscape had drizzled its magic upon each of them. For a short time, the children were able to forget the horrors of war. The Pope had sounded tired during his Christmas Eve speech, unable to give an inspired appeal for peace, love and harmony, knowing it would fall on deaf ears. Sassa suddenly pictured the Jewish man and the boy in her mind – had they made it? A hand slowly slipped into hers and she looked down into the smiling face of a young evacuee.

Isolina walked arm in arm with Sofia, while Gino remained back at the farm. Her decision was vindicated by the many Fascist militiamen watching people pass. Silent and intimidating, they stared into the faces of those who came to celebrate Christmas Mass. The flame from a match illuminated Carlo Sergi's features as he blew out a cloud of smoke. He noticed Sofia with her mother and tried to catch her eye. He smiled when he did, but she looked away.

Inside the church, the children sang 'Silent Night'. Isolina embraced Anna, who had spent the past week forming this choir. Sofia, too, smiled at Anna. Her outlook on life had changed these past few weeks. Father Mariano spoke about a strong nation, which chilled those inside the church. He called for a united Italy, one nation, and for all young men to come forward and join the new Republican Army. Vito Sergi grinned as the man sitting behind him slapped him on the back, took hold of his hand, and raised it. Most of the church ignored that moment.

Eva Pinto was one of those. She had still not heard from her son, Angelo, who was lost somewhere in Greece. It was common knowledge that Eva gave shelter to escaping soldiers, as well as food. The fact remained, though, that no one had been caught on her property, much to Vito's annoyance, but he now had her watched night and day. Not that Eva cared – what could they do to her that was greater than the loss of a son.

'Please, join me,' Father Mariano said in a voice that echoed off the walls. His eyes strayed to Vito Sergi's face.

'In praying for the innocent people of Pisa, who, on the eve of Christ's birth, have been bombed by our enemies in a cowardly attack. Let us also pray for the mothers and children who have been murdered in cold blood.'

Eva Pinto stood at this point and made her way to the central aisle. She stopped and gazed into Vito Sergi's face. 'Even here, in God's house, you spread your evil lies.'

'Facts, Eva … *Facts.*' He sat back and drew a deep breath. 'Unlike the lies those airmen you help tell you.'

Eva did not reply. Those around Vito grinned as the woman left. After pausing a moment, Father Mariano continued. 'We see with our own eyes what this indiscriminate bombing by the British has done. It makes orphans of Italian children. The children here before us were bombed out of their homes and brought here to live in safety.'

That was enough for Sassa. 'Father Mariano …' She looked up at the priest. 'You chose tonight to preach propaganda …We brought the children to our home for safety, that is true, but tonight, we brought them here to share Christmas with God.'

'Safety from the British bastards,' someone shouted from behind her.

Sassa ignored him. Fino reached for her hand and squeezed it. 'My home is a sanctuary for children, so they can be protected from adults … whatever nationality.'

'Does that include Jews?' another voice bellowed out.

'I see the person in need … that is all I see.' Sassa again saw the Jewish man and his grandson in her mind.

Fino squeezed her hand again. 'Let us go, Sassa,' he whispered.

'They are not human … so how can they be described as people?' Several men began to laugh. 'Why do you help the scum?' another shouted.

'Come on.' Fino rose from his seat and began to push her towards the central aisle. Before continuing, Sassa stopped, as had Eva, and looked directly at Vito.

'I see them as persecuted human beings … I feel it is my duty as a Christian to help and look after them.' She took a step closer.

Fino looked at Isolina, uncertain what Sassa was about to say or do next.

'Maybe one day … and in the not too distant future, you might become one of the persecuted yourself. And I will do my best to protect you.' With that she walked on, holding the hands of two of her children. Vito Sergi did not answer the Swedish woman. Father Mariano remained silent as he watched his church empty. Many came up to Sassa and hugged her, while all the time, the Blackshirts watched. The seamstress, Simona Piro, had tears in her eyes, which now ran the length of her thin face.

'Beneath it all, they are just cowards, Sassa.'

'Shh …' A woman placed a finger to her lips.

'I will do no such thing. I am not scared of these bullies, and soon the Allies will be here and *they* …' she pointed across to where the Fascist stood '… will soon become the hunted.'

'Come,' Alfonso and his wife gently directed the woman away.

Isolina and Sofia followed. Carlo stood outside smoking. Sofia felt his eyes scrutinise her body, making her feel uncomfortable.

'Are we to walk, Mamma?' Sofia asked.

Isolina heard the fear in her daughter's voice. 'Fino is going to take us home on his cart.' She smiled and kissed her daughter on the forehead.

'Good.'

Beauty attracts predators, she thought, finding Carlo Sergi in the crowd. The boy turned and caught her eye. They stared straight into each other's eyes for several seconds, before a smile broke across Carlo's lips, forcing Isolina to look away. The night air had a bitter feel to it. It was colder than when they had entered the church.

'I have to take Tobia and Arrigo … Sassa insisted! Anna would also like to come.' Fino was walking towards his cart. 'The woman will be the death of me,' he muttered.

Sassa waved as they got onto the cart. Just then, Vito Sergi left the church. He stood for a moment, staring at Fino's cart, then at the Swedish woman. He felt his anger rise; he would see them all removed if it was the last thing he did.

CHAPTER NINETEEN

He had seen the footprints in the snow, and knew they were not Sofia's, nor her mother's for that matter. They had come to a sudden halt on the far side of the barn. The backdrop was peaceful: a blanket of snow had enveloped the land, coating the trees that encircled the house. The gigantic moon overhead lit up the landscape, but it also highlighted the footprints, making his heart beat faster.

He thought of Sofia and, instantly, a calmness descended on him. When she was close, he felt safe, however much she teased him. Standing here now, he could smell her fragrance. His eyes once again settled on the newly made footprints. Surely no one was out in this weather – except, someone *was*. Perhaps standing on the other side of the barn. Could it be a Partisan? His mind flashed to the morning their car had become stuck: they seemed to have appeared from nowhere that day.

Suddenly, a shadow formed over the snow, and a cloud of smoke drifted into the air. His eyes moved to the road leading to the farm entrance. When would they return? He closed his eyes, wanting to clear his head. What should he do? Who was the shadow waiting for? Sofia? Her mother? Or were they just spying on the house? Had someone informed the Fascist that they had seen a boy on the farm? No, that could not be. The shadow was waiting ... but not for him.

Had they seen a light come on, Gino wondered, a silhouette in the window? He stepped back further into the room. Another cloud of smoke filled the empty space, and then he saw movement from beyond the trees. They were back. An old man sat proudly on a cart being pulled by a single pony. He manoeuvred it with precision, coming to a halt below his window. Gino's eyes moved to where the shadow was: nothing.

Sofia and her mother now stood on the frozen ground while the old man looked down, speaking. In the back, two other men sat quietly. A young girl, younger than Sofia, came and stood with Sofia's mother, who placed an arm around her shoulders. The girl then kissed Sofia and her mother before climbing back into the cart. They waved until they disappeared beyond the trees.

'Come inside,' Gino whispered to himself. '*Now.* Please ... it is not safe.' But they would not hear his plea or the panic in his voice. His eyes glanced again towards the barn, 'Move!' he said, annoyed with Sofia and her mother. Why didn't they come in? Why just stand there, to what purpose? At that moment, the shadow decided to step out into the open.

'I love the moon,' Sofia whispered.

'More than the sun?' Isolina tightened her hold around her daughter.

'Yes, I love the heat the sun gives off, but it cannot give this wonderful stillness we have right now. I forget what is going on around us. I look up and it's like an old friend looking down.'

Isolina smiled: her young girl was growing up. 'I do know what you mean.'

They heard the crunch of frozen snow, and, with hearts pounding, they swung round.

'Silvano?'

'Yes.'

'What is wrong?'

'I need to speak with you.'

Isolina squeezed Sofia's shoulder. 'Go inside and check on …' She stopped.

'Yes, Mamma.' Sofia had recognised the tall man who had come from behind the barn. She walked towards the house. Strangely, she was not alarmed at leaving her mother alone with this man.

'The girl is a credit to you … and very beautiful.'

Isolina felt her throat tighten.

'Thank you, she is a good child.'

Silvano smiled and took out a cigarette, offering one to Isolina. She shook her head. The flame from his lighter lit up his handsome face. He had remained youthful.

'Why are you here?'

'Fabia.'

'You have news?' Isolina took a step closer.

Silvano's face disappeared for a moment in a cloud of smoke.

'She has not been moved, as yet.'

'What do you mean?'

He took a deep breath and walked to the small picket fence, where she and Simon had stood a thousand years ago.

'We have managed to get inside.' He spoke without looking at her. 'She has been interrogated for many hours over the past few weeks … and I'm afraid tortured … until …'

'Go on …'

'Until she passed out … She has not told them anything.'

Isolina stifled a cry. 'I care little about that … Maybe she *should* talk … Maybe the nightmare would end sooner.'

'The only thing that would end is her life, Isolina.'

'What life has she?'

'She still breathes. And while she remains alive, we have a chance to get her out.'

'What will be left of her, Silvano? An empty shell where once a young girl lived?'

'Surely that is better than the alternative.'

'Is it?'

'We get her out. With love and care, the girl will return … It will take time, but the girl will return.'

'And carry the scars for the rest of her life.'

'Don't we all?'

Isolina stayed silent.

'We will wait until the time is right, then make our move, Isolina. She has not been forgotten, I promise you.'

'She is eighteen, a child, being tortured by Italians … What has happened to us?'

Silvano looked away, placing the cigarette back between his lips.

'If that were Sofia, I …' Isolina could not speak, struggling to hold back tears.

Silvano took a step forward. Isolina composed herself and held out an arm to stop his advance.

'I am fine … leave me be … A cigarette, if I may.' She sucked in its smoke and wiped her eyes before looking up to the moon.

'How are you, Isolina?' Silvano gazed at her face in the

moonlight. Age had not robbed her of her beauty. In fact, it had enhanced it.

'How do you think?' There was a sharpness in her voice.

'I do not mean this very minute ... I mean life, generally ... before all this.'

'Before?'

'Yes, before.'

'I can't remember before ... it does not exist. All the things that happened, they happened to another woman in another life; a life that will never be the same again. A life destroyed by evil men and their fight for power.'

'When can we talk, Isolina? When can we talk about the past and –'

'It is cold, Silvano, I need to go inside.'

He smiled. 'I understand, but can I say one thing?'

'If you must.'

'We both made mistakes. We both said and did things we regret now –'

'You might regret them, I do not,' she interrupted, throwing down the half-finished cigarette. She turned her back on him and walked towards the house. What had made her say those things? Anger, spite? Whatever it was, she had regretted saying them instantly. Who was she punishing but herself? Castigating herself for something she could no longer remember doing.

She turned and watched him disappear into the woods. He was hurt, and she had inflicted the pain. A needless act committed by the guilty party. Lies always came back to haunt you. They clung to you like leaches sucking the goodness from within. There would be little chance of sleep tonight: those memories were circling overhead like vultures.

She opened the door and entered the house. Let me face the agony, she told herself.

~ ~ ~

Severe snowfall greeted 1944, isolating almost everyone from the community around them. Sassa and Fino, along with what staff they had left, continued to clear the road leading to the farm. At Isolina's farmhouse, all three occupants remained inside. Sofia taught Gino how to play chess, but soon got bored of beating him with little effort. Gino, for his part, just wanted to be close to Sofia – he hated the game, and it did not cross his mind to take it seriously, thereby extending the game longer than needed.

He followed Sofia around like a faithful puppy. Her tongue could be as sharp as a butcher's knife, yet he always smiled in her presence. Isolina smiled: she had grown to like him, and often took his side in disagreements. Although, there were other times when he sat alone, watching the clouds drift across the sky. At night, as the stars sparkled in the darkness, he always remained deep in thought.

One evening, Isolina decided to sit next to him. His face was expressionless, his big brown eyes staring vacantly into the night sky. She studied his face. So sweet, so innocent; his face feminine in its construction, from the soft clear skin to the fullness of his lips … The boy looked lost. She sat and placed an arm around his shoulders, slowly pulling him towards her. He did nothing to discourage her.

Her fingers travelled inside his hair before coming to rest again on his shoulders. She looked at his face and found it covered in tears. Tenderly bringing his head to rest on her shoulder, she kissed it as the boy began to weep silently. Sofia chose that moment to come downstairs, stopping at the sight that greeted her. Slowly and silently, she retraced her steps.

~ ~ ~ ~

Sassa had sent a pony and cart to fetch Isolina. One of the children was sick with a high temperature and, although the thaw had begun, it was still too risky for Isolina to use her car. The harsh wind that blew down from the hills burnt the faces of both driver and passenger. Isolina diagnosed scarlet fever and quarantined the girl. It was moments like this that they missed their friend Simon. Isolina was no doctor, but she did her best. Although, in some circumstances, that was not enough.

Fino poured her a glass of wine. 'Ciano, Marinelli, Gottardi and Pareschi, those that voted against Mussolini, have all been shot, so we have been informed.' He refilled his own glass. 'And now more troops pour into the area daily, a thousand paratroopers, I'm told, are due to arrive soon. Where are they going to put them? That is what I want to know.'

'No more news of the Allied landings?' Isolina enquired.

'Livorno has been blown to pieces, the town has been emptied. The coast, we are told, is undefended.'

Sassa turned to Isolina. 'Maria?'

'She is very ill, Sassa. You must keep all the children away … We cannot afford to let it spread.'

Sassa looked drawn and pale. Fino worried about her taking every piece of news to heart.

'All you can do is your best.'

'Here,' Fino refilled his wife's glass. 'Angelo will be here soon with the shelters,' he said.

'Shelters?' Isolina asked.

'Yes, we will build two. Soon the bombing will begin here as they push the Germans back further. We can put the children in the cellar, but they will fill it, so the shelter will give some protection to the others.'

'Including British escapees and Jews,' Fino smiled.

'Whoever,' Sassa added.

~ ~ ~ ~

Her mother had gone to attend to the sick child at Sassa's, leaving her alone with Gino. As January edged closer to February, the snow showers began to decrease in frequency. Only at night did the temperature drop considerably. The days were bearable now, although the breeze had an edge to it. Gino had volunteered to fix the roof, despite not knowing the first thing about it. He hoped it would impress Sofia.

She watched him climb, shaking her head. Gino looked down and smiled, knowing Sofia would have that stern face. Sooner or later, she would let him know what he was doing wrong and tell him how it should be done. And, as always, she would remind him of how stupid he was.

'Remember my mother is at Sassa's … so if you fall, you will have to lie here and freeze, unless you're dead, in which case you won't be bothered either way.'

'Surely you would get a blanket and cover me?'

'Are you crazy? I'm not staying here freezing to death while you lie there and groan.' A smile crept onto her lips, knowing he could not see it from where he stood.

'Would you not kiss me before I died?' he shouted from the roof.

'Why would I do such a thing, you snotty-nosed boy.'

Gino touched his top lip: it was dry. He smiled.

'Come on, I'm freezing,' Sofia shouted, stamping her feet.

The boy climbed up and down the ladder like an overgrown monkey. He would do his best and hope it was enough. Up he went again with a hammer in his trousers and several nails between his teeth. For the next five minutes, he pounded the wood, causing a deafening noise that echoed around the barn. He shouted down to Sofia that he had finished, but received no answer. Either she had gone back to the house, or was annoyed with him over the time it had taken. He began his descent.

He touched ground to find a silent, pale-looking Sofia staring back at him.

'What is it now?' he smiled.

As the words left his mouth, he sensed that something was wrong. And the hand that clamped across his mouth confirmed it. His eyes made contact with Sofia's, just as a young German soldier came into view by her side, bringing his hand to rest on her shoulder. Panic quickly set in. Now another pair of hands took hold of him as he increased his struggle to free himself. The German holding Sofia led her to a post, while speaking to his two companions.

She had recognised him immediately: the face that had stared down at her on the bed. Her eyes searched for his friend, but he was not one of this trio. Her heart skipped a beat. She tried not to show any weakness as he shouted orders to the other two in German. They stood directly under the main beam that ran the length of the barn. The older of the two men held Gino, while the other one went outside. He returned a minute later with a coil of rope. He threw the rope over the beam and secured it to a post, then walked across to where the wooden stool lay on its side.

He placed the stool under the beam while the other soldier made a noose in the rope. Sofia stopped breathing, her mouth became dry, and the barn felt like it was revolving. Then her legs gave way, but the German increased his grip on her arm and held her upright. Gino had a rag inserted into his mouth and his hands were bound behind him. They lifted him onto the stool, where he balanced precariously. The two Germans stood with wide grins, turning to look at Sofia and their self-appointed leader.

The reality hit home. 'No!' Sofia screamed. 'NO! You cannot do this.'

One of the Germans holding Gino laughed, whispered to the other and undid Gino's trousers, pulling them down to his ankles. The boy felt his heart quicken and beads of sweat erupted onto his skin while a cold blast of air hit him, along with the realisation that he was naked below his waist. They placed the noose around his neck.

As Sofia watched, she gulped in mouthfuls of air, yet her lungs seemed to remain empty. She screamed, then screamed again, as the disbelief of what was about to happen hit home. She dropped to her knees as the soldier released his grip. Gino felt the rope burn his skin, felt it tighten around his windpipe. Panic swept through his body and he began to choke on the rag. A numbness entered his legs, making them buckle for a second. He sucked in air through his nose, gasping for breath, while at the same time desperately fighting to keep his footing. He tried to spit the rag from his mouth, as he felt one of the Germans touch his genitals and laugh.

A loud, clicking noise rose above the laughter, bringing an instant silence to the barn. The smile had gone from the faces of the Germans, while Gino remained balancing on the stool. Sofia looked up and saw the barrel of a gun resting on the lead German's temple.

'Sofia – move, now.' It was Mason's voice.

She wanted to scream with relief.

'Go and get your boyfriend down.'

'He's not my ...'

She moved swiftly across the barn and, helped by a couple of Mason's men, lowered Gino to the floor. There were a dozen Partisans inside the barn now, all armed, all looking in the direction of the German soldiers.

'Come, Gino.' Sofia placed an arm around the traumatised boy. They stopped for a second next to Mason, and he looked down at them.

'Get him inside, Sofia ... give him some of your mother's brandy. I'm certain she won't mind.'

'Thank you,' she whispered.

'A pleasure. Listen: it might not be wise to tell your mother about any of this.'

'Why?'

'I have my reasons ... Trust me this time, no questions.'

Sofia looked into his eyes and remembered another time in this barn. She looked away with a touch of embarrassment. 'Yes.'

'And Sofia ...'

She turned her head.

'I have never drawn a more beautiful young girl before, and I do not suppose I ever will.' She smiled, before turning her stare on the German boy. His face had turned pale, and he tried to force a brave smile, but without success.

Moments later Sofia and Gino were gone.

'What are we going to do with them?' a voice asked.

'Not here,' Mason said. 'The woods.'

Outside, Sofia and the boy took in a lungful of chilly Tuscan air.

~ ~ ~ ~

'Buongiorno, Roberto.' Sassa greeted the interpreter with a smile. He dipped his head in return. All around them were German troops, their boots crushing the gravel. They entered the farm buildings, Sassa's house, the clinic, and the building where the children played, before finally entering the now repaired stables.

'What do they hope to find?' she asked.

'They are looking for three German soldiers who have been missing for the past ten days.'

'I see. And they think they are here with us?'

'They are looking everywhere. The longer they are missing the more anxious they become … and the more forceful.'

Sassa watched as her maids comforted the children, all of whom had been brought from their warm rooms.

'Maybe they have deserted.'

The officer smiled at Sassa. She grinned and Roberto ran his fingers through his hair.

'I have no coffee, tell him … it has all gone.'

Isolina's car pulled into the yard. 'Can you remind the officer of our sick child,' Sassa turned to Roberto. 'Isolina is here to attend to her.'

Roberto turned to the German and spoke.

'He said a soldier will go in with her.'

'Is that really necessary?'

'Yes,' said the interpreter, not needing to relay that question on.

Holding her bag, Isolina walked across to them.

'One of them is to go in with you, Isolina.'

'Why?'

'You might have three German soldiers inside that bag of yours,' Sassa smiled. 'Have they been to your place?'

Isolina nodded. 'At the crack of dawn.'

'They found nothing?' Sassa asked.

Isolina returned from her thoughts. 'No, just me ... and Sofia.'

~ ~ ~ ~

He sat on what was left of a fallen tree and had not moved in almost an hour. Sofia pulled her coat tight cross her chest and placed her chin into the warmth of a woollen scarf as she walked to where Gino sat. He did not move or acknowledge her.

'I could have been a German,' she said, perching next to him.

He shrugged his shoulders. Sofia watched him with concern.

'I like the winter at night, when the moon looks down and there is no wind.' She decided just to talk for the sake of it, hoping he would at least tell her to shut up. 'Although, I like the warmth of summer, too. Maybe we are lucky to be living here in Tuscany – the seasons and landscape are so beautiful. I think we sometimes take it for granted how lucky we are ...'

There was still no response from Gino. He had been like this since the day the three Germans had come. She understood how he must be feeling: to have a rope tied around your neck must be the most frightening thing imaginable. Neither had known that help was on hand. He must have thought that he was going to die.

But now, he must try to forget it. He was alive, living here, and not back in that convent. He was fed, clothed and had a warm bed at night. What more could he want? Yet, he seemed to be going deeper and deeper into himself.

'Gino,' she whispered. 'Gino?'

He looked away.

'What is wrong with you? I prefer the stupid Gino, the crazy Gino. I do not much care for this Gino.'

His shoe continued to dig away at the earth beneath it, but he said nothing in response. She squeezed his hand before bending her head forward and smiling at him in the hope he would return it. Instead, she witnessed a waterfall of tears.

'Oh, Gino ... whatever is the matter?' She pulled him towards her. 'Surely it is not that bad? It's all over now, they will never come back here.'

He loosened himself from her. 'It will never be all right.'

'Gino ... *what* will never be better? They have gone.'

'You do not understand ... I wish they had hanged me, kicked that stool away from under me.'

'Now you are being stupid ... why would you want that? Why would anyone want to die?'

'Because that's how I feel.'

'I will tell my mother that, after she has taken you in and shared our food with you ... You ungrateful bastard, Gino ...'

'You don't understand!' he screamed.

'Then *tell* me!'

'You saw me.'

'Saw you? What do you mean, *saw* you?'

Gino put his hands to his face. 'You saw me! When they pulled my ...' He sniffled and began to cry.

Sofia understood, and her first reaction was to laugh. 'Firstly, I saw nothing, Gino. I promise you that. Secondly, I cannot understand a boy who would prefer to be dead because a girl might have seen his ... you-know-what. I find that strange, Gino ... like I find you strange.' She then began to laugh out loud, encircling her arms around his neck. Suddenly, she stopped and the two stared at each other. She could feel his warm breath on her face, and her lips moved closer to his until they met.

~ ~ ~

Two more logs were placed on the fire. The weather was bitter now that the sun had set behind the hilltops. Silvano had just led six men into camp, the rest sat huddled around small fires. They had packages with them, courtesy of the farmers. Not just food, but also clothing to help them survive the winter – whatever they could spare and, in many instances, what they could not.

The men left what they had brought in the snow and moved quickly towards the warmth of the fires. Kneeling, they placed their hands almost inside the flames; if only they could do the same with their feet.

'Luca,' Silvano shouted across the camp. 'There is bread, cheese and potatoes ... also some vegetables and wine.'

'No meat?' the boy asked.

'They have little of everything, Luca. They give what they can.'

'We caught a couple of rabbits,' said a voice from the darkness. 'Not much, but it will help.'

'Divide the bread and wine, Luca.'

'Would you like me to get a priest and have him bless them?' the boy smiled.

'Fuck off,' a man shouted. 'Most of them are Fascist.'

Silvano rested his back against a tree. He was tired and his legs ached. He rubbed his eyes and felt the soreness. He was hungry, too, and in desperate need of a good night's sleep. They had walked some distance today: supplies had been low, but it was also an exercise to avert boredom, which was as big a danger as the Germans, the Fascists and the cold.

He looked across the camp at this small army of men – mainly locals, but there had also been a constant stream of POWs, with the majority being British. The rest were Canadian, French, Yugoslav and Polish. Most got on, all having a common enemy. It was the hours spent sitting around that made his job harder. Until the Allies got closer, London wanted them to just sit tight. They blew up the odd railway line, maybe a bridge, which also helped to relieve the boredom, but it never felt as if the war was coming closer to an end. The Allied advance was slow, and becoming slower. The Germans were proving to be tough opposition, not retreating without a stiff fight.

The Allied advance meant more German divisions entering Tuscany, making Silvano's job tougher. Some were here because of the Allied landing at the beachhead at Anzio, where fighting continued. Another reason for the extra numbers was to search for the three missing German soldiers.

It had been almost five weeks since Mason had taken it into his own hands to execute them. Sooner or later, they would be found and the retributions would begin.

They would take it out on the weakest and most vulnerable first, those in the isolated villages: woman, children and the very old. The Fascist militiamen needed little excuse to inflict pain on their own. The Germans were in panic mode, which made them unstable. His Partisans were too weak to take on the might of the German army themselves, they needed the Allies to be closer. Richard Mason knew that, and yet, had still done what he had done. The Partisans were now left outnumbered, and the local population exposed to German retaliation. Anger consumed him. 'Always the Englishman … always.' He closed his eyes and thought of Isolina.

That first afternoon, the day after his visit to the hospital, he had looked up and seen her next to the fountain. He had stared for a few moments before waving. Her beauty had hypnotised him, along with that innocent demeanour that accentuated her magnificence. They spent an hour together before meeting up again two days later. He took her to the beautiful church of Santa Croce, with its magnificent marble façade – worrying that it might bore her.

Over the following weeks, they visited several other places of outstanding beauty. He explained that it was not the religious aspect that appealed, he wanted to be a great architect one day and it was the buildings themselves that captivated him. But, he felt intimidated by her looks, almost feeling inferior when standing so close to her.

Silvano opened his eyes and gazed into the flames. Her face stared back at him, a constant reminder of what he had lost. Time had sprinkled its dust on her, but had stolen none of her beauty. They had lost so much time, time that could never be replaced – and for what, a misunderstanding. He flicked the finished cigarette into the fire in frustration and blew out a cloud of smoke. How foolish, how blind, how arrogant had he been. To lose something so precious was unforgivable.

~ ~ ~ ~

It was the quick thaw that uncovered the graves. A patrol of Fascist militiamen found them and raised the alarm. All three had been shot in the back of the head, and then laid in their graves, still wearing their winter coats. It appeared that whoever did this did not want to touch a German uniform, even if it offered warmth. Inside two hours, the village was surrounded and all the residents brought out of their houses. German paratroopers went around pounding doors with their rifles, helped by the Fascists, who dragged people onto the street. There had been no warning, so while some wore coats, others just wore what they had on at the time.

Around eighty people stood shivering in the square, surrounded by Germans and Blackshirts. Two German officers strolled through the gathering wearing thick leather coats. They called over Vito Sergi and whispered in his ear, then stood back waiting for him to address the people.

'Look at the bastard,' Cinzia Bria said.

'Shh … He will hear you,' a woman holding a small child whispered.

Simona Piro stood with her fourteen-year-old daughter, Lisa. The young girl nervously bit her nails.

'Why are we here?' Alfonso asked.

'Rumour has it they have found three German soldiers buried out in the woods.'

'Good,' Cinzia said.

'Yes, but why are *we* here?' Alfonso repeated.

'They are probably robbing our homes while we stand here.' Mario from the garage spoke with a wide grin on his face.

'Shut up, Mario ... I do not like this one bit,' said Alfonso.

'Here he comes ... The bastard's going to address us. Who does he think he is ... the mayor?'

Vito stepped up onto a wooden box, cleared his throat, and surveyed the faces that stood before him. Beyond them stood around two hundred German paratroopers.

'You must be wondering why you have been brought here tonight,' he shouted. 'Today, three brave German soldiers were found murdered.'

'Brave my arse,' Mario whispered.

'The cowards who committed this hideous crime bound them before shooting each man in the back of the head.' He stopped to wait for a reaction, but none came, and that irritated him further. 'We know that no one here committed this crime ...'

'So why have you brought us here?' Mario was agitated.

'Mario, shut up, please,' Lorenzo whispered from behind him.

'This we know: the real culprits are the Partisans, the ones that live in the hills, those that you ... yes, YOU feed and clothe.' He pointed a finger at the gathering before him. 'Therefore, your finger is also on the trigger. If it were not for you, the Partisan would not be able to function, would not have food or shelter, and so would not be allowed to roam our countryside killing innocent soldiers in such a cowardly manner.'

Behind him a lorry pulled up and reversed. Moments later, German soldiers began unloading wood, ropes and tools. Vito turned and gave them a casual glance.

'We have to make an example, show them what will happen when they commit such acts.' Vito smiled as his audience looked beyond him to what was happening. 'The people who will pay the largest price will be those who help our enemies …'

'They are not my enemy, Vito.' Cinzia the seamstress took a step forward.

'Cinzia, stop this … I have my daughter with me, please do not provoke them.'

'Are you volunteering, Cinzia?' Vito asked.

Two German paratroopers came and took her by the arms, frogmarching her to where the soldiers had unloaded the wood. 'We have one … I need two more.'

'For what?' whispered Lorenzo.

Mario's smile diminished as the first two sections of wood were raised. 'They're going to hang them,' he whispered. 'The bastards.'

'No … that cannot be. Mario …'

'Look for yourself, Lorenzo … The bastards … An eye for an eye, they don't want to go into the hills to face the Partisans, they want to force them down here. So, for every crime they commit, it is we who will suffer.'

'But why?'

'Divide and conquer … it is simple. What he said was true: all of us give to the Partisans; without our support, they would not last a week … So, now the people have a choice:

help the Partisans and die ... or turn your back on them and live ...'

There was a gasp from those around them. Mario and the rest looked up. The gallows were almost in place and three ropes had been thrown over the crossbeam, with three wooden boxes placed under them. Mario was correct: this was just the beginning. Tuscany was about to be turned into hell on earth. The devil and his disciples had arrived.

CHAPTER TWENTY

Silvano walked towards the window, doing up his tunic. Dawn was at last breaking over Florence. He lit a cigarette and allowed his finger to touch the swastika on his arm. He shivered, and stared out into the darkness. In the distance, the Duomo's silhouette reached above the buildings around it, while the streets directly below his window remained quiet with the curfew.

He heard a voice drifting across the empty streets, a gramophone. A woman's voice sang and he tried to remember the opera, but was unable to recall it. She began to sing about a tragic love affair, but failed to tell of the outcome – silence came and stole her voice. He drew on the cigarette and continued to stare towards the city, closing his eyes, eager to hear the woman sing again. But silence prevailed.

He looked at his watch and stubbed out his cigarette in the overflowing ashtray. Matteo, the thin Sicilian, snored until the boot of Lauro made him stop. He sat up rubbing his eyes, disorientated, and looked around in the semi-darkness.

'You were snoring,' Lauro muttered under his breath, concentrating on rolling his tobacco. 'You would have woken the whole damn German army.'

The tanned Sicilian said nothing, just leant back and closed his eyes again. Silvano turned away smiling. They seem to show no nerves, he thought – and yet his own stomach was on fire, and his heart beat against his chest. He sat on a wooden stool and glanced at his watch, which was becoming an annoying habit. Aurele, the Frenchman, would be here soon. Fluent in German, he would lead them across the city dressed as an officer.

Lauro looked up. While placing the cigarette in his mouth he rolled the bottle of wine towards Silvano.

'Drink, just a little, it will help calm the nerves.'

Silvano poured out half a glass, lifted it to his lips and swallowed most in one gulp. It stung the back of his throat and tasted disgusting, but the man was right, it took his mind off what was to come.

He closed his eyes and saw Isolina: she was running to the door, buttoning up her blouse.

'I'm sorry, Isolina.'

'No, no ... it is not you, it is me ... I ... I ...' Her cheeks were tear-stained. 'It was the wine ... the meal ... the candles ...' She continued to struggle with her blouse.

'Here.' He walked across the room and took hold of the first button and gently guided it through the eye. 'There. Shh.' He pulled her to his chest.

'I'm sorry,' she sobbed.

'No, it is all my fault, I did not think. I went too fast and I did not know that you –'

'I am not yet twenty-one.' She spoke between sniffles.

He smiled: crying seemed to enhance her beauty.

'Do you hate me?' she whispered.

He tightened his grip on her. 'I could never hate you. And it is not important. I want to wait until you're ready. I want you to decide – until then, I will just kiss those lovely lips.'

'Is everyone here?'

Silvano awoke, the glass of wine still in his hand. In one swallow, it was gone. He winced and stood looking at Aurele in his smart officer's uniform.

'Five minutes.'

'Is this it?' asked Matteo.

'What we have here is the right number,' Aurele spoke with authority. 'Too many, and we will arouse suspicion.' He placed his gun on the table, checking the chamber before replacing it into the waist holster. Silvano knew the man had done this many times before, he was so clinical. The Frenchman adjusted his cap, before turning his focus on the men around him. 'Shall we?'

One by one they exited the room. Outside, a bitter wind awakened them; Silvano felt it sting his face. He took a deep breath before placing the metal helmet on his head. They set off with the sound of their boots echoing down the narrow, cobbled street. To his right, the River Arno gleamed in the moonlight.

They passed the beautiful Basilica of Santa Croce, and for a split second, Isolina's face stared back at him, before they turned down a side street which came out onto a checkpoint. The first examination. Two tired-looking German soldiers sat smoking around a fire. Silvano glanced nervously at Lauro as they approached. One of the guards looked up wearily, threw away his cigarette, yawned, stretched and finally stood.

'Papers,' he demanded, not looking up.

Aurele stared hard at him, and Silvano felt beads of sweat explode onto his skin. Aurele began speaking in German.

'What is going on here?'

His voice sounded harsh to Silvano, although he had no clue what Aurele was saying. He looked at Lauro, who shrugged his shoulders.

'Where is your helmet? You are a disgrace to the uniform, half asleep, half-dressed – I will have you transferred to the Russian front … All your brave colleagues fighting while you sleep, drink and smoke. Put your helmets on, stand upright, rifles at the ready … for all you knew, we could have been Partisans …'

'Sorry, Captain … it will not happen again.'

Silvano watched in amazement as the soldier stood to attention.

'I know it will not … I will speak with your commander in the morning.'

'Yes, sir.'

'Now, may we pass?'

'Yes … but can I …' A kick from the other guard stopped him asking. 'Yes, sir … *Heil Hitler.*'

Aurele barely raised his arm above waist as they all walked past two bemused faces.

'I can't wait to ask,' whispered Matteo.

They stopped in Via Dell, the narrow street that housed the former Monastery of Santa Verdiana. The yellow plaster flaked from the brickwork, giving it a look of decay. A large, wooden gate sat under an arched front that contained a small, solid wooden door. Aurele looked at his watch and a cloud of mist escaped from his mouth.

'Ready?'

The others nodded and followed him across the narrow road. Aurele pounded the door with his fist three times, while the others scanned the street in both directions. Florence remained asleep. A small hatch opened and a bleary-eyed man looked out. 'Yes?' he said in a gruff German voice.

Aurele met his eye. 'I have come to collect a prisoner.'

The man said nothing; his hand appeared and took hold of his unshaven chin, pondering the request.

'No one has told me of this – on whose orders?'

'I have it all here.'

'Let me see.'

'Here.' Aurele held up the papers in the dim early-morning light.

The man squinted at it; daylight was still thirty minutes away. 'Closer,' he ordered.

'Why not just open up. Here, you recognise the signature, don't you?'

Meanwhile, the three Italian Partisans stood nervously on the street, uncertain what was being said.

'Wait here,' said the guard.

Aurele put the papers back in his pocket. Was this a good sign? the others wondered. The hatch closed. It was now a game of chance: would the man phone his commander before opening up, or after? The sound of bolts being slid back from within brought relief and, moments later, the door creaked open.

Candles lit up a small reception area, which was decorated with portraits of religious events. Christ, his face full of despair, hung carved in wood looking down on a second guard who sat wedged behind a wooden desk.

'Who is it you wish to remove?' the first guard asked, picking up the phone.

'Fabia Grosseto.'

'Grosseto?' The man looked up; his face held surprise.

'Is there a problem?'

'She is a personal favourite of the Fascists. He wants her repaired, then sent back.' The man smiled. 'Why do they want to take her now? She is still unbroken.' He looked at the other guard and both grinned. 'I find that strange … Let me check those orders, there may be a misunderstanding somewhere down the line.'

'Put it down.' Aurele pointed his revolver at the guard.

The man behind the desk reached for his gun, except, Matteo was too quick and knocked him to the floor, smashing the butt of his own gun into the man's temple.

'Now, where is she?' Aurele asked.

The man shook his head. 'I will not tell you.'

'What is going on here?' They all turned to see the Mother Superior standing in the candlelight. The old woman stood erect with a young nun either side.

'Mother,' Aurele began, 'I have come to remove a prisoner you have here, a young girl named Fabia. She has been here for many weeks.'

'I know the girl you speak about.'

'Then, you will either show us where she is … or go and fetch her yourself.'

'For the time being, that is not possible.'

'Why not?'

The mother superior walked slowly across the room. Looking down at the bleeding German guard, she asked one of the nuns to fetch water and towels. As the young nun scurried away, Aurele looked at his watch: they were falling behind schedule.

The old nun smiled at him. 'Is your purpose to save one life so that many others are lost?'

Aurele stared at her with a vague look on his face.

'I do not understand.'

Three nuns returned with water and towels and began to attend to the injured German.

'Then let me explain … We have at least seven other political women held as prisoners. If you take this girl, what will happen to them?' She walked across to where a nun gently bathed the gash on the soldier's head. She bent down and whispered into the nun's ear, then stood to face Aurele again.

'You are asking me to take them all?' asked the Frenchman.

'Those are my terms … You could go and find her yourself, but there is no time – I have seen you stare at your watch four times. It would take you ten minutes, maybe more, to seek her out … It would be simpler to agree to my terms.'

Aurele took a deep breath: the annoyance was there for all to see on the Frenchman's face.

'All right, but you must move quickly, or more lives will be lost.'

'They are on their way,' the nun smiled.

Aurele returned it. The woman was a cool negotiator – perhaps God being on her side made that possible. Suddenly, a pitiful group of women arrived before them, each covered in cuts and bruises, each with a haunted look on their face. Silvano took a sharp in-take of breath; the others, too, were shocked at the sight before them.

The pathetic group stood silent, gaunt-faced, with lifeless eyes that sunk deep into their skulls. Their skin was almost transparent. Some could barely stand. Blankets had been draped over them, but still they shivered. Silvano searched for Fabia, trying desperately to recall what she looked like, for none of these woman bore any resemblance. Finally, his eyes settled on the young girl standing at the back – could it be her? Matteo confirmed it by whispering her name. But this was not the brave girl he had watched . Gone was the sweet, fresh-faced angel; gone was the carefree girl with the charming smile, who had acted the part of a lover so well. What stood before him now was just a shell. The Nazi vultures had fed on the rest.

'Come on … is he bound tight?' Aurele asked Lauro, who was gagging the other German in the chair. 'When we are well away, Mother,' Aurele turned to the mother superior, 'not until then.'

'It will be done.'

'Will you all be all right?'

'Of course … we have him for protection.' She looked up at Christ. 'Worry about yourselves, we will be fine. God speed.'

Aurele smiled.

'Fabia …' Matteo whispered. '*Fabia.*'

She paid him no notice. His anger got the better of him and, a second later, he withdrew his gun and pointed it at one of the Germans. Aurele was too far away to react; it was the Mother Superior who placed herself in the line of fire.

'Move, Mother,' Matteo shouted.

'No.'

'They must pay for their crimes.'

'Not by your hand.'

'Then by whose?'

'God's.'

'Why did he not come to this innocent girl's aid? Why did he allow this?' He looked at Fabia.

'Go, my child … let God punish those that have committed these crimes, do not commit another sin in this holy place … turn the other cheek.'

'Matteo,' shouted Aurele. 'Let's go … Come on, put that away.'

The seven women, including Fabia, found themselves outside moments later. They made their way down a narrow street as daylight broke. Aurele led the women quickly through the deserted streets; the realisation that they were free took time to register, but when it did, some began to help themselves. It was only Fabia who remained as they had found her.

Luck stayed with them – only once were they stopped, and Aurele dealt with it as skilfully as earlier. They reached the safe house, which was tucked down a narrow street off the Arno. It was owned by a rich art dealer sympathetic to the Partisans, but the man had not expected such a large group. Over the next three hours, all the women except Fabia, were dispersed to other safe houses dotted about the city.

Silvano stared at her, unable to take his eyes off the girl who sat silent with her hands clasped together. He wished Isolina were here.

'What are you going to do with her?' Silvano asked.

'Not certain,' said Aurele, smoking as he gazed from the top window. The art dealer had gone to buy some food. 'Her group splintered after the …' He stopped speaking. 'But they owe her, and said they would not forget … and have kept their promise.'

'But what now?' Silvano asked again.

'I was asked to get her out. There are other people to decide what fate awaits her.'

'Fate?'

'Sorry, wrong word – her … future.'

'I could take her back with me. Her cousin is a nurse and lives in the hillsides surrounding Florence.'

Aurele stabbed out the cigarette. 'Sounds fine by me, but it is not me who is going to make that decision, is it?'

'Then let's just take her now.'

'Kidnap her?' Aurele smiled. 'That should go down well with her friends … And how do you propose we get her out of Florence?'

'That uniform seemed to carry a lot of authority.'

'You want me to risk my neck a second time?'

It was Silvano's turn to smile. 'Why not? Is she not worth the risk?'

'Silvano … I see why you are the leader of your band of hillside brigands … You have the devil in you.'

Silvano poured two glasses of wine and rested his head back against the wall, glancing at Fabia and then back to Aurele.

'I think it is a good idea … But I need to think,' the Frenchman said.

Silvano moved across to where Fabia sat and gently laid her down, covering her with a blanket he had found in a cupboard. He sat back and watched her sleep, feeling his own eyes become heavy.

Twelve hours later, under the cover of darkness, the three of them moved silently through the back streets of Florence. The Frenchman had cleared it with the local Partisans, who would provide a car on the outskirts of the city, but the three of them would need to make their own way to the rendezvous.

'Good luck.' Silvano sat in the passenger seat an hour later. Pulling the door to, he looked at the Frenchman and raised a hand as the car pulled away. Aurele was already disposing of his German uniform. Silvano turned and glanced to where Fabia lay sleeping; he needed this time to clear his head. He had not thought about what would happen beyond this point. He tried to clear his head, but almost instantly, his eyes closed. Within seconds, he, too, slept.

~ ~ ~ ~

Sofia buried her head in her mother's chest at the sight that greeted them. Three bodies gently swayed in the chill breeze that swept down from the hillside. They swung from hastily built gallows in the village square. It was Cinzia Bria's contorted face that met Isolina's eyes first, making her grip her daughter and stifle a cry. What barbarity was this? Who had committed this savagery, and for what reason? Sofia was unable to prevent herself from looking again, and found herself retching at the sight.

'Why, Mamma … *why*?'

Isolina shook her head. 'I do not know, child.'

'Not a pretty sight.'

It was the voice of Carlo Sergi, who stood leaning against a telegraph pole, smoking. 'It has shocked you, I can tell.' He smiled. 'It has served its purpose.' He stood looking straight into Isolina's face, flanked as usual by two friends.

'And what was the purpose?'

'To stop you peasants helping the Partisans.'

'You did this to Cinzia and the others just to make that point?'

'Seems to have worked with you.'

'What normal human being would not be affected by this sight? Only a madman would look at this and smile.'

'Three young German soldiers were murdered.'

'So, this is an eye for an eye?'

Sofia suddenly became consumed by guilt. No, she would not accept the blame, this was neither Gino's nor her doing. Those soldiers brought it on themselves – except did they deserve to die? The honest answer … *yes*. Were they not going to murder Gino? The boy had done nothing. She knew what would have happened if the Partisans had not turned up: Gino would be dead. But instead it was them. No, she would not allow herself to feel culpable.

Mason had told her to say nothing and she had obeyed that request. Although, right now she would give anything to confess to her mother, to express the responsibility she felt at this moment, not for the murder of the soldiers but for those suspended from the ropes. She needed to explain – explain how they had made Gino feel, how he had relived that moment night after night; she wanted to tell her what Gino was going through because of those men … But it was too late for that now.

'You need to be careful, Isolina, there are rumours about you and an Englishman.' Carlo Sergi stared at her intently.

Isolina said nothing; he was casting his net wide in the hope of catching something.

'Unless it was a lover.'

The young man was trying to get a reaction, but she would not allow her anger to show.

'Is everything all right with you, Isolina?' said Mario Pinto.

'Go away, old man.'

'You do not own the streets yet, Carlo … or your father. At this moment in time, I am allowed to walk where I want, and speak to whoever I wish to.'

'Maybe my father will introduce a curfew …' The boy smiled. 'Just like the one in Florence.'

'How long do you, and your father …' he looked at the other two boys '… intend to lick the arses of your German masters? What will happen when they have gone? What does the future hold for you and your father here?' He turned his gaze to the three lifeless bodies as sleet began to fall. 'You will pay for the crimes you commit … No one in this village will forget what has gone on here, or the people who helped commit them. Italian, German, it does not matter, it is a crime against humanity and you will pay the price.' Mario stared directly into the eyes of young Carlo Sergi.

'Finished, old man? It all depends on how many of *you* are left.' Carlo Sergi watched the sleet fall. 'You are not worth catching a cold for …' He cast his casual glance at Sofia. 'Don't listen to this old man. You'll come running for my help, Sofia, mark my words … Let that over there be a warning to anyone who helps our enemies.' He pulled his coat tightly across his chest and began to walk away.

'I want to go home,' Sofia whispered.

'Not a sight a young girl should see.' Mario placed a hand on her shoulder.

'No.'

'Isolina,' Mario looked into her face, 'be careful … There are many who will sell their soul for some food, do not trust anyone here in the village … It makes me sad to say that, but this is no longer the Italy I grew up in as a boy. I am, in some ways, glad that I am old … notwithstanding the aches and pains in these bones, but I do not feel as though I could live in this new country.'

'I understand, Mario. I understand only too well.'

CHAPTER TWENTY-ONE

Gino sat staring at the girl lying on the settee. Her face was covered in cuts and bruises. One eye was partially closed, the other was bloodshot. There were a number of cuts on her lips, while a bruise as black as coal ran the length of her cheekbone. Her hair looked as if it had been cut with a blunt knife, revealing more cuts where her scalp was exposed. He also noticed what looked like burns down each arm. The tall Partisan leader looked at him.

'What is your name?' he asked.

'Gino.'

'Thank you, Gino, for letting us in.'

The boy gave a worried smile. 'I have seen you before … you are Sofia's mother's friend.'

Silvano nodded. 'Once again, thank you.'

Gino's eyes returned to the injured woman, who lay silent. Silvano studied the boy's face and knelt down. 'She is Isolina's niece from Florence,' he whispered.

'I see.'

'Do you expect them back any time soon?'

Gino shook his head. He watched as Silvano lit another cigarette.

'And you, Gino … how did you get here?'

'I ... I ... am ...'

Just at that moment a car pulled up outside. Gino dived to the floor, while Silvano went to the window, reaching inside his coat. His fingers brushed the gun's handle, but slowly he withdrew his hand on seeing that it was Isolina's car.

Both looked as if they had been crying as they entered the room. Isolina stopped and stared in surprise at Silvano. He looked away, and her eyes followed his gaze.

'Fabia,' Isolina screamed, and rushed across the room.

Sofia stood frozen to the spot. Gino came and stood close to her, uncertain of what to do next. Isolina was on her knees kissing the girl's face, bathing her with a deluge of tears. Fabia woke, startled, her face streaked with pain.

'Fabia,' Isolina whispered, before speaking to her daughter. 'Will you and Gino go and place another blanket on my bed please ... Rest now, Fabia.'

'Now?' Sofia asked.

'Yes ...' It was Gino who answered, realising Isolina needed to speak with the tall man. He took Sofia's arm and led her upstairs.

Isolina spun round to face Silvano. 'Thank you.' Words and tears came simultaneously, and then her eyes returned to the broken girl beside her.

'Do not thank me.' Silvano stood uneasy. 'She has had a torrid time, Isolina, I think the hard work is still to come.'

'I need to talk to her, find out what they did.' Isolina muffled a cry: this, after what they had just witnessed in the village, had begun to overwhelm her. Silvano almost took a step forward, but thought better of it and remained where he stood. He turned his head away to compose himself, a sense of frustration and anger consuming him.

'What is happening, Silvano?'

He said nothing.

'I have just left the village piazza where three bodies, three innocent bodies, hang from a rope.'

'What?' Silvano looked up, the colour draining from his face. 'When did this happen?'

'Yesterday, I think … I cannot be certain.' Silvano saw an image of Mason in his head. This was his doing; he might not have placed the noose around their necks but they were dead because of his actions.

'I am not certain Fabia should remain here.'

'Why not?'

'They could link her to you. Plus, think of your daughter, you don't want to attract danger to where she lives, and the boy, too. Remember, Isolina, Fabia tried to assassinate the head of the Italian SS; she is no ordinary assassin.'

Isolina looked down at Fabia and squeezed her hand. *Assassin*, he had called her. She smiled as she remembering holding this very same hand while walking to the shops all those years ago, Fabia's sweet little face looking up, excited about what they were going to buy. And now she is called an assassin. The world had gone crazy.

'What do you want me to do?'

'Could she go to Sassa's?'

'Don't you think Sassa has enough on her plate with the evacuees? No, that is asking too much of them.'

Silvano walked towards the window and gazed outside. 'Can you think of anywhere else, Isolina, somewhere out of the way?'

Isolina touched Fabia's hair and pushed it off her face, revealing a deep purple bruise on her temple.

'Maybe.'

Silvano walked over and knelt down, placing his face close to hers. She stared back into those dark mysterious eyes.

'The Stolfis.'

'Who?'

'A family, the other side of the village at the base of the hills; it's tucked away and they keep to themselves.'

'Sounds perfect.'

'Hold on, Silvano, they might say no. Don't go getting your hopes up just yet.'

'When can you go and see them? Would you like me to come?'

Isolina shook her head wearily. Right now, she just wanted to lie down and sleep. Mason, Silvano, this damn war, she just wanted it all to disappear. Fabia was all she cared about at this moment. Isolina suddenly felt herself begin to unravel, and it scared her.

'No, I will go alone tomorrow or the day after. Fabia is my first priority, I must see to her first.'

Silvano took out a pack of cigarettes. 'I understand. I am sure another twenty-four hours will not hurt – but no more.'

'Do not put pressure on me, Silvano … not like before.'

He inhaled the smoke, needing time to respond. He understood her words; they came from the past, a distant past, and yet it might as well have been yesterday. He quickly ran the events through his mind.

'I wanted us to be together. That was all. You had told me nothing, except that you would not marry me. What was I to think, Isolina? I wanted you to come to Rome with me. I had found you work, and still you told me nothing; how can you accuse me of pressurising you?' He spoke in whispers.

'I came searching for you.'

'You left me sitting at a restaurant table, Isolina … without any explanation.'

She was about to respond when she saw Sofia standing on the staircase, Gino behind her. How much had she heard? Silvano had seen Sofia, too, and smiled at the pretty young girl; how alike they were, mother and daughter.

'I will go now and come back tomorrow, Isolina.'

She acknowledged him before turning her eyes back to Fabia. Silvano walked to the front door; there was so much more he wanted to say, things she needed to know. He turned and looked at Gino.

'I know you're a young boy,' he said in a firm voice. 'But I need you to be a man and look after these women.'

'How?' Gino stared at him with a beleaguered look on his face.

'Be vigilant, keep your wits about you. I will keep people close by … but you are my man inside, so stay calm.' He glanced at Fabia before opening the door and leaving.

Sofia looked at her mother, a thousand questions going around inside her head. She opened her mouth to speak.

'Not tonight, Sofia,' Isolina stopped her, 'please … not tonight.'

Sofia said nothing. Gino placed a hand on her shoulder.

'Would you like us to help you get Fabia to bed?'

Isolina smiled at the boy. 'Yes, Gino, that would be a great help.'

Gino moved past Sofia and helped Isolina lift Fabia to her feet. The young woman screamed in pain, making Sofia rush forward. Isolina gently placed a hand on Sofia's arm; the smile was brief.

~ ~ ~ ~

Fino liked nothing more than to put his boots on and walk in the lower fields. He and Sassa had many plans for the house and the gardens surrounding it. They had visualised how they wanted it and had even hired a celebrated English gardener to carry out the work. Having worked on many country estates back in England, he had accepted Fino and Sassa's challenge. Except, war had brought a temporary halt to their plans.

Fino breathed in the fresh Tuscan morning air; it reminded him so much of when he was a boy. He saw himself running in the fields, climbing the tall chestnuts trees, and he was certain that, if he closed his eyes, he would hear the sounds of innocent youth: shouting, laughing and living. His face formed a weary grimace – how many are still alive? he wondered. He turned and walked slowly back towards the house, knowing Sassa would be watching him through the drawing room window, smiling as always, so beautiful, like a fine wine maturing. She would come out to greet him under the great oak, but not until he reached the second field. A kiss and a hug, it was their tradition – how foolish love can make you.

Sassa wrapped a woollen shawl around her shoulders. The cold chilled her bones a little more just lately, although the days had become warmer. She watched him; he walked slower now, she thought, as if carrying a huge weight upon his shoulders. The youthful spring in his step had gone, as if he had become older overnight. She turned away for just a moment and composed herself. That glint would still be in his eye, and she smiled to herself, before noticing three men emerging from the treeline.

Fino had seen them too and his walk had slowed as he watched their advance. He had not seen them before; they were certainly not Silvano's men. He looked across to where Sassa now walked. She, like him, had stopped and was staring at their progress. Fino walked on, never allowing the men to leave his sight, and reached where Sassa stood. The men continued walking, halting just short of where the pair stood.

The tallest approached, his clothes filthy and his jacket and trousers torn. He pulled off his knitted hat, sliding it slowly from his head down the side of his face. He was possibly in his early twenties, and the other two, at a guess, late teens. The tall one spoke. 'Buongiorno.'

Sassa and Fino said nothing, but allowed the man to continue uninterrupted.

'We have heard you are sympathetic to the cause.'

'And what cause would that be?' Fino replied.

'To rid Italy of the Fascists and Germans.'

Fino took out his pipe and tapped it on the palm of his hand; black ash drifted to the ground. 'I hope you have not walked all this way to just ask me that?'

The man laughed loudly – a little too loudly, Fino thought. 'No, no, we come to ask a favour.'

'And what favour might that be?'

'A small gift for the Partisan band in the hills …' He scratched his head, moving his hat from one hand to the other nervously. 'Eighty thousand lire to help the cause.'

Fino remained calm, but out the corner of his eye, he saw Sassa take a step forward. He knew she was angry, and had every right to be.

'So, what Partisan band do you belong to, may I ask?' Fino began to fill the pipe.

'We are new, we have come down from the north.'

The other two nodded their heads in agreement.

'New, you say,' Fino said out loud. He studied the men, wondering if they were armed, and caught a glimpse of a gun's handle poking from a waistband. 'Who is leading you?'

Sweat broke out on the man's forehead and he looked to the floor then towards the fields, unable to make eye contact with Fino.

'I tell you what I will do,' Fino began, before stopping to light up his pipe. His calmness seemed to unnerve the men. 'Show me proof that you are really Partisans and I will consider your request,' he finished, blowing out a cloud of smoke.

The men looked at each other. It was the youngest who backed away first. Fino stared at the one with the gun; just a boy he thought, and scared, his mind in turmoil.

'Well?' said Fino.

It was the turn of the tall skinny one to back away now. 'We will be back,' he whispered. He joined the others and they all disappeared into the woods.

'Will they come back?' Sassa asked.

'Maybe not them, but others will. The war has brought the best and worst out of people. So many are desperate, starving, exhausted and scared. So many lost souls, Sassa … so many.'

With that, he linked his arm through his wife's and began a slow walk back to the house. Only once did Fino look back, his heart pounding.

~ ~ ~ ~

Isolina had fed Fabia soup before going to bed. Her young niece kept drifting into a disturbed sleep so Isolina decided not to undress her. She had wrapped her arms around Fabia earlier, and had been shocked by how malnourished her body was. A foul odour came off her clothes; they smelt of damp, sweat and earth, amongst other less pleasant scents. She would attend to this first thing tomorrow, but right now, sleep was what Fabia needed.

She understood Silvano's worries: it would not be safe to keep Fabia here. She needed to drive to the Stolfi farm and hopefully enlist the services of Vincenzo. If anyone would be sympathetic, it would be him. Although, the task of convincing his father would not be easy. The old man did not want his family to become involved in the war and had turned a blind eye to it so far. But, without their help, Fabia would remain in danger.

The night had been a long one, she had drifted into a light sleep, one in which Silvano suddenly appeared. She watched him from a distance as he paced the platform of Florence train station. He kept looking at his watch; he was waiting for her. In her dream, she began running, taking in sharp mouthfuls of air. Exhaustion began to overcome her, but she continued to run – yet the gates got no closer. It seemed that the quicker her legs moved, the further away the station became. She saw him look at his watch again, saw the look of agitation on his face before he finally boarded the train. Breathless, she stopped and fell to her knees. She looked up and watched as the train pulled away. Awake now, she lay in the darkness next to Fabia, her cheeks stained with tears.

Early the next morning, she began to remove Fabia's clothes. The process was painstakingly slow and she had got

Sofia and Gino to heat up pans of hot water. Sofia brought in the metal bath and remained watching as Isolina removed Fabia's thin jumper and blouse. Sofia froze at the sight of Fabia's body, which was covered in tiny round red blotches. The burns went up her arms and across her stomach, a thousand tiny red blisters. Some, it seemed, had turned septic, and Isolina found more on her back. Sofia gasped at the sight. Isolina looked at her niece's back and noticed what appeared to be whip marks amongst the sores. She, too, had to stifle a cry.

'Go, Sofia,' she whispered, 'go.'

'Mamma.' Sofia allowed tears to fall down her cheeks. 'Why, Mamma ... why?'

'I cannot answer you, child ... now please go.'

With that Sofia fled from the room.

'Fabia, what have they done to you?' Isolina whispered.

Fabia lay naked as Isolina washed her body gently with soap and warm water. She felt her niece's body tense with each touch. As much as Isolina tried to be gentle, so much of Fabia's body was covered in wounds, it was impossible not to touch any. Seeing the extent of her cuts and bruises, Isolina become concerned for her mental state. How much had that been affected by this?

She moved the sponge up the inside of her leg. 'NO!' screamed Fabia, sitting bolt upright. Isolina took hold of her and gently eased her back down.

'Shhh, Fabia, it's all right. You're safe, child.'

Sofia's nervous voice came from outside the room. 'Mamma?'

'It's all right, Sofia, go and put some coffee on.'

She waited for her daughter's footsteps to depart.

'They took me, Isolina.' Fabia's voice sounded feeble. 'All of them.'

Isolina placed a hand over her mouth. 'Shhh, it's over.'

'They called me a whore ... but how could I be ... I was pure, untouched, until ...'

'Fabia, rest.'

Fabia could not stop speaking. 'They all watched ...'

'Fabia.'

'They laughed at me, touched me, did unthinkable things ... but I told them nothing.'

'It's over.'

'NO ... NO ... NO.' Fabia began to shake her head violently. 'It will never be over ... never ...'

Isolina gathered her up in her arms and slowly rocked her back and forth, feeling her shiver. 'Let me finish and dress you in clean clothes.'

Ten minutes later, the girl lay back on clean sheets, her head resting on a firm pillow. It was an improvement, as she looked and smelt far better. Sofia brought up coffee but remained in the hallway, peeking in every now and again, uneasy about entering.

'Thank you, Isolina.'

'There is no need to thank me, Fabia.'

'And the tall man.'

'Silvano.'

'Yes ... a gentle man.'

Isolina felt another wave of tears. Yes, she thought, Silvano was always gentle.

'Mamma ... Isolina, how is my mother?' She grabbed Isolina's arm. 'Does she know?'

'Yes ... she knows they got you out, and she is happy.'

Fabia sat forward. 'Never tell her what they did … you must promise me … She must never know.'

Isolina laid her back onto the pillow, kissing her forehead. 'I promise; now sleep, we will talk later.' She looked back at Fabia, before closing the door behind her. Sofia stood waiting at the bottom of the stairs.

'Will Fabia get well soon?'

'Yes … but she needs time.'

'What did they do to her?'

Isolina rested a hand on her daughter's shoulder and smiled. 'Another time, Sofia.'

~ ~ ~ ~

Vincenzo was almost as tall as Silvano. He stood with the sun beating down on his neck as he took a cloth from his pocket to wipe away the sweat.

'Yes, I want to help,' he said, replacing it.

'Your father,' Isolina added.

'Leave my father to me.' His smile was full of uncertainty, though.

Richard Mason blew out a cloud of smoke and flicked the finished cigarette away.

'You are sure about this?' Mason asked.

Silvano looked at Mason. 'Fabia cannot remain at Isolina's, it has already been three days and that is two to many.'

'What if you're wrong and they don't connect her with Isolina?'

'And you're willing to take that chance?' Silvano responded.

Mason did not answer. Instead, he leant back against the tree and removed a leather bound book. Vincenzo was not going to allow this opportunity to help pass. 'Let me take her,' he pleaded.

'Can she be moved soon?' Silvano said, looking at Isolina.

'Yes, she has been eating. I think she is strong enough now, and her injuries are healing well.'

'The fewer people who know about this, the better,' Mason said, looking up from the page.

'I agree,' Silvano added.

'How nice,' Mason's tone was patronising.

Isolina saw the tension between the two. 'When?' she asked. 'Tomorrow?'

'Morning?' asked Silvano.

'Yes.'

'That does not give this young man a lot of time to convince his family,' Mason added.

'They will be fine,' said Vincenzo.

'And if they are not?' Mason placed another cigarette between his lips.

'I said it will be fine.' Vincenzo stared at Mason, having taken an instant dislike to the man.

'Good,' Mason answered. 'Now, who is going to move her, Silvano? As I said, the fewer people who know, the –'

'Do you not trust each other?' Vincenzo interrupted, looking between both men.

'We live in strange times, my friend. No one has enough to eat, they have no money and watch their children starve; it is easy to be tempted.' Silvano looked at the man, wondering if he had explained well enough.

'I hear what you say … but I do not understand – surely the cause is greater and sacrifices must be made.'

'A bloody romantic,' Mason laughed. 'Every bloody war has one. People believe that the rest think as they do, but war also brings opportunity, my naïve friend … Those with low morals can be bought at any price.'

'As I said, I agree. I, you,' Silvano began, 'Enzo, Ambra and Tino will take her.'

'Enzo?' Mason shook his head.

'Put your squabble aside, Mason. Enzo is a good man to have in a dangerous situation.'

Mason held his hand up. 'I will say no more.'

'Good.' Silvano turned to Isolina. 'Have her ready for seven.'

Isolina felt apprehensive.

~ ~ ~ ~

Sassa was walking towards the clinic with one of her maids when two men in torn, dirty uniforms stepped out from behind the stables. The maid stifled a scream and stopped.

'Stay calm, Gina, walk on.'

The maid looked at her, then glanced at the men, clearly reluctant to leave Sassa alone with them.

'Go, Gina, and keep the children inside.'

'Should I tell –'

'No, just go on now, I will be fine.'

The maid finally did as she was asked, picking up pace the closer to the clinic door she got.

'Can I help you?' Sassa turned to the men.

Both men's uniforms were covered in mud. They looked as though they had not eaten in a while, and yet Sassa felt that all was not as it seemed. The younger of the two spoke, his Italian passable but tinged with a German accent.

'We are deserters from the Austrian army. We have not eaten in days and have no money. We are trying to get home.'

'I see.' Sassa pondered. 'Where have you been fighting?'

'Cassino. The line is about to break.'

'What is it you require from me?'

The other man spoke after glancing at his friend, his Italian not as good but adequate.

'I do not understand,' he began. 'Is this not the home of Fino Zotti, the rich industrialist?'

'I am Sassa, his wife.'

'Then why do you ask so many questions? Are you not the same people who help British prisoners and Italian deserters? The ones who feed and clothe those who come for help?'

Sassa remained silent. Then: 'I think you have been misinformed. I look after Italian children, evacuees from the bombing.'

The two men looked at each other before the younger one looked into her eyes. 'Are you telling us that you are not prepared to help?'

'I can give you some bread.'

'Money … surely your husband has money to spare so we can buy some food and clothing.'

'We keep no money here.' She smiled. 'What we have is spent on the children.'

'So, you refuse to help the Allies.'

'You have been fighting the Allies yourself, have you not? It is why you have deserted?'

The older man grabbed his jaw and scratched at the stubble. 'As I said, that line will not hold for long. Soon, the Americans and British will be here and they will get to know all those who refused to help the Allies, and you will be arrested as collaborators.'

With that, both men turned and walked back into the woods. Sassa walked towards the clinic. Inside, a British airman was being patched up to be handed over to the Partisans. Had she been wrong about those two? No, she felt certain.

CHAPTER TWENTY-TWO

It had been a slow and painful journey using the horse and cart Fino had supplied. They moved along narrow pathways, keeping close to the treeline, and across uneven rutted ground that caused Fabia to wince in pain. Isolina held the girl firmly. Fabia, wrapped in a blanket, leant against her cousin. They had been lucky the rain of yesterday had held off.

On reaching the outskirts of the Stolfi holding, they halted. Silvano and Mason went on alone to make certain all was well at the farm. They were met by Vincenzo and his brother Dario, both with rifles slung over their shoulders.

'Is everything well?' Silvano enquired.

The brothers briefly glanced at one another, then Vincenzo nodded. Mason blew out his cheeks as a bird let out a high-pitched cry from somewhere in the trees. Mason returned, accompanied by Dario, to tell Tino to bring the cart up.

Isolina helped Fabia down with the help of Tino. Suzetta rushed down the wooden steps to help too, before Gianni finally emerged pulling his braces over his shoulders.

'Lucia, get the bed ready,' Suzetta instructed, looking up to see her husband's face full of irritation. His shirt was dirtied with dried food, and old sweat stains formed shadows under each armpit. Gianni did not once look in her direction as she helped Fabia inside. Instead, he reserved his ugliest stare for his oldest son Vincenzo.

'You now head this family?' He spread his arms wide.

'No, Papa.' His son walked towards him.

'Then why have you gone against my wishes, boy?'

'Papa, I have not gone against your wishes.'

'Then, what am I witnessing? Am I dreaming that you have just taken that girl inside my house? Am I going to wake soon and find that my son is still obedient to his father?'

He walked down the steps and onto the dark earth, and dug his boot into the soil. He bent down and scooped up a handful of earth and held it out to Vincenzo.

'My land ... My soil ... Four generations.' He continued to stare hard at Vincenzo. 'This will be yours when I am gone, and one day you will have a son to leave this land to. I hope he does not make you feel as I do today.'

'Papa,' it was Fabrizio who stepped forward next. 'Vincenzo is doing what he thinks is best.'

Vincenzo and Dario smiled on seeing the youngest of them try to make peace. Vincenzo knew that his father's pride had been wounded; he also knew that the family could no longer continue to ignore a war that was on their doorstep.

'Why do you continue to bury your head in the sand?'

His father smiled and took a deep breath.

'Mister Stolfi ...' Richard Mason walked forward. 'Allow me to explain ...'

'I will not be lectured by an Englishman. Stay out of my business, or I will shoot you.' He gave Mason a fierce stare. The Englishman held up his hand and walked away, taking out his note book while doing so. He felt that the day would turn out to be a long one. Anyway, the old man was crazy, so he would watch the proceedings from a safe distance.

'Did you not see what they did to that girl?' Vincenzo launched his attack. It was his last chance to convince his father, whom he passionately wanted on his side. 'Your friend, Nico – both his sons have been dragged away and put into a lorry. That was only three days ago, and now Nico lies in bed with his head split in two.'

Gianni remained impassive. He turned his back on his son and walked several steps away. Those standing around remained silent. But Vincenzo was not finished; he took a step forward and began to speak to his father's back.

'You have always stood up against injustice, taught us good from bad. You and Mamma have brought us up well, we are strong and united, a good Italian family, a good home – but now danger has come to threaten us, and it will want to take Fabrizio, Dario and maybe myself away.' He stopped speaking and allowed his lungs to refill, but he was becoming angry with his father. 'Are you getting too old, Papa, is that it? Shall I place a chair and a blanket outside for you?'

In a flash the old man turned and drove a fist into his son's stomach. Vincenzo fell backwards, trying to steady himself, but his father's knuckles connected with his cheek. He sat trying to clear his head; the old man still packed a punch.

'No, Papa …' Dario screamed, and tried to grab hold of him.

Gianni threw him off as you would a small child, swinging another fist, only this time just missing Dario's head. It was the turn of seventeen-year-old Fabrizio next: the boy leapt onto his father's back and wrapped his arms around his neck, holding on for dear life.

Gianni tried to dislodge him, and Vincenzo finally got to his feet just in time to receive his father's size-ten boot between his legs, which brought him back to his knees. Moments later, all four lay panting, spitting blood, each covered in mud, dust and sweat. Silvano, reluctant to become involved in a family argument, stood some distance away. If the worst came to the worst, they would simply put Fabia back on the cart and take her … where?

Enzo spat at the floor, tired of these clowns: they were no better than the gypsies Hitler had exterminated, except they had a permanent home and money, things he did not.

Tino had stood on the cart clapping and shouting encouragement, enjoying the entertainment; it had been a long time since he had witnessed a good brawl. Blowing up bridges and train lines had its excitements, but you could not beat a good old-fashioned fight to get the blood pumping.

Mason's pencil had worked overtime, scribbling here and there to catch a fist flying through the air, a head rolling backward and the anger and determination on the faces of those involved. Now, he held out the sketch at arm's length: he had surpassed himself. He nodded with satisfaction as Ambra came up behind him.

'Very good,' she whispered.

'Thank you. I like to capture all your Italian customs – like family reunions.' He laughed out loud.

'Maybe I can show you another of our customs after dark.'

'No, not tonight … I'm tired.'

Ambra bit her top lip. It had been at least three weeks since he had allowed her under his blanket, and that had had more to do with the wine he had consumed. She felt anger rise inside her, thinking she had been used like a common whore.

'It's that woman ... Isolina. Every time you lay your eyes on her, it would not surprise me to find your penis grow hard.'

'Don't act like a spoilt child, Ambra.'

A second later he felt the blade of her knife resting against his throat. He needed to remain calm; there was nothing more frightening than a jealous woman, except a jealous woman with a knife. He stared into Ambra's eyes; she was serious, and he began to sweat. Twenty metres away, the men had picked themselves up.

'Go fetch two bottles of wine, Dario,' Gianni ordered. 'You, tall man,' he looked towards Silvano, 'come talk. Tell me what this young girl did to deserve being treated this way.'

By the fence, Ambra lowered the knife before kissing Mason, biting his lip and drawing blood as she pulled away. Mason breathed out and looked across to where everyone stood drinking wine. His eyes followed Ambra as she walked away without casting a look back. He laughed out loud. 'This country is fucking mad ... I hope they all get what they deserve,' he whispered under his breath.

~ ~ ~ ~

With Fabia settled at the Stolfi farm, Isolina discovered that Sassa was going to Florence. Perhaps this would be a good opportunity to go and see Fabia's mother, to tell her she was safe and recovering well. In the ten days that had passed, Fabia seemed to have regained some of her sparkle. Although, Isolina did wonder how much of that was simply for *her* benefit.

In lieu of the increased Allied bombing, Sassa wanted to bring another twenty children to her home. She had been deluged with requests from parents asking her to keep their children safe from the danger. She picked up Isolina early the next morning, and now they drove in silence. Her driver, Sandro, found it difficult navigating through the thick fog, which had settled along the valley. As it cleared, they came across convoys of German cavalry, and saw many tanks parked in adjacent fields. Lorry-loads of troops also lined the roadside.

They arrived at a five-star hotel near the centre of Florence, where Sassa had booked a room for the day. The foyer was filled with high-ranking German officers, making Isolina feel uneasy. Sassa had arranged to meet friends for breakfast, wanting to catch up with all that was happening in the city. After breakfast Sandro would drive Isolina to Savina's.

Sassa and Isolina went to their room to freshen up before they met the German vice consul, Wildt. The room was large and pleasantly decorated, except that there were empty spaces where pictures once hung, giving the appearance of a ransacked room. Sassa saw Isolina staring at the walls.

'Some have been stolen by German officers, the rest have been hidden by the hotel outside the city.'

'I see.'

'Let us meet with our German friend.'

Isolina thought about Sassa's strange use of words, our German *friend*?

Strangely, Wildt was a very nice old man – if you could see past the uniform. He spoke good Italian and seemed as weary of the war as everyone else. They discussed the evacuees, children aged between eight and twelve years of age. They would be brought by lorry from Genoa and Turin, where the bombing had increased one day to the next. He reminded Sassa that the Allies were bombing indiscriminately and that her home could soon become a target.

After their meeting, Isolina sat sipping a decent quality coffee. She held each mouthful, savouring the taste just that little bit longer.

'Nice?' She heard Sassa ask.

She must have had her eyes closed for a moment longer than she thought; on reopening them, she realised that the rest of the table was sat staring at her. She smiled back and blushed.

'You enjoy,' said an elderly woman, her hair swept back into a neat bun.

'Sorry,' Isolina whispered.

'Don't be,' another woman added.

'Wildt is a good man, Sassa.' An attractive middle-aged woman placed her cup and saucer down on the marble table. 'He helps with getting innocent Italian families out of prison.'

'How much does he charge, Vanna?'

The attractive woman looked up. 'Nothing, Alberta, there are still people in this world with a conscience.'

'My apologies, I am becoming cynical in my old age.'

Sassa looked across to Isolina and frowned. These people had not moved out of the city during the war, and knew nothing of hardship. None of their lives had changed since before the conflict began: they were well off, pampered, and always ready to gossip. They had their uses, though, she often told Fino, who did not have a good word to say about them. They tell me what's going on in the city, she would remind him; they get to know things the rest of us don't.

288

'Morning.' They were joined by a white-haired man who walked with the aid of a stick, without seeming to rely on it. A tiny set of spectacles balanced precariously on the edge of his nose.

'Morning, Clemente,' they said in unison.

He bowed his head and smiled. His eye caught Isolina's and his stare lingered for several moments.

'You look worried, Clemente,' said a woman in a wheelchair.

Lady Grimmes was the wife of an English diplomat (they called her Lady Grimmes, but no one knew for certain if her husband was a sir).

'You know the village of San Pancrazio?'

'Yes,' said Vanna, 'my husband and I have passed through it several times on our way to the coast.'

'It's been burnt to the ground.'

'What?'

He took a deep breath, looked up to attract the attention of the waiter, and ordered coffee.

'San Godenzo?' His eyes surveyed the table.

'Yes,' some said, while others nodded.

'At least six women have been raped and a young child killed. Everywhere, farms have been burnt, food stolen, cattle and pigs taken.'

'This cannot be.' Lady Grimmes took a handkerchief from her sleeve.

'I do not lie, Lady Grimmes, the Germans are panicking.' With that, his eyes searched for uniforms within hearing distance.

Isolina suddenly felt ice flowing through her veins. She thought of Sofia and looked across to Sassa.

'I will get Sandro to take you at once, then we will have a spot of lunch and return.'

'Thank you.'

Savina had aged dramatically. Isolina held her in a tight embrace, as if afraid she would slip away and be lost.

'Fabia … tell me how she is?'

Isolina wiped away her tears and smiled. 'She is growing stronger by the day.'

'Do not lie to me, Isolina: the truth – *always* the truth.'

'I would never lie to you; she is as I tell you. She is eating and resting, and she is surrounded by good people.'

Savina rested her head on Isolina's shoulder and took a deep breath. 'Thank God,' she whispered. 'Sweet Mary, I love my daughter, Isolina. To lose her would end my life.'

Isolina gently rubbed her aunt's back.

'Tell me …' Savina looked into her niece's eyes. 'Is she whole?'

Isolina had promised Fabia, but the delay in her answer was noticed.

'I see.'

'I'm –'

'No.' Savina held up her hand. 'She is alive and that is more important to me. But we have to expect that it will take longer to heal what we cannot see.'

Isolina nodded her agreement. Savina pulled away. 'Coffee? Those nice men brought me some.'

Isolina smiled; they had remained true to their word.

'The tall one,' Savina spoke without looking. 'Was he, by any chance, the one you painted your face for all those year ago?'

'I never painted my face.'

'You did, and always put on a clean blouse and washed your hair. I knew the signs.'

She placed two empty cups down in front of Isolina.

'You never said.'

'It was none of my business, and you looked happy.'

'Did I?'

'Yes, very.' Savina stared at Isolina. 'What happened?'

Isolina shrugged her shoulders. 'Nothing.'

Savina watched the flames grab the underside of the coffee pot.

'We drifted apart. Father was not well …' She looked at Savina. 'There were lots of reasons.'

'You changed before my very eyes, Isolina.'

'I returned to see you.'

'Yes, but something had happened and I couldn't understand it – if he made you happy, why did you part?'

'Have you a cigarette?'

'It cannot be that bad.' She went to a drawer and handed Isolina the pack and sat down again.

'Father was growing weaker by the day, it was so sad to watch.' Isolina drew on the cigarette. 'The debts were mounting.'

'Fausto.' Savina almost spat out his name. She had met him once and had taken an instant dislike to him. He was, in her words, a *Fascist pig*. 'Was he not helping?'

'Yes … but …' Isolina pictured her late husband staring back at her. 'He offered to clear all the debts.'

'So, he did have a heart … that does surprise me.' She sipped her freshly made coffee.

'It came at a price.'

Savina looked up.

'Me.'

'You?'

'He would clear everything, but only if …' She stopped for a moment to compose herself. 'I married him.'

Savina rose from the table. 'I knew it. I knew marrying that man was nothing to do with you. But *why*, child?'

'He knew father worried about me. So, Fausto played on those fears and made father talk to me, made me promise him that I would marry Fausto; but then father died.'

'Then why did you stay?'

'I never intended to. The wedding was set for February. In January, I came to visit you and I met up with Silvano.'

'Had you not told him about Fausto?'

'No.'

'Why?'

'I feared losing him.'

Savina sighed. 'Did you tell him when you met with him?'

'Yes.'

'And?'

'He was like a firecracker.' Isolina now smiled. 'I had to calm him.'

'How?'

'I told him I would go to Rome with him. I was to meet him at two o'clock on the thirtieth.'

'But you …'

Isolina took hold of her aunt's hands. 'I went home to get what little money I had scraped together, some clothes and other family mementoes to remind me of my family: I was not certain I would ever return. What I did not know –' she stopped for a moment '– is that Fausto had brought the wedding forward, to the very day I arrived home.'

'I see.'

'No, you don't ... I refused to marry him.'

'What did he say?'

'It was more what he did ... He hit me.' Tears spilt down Isolina's cheeks.

Savina gripped her hands and allowed her own to fall. 'Poor child,' she whispered.

'He hit me several times, then showed me the debt. He had found all my money; I had nothing. I was scared and so alone, Savina ... and so I married him. Two days later, Silvano waited for me before boarding the train for Rome, convinced that I had chosen Fausto over him.'

'Could you not get a message to him?'

'How? I had nothing. But I began to plan my escape: I was going to follow Silvano to Rome and marry him ... But then I found out I was pregnant, and that changed everything – how was I to escape with a newborn baby? He would never have allowed me to take the child. Although, he cared very little for Sofia. At home, he would drink and abuse me, but in the village, he was the perfect husband and father. He made certain that all the bruises were hidden from sight.'

'So you remained.'

'I was very ill after having Sofia. It took about five months before I began to feel better.'

'I remember ... The bastard would not let me see you.'

'When Sofia was six, I met Simon Stein, the village doctor. He was new and treating Fausto for some ailment. He needed a nurse and found out I had trained to be one. So, he made a deal with Fausto: he would treat him for nothing if I could work a few hours a week for him.'

'And Fausto agreed?'

'It was a business arrangement, of course he agreed.'

'I see.'

'It was only a matter of time before Simon saw the bruises on me, and it was then he told me.'

'Told you what?' Savina leant forward.

There was a loud knock on the door and both women froze. It was Sassa's driver, Sandro: they needed to be going. Isolina hugged and kissed Savina at the door, and moments later Isolina was gone. Savina closed the door and leant her back on it. 'What were you going to tell me, Isolina?'

~ ~ ~ ~

Sofia looked towards the ceiling, uncertain if the last hour or so had been real. She looked to her left and saw the smooth, naked back of Gino; her fingers had danced across it only moments ago. Sofia looked down at her own naked body, and her hand touched a breast. Closing her eyes, she remembered his hand doing the same, and she recaptured the moment he entered her, the pain, then the joy – and the scared look on his face.

Neither was experienced. She had tried to slow him, running her fingers down the side of his face, but then she, too, had become caught up in the passion. They had kissed at that moment, their bodies joined as one: tongues, legs and arms interlocked. The entire German army could not have parted them at that moment. She smiled and a tear left her eye. Just for a moment, she felt ashamed at what they had done, but then Gino turned to face her and the feeling left her. He laid his head on her breast, kissing her neck and ear while she ran her fingers through his hair.

'Are you …?' He stopped, not certain what to say next.

'I am fine.'

'Are you sure?'

'Yes.'

'Did I … was I …?' Again, he was lost for words.

Sofia remained silent, making Gino a little uneasy. This had been a new experience for both, and they seemed a little subdued, overwhelmed perhaps. From overhead came the sound of plane engines. Gino, naked, leapt from the bed while Sofia merely studied him, totally ignoring the humming noise growing closer. His body was magnificent, firm and beautiful, like a Greek god. She smiled as he turned to face her.

'I think that they are …' He stared at her. 'Why are you smiling?'

Sofia shrugged her shoulders, the smile still on her lips. He returned to the bed. Sofia could see he was aroused again. She rolled away and stood looking down at him.

'My mother will be on her way back, and you never know where those bombs will drop. Besides, I don't want to be found naked with you.'

'Why?'

'Why? Because I am too young and my mother will cut off your …' She looked down his body.

'Ouch.' He smiled.

'Now come on, Gino.'

~ ~ ~ ~

Isolina stopped in the village on her way home. She felt happier about Fabia, who had begun to look better and was eating at last. On the outside, she looked almost back to normal, but there were times she caught her staring into the distance. What was she thinking? Could she be reliving those months in that prison? If so, what experiences did she recall?

She had only just stepped from her car when a German lorry carrying troops stopped, its brakes releasing a high-pitched squeal. Paratroopers leapt in twos and threes from the back, their boots pounding the concrete ground. A staff car with two officers in it pulled up behind. The troops kicked down Eva Pinto's door and forced their way inside, where they were met by a loud anguished scream. Isolina watched the incident unravel from across the street, unable to understand fully what was happening, until Mario came to join her.

'What has the poor woman done?' Isolina asked.

'Been hiding her son.'

'Angelo … he's back?'

'Been back several weeks or more, so they say.'

'Who gave him away?'

Mario frowned, and stared beyond Isolina. Several metres away, Rosalba Calvi and Father Mariano stood watching.

'Rosalba?' Isolina whispered. 'But why would she do such a thing?'

'Who knows; this war is driving us all insane.'

'That is not insanity, Mario, it is sheer hate.'

'There's a difference?'

Two paratroopers dragged Eva Pinto from her house. Behind her followed a pale-looking Angelo. Isolina hardly recognised him, he had lost so much weight. He had a vague expression on his face, as if unable to grasp the seriousness of his position. Angelo stumbled forward, and his hysterical mother tried to reach out to him, but was restrained by the two burly paratroopers.

A second lorry pulled up and two soldiers jumped down to lower the tailgate. Inside, a dozen or so people sat facing each other, silent, with stony faces. Isolina recognised one of the young boys. She recalled his mother pleading with Simon at Sassa's once. They made eye contact. The boy stared back with an ominous look before suddenly leaping from the lorry and barging one of the German guards to the floor. He began to run. Isolina saw a soldier going down on one knee and taking aim. She looked towards the boy, wanting to scream for him to run faster. Then came the sound of a single shot, which echoed through the street.

The boy stopped instantly and remained upright for several seconds. Isolina and those around her held their breath. A red stain began to appear on the boy's white shirt. It started to grow, like a rosebud opening to the sun. He then fell forward in silence. A cheer came from the German soldiers. Mario lowered his head.

Isolina knew that there was nothing she could do for the boy. She walked across to where Rosalba stood with the priest.

'Are you happy now, Rosalba?' she asked.

'I am not responsible for that.'

'For the boy, you mean?'

'Yes.'

'Eva?'

Rosalba said nothing.

'And you, priest, you call yourself a man of God but you don't even go to say the last rites. Are you afraid, Father

Mariano? Afraid of what your Fascist friends will think if you did? Are we not all part of your flock? Is he not one of God's children? Why not give his soul some peace?'

The priest looked down at his shoes and coughed nervously, but did not utter a word in his defence.

'You are a coward, Father.'

'Do not call him that,' Rosalba answered for him.

At that moment, Eva was bundled into the lorry and driven away. Her son was placed in the other lorry, in the space vacated by the dead boy.

'I thought she was your friend. Not long ago we all sat together drinking coffee. *Why*?'

The woman gave her a stern look. 'Maybe, Isolina, you should look where your loyalties lie ... Eva's fate could one day be yours.'

'Are you threatening me?' Isolina smiled. 'And you, priest, you still have nothing to say? You just stand there, Vito Sergi's puppet?' She shook her head as the lorry departed, followed by the staff car. She turned her back on the pair and felt tears prick her eyes. She would not give them the satisfaction of seeing her cry as she walked the short distance back to Mario.

~ ~ ~ ~

'Cassino has fallen,' Sassa said, greeting Isolina and Sofia.

'The so-called Adolf Hitler Line is strong, so we must not get carried away,' Fino added.

'Where are you going?' Isolina asked.

'To greet our new arrivals. Our evacuees are on their way. We are driving out to meet them outside Arrigo's farm.'

The four got into Fino's old car. The day was grey but, behind the clouds, the sun was trying to melt away a low mist. Fino drove slowly through their grounds, coming to the first of two gates. A small group of people sat together by the roadside, their faces unfamiliar to both Sassa and Fino. Italy was now full of nameless faces, refugees of war: Italians, Poles and many more nationalities were scattered all about the countryside. They looked half-starved and dirty, and a baby lay lifeless in its mother's arms. Further along, two Italian soldiers sat smoking, their uniforms no more than rags stained with sweat and dirt.

They were greeted by a similar sight at the second gate. A boy no older than ten, sat perched on a battered old suitcase. A woman with a child either side of her held out a hand. Fino sped up as Sassa wept next to him, ashamed of what Italy had become. Isolina had also seen Italy coming apart at the seams, its people traumatised, without homes, food or hope.

They passed two columns of German military heading towards the Hitler Line. As they approached the meeting place, they saw the planes appear above the horizon. Sassa gripped Fino's arm.

'What are you going to do, Fino?'

Fino shook his head. Three German trucks passed them at speed. Five hundred metres ahead, Fino spotted the lorry containing the evacuees, parked by the side of the road. No one seemed to be in the cab. Suddenly, all around them, the ground shook with explosions as the planes swept low, dropping their loads on the targets below. The first few fell a good distance from Fino's car, but one exploded less than a hundred metres away. One of the RAF planes broke away from the rest and came in low, machine-gunning the German lorries that had tried to make a break for it.

'Fino, we must get out … for the love of God.'

Isolina had gripped Sofia, whose face had drained of colour. She opened the door before Fino had brought the car to a halt. All four scrambled out and now stood in the open. All around, the ground trembled, pieces of earth were hurled skyward, and a lorry exploded sixty metres away. Men covered in flames jumped from it. Machine-gun fire now came from the troops on the ground.

'Off the road,' Fino shouted.

All four lay face down in a ditch, but Sassa was unable to take her eyes off the lorry containing the evacuees, searching to see if anyone was in the driver's seat. The back doors seemed to be locked. Surely the children were not still inside? She suddenly felt nauseous and panic got the better of her. She climbed from the ditch.

'What are you doing?' Fino shouted, and took hold of her.

'The children, Fino … they could still be in there.'

'There is nothing you can do, Sassa … stay down …'

Fino clung to her arm, pulling her back into the ditch with Isolina's help. Sofia kept her eyes closed and her head buried in the dirt. An explosion almost hit Fino's car as Sassa fought to free herself. The air filled with smoke and the smell of burning petrol.

Finally, the noise level began to decrease: it seemed that the planes had exhausted their stock of ammunition. One final eruption made them bury their heads again, before silence finally came.

Slowly, they got to their feet, brushing dirt from their clothes.

'NO!' Sassa screamed.

She stumbled forward and began running, catching Fino by surprise, but then he, too, saw it. The lorry with the evacuees had been hit. It was now a ball of fire. From inside came horrifying cries, a sound that would live with those who heard it for their entire life.

'No, Sassa,' he shouted. 'Stop, Sassa … please.'

The three of them went in pursuit, catching her before she got too close to the inferno. Fino held her back. Yet, even at this distance they could feel the fierce heat. The cries had ceased; no one inside could have survived.

'Come, Sassa, there is nothing you or anyone can do.'

'I must look.'

'Sassa, there is nothing you can do.' Isolina took hold of her arm.

Sassa turned to face her. 'I must look … I cannot abandon them like the cowardly driver did.' Sassa's face was a mixture of tears and dirt. Sofia came forward and silently placed her arms around her. Isolina and Fino joined in the embrace. Beyond them, the lorry sent up a cloud of black smoke high into the Tuscan sky.

A German troop-carrier arrived at that moment. An officer jumped out and worked his way around to the lorry's side. He appeared several moments later, shaking his head, and then looked across to where Sassa and the others stood huddled together.

'Go,' he shouted. 'Nothing can be done here.'

CHAPTER TWENTY-THREE

It was a warm, sticky night. A thousand stars sat gleaming against an inky black background. Gino closed his eyes; everything he imagined this would feel like had abandoned him. Now, he was gripped by a deeper fear. It had been easy to make up his mind to become a part of this war, to join those that struggled in the hills. The hardest part had been telling Sofia.

High above him, a squadron of planes flew in formation, heading north-west towards the German lines. Maybe another bombing mission on Milan? he wondered. In the stillness, he thought of Sofia. She had cried into his shirt for almost an hour as he had held her. But, however guilty he felt, he knew he was doing the right thing. He knew he would only feel guiltier later, if not.

Now, he found himself on his first mission, and all those doubts had come flooding back. Sofia was a fixture in his mind: her beautiful face, her naked body – right now he desperately missed her. He never thought he could miss someone as much as he missed Sofia. He took a deep breath, hoping to catch a trace of her scent, and a hand lightly touched his shoulder.

Silvano stared down at him, making him sit up.

'Shhh.' Silvano placed a finger over his lips. 'Come, let's get closer to the bridge.'

The German guard stubbed out his cigarette, blowing out a cloud of smoke as he did. He was bored.

'Otto ... what is the time?'

Otto sat playing solitaire, a cigarette balanced on his bottom lip and his rifle resting against the wall. His helmet sat on the floor next to it.

'Almost eleven ... It's the last time I'm looking, Schmidt. We won't be relieved until midnight, so stop asking every ten minutes.'

Otto turned away. *Fuck you*, he thought as he looked towards the surrounding hills, which formed a jagged silhouette against the night sky. He liked Tuscany, it was pleasing to the eye. Maybe, when this crazy war was over, he would bring his family here on holiday. He reached inside his coat and removed a badly creased photograph. Slinging his rifle over his shoulder, he held it between both thumbs, attempting to smooth out the creases, but it was beyond repair.

A smile came to his lips. Hedy, his wife, sat surrounded by three young children. Little Elise, not yet three, was just a four-week-old baby in her mother's arms when this was taken. He looked up and breathed in deeply, wiping away moisture from his eyes. He then gazed across to where Otto continued his game. On one side of Hedy stood his son, Claus. Even at seven, he held himself with confidence, his blonde hair swept to one side – how handsome he looked. Agna, his sister, like her mother, was so beautiful. He traced their faces with his finger, closed his eyes and imagined he was with them.

He replaced the photograph inside his pocket. How long had it been since he had seen them? He had lost count

– two, three years? Maybe less, maybe more. Either way, this senseless war had robbed him of some of the best years with his family. He cursed Hitler under his breath. He was a madman. How foolish they had all been to follow him. How bloody stupid could a whole nation become?

'Would you like some coffee, Schmidt?' asked Otto.

'Yes,' he answered wearily, knowing how awful it was going to taste. 'Have we no schnapps left?'

Otto just stared at him. Like his friend, he, too, was bored, tired, hungry and homesick. He stacked the cards to one side and began to heat the coffee, stretching his arms wide to yawn. He wondered if he should go down and ask Kurt if he wanted one – he was pacing the other end of the bridge by himself, since Sepp had gone sick. Why the hell were they bothering to guard this bridge? It played no strategic part in the defence of Italy. He shook his head. Oh well, they knew best: the generals who were right now either sleeping in comfortable beds or drinking good coffee. Bastards.

He poured out two cups and immediately felt guilty about Kurt. Picking up both mugs in one hand, he grabbed his rifle with the other. He was about to shout to Schmidt when he saw movement from the trees behind him. The tin mugs fell to the floor with a crash. In seconds, his rifle was hoisted to his shoulder and he shot blindly into the thicket. Meanwhile, Otto had dived to the floor and crawled across to a post for some protection. Schmidt got off two more shots before he heard footsteps come from behind. He turned to see Kurt running towards him.

Another shot, and Kurt fell backwards. Schmidt was unable to see how bad his injury was as the man lay in the darkness, groaning. He looked towards where their three bikes were parked. They were too far away to get to without being shot. Schmidt ran his tongue the length of his top lip. Kurt groaned again somewhere in the darkness.

'Shut up, Kurt … just shut up.' Schmidt felt bad the moment he spoke, but he was scared and confused, unable to think straight.

'Otto,' he whispered, 'how many?'

'How the fuck should I know.'

Schmidt looked down at the water below; the fall would properly kill him, so what did he have to lose? Unless he just gave himself up … but that was not the German way. Anyhow, there might only be two or three of them. Kurt groaned again, and the light from the large moon made the blood coming from his wound glisten as it seeped across the surface of the bridge.

A shot exploded above Schmidt's head and another to his right, and then two more came, close. Otto was too far back, Kurt almost dead … again he looked to the bikes. It was then that sheer panic took over, and he found himself running towards them.

Richard Mason took aim and fired, taking the right side of the German's head off. Mason stood calm, pleased with his aim, and at night, too – probably his best shot yet. He walked forward and stood over the body. Blood oozed from the wound his bullet had inflicted; a second man lay further away. He walked towards him and poked him with his boot.

It was at that moment he heard the noise. Ambra had leapt onto another German soldier as he was taking aim. They had rolled across the bridge, and the German let go of his rifle. The soldier looked up, surprised to see that his attacker was a woman holding a knife. For a moment, it

305

filled him with hope. He should be able to overpower her and make a break for it towards the edge – it was his only chance. He rolled on top of her and looked into her eyes. The woman smiled, and Schmidt almost returned it with his own. He looked up to see several shadowy figures coming from the darkness. Then he looked to his left and saw that he was less than a metre away from the edge, and safety. It was then he felt the blade enter his abdomen.

Schmidt drew in a deep breath and looked down. She held the handle tightly, feeling his body begin to shake. He looked back into her eyes and smiled, but it was not Ambra's face he saw, it was Hedy's. He felt the strength slowly flow from him. He suddenly needed to know how old little Elise was – he had forgotten … How could a father forget something like that?

'Take care of our children,' he said out loud. 'I love you.'

Ambra gave him a strange look before rolling him to one side.

'Did he speak?' Mason said as he joined Ambra.

Ambra shrugged her shoulders. She observed Mason for a few seconds before speaking. '*Thanks for saving my life, Ambra – how are you?*' There was no smile to accompany her sarcastic words.

'I'm grateful, Ambra … but I wondered if it crossed your mind to let him shoot at me first?'

Now the smile came to her lips. 'That would be telling.'

Silvano dispersed his men to unpack the explosives they had brought. He looked at his watch and saw that they were behind schedule.

'Gino, take the reels of cable down to the far end.'

Gino picked up the one nearest to him and began to run,

stopping only when he came to one of the dead Germans. The man's coat was undone, and he lay with open eyes looking out towards the river. Gino had never been this close to a dead person before and froze, hypnotised. He suddenly felt ashamed, as if staring at the soldier was akin to humiliating him. He began to walk away, but then noticed a photograph sticking out of his pocket. He put down the reel of cable.

His hand reach across the body and took hold of it. He looked around to see if anyone was watching: no, everyone seemed busy. He brought it close to his face and stared at it. A woman holding a young child stared back at him. Either side of her stood two older children, a boy and a girl. Was this the man's family? Gino looked down at the dead German and crossed himself; he would like to have said something, but an angry voice from further down the bridge shouted to him that they needed the cable, *now.*

He stood and realised he had tears running down his cheeks. Wiping them away, he began to walk. He handed over the cable and walked back. Gino stopped halfway down, leant over the side and vomited into the river. He felt a hand rest on his back and turned to see Silvano looking down at him.

'War is ugly, Gino. I'm glad it makes you sick, it means you still have feelings, that you're still human.' Silvano smiled and looked towards the hills. 'War makes animals of men.' He stared into Gino's face. 'Go and get some water, wash your mouth out and continue with your work.'

Gino set off. How he wished he was lying safe in Sofia's arms tonight.

~ ~ ~ ~

Fino stared across the room at a sleeping Sassa and rubbed his eyes. Either old age or the light had made them moist. Isolina noticed, but said nothing.

'How has she been, Fino?' Isolina whispered.

'Like now: quiet. She just sits and reads all those letters, over and over again.'

'What letters?'

Fino almost laughed. 'The letters that were sent on behalf of those that perished in the lorry. The letters begging Sassa to take in their children so they would be safe.'

Isolina could not think of anything to say. Sassa blamed herself for what happened. But she knew the risk they were taking. It could have happened anywhere along the journey and it was just pure bad luck that it happened so close to safety. No one was to blame.

Isolina's mind switched to her own daughter, whose relationship with Gino had grown closer. Watching them at times, she wondered just *how* close, although she was certain that Sofia was a sensible girl. Gino's decision to go and fight with the Partisans had left Sofia distraught, and all her attempts to talk to her daughter had sent her deeper into her shell. Before, they would talk about almost anything; there had been no secrets. Now, everything seemed so guarded between mother and daughter.

'Yes, Maria.'

Isolina snapped from her thoughts as she heard Fino's voice.

'A German chaplain would like to see you. I have taken him into the study.'

'Thank you, Maria. Please go and tell him we will be

there in five minutes.' He smiled at the girl. 'Come with me, Isolina. I am in need of support myself.'

He stood tall, his uniform covered in dirt and his collar stained with sweat. He clicked his heels as every good German did, bowed, and took the hand of Isolina, kissing it gently. She looked towards Fino, who just shrugged his shoulders; nothing surprised him anymore.

'Your wife is not going to join us? Or maybe this is –'

'No,' Fino put up his hand. 'This is Isolina, our nurse. My wife is … busy at the moment.'

'I see.' The chaplain walked across the room and looked out of the window.

He remained there, silent. Isolina and Fino looked at each other again.

'Sorry.' He turned around and started to speak. 'Tomorrow, you will have German troops stationed here.'

'So we have been told … it won't be the first time,' Fino replied.

'They will be the Second Division of German paratroopers, men who were at Anzio. I'm afraid they do not care much for Italians, soldier or civilian.'

'Why?' asked Isolina.

'Why? It's simple. One day, they sat eating and drinking with Italians. The next day, those same Italians attacked them. They had many casualties. From that day, the Second Division has been almost uncontrollable. Their captain has little authority, and they have no respect for anything or anyone Italian.'

Fino walked towards the table where a bottle of wine sat. He poured out three glasses, handing one to the chaplain and one to Isolina. The German swallowed almost all of his in one go. Fino waited, then refilled the man's glass without speaking.

'So, what are you telling me?'

'I am warning you, it is all I can do. These men are almost out of control. This war is lost, and they are on their way back home, determined to wreak as much havoc as possible on their way.' The chaplain finished his wine in one again. 'I suggest you remove everything you value, and keep your women close.' He looked at Isolina. 'Make certain those children are with someone at all times.'

'They are just young children.'

'Do you really think that will bother these men? They have no soul. It is as if they have made a pact with the devil himself … These are not men, these are the living dead.'

'Why are you with them?'

'To try and save as many people as possible, the ones who cross their path … people like you.'

After the chaplain left, Fino and Isolina hurried down to the clinic, where they were greeted by Anna. Her hair had now grown to shoulder length.

'I have just finished that last book you lent me,' Anna said as she greeted Isolina.

'I have not come for that, Anna. We are moving you all into the main house.'

'We want to do it by bedtime, Anna,' Fino added. 'Could you and a couple of the older ones help?'

'You are worrying me.' Anna's smile had gone; she looked up at Isolina. 'What is it?'

'A company of German paratroopers are coming first thing in the morning. Anna, we feel it is best you come inside the house. If there is an air raid, we can all go down to the cellar.'

Anna nodded her agreement, but left with a puzzled look on her face. Fino turned to go and came face to face with Sassa.

'What on earth is going on, Fino?'

'We're moving the children into the house.'

'Whatever for?'

'The Germans are coming.'

'And they will sleep in the stables like before.'

Fino looked at Isolina.

'What is it, Fino?' Sassa's face was stern.

He had always found it hard to lie to her. She needed to know. 'We must take the cow up into the meadow – we must have milk for the young ones.' Sassa's instant reaction was to take control. 'Valuables to be buried in the flowerbeds. Hide everything else of value under the floorboards. We must lock every door. Fino, there is no time to lose.'

The three hurried in separate directions.

~ ~ ~ ~

Isolina reached home before dark. It seemed that the whole valley was filled with German troops, including outside her own front door. The Germans had placed two gun batteries there, and more in the surrounding fields, thus making her house a prime target for the RAF. Three soldiers watched her walk towards the house. She could feel their eyes upon her. Inside, she took a deep breath and rested her head against the wall. The shadows lengthened as the sun began to set.

'Sofia,' she shouted up the stairs. 'Sofia?'

She heard the sound of feet, but no answer came. Isolina warily began to climb the staircase. On reaching the landing, she went to Sofia's room.

'Sofia,' she whispered.

Sofia lay face down on the bed. Isolina moved slowly around it.

'What's wrong, Sofia?'

Sofia remained silent.

'Is it Gino?'

With that Sofia flung her arms around Isolina's neck, sobbing.

'Sofia, you're scaring me ... what is wrong?'

'He's gone.'

'Who?'

'Gino.'

'Where?'

'With *them*.'

'You knew this already, Sofia.'

'But he is too young, Mamma. He is just a boy and he will be killed, I know he will – I have seen it.'

'Seen it?'

'In my dreams ... like I saw Papa ... when he came back.'

Isolina went cold. 'Papa coming back was a nightmare, Sofia, just a nightmare. Why are you acting like this? Gino will be well looked after. He is probably safer up there than he is down here.'

Sofia pulled away and looked into her mother's face. 'But I love him, Mamma.'

Isolina went cold.

~ ~ ~ ~

Sassa heard the vehicles arrive and looked at the clock; it was just before midnight. Fino snored next to her and she smiled at the familiar sound. He had worked relentlessly this afternoon, and now, it seemed, it had caught up with him. Suddenly, she felt a twinge of guilt: since the death of those evacuees, she had allowed her thoughts be consumed by them; not once had she considered how Fino felt. The tragedy must surely have touched him as well, and yet, she had not taken the time to speak to him. She closed her eyes and allowed the feeling of shame consume her.

Suddenly, she heard loud shouts in German. The front door was rattled several times, but the bolts held firm, for now. She lay looking at the ceiling, restless, feeling every muscle in her body tighten at the smallest noise. Finally, she got out of bed. A glance at Fino and another loud snore told her all she needed to know. She wandered down the hallway. She could still hear voices coming from outside and, intermittently, the sound of an engine starting up. She hoped it would not disturb the children.

Holding a candle, Sassa opened the first of two doors and peered inside. All she heard was the sound of soft breathing. She slowly shut the door behind her and moved to the next. There, she was greeted by a voice.

'Sassa.' It was Anna.

'Go to sleep, Anna,' Sassa whispered. 'Don't wake the others.'

'I can't sleep,' said Anna. 'I keep hearing them. I'm afraid they will come in.'

'They will not, now please go back to sleep.' She began to back out of the room. 'Buona notte, Anna.'

'Buona notte,' Anna whispered back.

Sassa began to make her way back to Fino, but the sound of breaking glass brought her to a halt. Her heart quickened.

She looked towards her bedroom door and wondered whether to wake Fino. No, she decided, and took a step towards the stairs instead. She stared down into the darkness; candlelight only lit up the top steps, and the shadows it created gave the place an eerie feel.

She descended slowly. She heard nothing at first, but then a noise came from the kitchen. The candle flame flickered – it seemed a breeze was coming from somewhere. She moved towards the open kitchen door. She noticed the glass on the floor first, before her eyes caught sight of the broken window above. The back door was open. Without thinking she walked across to close it. It was then she saw them: two tall German soldiers were eating bread and olives, and drinking from a bottle of wine. They stopped and stared at her.

'Good,' one said in Italian, holding up the bottle.

'I know … it's mine,' Sassa replied.

His mate just stood there, grinning, as if Sassa were not there. They passed the bottle between them, with the occasional glance in Sassa's direction. She suddenly felt foolish standing in her own kitchen. The German chaplain suddenly filled the doorway. Both men acknowledged him but continued as before.

'Hello,' he said to Sassa. 'I will see what I can do.'

'If you would not mind.'

He looked at the broken window. 'And repair that.'

'Please do not worry about that. Just get these two out, the children are asleep upstairs and I cannot leave these two wandering around the house.'

'I understand.'

The chaplain turned to the two soldiers and began to speak in German. It was twenty minutes before both men left, each carrying a bottle of wine, as well as pocketfuls of Sassa's food.

'I'm sorry,' The chaplain said, shutting the door behind them.

'I'm grateful to you, and it is not your fault.' Sassa knelt and began to pick up the glass.

'Please allow me.' The chaplain's face was close to hers. 'We cannot get this window fixed tonight, so let me sit here until morning. Tomorrow, either you will find someone, or I will ask so we can fix it.'

The chaplain acted nervous and spoke too fast; but Sassa had to trust someone.

'You cannot do that.'

'Please, I am not tired, and I would very much like to. I do not want you to think that all Germans are like those two.'

Sassa gave a weary smile. 'I judge each on merit ... But thank you, I will sleep easier now.'

'Good,' he smiled. 'Sleep well.'

Sassa made her way back to her room in need of sleep, although, whether that would happen was another matter.

~ ~ ~ ~

Isolina sipped her coffee, looking at Sofia. She had expected a visit last night, but the other side of her bed had remained empty. Sofia chewed on a piece of bread, staring at the whitewashed wall opposite. Outside was a hive of activity, soldiers running here and there. Isolina took out a cigarette.

'Sofia,' she said in a faint voice, 'how do you know that you are in love?'

Sofia stopped chewing and reached for a glass of water.

'I just do.'

'Have you told Gino?'

'He loves me.'

The reply was fervent. It left Isolina in no doubt.

'How do you know it is love?'

'Because he does not hit me.'

The answer tore at Isolina's heart. She felt her body go limp and tried to gather her thoughts.

Sofia stared at her, then stood and walked around the table, her eyes never leaving her mother's face. She could see the pain she had inflicted. She placed her arms around her mother's shoulders and began to whisper. 'Sorry … sorry … sorry. I did not mean it. I feel so angry … all the time. I am angry with the world, with Gino, with you, with myself … I hate everything.'

Isolina squeezed her tight; it felt good to hold her child again.

'That's fine …' She kissed her daughter's cheeks. 'Sofia?'

'Yes.'

'You and Gino … you have not … nothing has happened?'

Sofia closed her eyes and bit her bottom lip before replying. 'No, Mamma … No.'

'Good.' Isolina kissed her again, relieved by her child's answer.

CHAPTER TWENTY-FOUR

Maria fled from the laundry room in tears. Inside, four naked German soldiers stood washing. They laughed and shouted in German after the girl; it was the third time this had happened in as many days. They had raided the storeroom, taken a leg of lamb, all the eggs and the last of the bread and milk. Outside, those who were awake, sat around drinking wine, smoking and eating whatever food they could find.

The chaplain had informed Fino that they had been given instructions to move out today. They were needed east of Florence where attacks by Partisans had increased. They were due to begin what they called a mopping-up campaign, which Fino interpreted as going from village to village persecuting innocent people. He counted down the minutes until they were gone.

Sassa had lost her sunglasses, a silver salver and two bottles of brandy. And they were just the things she had noticed – God knows what else had been stolen. She had walked into the lounge only yesterday to find three of them with their feet on the coffee table, smoking Fino's good cigarettes. This morning, she had sent Anna to get milk for the little ones, making certain she slipped out from behind the stables unnoticed.

The cow remained tied to the tree with a long rope, allowing the animal to move around quite freely and eat to her heart's content. Although early, the sky was a deep blue, and Anna could tell that today was going to be a warm one. On reaching the treeline, she had looked back to make certain no one had followed her. With every stride, she felt more confident. From the trees, she saw the cow grazing happily in the meadow. Anna listened, her eyes on the surrounding trees. Nothing moved. With the bucket in her hand, she moved out into the open.

She sat for a minute, cross-legged, before lying back in the long grass. She closed her eyes and plucked a blade of grass, placing it between her teeth. She felt the warmth of the sun caress her skin; the war and all its ugliness seemed to evaporate in this small meadow. She had decided to become a nurse, to be like Isolina, to help people. If she kept on learning, one day she could become a doctor, a real doctor. She smiled, her eyes closed against the warm sunshine. Eventually, she got to her knees and placed the bucket under the cow.

In that instance, a hand covered her mouth. It smelt of soil and tobacco, and it forced her onto her back. Now she was being dragged backwards through the long grass. A hand took hold of her right ankle, another her left, and she felt her legs being pulled apart. Up until now, she had had no time to panic, but now it came in one gigantic surge and she began to kick out in fear, flinging her arms and legs left and right. More hands joined in, and soon she was unable to move at all. A knife sliced through the fabric of her dress. She watched in horror as it was ripped apart. They used the same knife to cut off her pants before spreading her legs wide. The pain when it came was almost unbearable.

~ ~ ~ ~

Luca's job was to get as close as he could to Sassa's place and keep watch on the German paratroopers' movements. If they began to move out, he was to send Filipo or Gino to Mason. They needed to know what direction the Germans were heading. The paratroopers were too strong for the Partisans at this moment in time, although the balance of power was beginning to shift their way.

'Down,' Luca whispered, pulling the boy with him.

'What?' said Filipo, spitting out dirt.

'Something moved.'

'Where?'

'Thirty, forty metres to our left.'

'Germans?'

'I'm not sure … Stay here.'

Luca crawled forward through the long grass, keeping his body close to the ground. He had left his rifle with Filipo – not a wise thing to have done, given the circumstances. He wished he had brought Gino with him as the boy was far more capable. But, for some reason, he had failed to turn up this morning. He moved towards a small clump of bushes and saw it. A cow. It was tethered to a tree and stood munching grass. Luca looked around to see if anything moved, before making his way back to Filipo.

'Well?' Filipo asked Luca on his return.

'A cow … it's a damn cow.'

'A cow?'

'Yes.'

'What is a cow doing up here?'

319

'How the hell should I know, I'm not a fucking farmer, Filipo.'

Luca reclaimed his rifle and set off slowly. Filipo followed. They came to a halt twenty-five metres from the animal. Again, Luca looked towards the surrounding trees. He saw no movement and yet he felt an uneasiness spread through his body. He moved another three metres before stopping, which was when he saw the bucket on its side.

'What's happening?' Filipo asked.

'Shut up, let me think.' Luca's answer was sharp.

Other than the cow, nothing moved. He lifted his head and surveyed the ground in front of him before lowering himself down quickly.

'You saw something?' Filipo asked. 'Germans?'

'Filipo, shut up … I'm not sure what I saw, but something is there in the grass and I do not think it's a German.'

'Well, what could it be?'

'I don't fucking know.' Luca was becoming annoyed. 'Look, Filipo, can you shoot this?' He pointed at the rifle.

'Yes, of course.'

'Good. I'm going to see what it is. You see anyone in a uniform, shoot and ask questions later.'

Luca moved quickly across the ground. If there had been a German marksman in the trees, he would surely have been dead by now.

Where the grass grew taller, he could see something, but could not make out what it was. It had not moved in all this time. There was a touch of colour: red … and black, like someone's hair. He thought. The bucket, the cow? It was then he knew. He moved forward with haste before coming to an abrupt standstill. Luca stared down, transfixed.

The girl lay at his feet on her back, naked. Luca remained riveted to the spot. He heard footsteps coming up from behind but ignored them. Filipo stood by his side and turned as white as a sheet.

'Is she …?'

'I don't … I'm not …' Luca wanted to be sick.

Just then the girl groaned. Without thinking, Luca took off his jacket and covered her. Filipo had fallen to his knees and vomited.

'Filipo, go to Silvano, tell him what we have found.'

Filipo did not move.

'Did you hear me?' Luca asked, angry. Then, as he turned his head, he realised they were surrounded by Fascist soldiers.

'Stand up,' said one. 'Move away.'

Luca stood, leaving his rifle lying on the ground.

'You bastards,' said one man looking down.

'That was not us!' Luca began to protest.

A rifle thudded into his face, knocking him to the ground. He tried to stand, only for a boot to thunder into his kidneys.

'It was not him,' Filipo shouted.

'Then it must have been you.'

'No … it was neither of us.'

'I see no one else … just two enemies of the State.'

Luca finally got to his feet, spitting out a mouthful of blood.

'She will tell you … she is alive. You need to take her to the farm below, let her tell you it was not us.'

The Fascist leader looked to one of his men. 'Check.'

The man moved to where Anna lay and studied her bruised and battered face. Slowly, Anna opened her eyes and stared back at him. The man gazed back at his leader, who dipped his head. The man then placed his large hand over her mouth and nose. He squeezed until life left the girl's body.

'No, Pino … She will not tell anyone anything. They have done a good job on her.'

'No!' Luca screamed. 'You bastards … you Fascist bastards …'

'Tie them up and take them to Vito Sergi.'

'What about the child?'

'Two of you take her down to the farm of the Swede.' He smiled and spat at the ground. 'Vito is going to love this: Partisans murder a young girl – who will want to help them now? Let's move.'

~ ~ ~ ~

Silvano had only eighteen at his disposal, having sent Luca, Gino and Filipo to keep watch on the division of paratroopers at Sassa's. He moved quickly, the sun already radiating more heat than usual for this time of the day.

Silvano cursed that he did not have Enzo with him, who had injured his leg on the way to warn him about the Fascist raid. Mason jogged behind, deep in thought, finding it difficult to keep up with the long-legged Italian. His own leg continued to give him trouble over the hilly ground. Not that he was overly keen to arrive at the Stolfi farm; something was not right, although he was in the minority who thought that.

'Silvano,' Mason shouted to the man ahead, sweat pouring from every part of his body.

The tall Italian took no notice and continued to eat up the ground in front of him.

'Silvano.' More a scream now.

Silvano finally stopped and faced the Englishman, his face crimson and covered in sweat. He looked beyond Mason to the long trail of men behind.

'Rest,' he said in a low voice. 'Five minutes – check your rifles.'

Silvano turned away from Mason and walked to the top of a small hill. He stood and allowed the breeze to dry the sweat from his face. Richard Mason stared up at him, anger growing with each passing second.

'Have you no brain, Silvano?'

The Italian ignored him and drank from his flask.

'I said –'

'I heard you the first time,' Silvano interrupted.

'Then be good enough to acknowledge me, Silvano. I'm not one of your peasant army.'

Silvano spun round, taking one more mouthful. 'What do you want?'

Richard Mason placed a cigarette in his mouth and lit it, calming himself, wanting to present his argument in a composed manner.

'Don't you find all this a bit strange?'

'Strange?'

'Enzo.' Mason drew on his cigarette. 'He knows where they're going to strike – the time, the place … and that leg injury … Don't tell me you fell for that?'

Silvano spat on the ground as Ambra came to joined them.

Mason turned to her. 'Ambra … What do you think?'

The woman used a cloth to dry her skin, first her face and neck, before removing the tiny droplets of sweat from between her breasts. Mason caught a glimpse – but now was not the time.

'I follow Silvano.'

Mason laughed out loud.

'Why do you laugh? Do you not follow orders from London?'

The laugh turned into a smile. 'So, you cannot think for yourself, Ambra? Did you ever think that Silvano might have got it wrong? None of us are perfect, we all make mistakes.' Anger had again got the better of him. 'God, you people don't deserve to win this fucking war.' He walked towards Silvano and stopped. 'Just hear me out, Silvano, please.'

Silvano blew out a mouthful of smoke; it caught on the breeze and floated skyward.

'Go on … I will give you the next minute.'

Mason drew breath. 'It is all too good to be true: what road they are taking, how we must approach the farm … That we must come up through the orchard is bullshit. Firstly, its across open land … Tell me, Silvano, is that a good thing? All of us out in the bloody open, with only our arses as cover?' He felt his mouth become dry and he craved a mouthful of water, but he needed to keep talking. He looked at Ambra and hoped he had her attention.

'If you had not been told how to approach the farm, would you have done so this way?'

Silvano remained silent for a moment. 'No.' The answer was whispered.

Mason turned to Ambra. *Say something*, he wanted to scream. Instead, he just glared at her in the hope.

'Silvano,' she broke her silence, 'maybe …' she stopped.

'So, Mason, what are you suggesting?'

'The opposite of what Enzo wanted you to do.'

'Do you accuse him of treachery?' Ambra asked.

'If I'm wrong … shoot me.'

Ambra smiled and pulled out her knife, 'I have a much better way of disposing of you.'

Mason returned the smile with a wide grin. Silvano ran his thumb across the stubble on his chin.

'Then, let us do that, but let's move now … time is short.'

Mason allowed himself a feeling of triumph, but made sure it was not obvious to the other two. Hopefully, he would have all the time in the world to gloat later. Ambra walked past him and whispered into his ear. 'If you're right, I will suck your cock tonight.'

Mason smiled. 'If I'm wrong, I might not have one for you to suck.'

Ambra laughed and placed the knife in her belt.

~ ~ ~ ~

Gianna went outside. His body stank of sweat and his vest was stained with everything he had eaten this past week. The man was built like a bulldog, his arms a mixture of firm sculptured muscle and mounds of fat.

'Fabrizio,' he shouted, 'help Dario move some of the unwanted stones.'

The boy looked disheartened. All he wanted to do was just dip his head in the barrel. They had been working since five this morning, sweat was stinging his eyes, and his belly needed filling. His mother was on the warpath, too: nothing had been done to the new part of the house in five months and she had had enough. Moaning constantly at Gianna, he had finally given in to her demands. Nothing would be done in the fields today. Instead, they would all work on the building.

Inside, Fabia sat next to Cristina; they had become firm friends. Little Paolo sat on her lap playing with her hair. Vincenzo came into the room and kissed his wife, Lucia.

'What was that for?'

'My child.'

'Yours? It has nothing to do with me?'

'I think that two people –'

'Mimi,' shouted Suzetta, 'enough, you're too young.'

'Too young? I know about –'

'Mimi, I'm warning you.'

Vincenzo and Lucia looked at each other and smiled.

'Have you finished your work, Vincenzo? I thought not. Your wife will be fine here with us, I will take care of her welfare while you take care of my new room.'

Vincenzo kissed Lucia and left.

'Is Isolina coming to see you?' Cristina asked.

Fabia smiled. 'Yes, but soon I must go back to Florence. I cannot remain here.'

'They say the war is nearing its end,' Vincenzo spoke from the new room. 'Another month, six weeks maybe, and Florence will be safe to return to.'

'How can you be certain?' Cristina asked.

'I spoke with Silvano three days ago.'

'He's nice.' It was Mimi who spoke.

Suzetta gave her a look of annoyance. 'For heaven's sake, Mimi, whatever has got inside your head, child?'

Fabrizio was halfway across the yard when a shot rang out. The boy collapsed to the ground, holding the lower part of his right leg.

'Fabrizio,' his father shouted as two more bullets exploded into the wall next to him.

Fabrizio began to crawl towards the house. Vincenzo and Dario burst out of the front door together, firing their rifles indiscriminately. Gianni took the opportunity to go and help his youngest. He took hold of the boy's shirt and began to lift him, before a bullet drove into his upper arm. From the window came screams; Vincenzo turned and shouted for the women to get inside.

'Father.' Dario let off two more shots.

Suzetta came out of the door with two more rifles, handing them to her sons.

'Mother, back inside – get them into the middle of the house where it is safer.'

Gianni and Fabrizio collapsed at the top of the steps; Dario and Vincenzo fired two rounds.

'*Inside*,' Vincenzo screamed, kicking the door to behind them.

Dario moved to the nearest window, smashed the glass with the butt of his rifle and fired towards the fence.

'Father, are you all right?'

'Yes, it passed through my shoulder. Give me a rifle, I will cover the new room. Vincenzo, take over from Dario, he can cover the left side.'

Mimi watched, crying, as Cristina and Lucia attended to Fabrizio. Meanwhile, Suzetta was trying to clean up her husband's wound.

'Remain calm.'

'Off me, woman, there is no time for this horseshit.'

Fabia sat on the bottom step. It was all coming back now: the café, the bomb, running away, the room, men and the laughter. She let out a scream.

'Fabia.' Cristina got her to sit, pulling her into her chest and desperately trying to stop her panicking.

'Take her upstairs with little Paolo,' Gianna shouted from the other side of the room.

'Come.' Lucia picked Fabia up.

Cristina took hold of her son. 'Mimi, come on upstairs.'

'Can't I help here?'

'You're a brave girl, but I need you upstairs.'

Mimi smiled, but tears filled her eyes.

'Fabrizio, can you shoot?' Vincenzo asked.

'It's my leg, brother, not my hand.'

Vincenzo smiled. 'Good to hear. Now, go and cover the upper fields.'

The boy limped towards the other room while Lucia crawled across to Vincenzo.

'What do you want me to do?'

'What are you doing back here? Go upstairs, please.' He kissed her.

'I want to help.'

'No, Lucia, keep our child safe.'

'I am staying with you, husband.'

Vincenzo looked at her: she had never looked more beautiful. He knew it was useless to argue. 'Load the guns.' He smiled.

Now it was Cristina's turn to return, making her way to Dario, who just shook his head.

'Do women take no notice of their men anymore?' Gianni shouted.

His wife smiled as she finished placing the bandage on his arm. She felt proud of her sons' wives.

'Gianni Stolfi.' A shout came from outside. 'Gianni Stolfi,' the voice repeated.

'Yes?' he shouted back.

'We know you are a good honest Italian, hard-working, one of the men who helped make Italy strong again under Il Duce. We know that you never wanted any part of this, that others talked you into it. You were misled by your sons, by those in the hills, who have no respect for you as we have.'

Suddenly, there was a pause. Gianni, his head bathed in sweat, looked around the room; all eyes were on him. The man was correct: he never wanted any part in this – but they had shot his son, *shot him*. That was no way to treat someone you respected.

'Gianni.' The voice returned. 'Send out the girl, Fabia. She means nothing to you. What is the point of dying for someone you don't know.'

Silence.

'Send us the girl and we will leave you in peace, Gianni, that is all we ask. Let us stop this now and put our guns away. Send out the girl and we will leave, you are outnumbered, Gianni. We have twenty men out here and we can remain here for a week if it takes that long to make you see sense. But we know you are not a stupid man – protect your family, Gianni, send out the girl.'

'Vincenzo,' Gianni shouted. 'Get the girl.'

'Father, you cannot mean that.'

'We are outnumbered, Fabrizio is hurt …'

'I am fine, Father,' Fabrizio shouted from the other room.

Suzetta, with a look of disappointment on her face, stared at her husband. 'No, Gianni, you cannot do this.'

'I have to do what is best for this family –'

'But –'

'Your husband is right, you have all done enough.' Fabia walked down the stairs. Paolo sat with Mimi at the top.

'No, Fabia, I will not allow it,' said Vincenzo, looking at her. 'Go back.'

'Gianni, I need an answer,' the voice came again.

Fabia began to walk towards the door. Dario stood to block her path as a rifle was discharged and glass shattered.

'Dario,' Cristina screamed.

He fell forward with a hole in his back. Vincenzo fired from the window and, suddenly, the house was peppered with gunshots that came from every direction. Wood splintered, cement fractured and the smell of gunpowder filled the air.

'They're coming,' Fabrizio screamed.

Vincenzo looked away from Dario's motionless body in time to see two men step forward, preparing to throw hand grenades. He fired, hitting one, who fell backwards, dropping the explosive. The other grenade bounced across the wooden porch before exploding.

Wood, glass and earth flew into the house, while the dropped grenade killed five advancing Fascists. Inside the house, people coughed and desperately tried to see through the thick smoke. A rifle fired and Vincenzo shot blindly through the haze at anything that moved; his eyes watered and he spat out dust, reloaded and fired again. Then came another explosion, and another. He turned and, through the smoke, saw his father cradling his mother.

Silvano wondered if they had arrived too late. If he had followed Enzo's directions, they might not have got here at all. Mason had been right, the Fascists had lain in wait for them. Enzo had betrayed them.

Uncertain of what was happening, the Fascists that surrounded the house began to run as the odds suddenly changed. In the yard lay at least a dozen dead bodies; several more had limped away. Silvano looked towards the house, where smoke rose into the sky. The front looked completely destroyed. There were no windows and no door, just a gaping hole. Silvano, joined by Ambra and Mason, walked slowly towards it. The dust that hung in the air drifted across the front of what was left of the house. It was hard to see further than three metres ahead. Nothing moved, until finally, shadows began appearing, slowly taking human shape.

Silvano felt as if the world had stopped. The light breeze that had stirred his hair only moments ago had gone, and the birds had stopped singing. He blinked and spat out dust. He allowed his eyes to become accustomed to the chaos and damage around him. The first person he saw was old Gianni, and next to him his wife, her lifeless eyes staring towards the hillside. Fabia, who lay motionless for several seconds, began to get to her feet. Mason moved quickly over the rubble to help her up. Cristina held Dario's head in her lap and hummed a tune whilst playing with his hair. Vincenzo got to his knees; his head ached and every joint in his body began to throb.

He struggled to focus on the room around him. Particles of dust fell like snow, drifting down onto those below. Vincenzo could taste the dust in the air; it made him cough. He crawled forward on seeing Lucia sitting a metre away. He reached her, but she did not move. Instead, her eyes just gazed down to her stomach, where a long sliver of glass protruded. Her hand was clasped around it, blood seeping through her fingers, staining her dress and the floor below her. Vincenzo's eyes widened, colour drained from his face and a look of despair came across it.

'No!' he screamed. 'NO … NO … NO …'

Silvano looked across, an icy chill coming over him.

'I love you,' Lucia whispered. 'I will always love you.' She placed a hand on his cheek, and held it there for several seconds until it slipped slowly from his face, leaving behind a bloody smear.

~ ~ ~ ~

Amongst the noise of the paratroopers leaving, Sassa wept uncontrollably. Anna, wrapped in a blanket, lay on the back of a cart. Fino had had a grave dug in the lower field under the tall oak tree, while the children, unaware of what had happened, had been kept inside. The German chaplain came and said a few words before walking away, ashen-faced. Laughter came from some of the troops, while others gazed casually towards the scene. This was war in all its revulsion, and yet it was just part of Tuscan life.

Fino brought Sassa to the cart, but she refused to get on, wanting instead to walk behind. Fredo got up behind the pony and took hold of the reins. He gazed at Fino, who nodded and slapped the pony. Fino held onto Sassa to keep her upright and they stared in silence as the small body wrapped in the blanket gently rocked. Fino had been told of Luca's arrest, but he did not believe a word of it.

The pony travelled slowly towards its destination under a clear blue sky. Birds flew in and out of the surrounding trees, singing loudly, unaware of what was happening below them. Maria came to assist Fino. Sassa, on two occasions, had almost collapsed, but still she refused to ride on the cart. Fino looked at the body and wondered how such a short life could be lived in so much pain. He remembered the birthday party, the shaving of her head, the day she heard about her parents' death, and the moment she ran from the house. But he also remembered the courage she shown after the stables had been hit.

Fino closed his eyes and shuddered. Isolina: someone needed to go and tell her. To Isolina, Anna was a second daughter. Fino hung his head low, realising it would fall to him. He would go this afternoon when all the Germans had gone. They reached the oak tree, where a hole had been neatly dug. A mound of damp earth sat to one side. The cart came to a halt. Fino and Fredo moved towards the tightly wrapped bundle that was Anna. They gathered around the grave in silence. Fino took one more look skyward before beginning to speak; he had not planned the words, they just came in one long procession. Above, the birds continued to sing and the sun continued to send down rays of sunshine. Another young casualty of this senseless war was laid to rest in the Tuscan earth.

~ ~ ~ ~

Luca walked up to the door for about the fiftieth time and stood for a moment before walking back. He repeated this action for another ten minutes while Filipo sat on a wooden stool watching him. Outside, Luca could hear voices, and doors opening and shutting, while, in the distance, he heard bombs being dropped. He was not pacing with worry; it was the girl that troubled him. He remained haunted by the look on her face. What they had done was barbaric, and he found it difficult to control his anger. The pain inflicted on him was nothing compared to what they had done to her. Each day, the Allies were getting closer and that pleased him. He saw fear in the faces of those who had arrested him: they were already looking over their shoulders. He suddenly came to a halt, making Filipo look up.

'We are the reason,' he said out loud.

'What?'

'They took her life because of us.'

Filipo was about to defend himself but stopped. Luca was right, the girl could not live, how could they let her talk.

'I need a piss,' he shouted, kicking the door at the same time.

'Shut up, Luca,' a voice said from the other side.

'Eligio … is that you?' Luca pressed his face up against the door.

'Yes.'

'Then let me go for a piss.'

'Use the bucket in your room, Luca … Now shut up.'

'There is more on the floor than in the bucket, come see for yourself.'

There was silence.

'You and Filipo stand against the back wall where I can see you.'

The lock clicked and the door swung open. A young man stood in the doorway and another stood behind, pointing a rifle.

'Come, bring the bucket. You stay there, Filipo.'

Luca, holding the overflowing bucket, stood in the corridor before following Eligio's extended finger. In the washroom at the far end, Luca emptied the bucket before undoing his trousers. Eligio remained at the door, watching nervously.

'How did they know where we would be, Eligio?' Luca asked.

He received no answer.

'We used to go stealing figs, Eligio, when we were young ... and that was not so long ago.' He stared at the wall, urinating. 'You, me, Satato, too ...'

'Yes ... yes ...' said the boy holding the rifle. 'I remember.'

'Then you know that I did not do what they say I did.'

'Well, who did?'

Luca turned, doing up his belt. 'You damn well know who did.'

Eligio shook his head.

'She was alive when we found her.'

'Alive?'

'Yes, and if she were here now, she would tell you I had nothing to do with it.'

'You're telling me that someone ...'

'Yes.'

'That can't be.'

Luca laughed. 'She was alive, Eligio, as you are now.'

'Enzo said ...' The boy stopped before he said anymore.

'Enzo? What has Enzo got to do with all this?'

'We must get back ... Pick up the bucket.'

'Tell me ... please ...'

'Enzo has been paid by Vito Sergi to give all of you away. The rest of your band were ambushed at the Stolfi farm this morning.'

Luca suddenly became angry. He took two paces forward, until the end of Eligio's rifle stopped him going any further.

'I've said too much, let's go … now!'

Filipo sat alone; the vile image of the girl had become lodged in his mind. He felt increasingly fearful of being on his own as he heard people coming down the corridor … Luca returning, hopefully, he thought. A man now stood in the open doorway, partly obscuring another. When he stepped to one side, Filipo recognised him.

'Enzo – they have you too?'

Carlo Sergi's face came into view.

'Fool,' he whispered.

Enzo turned to face him. 'No, you're the fool – or whoever allowed this to happen.'

'Where is Luca?' Carlo Sergi asked the other guard.

'In the washroom with Eligio.'

Carlo turned to the two men behind him. 'Go and get them,' he said, 'but bring him with us.' He pointed to Filipo.

Moments later, Luca appeared, returning to his cell surrounded by three guards.

'Where's Filipo?' he asked.

They all shrugged their shoulders before closing the door behind them.

~ ~ ~ ~

Gino watched as Isolina walked towards the hall cupboard. He stole a quick kiss from Sofia at that moment, cheekily squeezing her breast.

'Gino,' she whispered. 'That is unfair.'

'You're so beautiful, I want to touch you all the time.'

'Control yourself.'

'Tell your mother we are lovers … or I will.'

'No, not yet.'

Gino smiled at her. 'I must go now.'

'No.'

'I must, I am already late … I should have been at the camp an hour ago.'

There was a loud hammering on the door. Isolina appeared at the doorway and turned to the couple. 'Out!'

Gino made his way upstairs while Isolina walked slowly towards the front door. Another loud thud and Isolina finally opened the door on Vito Sergi.

'Buongiorno, signora.' He lifted his hat and a smile grew.

She did not acknowledge him.

'I will wait, Isolina.'

'Wait? Wait for what?'

'This.' He gestured towards the barn.

Isolina looked in the same direction. It was then two men came, holding Gino by his arms, his nose bleeding and his shirt torn.

'Gino,' Sofia screamed as she ran from the door.

'Sofia,' Isolina shouted.

The girl flung her arms around him, smearing blood on her dress.

'What have they done to you?'

'Get her away,' Vito Sergi ordered. 'Put him in the car,' he said to the men. He turned to Isolina. 'How touching.'

Sofia was on her knees, sobbing. Isolina went across and desperately tried to lift her onto her feet. The German soldiers looked on, bemused.

'Where are you taking him?'

'Just a few questions … before a nice short trip to –'

'Bastard,' Sofia shouted. '*Bastard.*'

Isolina watched them bundle Gino into the back seat of a car. Vito came and stared at the women. 'I should really take you in for questioning, Isolina … for harbouring a fugitive.'

'A fugitive?' She laughed out loud. 'He is just a boy.'

'I'm certain your daughter does not think that way.' The smirk grew on his face.

Isolina kissed Sofia's head and held her tight. 'Then why don't you take me as well?'

'Oh, no … I owe it to my friend's memory – your late husband, I mean. Honour prevents me from arresting you today. Call me an old-fashioned romantic. Maybe tomorrow I will allow your daughter to join the boy.' He smiled and walked to the car. 'Oh – by the way …'

Isolina looked up as Vito Sergi looked at his watch. 'At this moment in time the Stolfi farm is under siege, with your niece inside … And, before you are filled with too much hope … your Partisan friends, including the Englishman …' his grin expanded '… were ambushed on their way to help. It's been a productive day.'

Fabia came to Isolina's thoughts, along with an image of Silvano lying dead in a field. She tightened her grip on Sofia as she watched the cars drive away. She tried to absorb the news, wanting to remain calm for her daughter's sake, yet, inside, her world was collapsing. It was then a young German soldier came across carrying a water bottle. Isolina looked up and forced a smile. He returned it. They stood up and Isolina placed a hand on the boy's arm.

'No, thank you.'

Her words were in Italian. Unable to understand, the boy just stared at the pair of them. Isolina reached up and ran her thumb across his smooth cheek. The madness that rules this world makes us lose hope, she thought; and yet, just a small act of kindness encourages us to keep going.

CHAPTER TWENTY-FIVE

Silvano lit up his second cigarette, turned his back to the road and lay looking up at an almost cloudless sky. He blew out the smoke and yawned.

'Not sleeping?' Mason sat with his pencil in hand. 'Me, I slept like a log.'

'Good,' Silvano answered, keeping his eyes closed.

'Twenty minutes and they will have the explosives in place.'

'Good.'

'Talkative this morning.' Mason laughed and continued to draw.

He had caught Silvano's likeness perfectly: the worry, frustration and the growing tiredness that was catching up with him, all captured on paper. It surprised him. True, he had achieved this before, but only with beautiful women, never a man. He knew the reason for the worry: it had been more than two weeks since Luca and Filipo had been incarcerated in the Fascist barracks, along with a division of German paratroopers, making the place impregnable. Mason shaded under the eyes, further emphasising the Partisan leader's tiredness. As much as the tall Italian continued to annoy him, he felt a certain amount of sympathy for the man. Silvano had attended the funeral at the Stolfi farm, something he himself was glad to have missed. He felt certain Silvano had visibly aged in that short time: he had returned with the look of a ghost. Isolina had come to see him that day, and they had argued, which had pleased him. He could never look at Isolina without wanting her; no other woman had made that impression on him, and he had drawn many beautiful women in his short life.

He flicked through several pages until her face stared back at him. Even from memory, he could sketch her. Every detail was set in stone, every curve, the sharpness of her bone structure, her ample lips – he knew her features better than she did herself, he thought. That striking face filled an entire page. He used his finger to gently trace her features, then closed his eyes and imagined himself looking down at her while they made love, her face a mixture of passion and lust, her fingers playing with his hair. Silvano coughed and Mason opened his eyes; he felt a stiffness between his legs and adjusted himself.

Silvano was exhausted; this war was bleeding him dry. He continued to think of his imaginary villa, which he had built a thousand times in his head. He tried again to see inside the rooms, but found the images blurred. Everything was going out of focus, like Italy, like Tuscany, like himself. The villa had become a ruin and not the inspiration it had once been, and now he struggled to conjure up something new in his imagination, devoid as he was of ideas. The realisation that he had nowhere to go to escape this chaos, terrified him.

He remembered standing around the grave at the farm, closing his eyes as they brought out the coffins. In that darkness, he tried to find some respite, a little peace, but the images circled in his head: he was looking into that room again, seeing the horror once more. Dario's blood-stained shirt, Gianni holding his dead wife, the sliver of glass that took the life of Lucia and her unborn child. For the first time, he questioned whether it was all worth it.

Isolina worried him, too. At the Stolfi farm, she had fainted twice and almost had to be carried back to the house. The death of the evacuee girl had devastated her; she looked frail, colourless and without energy – he had not seen her like that since the death of her father. He had stood, frustrated, unable to comfort her. Their eyes had met, just the once – had he seen loathing and disappointment in hers? He had thought back to another time, one he prayed would come again … Right now, though, he needed to hold onto something positive.

He found himself questioning every decision he made; all confidence had drained from him. After the funeral, she had come to see him about Gino, but he had been unable to give her answers. In reply, her voice had sounded harsh. He tried to explain that Luca and Filipo were also prisoners, and that he could do little for them either.

He felt as if he had dived into a cold lake and was sinking deeper into its icy depths. Suddenly, he was gasping for air, unable to breathe, water was filling his lungs and he was choking. He sat bolt upright.

'Wow!' Mason stared at him. 'Nightmare?'

Silvano fought to calm himself, controlling his breathing with difficulty. 'Dream.' He stretched out his legs and felt the sweat soaking his clothes.

'If you say so,' Mason muttered under his breath.

Shells could be heard falling in the distance. It seemed the Allied advance was in full swing.

'What did your man have to say?' Silvano asked, removing a cigarette.

'The American Fifth Army are not too far from San Gimignano; our Eighth have pushed up past Montepulciano, moving towards the Chianti Hills; Florence has been declared an open city.'

Mason stopped and looked at Silvano; the man was on the edge, he thought. 'We are to cause the retreating German army as much disruption as we can. I think that is it in a nutshell.' Mason smiled.

Silvano drew in the smoke and stared out across the valley.

'Look,' Mason began, 'this is war, things happen. You can't go around blaming yourself every time someone dies.'

'Who said I was?'

'It written all over your face, Silvano.'

'I'm tired.'

'Please yourself.'

Silvano stood, brought the binoculars to his eyes and began to follow the winding road down to where they were. Suddenly, something caught his eye.

'Here.' He held them out to Mason, who got to his feet wearily and walked over.

'Interesting.'

'The car?'

'Yes.'

'What about the troop carrier.'

'Take that out with explosives ... The car we can take care of ourselves.'

'Let's do it.'

The car moved a lot faster than the following lorry, and a good hundred-metre gap now separated them. Silvano had two charges placed one hundred and fifty metres apart. Everything was ready. Ten minutes later, the car sped past the first explosive. Just as the lorry came alongside, the explosive was detonated, tipping it onto its side. Those who survived ran from the burning vehicle, only to be machine-gunned down.

The occupants of the car heard the explosion and it began to slow down. It was at that point that the second detonation went off, only this time with far less explosive charge. The car careered off the road and hit a tree. The driver continued his journey via the front windscreen, killing him instantly, while his passenger remained unharmed. The vehicle was surrounded in seconds and the passenger stood beside it with both hands held aloft. He looked shaken, but had no noticeable injuries.

'Well, well, a real life general,' Mason laughed.

~ ~ ~ ~

Sassa pulled the crying child closer. The walls, ceiling and floor shook as another explosion took place somewhere above. One of the children crawled across to be closer to her, while Gina and Daniela also sat with children clinging to them. Some of the older ones helped by comforting the youngest, but they, too, had panic in their eyes. Fino smiled at Sassa from across the cellar to reassure her.

They had been down here now for almost four hours, with blankets, toys, food and candles. At first it had been an adventure, they sang songs and the children had laughed, but all that had changed with the growing noise above. They knew that sound so well, having heard it a hundred times these past few weeks. The first explosion had brought blind panic; screams had filled the room, making old and young alike search for someone to cling to.

The next explosion seemed more distant, like a crack of thunder way off in the next valley, while the ensuing one faded in its severity. Sassa squinted through the gloom to search out faces. Some tried to force a smile, while others rested their heads on the shoulders of those next to them. Sassa thought of Anna; if ever there was a time for her calmness, it was now. The children missed her; they had been told she had gone home. They had lied, something Sassa had said she would never do, but, right now, it seemed the best option.

The burden of having to remain strong was weighing heavy on her shoulders. She felt tired, and yet found sleep almost impossible. When she did sleep, the nightmares came with a ruthlessness she had never experienced before. She had been told that the two Austrian deserters were really German SS, tricking those naïve enough to fall for it. Several of the surrounding farms had people forcibly removed, their homes ransacked or burnt to the ground.

Half an hour passed without a single explosion. Then the sound of boots like stampeding cattle came from above, with men shouting in harsh German, while engines were started up.

'Let Gina and Daniela stay here with the children while we go upstairs,' said Fino.

'No!' screamed three of the children, desperate to hold on to both guardians. Sassa calmed them down, kissing their heads and promising she would return.

'Anna never came back,' said a pretty, round-faced child.

'I will, Francesca.'

'But –'

'I said I will come back.' Sassa looked into the frightened girl's face and smiled. 'I will bring some food.'

Objects littered the ground floor: glasses and bottles had fallen from shelves and tables. In the kitchen, plates, cups and saucers were in fragments across the tiled floor. The dust was just settling on the furniture.

'Well,' said Fino, his hands on his hips, 'it could have been worse.'

Sassa stared at him, unsure whether to laugh or cry, but chose neither. She looked out of the window. It was remarkable how almost everything else remained undamaged, except for a German lorry that was on fire. Sassa stepped away from her back door, where two men lay on stretchers, a German medic working frantically on both.

She walked towards the man. 'Is there nothing you can do for him?'

The German looked up before crawling towards the second man. 'No.'

'But he is alive.'

'For now, yes.' The man struggled to find the right Italian words.

'Then why do you not help him?'

'He is beyond help.'

The medic rubbed his eyes; he looked close to exhaustion.

'Surely if he is –'

He cut her off. 'His gut is hanging out and I have no blood to give him.'

'At least relieve some of the pain?'

'With what? I have nothing … The last consignment was blown up by the Partisans, with all my medical supplies. I have nothing. Until another shipment gets through, all I have is what is in my case. I'm sorry if my answer is not what you want to hear … but, like my Italian, it is not all my fault.'

Sassa looked down at him. The desperation in his voice made her feel ashamed of herself.

'Your Italian is very good … much better than my German.'

'You speak German?'

'No.'

The German smiled. Sassa took a step back to allow him to attend to the other casualty, a young boy whose face was covered in sweat.

'He is in shock.' The medic pulled back the blanket to expose the thin piece of metal embedded in his chest.

'He is asking for a drink of water.'

Sassa went to fetch some. On her return, she observed as the medic tried to stem the flow of blood.

'Here.' Sassa held out the cup.

'You give it to him while I attend to this.'

She let the cup rest on the boy's bottom lip and slowly tilted it, allowing just enough to trickle over his tongue. He still choked a little as he swallowed, before reaching up and gripping the fabric of her dress. He stared into her face, beads of sweat covering his own, and whispered in German before his final breath left him.

'What did he say?'

'I can sum it up in one word: *Why.*'

Sassa gently closed his eyes. 'Madness … sheer madness,' she whispered.

Fino bent down and lifted his wife back onto her feet. He kissed her cheek and wiped away her tears, something he was doing with great regularity lately.

Across the yard strolled Lieutenant Bergmann, the only man in authority left at the farm.

'If I may be permitted to give you some advice,' he began, 'take the children, your staff and anyone else who wants to leave here.'

'And where do you suggest we go?' Fino asked in broken German.

'Away from us, the German army, from our troops, our guns, our vehicles ... While you are around us, the children's lives are in danger. The British bombing is quite accurate, but the Americans seem to drop them wherever they like. Go, and go soon.'

Fino looked at the man, weighing things up.

'My wife and my son have both been killed ... A bombing raid in Berlin,' Lieutenant Bergmann continued.

'I'm sorry.'

'Why should you be? We brought it upon ourselves ... Did we not?'

'No ... One madman did.'

Bergmann smiled. 'Yes, a madman ... and if my men could hear me now, they would shoot me ... Mad or not, so many still want to lay down their lives for him.'

'And do you, Lieutenant?'

'I just do my duty like a good German officer ... Now, gather what you need, I would say we have at least a two-hour wait before they come again.'

'What about you?'

'Our orders are to hold, retreat, hold again ...'

'And, like a good German ...'

'... I will follow those orders.'

Fino blew out his cheeks; it all seemed so senseless.

Over the next hour, Fino, Sassa and their staff gathered what they needed. It was decided they would take only essentials that could be carried easily. The only clothes would be those they wore, and for the children a change of underwear, which they placed inside several prams, along with food and water.

Bergmann came to see them off. 'Go towards the village of Certaldo, the Eighth Army are likely to take it in the next forty-eight hours, but let me remind you, all the roads have been mined.' He stopped speaking to allow what he said to sink in. 'This is important: stay in the middle of the road and keep spread out. If not, you will attract attention from the air. And keep moving.'

'Thank you.' Fino came and shook his hand. 'You know the war is lost.'

Bergmann smiled. 'Germany will never be defeated.'

Fino stared at the man before slapping his shoulder; there was nothing left to say.

Finally, thirteen adults, seventeen children and four prams set off down the road. Some of the younger ones played, while others sat on the shoulders of the adults. Sassa turned to look back at their house. Fino came and stood next to her.

'We will be back,' he whispered.

'Will we?'

'Come on, Sassa, this is not like you.'

'I'm tired, Fino. I'm tired of having to be strong for those around me, I'm tired of trying to understand why people make war …' Tears flowed from her eyes and down her cheeks, falling onto her dress and staining it dark.

Fino placed his arms around her and kissed her forehead. 'Come on, I hope you're not tired of me.'

Robert Fowler

'I could never be tired of the man I love.' Sassa smiled, took one more look at the house and began to walk.

~ ~ ~ ~

Isolina saw Anna walking towards her. She came through the meadow, with the hills behind. All around lay the land with its lush green rolling hillsides and fields of golden wheat. Vast vineyards, neatly planted, grew in military lines either side, while tall cypress trees formed a guard of honour. Anna was smiling, a basket of blackberries over her arm. She waved and kept walking towards Isolina. Suddenly, Anna stopped, her smile now replaced by a look of fear. Behind Isolina stood an army.

The bombs began to fall and the army advanced. The ground where they marched was scorched black, the floor vibrated, the breeze became a squall, and rain now fell as sleet and snow. 'Wait!' Isolina shouted, 'I am here, stay with me.' Her nostrils became filled with a sickly stench and her eyes watered as smoke drifted into them. 'Wait!' she screamed again, trying to catch Anna's attention. 'Wait … wait … wait …'

'Mamma … Wake up, Mamma.'

Isolina looked up into a face full of concern: Sofia's face.

'Mamma, are you ill?'

Isolina sat up. Everything seemed unfamiliar, until she remembered they had slept under the staircase.

'Yes …yes, I'm fine,' she whispered. 'A bad dream.'

'You called out Anna's name.'

'Did I?'

Isolina recalled parts of her dream and reminded herself that Anna was dead. She reached across and held Sofia. In the distance, she heard an explosion, and the sound of engines just on the other side of their wall. German shouts, German boots, and the throbbing noise of a squadron of planes overhead. She struggled to her feet, lowered her head and stepped out into her front room.

The shadows were long; it was not yet midday. She put her hand to her forehead and felt the moisture; she felt a little sick. The sickness grew, her mouth went dry and her head began to spin. She ran to the kitchen and vomited into the sink. Four times her stomach pumped bile into her throat, until there was nothing left to bring up. She pumped the water tap and waited for it to turn from brown to clear before placing her mouth under it.

'Mamma.'

She felt Sofia's hand on her back, rubbing it gently.

'I'm fine,' she said, trying to reassure her.

'Mamma, please.'

She had failed. The anxiety in her daughter's voice made her feel ashamed. It had been her job to comfort her daughter, to keep *her* safe, not the other way around. Now came the realisation that they were the only ones left. Simon was gone, Silvano lost to her … maybe she should have kissed the Englishman and taken him to her bed.

'Put the coffee on.'

'Mamma –'

'I will be fine.'

Suddenly, someone was pounding on her door. Isolina's first thought was that Vito Sergi had returned to take her away.

'Isolina …' From outside, her name was called. 'It is I, Roberto the interpreter, from Milan.'

At first came relief, but that was soon replaced by trepidation. Sofia walked to the door, but waited for her mother to permit her to open it.

'Buongiorno.' He lifted his hat. 'Is your mother …?' He saw Isolina standing in the kitchen doorway.

'Isolina, you must go.'

'I know.'

'Go now, and I mean today.'

'Why today?'

'Just do as I ask.'

'Where do I go?'

'South, away from the German lines. It is not safe to be an Italian here. I have seen it with my own eyes, Isolina, take your daughter and go, please, for her sake if not yours.' He was almost crying now.

'Calm down, Roberto. I know we have to go from here, I am not a fool, but why are you speaking in this way?'

'Because you have not witnessed the things I have these past two weeks.' His face lost colour and he took out a cigarette. 'May I?' He pointed to a chair.

Isolina nodded.

'Orders have been issued, orders which some officers think translate to them doing as they like.' He blew out a cloud of smoke. 'I was in a village.'

'What of it?'

'The Partisans had tried to blow a stone bridge. It was pointless chasing after them into the mountains. That is where they are at their strongest. Instead, our commander came across the church, where men woman and children of that village were saying mass … Can I have a drink please?'

Isolina handed him a glass and filled it with wine.

'Grazie.' He took a few sips. 'They went inside and shot them all.'

Isolina placed her hand to her mouth.

'If that was not enough ...' the interpreter began to cry, rocking back and forth '... they went around the village shooting anything that moved. They left with the whole village ablaze.'

'How many?'

'Forty, fifty – who knows; they all died that night. Now do you see why you have to go? Get away from here, head towards the Allies ... I've seen these Germans, their eyes are full of hate and vengeance ... I will not tell you the other stories I've seen and heard.'

'Come, Sofia, let's get some things together.' Isolina walked towards the stairs.

'I have a car,' the interpreter said, 'I can take you to the Swedish woman's house. You will be stopped if you go on your own.'

'Sassa,' Isolina said under her breath – where else was she going to go.

Sofia walked across to her. 'Mamma ... Gino?'

Isolina had forgotten him and felt guilty.

'Who?' asked Roberto. 'The boy being held by the Fascist Vito Sergi?'

'Yes ... have you news?'

'Only that the Germans are not interested in him, or any of the other Partisans; their only concern is for Kruger.'

'Kruger?'

'The general taken by the Partisans – have you not heard?'

Isolina shook her head.

'It's the people in the village you should be concerned about. The Germans want him back and they will use anything at their disposal to achieve that.' Roberto walked up to the pair. 'This Gino is safer where he is than they are: Partisans are supposed to die for their cause so what's the point in shooting them ... No, they will use the innocent to bargain with.'

'I can't go.' Sofia took a step back.

'Sofia.' Isolina placed a hand on her daughter's shoulder. 'Please.'

'You go, I will wait.'

'Wait?' said Roberto, angry now. 'Wait for what? He could be halfway to Florence or Germany by now ... You might sit here and wait for the next ten years ... I'm sorry to sound so harsh, child, but if you remain here you may never see him again.'

Twenty minutes later, a tearful Sofia walked to the car as the German soldiers stared at her from their battle stations. She sat with her head bowed in the back seat. Isolina was pleased to be leaving the house: it held a multitude of black memories within its walls. She walked and joined her daughter without looking back.

'Wait.' Sofia pushed open the door and ran back to the house.

'Sofia,' Isolina shouted.

Sofia returned with a coat over her arm. 'For when it's cold,' she said, breathless, getting back into the car.

~ ~ ~ ~

Father Mariano looked sheepish; he had delivered his message to Silvano and now waited for the reply.

'So, the lives of those in the village for this general?' Silvano paced across the floor.

'Must be important.' Mason had finished a quick sketch of the priest. He had given him an exaggerated nose, bulging eyes, and had him standing holding a sickle. Mason smiled to himself.

Ambra smiled too, looking over his shoulder. There were times the Englishman made her angry, yet she always found herself forgiving him.

'He wanted you to know,' the priest fumbled for the words, 'that if you thought he might be bluffing ...' Again, he paused, nervous about what he was going to say. '... At three, five people will be executed ... then a further five every half an hour, until the general is handed over.' His ordeal finally over, Father Mariano walked away from the tall Partisan leader. 'Could I have some water?' he mumbled to one of the men.

Silvano nodded.

'Call his bluff, Silvano.' Mason spoke while still looking at the sketch, turning it this way and that with a smile.

Silvano stared down at him stone-faced and ran the palm of his hand over five days of stubble.

'Don't even think about it, Silvano.' Mason got to his feet. 'You know our orders. Keep this general here so our people can pick him up ... This man is valuable, Silvano, he could be the key to ending this part of the war.'

'Is he more valuable than the people of the village?'

Mason bent down and picked up a half full bottle of wine, pulled out the cork and cleaned the dirt from around the neck. He lifted it to his mouth, allowing some to escape down his chin, which he mopped up with his sleeve. It bought him the time needed.

'I know things have been tough for you. I'm not blind and not without feeling –'

'You surprise me,' Silvano interrupted.

Mason ignored him. 'But if we are to bring this war to a swift conclusion,' he went on, 'then tough decisions need to be taken. This man could be the key to finding out what the Germans are up to, what their plans are, where they intend to hold the next line ...' He stared at Silvano. 'You're going to have to hope that those Germans down there are bluffing.'

'And what if they are not?'

Mason grinned. 'That general *will* be handed over to our people. You need to get that inside your thick head, my friend.' He brought the bottle to his mouth again, his stare never leaving Silvano.

The priest sipped his water while Ambra stood next to him, glad that she preferred to follow than lead.

'This is so simple for you.' Silvano looked at Mason. 'These people mean nothing to you, these Italians, these peasants, some of whom fought against you not so long ago. It comes so easy for someone like you.'

'Don't make me out to be the cold-hearted Englishman, it has nothing to do with that. This is war, and people have to make decisions – decisions that might cost some lives initially, but, at the same time, might save thousands later.'

Mason took out a cigarette.

The priest stood. 'I need to be going back now.'

'And just what does the man of God think?' Angry now, Mason turned to him.

'I am merely the messenger.'

'You're a Fascist, too, are you not?'

Father Mariano began to speak, but Mason did not give him a chance.

'Will you help pick the five? Will they be blessed by you before being taken out to be shot?' Mason walked towards him. 'And what does God think about this situation?'

'I ... I ...'

'He does have an option ... yes? God, I mean, not you. You're the shepherd ... for all your flock – is that not so?'

The priest had become anxious; sweat began to form on his top lip.

'Is God a Fascist?'

No answer.

'I said *is* God a Fascist?'

'Why do you ask?'

'Well, I want to know if God is with our friend here ... Silvano.' He circled widely around the tall Italian. 'Or, is he with your German commander down there ...'

'He is everywhere.'

'So, he is with you right now?'

'Yes.'

'So, ask him.'

'Ask him what?'

'What Silvano should do.'

The priest swallowed, wishing he had something stronger than water to drink. Mason stared at the man.

'Go. Get out of my sight, you fucking hypocrite. As for all you religious people, God is who you want him to be. You tell yourselves that He will forgive because He is merciful.'

'He is,' the priest suddenly said. 'I am certain it is just a threat.'

'So, when your flock is murdered today, you will tell them that God will have mercy on them, and he will come and shine a light to lead them to the Promised Land.' Mason in a flash withdrew his gun and placed it on the priest's temple. None there had time to react.

'Mason,' shouted Silvano.

'What's the problem, Silvano? They take a life, we take a life …'

The priest was dripping with sweat, unable to speak.

'How could someone like you deliver a message like this, as if it were just a business transaction? I thought you people dealt in life, but all you have done is speak of death.' Mason clicked back the hammer.

'Mason, please …' Silvano took a step forward.

'I should blow your fucking brains out, *priest*. See him over there – I might not get on with him, in fact he would love to do to me what I'm doing to you …' Mason was almost whispering in the priest's ear. 'But he is a much better man than you will ever be. He is closer to God than you will ever be. So, go back to your Fascist and German masters … and lick their arses. Then do everyone a favour and blow your brains out.'

Mason lowered the gun in total silence. He walked back to where his book and pencil lay and sat cross-legged. He did not watch Father Marino leave – he didn't want to; all that worried him now was the decision Silvano was about to make.

CHAPTER TWENTY-SIX

Fino pushed the pram down the middle of a dirt track. Zita, only seven-years-old, walked beside him. She occasionally looked up and, when Fino caught her eye, she smiled, her cheeks reddened and she quickly looked away. If this little game made this child forget about the war, albeit for a short time, then he would continue to play, for it also helped to ease his own anguish.

The party remained spread out, adhering to the warnings they had been given. That was how they had journeyed for the past three hours. The war seemed to have vanished for the time being; they had not seen or heard planes above them. Fino, every now and again, would look back at Sassa, who would smile back at him, but neither exchanged any words. The procession turned and began to drop downhill. At the bottom was a small farm.

'That's Giosue's place, Fino,' Sassa shouted from behind.

'Yes, it's been a while since we last saw him.'

Clouds began to appear in the sky, floating lazily across a deep blue background.

'Mimi,' Sassa shouted to a small barefoot girl wearing a thin summer dress. 'Stay in the middle.' Gina was already there clasping the small girl's arm to bring her back.

'Thank you, Gina.'

Giosue's little house sat in a dip. From behind the house, the tops of three oak trees rose above the roof. The stone wall that used to run the width of the house was now gone. The barn's roof tiles lay scattered on the ground and the walls of the house had paint peeling off in places. This house has not been lived in for many months, Fino thought. They came to a halt outside the open double gates.

'Let's rest here, the barn will give us some shade. The children have the hill to climb next, so make sure they drink and rest.' Sassa spoke to Gina and Daniela. 'Amedeo,' Sassa looked towards her gardener, 'remain at the gate and do not let any of the children past.'

The old man dipped his head in acknowledgment and lit up a cigarette. Fino was trying the front door when Sassa reached him.

'Locked,' he said.

'He lived here with his sister, did he not?'

'Silvia, yes, an outspoken woman … a teacher.'

'The last I heard she moved to Florence or Lucca.'

Fino banged on the door and rapped with his knuckles on the windows, but nothing within stirred.

'No one seems to be here.' He looked back towards the assembled group, who sat around in the shade. One or two of the children ran around the yard, but more sat with an adult, drinking water or eating a little bread. 'Let's see what's around the back.'

At that moment two girls came running past. They stared through the windows as Fino had done, and he ruffled the blonde one's hair. 'Little miss mischief,' he said.

The two girls, holding hands, took off again, running towards the end of the building. Sassa and Fino moved a little quicker: Sassa never liked it when the children were out of her sight. Fino understood why and quickened his pace.

The bizarre stillness of the day was suddenly shattered by the tormented screams coming from the two girls. Fino and Sassa stopped and looked at each other before moving with as much speed as they could muster. Down the side of the house they dashed, before turning the corner, where the girls stood staring up into a tree.

A tall oak grew behind a wooden fence. A thick branch reached over the fence and stretched out towards the house. Two bodies hung from it. Frozen by what they saw, unable to remove their eyes for their revulsion, both girls remained standing side by side.

'Get them out of here,' Fino said, walking past both. 'Get them back to the others and send Amedeo and Naldo to me.'

Sassa took hold of the children and walked them back; she was met halfway by Gina and Maria.

Fino went across to an old wooden outbuilding where the door hung on one hinge. The roof was covered in bird shit; the wood itself was crumbling. He laid the door on the grass and looked inside the building, where he found two shovels. A rusty knife lay on a small wooden shelf. Fino forced himself to stare up at the two bodies hanging above him. He walked towards them as a breeze swept in from the hillside, gently turning the bodies so that both now faced him. Giosue, like his sister, had no eyes: just dark holes, the local bird life had seen to that. The breeze also brought the odour of rotting flesh and the redolence of human waste.

Fino suddenly felt embarrassed on her behalf, although she had long ago stopped worrying about being presentable. Somehow, it did not seem right to stare at these people –

not now; it was not their fault. He would get the younger man, Naldo, to climb the tree and cut both down and they would dig two graves, deep enough to stop any of the Tuscan wildlife getting to them. Like the humans in this part of Italy, starvation was a threat to the animals as well.

Fino tried to remember Giosue; his face was unrecognisable now. He had a vague memory of lending him a tractor to plough his back field, but that was a long time ago. He stared at the tractor: grass, weeds and sunflowers covered it. He found it hard to recall that conversation or even where they had had it. Silvia? He could not recall ever meeting the woman, yet they lived a short drive up the road. The thought saddened him.

The sight that greeted both men took their breath away, but they seemed unable to remove their eyes from the vision above them.

'Poor bastard,' said Amedeo, removing his cap.

'Did you know him?' Fino asked.

'Yes, we sometimes bought oil from him.'

Fino felt even more ashamed: they did business together and he never knew. What else had slipped by him?

'Could that be his sister?'

'Yes – Silvia; she got married about ten months ago.'

Fino directed Naldo up the tree and five minutes later, both bodies lay covered by empty sacks from the outhouse. They bowed their heads and said a few words. Afterwards, Naldo and Amedeo crossed themselves and made their way back. Fino remained for several minutes, looking down at the graves. What had this country become, Italian killing Italian … He, too, crossed himself and walked slowly back to where Sassa waited for him.

~ ~ ~ ~

The man with his outstretched arms stepped out into the middle of the road.

'What's happening?' Isolina asked.

'Fascist road block … they're everywhere.'

'What do they want?'

Robert never got the chance to answer; the Fascist soldier came to the window and looked in.

'Papers.'

'I'm with the –'

'*Papers.*'

Roberto stopped mid-sentence, knowing it would be useless to argue. He might be driving a German military car, but he was still an Italian. The man unfolded the sheet of paper. It was badly creased and torn at the corners from too many hands touching it these past three years.

'Interpreter,' the man said aloud. 'Going where?'

'The Zotti farm.'

'Why?'

'This woman is a nurse.' He glanced to his side at Isolina. 'She is a nurse and is on her way to see to some injured German soldiers.'

Isolina stared at him: his lie had come as a shock.

'And the girl?'

'Her daughter.'

'Nurse also?'

'No.' Roberto knew instantly that he had answered incorrectly. He clenched his jaw until it hurt.

'Out.'

'What?'

'The girl … Out!'

Isolina leant across Roberto. 'No, she comes with me.'

Sofia sat silent in the back seat; her thoughts had turned to Gino. 'Mamma, it is fine.'

Isolina swung her head around, a look of amazement welded to her face. 'No, Sofia.'

But her daughter was already climbing out of the car, her coat hung over her arm. Several of the men looked up and fixed their stare on the attractive young girl. One whistled and another made a comment under his breath. Isolina opened her door but the Fascist captain told her to remain where she was.

'She will be safe, don't worry. I have a daughter her age, but these are my orders. Unless you are a German or Fascist or on government business, you are to be detained.'

'But she is a child,' Isolina shouted.

'A bomb was planted at one of our barracks only a month ago … two fifteen-year-old boys did that. Age means nothing anymore.'

'Mamma, stay, go to Sassa's … I will be fine, I promise.'

A man came and pushed Isolina's door shut, and then leant against it.

'Drive on, interpreter. I will personally take your daughter to the village,' he said to Isolina directly.

Panic consumed Isolina. The warmth of the morning now had a chill to it: June had turned into December in the blink of an eye – and yet Sofia remained calm. But this did little to put Isolina at ease; she twisted her head around and watched her daughter fade into the distance, and then placed her hand on the door handle.

'No, Isolina … NO!' Roberto reached across, grabbed her arm and held it down firmly on her lap. 'I will stop in a moment, please don't try to do that again. You will only hurt yourself.' He stared at her with pleading eyes. 'Breathe slowly, short breaths – slowly, Isolina, I will stop in five minutes, I promise.' He began to perspire. 'I will go and see my new commander, I'm certain he can help.'

Isolina stared at the road ahead as it slipped beneath the car. Her mind was in turmoil, and now the landscape around her began to spin, causing the sky and land to become one. She swiftly felt very sick and leant forward, her head too heavy for her neck. She rested it on the dashboard, until, suddenly, there was darkness.

~ ~ ~ ~

Sofia sat silent. The driver's uniform emitted a strong, unpleasant odour. He drove faster than her mother, resting his elbow on the open window ledge and he allowed his cigarette to burn until it almost touched his lips, before tossing it out of the window. He spat, and smiled, wiping the residue from his chin.

She turned her eyes to the passing countryside. Two swallows glided on a warm cushion of air, keeping pace with them. She wondered why she had remained so calm and in control of her senses; could it be that, instead of going further away from Gino, she was now moving closer to him? She felt some trepidation, as well as a certain amount of guilt about her mother. There was an increased presence of German troops as they got closer to the village.

'Why so many?' she asked.

'A German general has been captured by the Partisans in the hills.'

Sofia saw Mason in her mind, sitting with his paper resting on his knees, the pencil distributing lines over a white sheet of paper.

'They want him back and quickly, as they should have moved by now towards the Arno.'

He spoke as he lit up another cigarette, while Sofia tried to remember what she had been doing the day before Mason came.

'And you?' she asked.

'Me?'

'The rest of the Fascists.'

'Yes, we will drop back. What is left for us here? Most have already gone north to join the new Italian Republican Army.' He placed his elbow back into the sunlight. 'The Partisans have made a mistake.'

'Mistake?'

'Yes … the bastards attack us and the Germans do nothing; one of theirs go missing and all hell breaks loose.'

'And this general … they will give him back?'

The man breathed in a cloud of smoke and looked at Sofia.

'Who knows?' He looked away as the breeze took the ash from his cigarette. 'Who knows,' he whispered under his breath. 'Me, I am going to take my wife and daughter and run.'

Sofia said nothing and looked out onto the village, which was unusually empty today, except for the many German uniforms. Some of the soldiers turned their heads to watch their vehicle, but showed little interest. Ghosts, Sofia thought, they reminded her of faces in a nightmare. Their car drew up alongside the small church, bringing back memories of Fino and Christmas Eve, of Anna, of her jealousy. How stupid and childish she had once been.

'Out.'

Sofia was roused from her thoughts. Outside, orders were being screamed, and the sound of boots crushing the gravel filled the air. She blinked as the sun dazzled her eyes and its warmth embraced her skin.

'I don't think you're going to need that.' The man pointed to the coat draped across her arms.

'At night.'

'Please yourself,' he mumbled, then asked her to follow him.

She looked around and wondered where Gino was being kept – or had he already been taken? The interpreter felt that he could have been moved by now, but instinct told her he was still here. She followed the man from the church to the old Carabinieri building, each step seeming to bring her closer to her destiny.

The man pushed open the first door they came to. Mussolini hung on the wall opposite, his bull-shaped head and piercing eyes stared back at her. The same wall had a closed door, and there was a single desk with dead flowers in a chipped vase; everything else had been taken: pictures, files, phones and paperwork. Sofia heard the door open behind her and she turned to see the smiling face of Carlo Sergi.

~ ~ ~ ~

Cool moisture touched her lips and she swallowed until she had to spit out the last mouthful.

'Slowly … slowly …' Roberto's voice sounded distant. A hand helped her to sit upright. She heard a door open and the sound of footsteps moving with urgency, before sunlight rushed inside the car, illuminating her legs and arms.

'Swing your legs out.'

She did as he asked and sat with her feet planted firmly on the ground.

'You fainted.' He forced a smile. 'But we are well away from them now.' He looked back in the direction they had come.

At first Isolina felt relief, but then came the realisation of where they had left Sofia.

'Let me stand.'

Roberto held onto her arm.

'Are you all right?' he asked.

'I am fine.'

She began to walk forward breathing deeply, removing her arm from his grip. Isolina desperately needed to clear her head, but knew panic would follow. She looked around her, trying to determine her location.

'I need you to take me somewhere.' She spoke without looking at him.

'To the Swedish woman?'

'No ... somewhere else.'

Now his face had a troubled look to it.

'I am the enemy, Isolina. I have taken a chance bringing you this far. I will take you to the farm, but there I must leave you. I am risking my life by being here ... You of all people should know that.'

'But all those things you have witnessed, Roberto, what they are doing to our people – surely you cannot go back to them ... The war is lost, Roberto. Change sides now while you can.'

'Change sides.' He stared at her. 'I could not change sides even if I wanted to. It is like a tattoo and everyone in

Italy carries a mark … We will be hunted down and …' He stopped.

'Roberto, you make it sound as if we are at war with our own people.'

'A civil war, you mean?'

'Yes.'

'It started the day we signed the armistice. Open your eyes: Italians are killing Italians across Italy; a hundred Fascists were machine-gunned down near Naples; in another place, I saw fifty hanged by the roadside … It is not just the Germans who want their pound of flesh, so does the rest of Italy. They want to wipe out anything and everyone who supported Mussolini.'

Isolina stared at him, feeling numb.

'You make it sound like all I need to do is change my clothes.' His smile was filled with fear and sadness. 'I have to live with my crime.'

'Crime?'

'Working for the Germans … being a Fascist.'

'Surely you were forced?'

He almost laughed out loud. 'Forced? No. I volunteered. I am a coward, Isolina. I thought it would be better than fighting, shooting a gun, marching, digging trenches; this way I got to drive with the generals, drink good brandy, sleep in comfortable beds … That's what cowards do, they take the easy route. Back then, I was on the side that was invincible, all this was going to last a thousand years … but now that has all changed. From those doing the hunting, we have become the hunted.'

'Roberto, you are a good man.' She touched his arm gently. 'If that was not so, I would not be here now. But I have to think of my daughter, and I must do everything to get her back. I am sorry this places you in danger, but I can talk to them about you.'

Roberto looked at the attractive woman before him. How naïve she was, he thought.

'My daughter's life means more to me than –'

'Mine?' He cut her off.

Isolina looked up suddenly. Beyond the dip where the land rose to meet the road, there were five or maybe six of them. They moved spread-out in a line, each holding a rifle. Roberto had followed her gaze. Seconds later he was sprinting to the car.

'Get down,' one of the men shouted.

'No, wait,' she screamed, holding her hands up.

'Down,' another shouted.

Isolina looked back towards the car, where Roberto was grabbing a rifle. 'Do as they say, Isolina,' he said, staring at her.

'No, Roberto ... no.'

'Your daughter needs you ... get down.'

'No, Roberto ... stop!'

He did not use the car as cover. Instead, he went down on one knee, hoisting the rifle to his shoulder before firing. Four shots came in reply. Roberto fell onto his side, the rifle slipping from his grip. He was still alive when blood began to stain his shirt and trousers. He tried to move his left arm in a futile attempt to reach his weapon.

Calmly, Isolina got to her feet and walked to where Roberto lay. His fingers continued to stretch for the rifle, and blood stained his lips. Isolina looked at his stomach, where blood escaped from two holes in his shirt. There was no way back for him, so she knelt down and gripped his hand.

'Roberto,' she whispered. 'Why? Why did you do that? Why did you not stay beside me?'

He struggled to speak, breathless and in pain. She moved her ear closer to his mouth in an attempt to hear him. Roberto's eyes looked beyond her, to what created the shadow that covered them. Isolina looked up to where a man stood pointing a pistol at the dying man.

'No,' she roared.

The man ignored her and fired a single shot into Roberto's forehead. He lay motionless, his eyes staring into the cloudless sky. Isolina tenderly closed them, resting her hands there for a few seconds longer.

'Why did you have to do that? He was almost dead.' She did not look up; the shadow told her his assassin was still there.

'Then what is the problem? I put him out of his misery like I would a dog or any other animal.'

'But he was not an animal.'

'He was a Fascist pig ... which makes him as good as.' The shadow moved and Roberto's blood glistened in the sun. 'So, get up and be thankful we were here.'

'Thankful ... Thankful for what? I'm not thankful to any of you: Partisan, British, German or Fascist.' She looked back down at Roberto's face. 'You all seem to forget who you are, who you were before all this began. Life means nothing to any of you anymore; he is a Fascist so you shoot him. But you forgot he was an Italian first.' She stood and looked into the man's eyes for the first time. But this was no man: more a boy, perhaps twenty at most. Across his chest was a strap filled with bullets, while over his shoulder hung a rifle. He replaced the pistol into his waistband.

'Taking a life is nothing to you.'

'I do what I do to stay alive.' He took a cigarette from behind his ear and lit it. 'Have a look in the car boot, see what's in there.' He spoke to the men with him.

'Will you bury him?'

The boy began to laugh. 'Bury him? No, I will not bury him … If you want to, go ahead.' He then spat on Roberto's shirt. 'He is a piece of shit as far as I am concerned. I have no father or sister because of him.'

'Him?'

'Not him, but the Fascists – we should kill them all.'

Isolina remembered what Roberto had said about civil war and knew how right he was: it had begun already, fuelled by the youth of Italy. Everywhere was hate. It lived in people's eyes and their hearts; it ate away at them. He was a Fascist, but not by choice, by circumstance, simply to stay alive.

The boy began to walk away.

'Could you take me to Silvano?'

He stopped and slowly turned around. 'Now I remember you. I knew I had seen you before … Yes.' Smoke escaped through his nose. 'Explain to me, if you can … Are you his mistress or the Englishman's?' He burst out laughing, and two others joined him.

Isolina felt her face flush. She looked towards the hills, wishing she was away from this madness.

'Well? Can you?'

'Yes.' He nodded. 'But you better bury him quick, your friend there, because we will be gone in two minutes.'

'I cannot bury him in that time.'

'Then get inside the car now.' He threw the finished cigarette to the floor and walked towards the car.

Isolina looked down at Roberto. She placed his hands together across his chest, closed her eyes, and said a few words, crossing herself at the end. They watched her from the car with blank expressions. There was no compassion in their faces: these were the faces of war and it left no room for sympathy, for understanding, mercy or tolerance.

One last look at Roberto, the seller of books, with a wife, now a widow, in Milan … She was glad he had never spoken of children.

'Well?' the boy shouted. 'We have not got all day … get a move on.'

Isolina walked to the car. Overhead, she heard the sound of planes and looked up to see more death and destruction on its way.

CHAPTER TWENTY-SEVEN

Fino and Sassa looked up at that same moment; they had heard the gentle humming of planes before they saw them. They had been walking for almost an hour since stopping at Giosue's farm, mostly in complete silence, when they felt the first explosions: the ground beneath their feet winced in pain, and they witnessed smoke rising, five or six kilometres away.

'Get everyone off the road,' Fino shouted.

'The mines,' Sassa responded.

'Let's take our chances … It's better than staying out here in the open.'

The children and adults moved into the ditches either side of the road. The first bomb to fall caused panic amongst the children; some screamed in terror, while others tried to stand. Fear had unnerved them, so some of the adults began to pray with them, their words mere whispers on the light breeze.

Amongst the explosions, another sound could be heard. From around the bend came a German convoy of half a dozen trucks. Their occupants, German boy soldiers, looked just as scared as those in the ditches. An officer in the lead staff car got to his feet.

'What the hell are you people doing out here?' He spoke in broken Italian.

Sassa left the ditch where she had been lying. 'We have had to move because of the shelling; our house has one of your divisions stationed there.'

The officer shook his head, nothing shocked him anymore. 'And they think it is safer out here?' His words seemed meant more for himself than the woman in front of him.

'We have laid mines back there.' He pointed. 'In the fields either side, and some close to the roadside. The trail stretches back six kilometres. For Christ's sake, stay on the road.' He shook his head. 'Crazy.' Then he signalled to his driver to continue. 'Good luck,' he said, glancing back.

Four American planes flew over at that moment. Two broke away and came in low but held their fire; instead they dipped a wing and turned away.

Fino took hold of the pram. 'Quick, let's get out of here now.'

The last lorry had passed and the planes had not returned. It must have been a good ten minutes before they heard more explosions. Sassa turned and looked in the direction the convoy had taken, and saw smoke rising. She could not help but feel sorry for the officer and his men. The sky was filled with planes filled like swallows on a summer evening. The war continued back there; here, there was just silence, with only the sound of shoes scraping on the ground and the odd whimper from one of the younger children. War had its own strange silence, which was sometimes more threatening than the sound of battle itself.

It was reaching the hottest part of the day. The distant sound of bombing had finally ceased, leaving only the sight of smoke climbing steadily into a clear blue sky. They walked in single file as the road twisted around another tight bend. Suddenly, they came to a halt. Fino walked to the front to investigate. Naldo and Amedeo stood staring ahead to where a German troop carrier lay on its side, blocking the road. Black smoke still rose from the burnt-out vehicle, and Fino could see several bodies lying in the road.

'Let's take a look,' he said, walking forward.

They could feel the heat, and a putrid smell filled their nostrils. As they drew closer, so came the sudden realisation of what it was: burning flesh. Naldo turned away and vomited, while Amedeo pulled him out of view of the children.

'We cannot let them see this,' Amedeo said, rubbing the young man's back.

'We can't go back.'

'I know.'

Fino's eyes settled on the face of a blonde boy, no more than eighteen, his blue eyes open. A life ended far away from home, like so many, the enemy. Fino looked again at the bloodstained uniform – not *his* enemy, just someone's son, who would lie here rotting before being slung into a hole. He felt guilty that no one had the time to bury the dead, not even him; everyone was too busy trying to stay alive.

They removed those in the road and concealed them. Then they moved the children through quickly. Sassa made them sing, forcing the adults to join in. This seemingly merry band of travellers smiled, sung and laughed, while only metres away, young men and boys lay dead.

~ ~ ~ ~

Silvano felt the stubble scrape the palm of his hand. He could smell his own foul body odour, and it made him feel sick. He could not remember the last time he had washed with soap; his only way of keeping clean was to dive into a stream. One scent remained with him: Isolina's. He drew on his cigarette and allowed the smoke to drift from his nostrils as he saw her lying naked with her black curls unfurled across a crisp white pillow. She was beautiful, young, her skin smooth – his fingertips retained the memory of their touch. He smiled. She had asked him to make love to her.

The memory made him tremble. The past was as painful as the present. That was fifteen years ago, on a damp, cold day. A solid crust of grey sky hung over the city, and he remembered entering the room, tipping the maid and closing the door. They stood staring at each other for a full minute, both waiting for the other to do or say something.

Finally, he had walked across and closed the green wooden shutters, and then lit the candles on the table before distributing them around the room. For some reason, he kept his eyes from her. Satisfied, he stopped and took a deep breath; nothing existed outside this room; no friends, no family – only the two of them.

He had undressed her slowly, gradually revealing what had been forbidden. His fingers became clumsy, but she remained staring into his face. He kissed her neck whilst removing her dress, allowing it to fall gently to the floor around her feet. He remembered the breath being forced from his lungs as his eyes fell on her nakedness. They made love three times that afternoon; darkness filled the night sky when they finally lay exhausted in each other's arms. He had felt a responsibility towards her that day, an accountability for his actions. And now he felt the same for those down in the village.

The sun penetrated the trees, forming strange elongated shadows on the grass. He hardly knew anyone in the village, for Fino and Sassa were his only contacts outside these hills. He let those familiar with it go and gather the information, except, he now held their life in his hands. The responsibility hit him like a bullet from a gun and he dropped to one knee. He did not need this responsibility; he was a simple architect, he wanted it passed onto someone else … Mason. Yes, Mason could take it.

Thinking about the past had been a distraction, a smokescreen, a means of ignoring the reality of the situation now. His people waited for him, ready to hang on to his every word. But he had no plans, no orders to give. He could think of nothing that would save the lives of those in the village. He knew that releasing the general would not bring an end to this: the Germans would never demonstrate any show of weakness, and the Italian people would need reminding who was in charge.

Thinking about Isolina became a distraction, a cowardly escape from the decision he needed to make. He walked out into the sunlight and felt the heat burn his skin. He looked down into the valley below and saw his imaginary villa, pictured Isolina with their four beautiful children and heard them calling his name. He opened his eyes and saw the mountains in the distance, the hills in the foreground and the movement of a bird above. Nothing had changed, he was still here with the same responsibility, the same choices, and the same overwhelming feeling of desperation.

He reached for another cigarette and felt the acid burn his throat. He lit it, and cursed himself for not bringing water with him. Isolina was real, but the villa was a dream, and dreams would do nothing for those poor bastards down in the village. The weakness in his legs quickly spread throughout his body. He tried to clear his mind of all other thoughts, while his mouth became dryer. He had come up here to make a decision. It was his duty.

He began the walk back down the hillside. He had made up his mind. Except, his thoughts returned yet again to Isolina, and how hard it must have been for her to tell him about Fausto and the wedding. He remembered going crazy, and her calming him. After, they had made plans to go to Rome together, to marry there. They parted speaking of love, making promises that only lovers made, dreaming of that villa. They needed to wait only three days and all this would come to them.

He stopped and placed a hand on the nearest tree. She had lied – why? He had waited on the platform as planned, right up until the last moment, when the train began to pull away. He had jumped on board at the last second and his eyes had searched for her, but she had not come. He had slammed the door shut and cursed her, God forgive him, his anger got the better of him. How foolish he had been back then.

He began to walk back through the trees with more intent. He would not barter this German general. Instead, he would hand him over to the British and that would be that.

~ ~ ~ ~

'Would you like a drink … some wine maybe?' Carlo walked around the desk and sat in the leather chair. He opened a drawer and removed a bottle and two glasses before slamming it shut. Looking up, he poured brandy into both. 'Sit.' It sounded like an order. He stared at her while swallowing a large mouthful of spirit. 'Uhh, the Carabinieri had good taste in drink if nothing else.' He refilled his glass and emptied it in one swallow.

'Your mother has gone to that Swedish bitch ... or maybe to the English spy who's been fucking her.' He sat back in the chair waiting for a reaction.

Sofia just returned his stare. He was drunk, and that frightened her. She had not thought any of this out – only that she needed to find Gino.

'Did you remain in your room, Sofia, while he took her? Did you want to have a peek?' He swallowed another mouthful and topped the glass up again. 'Maybe you thought about joining them. I'm certain your mother would have let you.' He laughed.

She would not let her anger show, not if she was to find Gino. When he got drunk, Carlo became hateful, vicious and more vulgar.

'Silent today.' Carlo rose from the chair. 'Have you been struck dumb, Sofia? Or ...' He stopped and picked up the glass, sweat forming on his forehead.

'I know now ... It's the boy ... What's his name?' He laughed again. 'No, Sofia, surely not him ... he's just a boy, thirteen, fourteen ...' He slumped back into his chair, a grin firmly fixed to his lips.

The door opened behind him and a young man walked into the room holding a box. His eyes gazed at Sofia before turning to Carlo.

'I've come to clear –'

'Fuck off.'

'But I have been told …'

Carlo reached into the drawer and pulled out a gun.

Pointing it at the boy, he spoke. 'I said fuck off … did you not hear me?'

The boy's face drained of colour. 'Yes, I am sorry. I will not disturb you again, I'm sorry.'

Sofia watched, wondering how she had once held his hand, this pig.

'So, where were we?' His eyes went to her coat. 'A coat in this weather, are you crazy?'

'For night-time.'

'It's damn hot then as well … Oh well.' He lit a cigarette and blew out the smoke. 'Was he good, Sofia? Was he gentle? Or was he rough with you?' The grin remained as he spoke. 'So, have you come to say goodbye?'

Sofia did not react. Outside a car horn sounded and both looked up; she saw annoyance in his face for the first time.

'We wanted to shoot one and send the other to Germany … They decided on Luca, never lucky, that boy.' He now studied Sofia more closely. 'I have the final say,' he poked his chest, 'and I could, if I wanted, change it around.' He took another mouthful of brandy.

'I'm bad with names.' He drew in a mouthful of smoke. 'Well, anyway, they said: *if that's all right with you, Carlo.*'

Carlo had lost weight, Sofia thought. His face was drawn and pale, his eyes looked deprived of sleep and he seemed constantly agitated.

'I just might change my mind and have him shot.'

'No!' Sofia's reaction was instant and it brought a smile to his lips.

'No? … Is that all? … Just a NO?'

'Send him to Germany if you must.'

'What difference will that make, he will die whatever I decide. Only, one means he suffers longer.'

She clenched her jaw and felt her breathing become shallow; the room whirled. Not now, she said to herself, please don't let me faint.

'So, what are you prepared to do to save him, Sofia? Let us say, I could do with him what I wanted, send him to Germany or to his death here … Or maybe …' He smiled at his little joke. 'Tell me, how far you would go to save this … this …'

'Gino.'

'Uhh, now I remember, thank you. Yes, the boy, Gino … how far will you go to keep him alive.'

He stood and walked around the desk, stopping in front of her.

'I will ask you again: what would you do to save him?'

'Anything,' she whispered.

'Anything?'

'Yes.'

He pulled her closer, and now she smelt the brandy on his breath. He brought his hand to her chin and lifted it.

'*Anything*?' he whispered.

'Where is he?'

'Close.'

'How do I know you're telling me the truth? You might have sent him away already.'

'You'll have to trust me.'

She shook her head. 'Not good enough.'

The force of his open hand took her by surprise. She stumbled but managed to remain on her feet. Her coat dropped to the floor and she steadied herself, her tongue tasting the blood on her lip.

He stood with a look of regret on his face, but she was certain he regretted nothing. He picked up his brandy and emptied the glass in one, and then, lifting a finger to her lips, making her flinch, he smeared blood across her cheek. He seemed to find this exciting. His hand continued down her neck, stopping as it reached her top button. He undid it. She remembered Mason doing the same thing. Carlo opened her blouse to unmask her breasts. He began to slip the blouse over her shoulders.

'No! I want to know where he is,' she whispered.

'And I want a deposit.'

'No,' she pushed him away. 'No more ... I want to see Gino.'

'I could just take you here and now,' Carlo spoke angrily.

'But that's not what you want, Carlo, is it. You want me to want you back. You want to hear me moan.' She leant forward and kissed his lips. 'That's what you want, all of me, not just a part.'

'Yes,' he moaned, 'yes, all of you ... every bit, every single piece of you.'

He stood up and refilled his glass. 'I will take you to him, will that do?'

'I want to see him leave.'

'You want what!'

He became angry again. 'I will not play games with you, Sofia ... Or I will put you with the rest.'

'The rest?'

'Nothing.' He emptied the glass. 'Wait here, I will be back soon.'

Sofia began to button up her blouse, pleased with how strong she had been in his presence. But seconds later, she broke down and wept.

~ ~ ~ ~

Mason shielded his eyes from the sun. It was high up, meaning the day was more than halfway through, and they were closer to the German ultimatum. Silvano had been gone some time now, but he understood the reason why. He had amused himself by drawing Ambra naked; he smiled, thinking of Enzo and their little scrap not so long ago. A rustle came from the bushes behind him; Ambra, opposite him, rose with a smile on her face and Mason assumed her leader was back. He remained sitting, flicking through the pages of his notepad.

'When are your people coming?' Silvano asked.

Mason looked up. 'Tomorrow.'

The big Italian ran water around his mouth before spitting it out. 'Okay.'

'Do I take it you have reached a decision?' Mason closed the notepad.

'Yes, but I do not intend to stand back and do nothing.'

'So, what *do* you intend on doing?'

'I'm not sure … Maybe …' He stopped.

Mason looked away, unable to watch him struggle with his conscience. It was too painful; he understood the reasons, because he, too, had been there.

'Let me go into the village,' said Ambra.

'What will that achieve?' Mason retorted, not looking up.

'It is better than sitting here doing nothing.'

Mason drew on his cigarette. 'They outnumber us ten to one. They have tanks, we have two beat-up cars. They also have machine guns, and not these.' He held up his battered rifle.

'Why have you not got us better weapons, machine guns like they have? Why have they left us unsupported?'

Mason stood. 'First, we invaded France and we needed all the weapons we could lay our hands on. No good running onto a beach with only your dick in your hand.' He stubbed out the remains of a cigarette. 'Second, you lot haven't worked out what fucking side you're on. One minute you're fighting with the Germans, the next you want weapons to kill them. And third …'

'What is it you say?'

'Enzo, remember him? The traitor. For a couple of bob, he nearly got all of us killed.'

'We are not all like Enzo.'

'Really.'

Ambra rushed at Mason. Silvano caught her around the waist and tried to contain her.

'Not now, Ambra, not now,' he shouted.

Mason turned his back and walked away. He sat down and removed a bottle of wine from his bag. Ambra straightened her shirt, ran her fingers through her short hair and walked away to sit alone, her back turned to Mason.

'Look, Silvano, if you can think of something, then fine, I'm willing to help, but the odds are against us. All I ask is that you don't get us all killed on a whim.'

Silvano remained deep in thought.

Isolina walked behind the young man as they entered the camp.

'She wanted to see you,' he said, looking at Silvano. 'We also have some new transport, courtesy of the Germans.' He smiled, but found himself surrounded by solemn faces.

Mason's eyes widened at the sight of her, while Ambra, on seeing his reaction, spat on the ground.

'I needed to see you.' Isolina looked at Silvano.

She wanted to raise Roberto's treatment, but right now that seemed insignificant, considering the reason she was here.

'At the checkpoint … they took Sofia.'

'Where were you going?'

'Sassa's.'

'They left early this morning, all you would have found was a German garrison there.'

'Oh.' Isolina bit her bottom lip. 'They have taken her back to the village for some reason. Roberto said something about a general you have captured.'

Mason caught Silvano's eye and Isolina suddenly felt troubled.

'What's happening? Tell me.'

'It's simple, Isolina.' Mason relished saying her name, it felt good, almost as good as looking into that beautiful face. 'We have their general … and they want him back.' Sunlight came crashing through the treetops, splintering into a thousand golden shafts of light, one of which lit up Isolina's face. Mason cursed, unable to capture the moment.

'What has that to do with the village?'

'If they don't get him back before this evening …' Mason stood and walked across to the water. 'Best you tell her the rest, Silvano.' He filled a metal cup and drank, glad it was not him having to explain the situation.

Isolina gave Mason an inquisitive look. Mason, in turn, stared back at Silvano. 'Is anyone going to tell me what is going on?' she demanded.

It was Ambra who spoke, with a trace of a smile on her lips. Mason spat out a mouthful of water. Ambra glanced at him before looking at Isolina. 'They will begin to shoot five people from the village every half hour if he is not returned by three o'clock.'

Isolina looked at Silvano as the colour drained from her face. 'You will not let this happen, surely?'

'We are at war.' Ambra, again, spoke before anyone else.

'Ambra,' Silvano said sharply.

'It is how it is, Silvano,' Ambra began. 'People like her get us to do all the dirty work … It is we who take all the risks, who live in this filth …' She walked up to Isolina and stood eye to eye. 'Did you sleep in your own bed last night?' She waited for an answer, and smiled. 'I lay on the floor here, pissed this morning in the woods, had a piece of bread for my breakfast – I am certain you had a nice coffee.'

'Ambra, enough.' Silvano walked over to where they stood, but she ignored him.

'There is a whole village down there. Are you suggesting we save your daughter and just forget about the rest?'

'No … no … I did not say that.'

'Then what is it you're asking?'

'I want …' Isolina's words suddenly dried up.

'Don't you think Silvano has thought about this? We all want to save those in the village, but it is beyond us.'

'But you can't let them just …' She turned to Silvano, who stood running his hand through his hair. 'You're not going to do anything, are you?'

Mason saw what Ambra's words had done. 'Leave it, Ambra. Shut your mouth.' He walked across to her. 'Come on, Ambra, the people on this mountain are here for many different reasons, not just the reason you're here. Let's face it: how many vendettas have taken place that were nothing to do with the Germans or Fascists?' He laughed out loud. 'Communist Italians kill Socialist Italians – those people down there are paying the price for us, not her,' he pointed towards Isolina. 'We took their general, we have him here; if anyone dies in that village, then all of us will have blood on our hands, not her.' He walked away and sat cross-legged, took out his book and pencil and began to sketch.

Silence took centre stage. Mason's words needed digestion. A bird cried out high up on a branch and, except for several thin vapours of white, the sky remained clear.

Isolina turned to Silvano. 'Can we go somewhere?'

Silvano nodded and walked towards a group of tall trees.

'This general, he is very important ... yes?'

Silvano remained silent, needing to choose his words well.

'What is it like to hold so many people's lives in your hands?' She spoke without looking at him. 'How many of those in that village do you know personally?' They had gone a good distance from the others now. 'I know each one. I've laughed and cried with them, embraced and kissed them ... it makes a difference.'

'Does it?' Silvano whispered. 'Some of the people with me are like you, they have family there, mothers and fathers, aunts and uncles, and yet none have come to me and asked me to hand the general over ... They know why.'

'Do they?'

'What?'

'Is it not just a sense of duty. They have respect for you, I can see that. I see it in their eyes and in how they become silent when you speak. You captivate them like you did me.'

He smiled. 'And just when did I do that?'

'The first time I set eyes on you.'

'Really?'

'Yes.'

Both became silent. Images flashed through their heads, memories, fragments of a life, tiny pieces lost, never to be recovered.

'Is there nothing you can do to help those in the village?'

'Don't you think I would? I know how hard this must be for you, especially now with your daughter being there. I am truly sorry, but as the Englishman said, I have many here who have friends and family down there. I can only guess how you must be feeling.'

'Only guess? What if you had someone there, one of your family – would that change how you think?'

He took a deep breath. 'I try to think like that, so I can understand … But it is difficult … I'm sorry if that does not answer your question.'

Isolina leant against a tree and wiped away several tears. Silvano felt helpless, wanting to go and comfort her, knowing he had the power to relieve her pain.

'Isolina.'

She shook her head and turned away, unable to speak.

'Isolina.' There was pleading in his voice. She remained silent. He finally walked across to her, lifted his hand to her cheek and gently wiped the tears away. He stared into her moist, sorrowful eyes; it was as if nothing had changed, except it had.

'Silvano,' Isolina whispered.

He lowered his head towards her lips.

'No.' She pulled away.

Silvano closed his eyes and felt foolish; what made him behave so stupidly? Her daughter in danger, and here he was attempting to seduce her.

'I'm sorry, that was wrong of me, Isolina, forgive me.'

She looked up and saw a man drained of energy, exhausted, the sparkle in his eyes gone. And now she was about to add to his anxieties – in fact she was about to deliver the decisive blow. Guilt consumed her.

'Silvano.'

He looked up. 'Yes?'

'I need to tell you something.'

'Very well ...'

'Sofia ...' She stopped and caught her breath.

'Your daughter.'

'Yes ... But she is also your daughter.'

CHAPTER TWENTY-EIGHT

Father Mariano sat behind the oak desk inside his office. The church was filled with people, his people. He took a mouthful of brandy, the only spirit he could face at this moment in time; the burning sensation his atonement. He clasped his hands together, fell to his knees and looked up into the eyes of Christ.

'Dear Father, please send an army of angels to stop this madness. Send the rains like you did with Noah and drown the evil that walks this earth. Give me, your obedient servant, the strength to stand up and fight this wickedness.' The realisation that he had been part of this sin had finally dawned on him. Just like for Peter, the cock had cried a third time.

He stood, needing to somehow make this right. The Englishman's words had felt like a thousand lashes that had cut deep into his flesh. He filled his empty glass with brandy and stared up at the wall to see the blood dripping from Christ's crown of thorns; like his master, he needed to find inner strength. He took a deep breath before stepping into the corridor.

'Father.' It was Alfonso the shopkeeper who had called him. 'What is happening?'

He shook his head but said nothing as he continued towards the back door.

'Father,' another man shouted.

'Father,' a woman called.

The priest felt what little strength he had amassed when inside his room, melt away. His forehead became moist with sweat, his undergarments stuck to his skin. He wanted to turn and face those voices, and he almost did, but seconds later, he stood outside in the sun. He stared at a young German soldier and, as he walked away, he heard the sound of laughter coming from behind him.

He found Vito Sergi directing the loading of a lorry.

'Vito,' he shouted as he walked towards the man.

'Father.' No eye contact was made. 'I'm a little busy.'

'Why has everyone been assembled inside my church?' the priest asked.

'Maybe they are waiting for you to give them a sermon.'

Again, the sound of laughter came from all around him. It seemed he had the ability to make everyone laugh today, Italian or German.

'I need to know what is going to happen to them. You led me to believe that this was a mere threat.'

Vito Sergi now looked at the priest. 'Your conscience getting the better of you?'

'I demand an answer.'

Sergi stood motionless for a moment, before walking the five metres to where the priest stood. He looked into his eyes, and the beginnings of a smile formed on Vito's lips. Seconds later, he smashed his fist into the priest's jaw, sending him to the floor.

'Never speak to me like that again, priest.'

Father Mariano lifted himself onto one arm, smearing blood across his chin and cheek with his hand. The bitter taste of blood settled on his tongue. Vito had walked away by the time he got to his feet.

'What is happening, Vito?' The priest felt the hot sun burn his exposed scalp.

'We are moving north ... you know that.'

'I'm not talking about us, Vito.'

Vito Sergi smiled and turned to face what he considered to be a weak man, one he despised. 'The Germans are waiting for their general, and when they have him, we are all moving towards Florence and the Arno.'

'And they are guaranteed this general?'

'I think the Partisans will give in sooner or later.'

'And if they do not?'

'Then when you next say mass, the congregation might be a little thin on the ground.'

Father Mariano felt the anger rise in him. 'You will allow this?'

'Was it not you who delivered the message to them?' His eyes looked towards the hills.

'I did, but ... God help me.'

'God help us all, Father.'

'He is looking down on us, Vito. He is seeing what we are doing ... the evil we are embracing here today. Let him see us save our souls. If we do this evil thing, we will never pass through the gates of paradise ...' The priest dropped to his knees and began to pray. All around, Vito's men watched him rocking gently back and forward.

'Come, Vito, join me and save yourself.' He looked all around. 'Come, all of you, pray with me, let us ask for His help ...'

No one moved except Vito Sergi, who stepped forward six paces, took out his gun and shot the priest in the forehead. He lay still, his eyes open and his head turned to one side, blood seeping from the small hole and soaking into the dirt.

'Amen,' whispered Vito, taking out his handkerchief and wiping the back of his neck.

'Father.'

Vito turned to see Carlo standing in the shadows. The boy's eyes moved from the dead priest to his father.

'What is it, Carlo?'

Carlo walked into the sunlight.

'When we go ... I want to take Sofia.'

His father studied him. 'You're drunk.' He laughed. 'When you say *take* ... you mean ...'

'I mean take.'

The smile left Vito's face. 'I've just shot a priest, boy ... do not make me shoot my own son. That greedy bastard Enzo is waiting for me to pay him the rest of his money because you let him play with you ... You're weak, Carlo, always were ... No: you go back to her and *take* her before we go, then throw her into the church with the rest. When the Germans move, so do we ... understand?' He stared at his son for several seconds before walking away.

Carlo looked down at the corpse and felt sickness rise into his throat. He belched and tasted the bile mixed with the brandy. Sweat ran down his face and soaked into his clothes, and he smelt its rancid odour. It was all changing: the Allies were just on the other side of the hills, and it was almost time to become the hunted. He laughed out loud, making several heads look his way. His father was right, he would take his pleasure with Sofia, then get the hell out.

~ ~ ~ ~

'When? How?' Silvano found it hard to think straight. He walked up to the nearest tree and rested his head against the bark. Isolina watched his pain and felt a deep sense of guilt. 'Why did you not tell me?'

'I wanted to.'

'You had so many chances.' He took out a cigarette. 'How do I know you have not made this up to save your daughter?'

Isolina walked up to him and slapped his face.

'You doubt me? You think I could do such a thing?' She shook her head. 'I loved you, Silvano ... I would never, never do such a thing to you.'

'I'm sorry.' Silvano stared at her, wanting to say more but saying nothing.

'It must have happened that first time, the time I told you about Fausto ... when you went crazy ... remember?'

Silvano nodded.

'I know what you would think ... could the child be his?' She smiled. 'No, I thought that also, but at the time I was working for a doctor named Simon Stein.' She saw Simon's face for a second. 'He was treating Fausto, for what I cannot remember, but he told me one thing: Fausto could not have children.'

'But you stayed.'

'Simon saw the marks of our marriage, on my arms, my neck and my wrists.'

'He hit you?'

'From the day I returned ... When I told him I was getting my things to leave, he hit me and never stopped.'

'But –'

'I came searching for you later with the intention of telling you. Sofia was older and I wanted to start again, explain everything; I even imagined how you would react. The three of us would all be together.'

'But you said nothing.'

'You began to talk about Nicia … On and on you went, how you met in Rome and were to be married … I was angry. It had been seven years and when I saw you all those feelings came back … Not that they had ever truly gone … And listening to you speak about Nicia, I knew you had moved on.'

'But you were wrong.'

'Was I?'

'Yes … It was you who had got married, not me. You had moved on with your life and I was left hurt. I, too, was angry … I loved you.' He reached up and touched her neck. 'I never stopped loving you, not a day passed when I did not think of you.'

'While you were lying next to her?'

She hit out blindly.

'And you next to Fausto?' It was a petty retaliation that he regretted instantly. 'Sorry.'

She stood silent for a moment. He reached out and pulled her into his chest and held her there. For the first time, he had felt her come willingly.

'I have a beautiful daughter,' he whispered, his chin balanced upon her head. 'She is so like her mother …'

'Why are you not angry, Silvano?'

'Do you want me to be?'

'Yes.'

'Why?'

'To make me feel better.'

'Too much time has been lost to waste more on anger.'

'She has your eyes, your smile,' Isolina replied.

Mason approached. 'Sorry to interrupt this grand reunion, but I think you need to address what is happening, now.'

Silvano moved Isolina from his chest. He was not angry with Mason. In fact, for some strange reason, he felt no anger towards him at all.

'Sofia is Silvano's daughter,' Isolina said without thinking, as if it was right that the Englishman should be the first to know.

'Surprise, surprise ... Today is full of them, so it seems. Congratulations are in order.' Mason looked up towards the sky. 'I suppose that changes things.'

~ ~ ~ ~

Vincenzo gripped the rifle and squeezed himself behind a concrete pillar. He stifled a cry as the corner of a wooden box dug into his kidney. He listened as they helped themselves to what was left in Alfonso's shop. Now, they were pulling the racks apart in the main shop. The storeroom had no window, which was just as well. He had removed the lightbulb, checking that there were no more to replace it; only the brown cord now hung from the cracked ceiling. Paper and cloth was about all that was left in here; empty boxes lay across the floor, powdered milk and oil – nothing that would interest a retreating German soldier.

They spoke in that harsh tongue, laughing and whistling without a care in the world. He had done that himself with his brothers when working in the fields or house. He pictured his home bathed in sunshine, closed his eyes and saw the mountains rising up behind the hillside. His mother stepping into the sunshine, calling for her boys to come in for lunch. An uneasy smile formed on Vincenzo's lips, and faded just as quickly. The image in his head altered: he now saw her staggering blindly through the ruins of their home, her clothes soaked in blood.

Something heavy fell to the floor, shaking Vincenzo back to the present. Surely there was nothing left to take now. The door handle began to turn and his heart beat with increasing velocity. He tightened his grip on the rifle and wondered if this was a poor choice of hiding place. The door opened and a soldier stood in the doorway.

He spoke while lighting up his cigarette. He tried the light switch several times before realising that there was no bulb. Vincenzo dug his boots into the soft wooden floor and eased himself further back, except the wall became an unmovable force: he was back as far as he could go. The smell of tobacco filled the room and he thought of Lucia at that moment, smelt her fragrance, heard her breathing. His chest became tight and moisture filled his eyes. His arms would remain empty for the rest of his life, without a wife or child to fill them.

His confidence grew in his mission to avenge Lucia and his unborn child. He would also seek justice for the death of his mother, and his brother Dario. All those hours spent in the fields, the sweat, the pain – what was it all for? Lucia had made it all worthwhile – sitting in each other's arms, looking ahead and planning their lives. As much as he grieved for his mother and brother, the passing of Lucia had devastated him; a light had been extinguished.

Hate drove him now and it all centred on one man: Vito Sergi. He would look him in the eye before placing a bullet in his brain. So what if they came, what did he care? His life was over, they could not kill him, because, in a way, he was already dead.

He suddenly realised the shop was silent. He had become lost in the thoughts that imprisoned him night and day. He kept clear of people and refused to speak with his father, who lived with his own grief. He knew his father blamed him for what had happened – he felt they all did. They might not say it, but he knew.

He eased himself out and felt his muscles and joints ache. He saw Lucia standing at the other end of the room, smiling as always. He would remain a little longer; he closed his eyes. Mother had called them for supper; Dario sat and smiled at Cristina, who bounced baby Paolo on her knee. His father clipped Fabrizio around the ear for making some silly remark, and Mimi laughed. His mother looked down at them all with a contented smile on her face, until her stare met his. She nodded and he smiled; this was how life was supposed to be. The storeroom filled with the sound of a man weeping.

~ ~ ~ ~

Lorenzo Ales felt uneasy. He looked around the interior of the church, at Christ in his many different facets. The sun then caught the stained glass windows and formed a washed-out rainbow on the tiled floor. He rubbed his eyes to clear the distortion and came face to face with Jesus. This, for some reason, filled him with unease. Surely some other positive spiritual sensation should have taken hold of him. He was in the house of God, surely he should feel protected? Instead, the church suddenly felt like a sinful place to be in.

He wiped sweat from the nape of his neck, uncertain what had caused it, the abrasive heat or fear. The garage owner, Mario Pinto, came and sat beside him. The old mechanic looked his age today, his skin wrinkled like old leather after a lifetime spent in the Tuscan sun.

'Father Remo is coming, so someone said,' Lorenzo whispered.

'More rumours, Lorenzo,' the old man smiled. 'We have had twenty years of rumours, no one tells the truth anymore. It seems to have gone out of fashion.'

Lorenzo remained silent beside him, fear eating away at him.

'Are you feeling all right?' asked Mario.

Lorenzo nodded, but he felt fatigued. The old man placed a hand on his knee.

'Don't worry,' he whispered.

Lorenzo felt tears gather as he tried to compose himself. A small child came and stood in front of him, staring.

'It's Sonia's child … Franca.'

'Uhh, so it is.'

'Where is your mother?' Lorenzo asked.

The girl pointed a tiny finger to where Sonia sat in conversation with several other women. The girl had deep blue eyes and blonde curly hair that rested on her shoulders. Mario leant across and lifted her onto his knee and began to make the sound of a horse, moving his leg up and down in rhythm. The girl smiled and both men began to hum and sing. Franca began to giggle and clap her hands, the war forgotten.

Mario stopped abruptly and stared into the child's face. He suddenly felt concerned for her future: life had not yet begun for her. He himself had drunk too much, married and embraced life to its fullest, and, although he had never left Italy, he felt he had seen the world through the many people he had met. Yet, this child had sampled none of this.

He kissed the child's head and placed her on the ground. He watched her run off towards her mother as two German soldiers appeared with a woman pushing a trolley.

'Water,' the woman shouted.

'What do you think will happen?' A woman sat holding a child, facing Lorenzo and Mario.

People surrounded the trolley and drank from the chipped metal cups and bowls. The child sucked at the woman's breast and Lorenzo looked away, while Mario watched the wonder of life. What better place to feed your child than in a church, he thought.

'I don't know what will happen,' she whispered. 'Will you take her?'

Mario thought about his answer. 'It will not come to that.'

The woman looked down at her child.

'How do you know? I have heard stories ...'

'Rumours ... Just rumours, nothing else.'

'Every rumour has a certain amount of truth ...'

'Stay with your child, and try to stop worrying. It will all turn out fine.'

'Like for those they hanged in the square?' Lorenzo intervened.

Mario was surprised when his friend spoke, and saw the distress it caused the woman.

'Do not listen to him.'

'But he's right … Why have the Partisans not returned the general? That is why we are here, isn't it? Why don't they give him back so we can go back to our homes? I wish I had not given them anything in the past, I should have slammed my door shut.'

'You are wrong, although, I understand how you feel. To fight the beast, some will fall, but if we want to be rid of it … then we must expect to make sacrifices.'

The woman gazed at Mario. 'My child's life … is she my sacrifice?'

'The enemy is the one who locked us in here, not those in the hills.' Mario felt the blood flowing through his veins.

Lorenzo watched as his friend fell silent. The woman rose to her feet and went to speak, but chose to walk away instead.

~ ~ ~ ~

Mason tried to wipe away the image of Sofia sitting on the stool, and the stolen kiss. He shuddered. Silvano's daughter – well, well. He had almost laughed out loud. She had been right about one thing: it was far easier to make decisions when you knew no one. Attachments changed everything. He smiled to himself and thought about Isolina then.

'How you going to play this?' he asked, shielding his eyes from the sunlight.

'Put him in a car and drive … I've already sent Father Remo to the village.'

'And just who is going to take the general?' Mason followed the Italian's eyes. 'No … you can't.'

'Who else? She is not part of us.'

Mason stared at Isolina as he spoke with Silvano. 'There is a very good chance … and I mean a *very* good chance, that the Germans will take the general and renege on the deal.'

'Have you a better suggestion?' Silvano was angry; he liked this less than the Englishman.

'Enough.' Isolina strolled forward. 'Our daughter is down there, along with many other innocent people – did you expect me to stay here and do nothing?'

'This is madness … Tell her, Silvano.'

Silvano stared at Isolina. 'Ready?'

'You're crazy.' Mason turned his back on them.

'What time have you got?' Silvano shouted.

'Two thirty, almost … You can't let her do this.'

'Let's get moving.'

'On your head be it, Silvano.'

'Mason, get your rifle and go.'

Mason realised it was a pointless exercise to argue.

The German general looked bedraggled, his hair untidy, dirt and dust covered his once pristine uniform. They put him in the back seat and closed the door. He sat upright and proud; even blindfolded, he knew they would be watching him and he would show them what a German officer was made of. Isolina stared at the car, half expecting to see Roberto in the front seat waiting for her.

'Are you sure about this, Isolina?' asked Silvano.

Mason said nothing. Even now, he felt uncomfortable seeing them together. He gripped the rifle tighter and felt jealousy burn a hole in his gut. Given half a chance, he would shoot the big Italian. He watched as Silvano placed an arm around her shoulder; it was Mason's cue to turn away.

Silvano felt her soft skin under his rough hand and pulled her close.

'I'm sorry, it was a wicked thing I did,' she whispered.

'Shh ... we both acted badly. We both said and did things that we are not proud of ... but those things cannot be changed, what has happened has happened.'

'I thought you would hate me, I denied you so much time with Sofia ... time that cannot be replaced ... I'm sorry.'

He could not deny a certain amount of frustration.

'The taste is bitter, I agree, but now I want to look forward, not back.' He forced himself to believe what he was saying, but knew the wounds and scars would take time to heal.

Isolina began to walk towards the car.

'Mason?' She turned.

'Gone.'

'Let's hope ...'

'Believe it or not, I trust him.'

Isolina smiled. 'So do I.'

She sat behind the steering wheel of the car. It was like sitting in an oven. The men had left all the windows up for the benefit of the general. She turned and saw the sweat pouring down his face, dripping from his chin and staining his uniform. Should she offer him some water? Maybe, when they were out of sight.

Silvano watched with his heart pounding. He agreed with Mason that this was madness, but they had no plan B. Isolina pulled away slowly, leaving a cloud of dust. Silvano watched the car disappear: he was back on that railway station in Florence, waiting, watching and hoping.

~ ~ ~ ~

The road narrowed ahead. This is where the mines began, thought Fino, staring into the distance. It almost became a single track, which snaked its way around and through the hillside.

'We need to be extra careful from here, make sure we keep hold of the children. Don't let any of them run off.' He turned to face those behind him. 'You make certain you hold onto these children, do not let go for one second.' He spoke forcefully, leaving no one in any doubt that he meant what he said.

He picked up little Zita and placed her on the pram. 'There, little one, time you had a ride.' He smiled reassuringly at the child.

'The children are complaining that they are tired and thirsty, Fino.' Maria spoke while holding the hands of two small girls.

'No, we don't stop.' Fino was abrupt in his reply, before forcing a smile. 'We have no idea how long this goes on for, and I don't want to do it when the light is fading.'

Maria smiled and nodded her agreement. Sassa took hold of her husband's hand and squeezed it.

'You look tired,' she whispered.

'No more tired than anyone else. Let's get through this, then we can rest.'

Sassa smiled, but the light had gone from his eyes. For the first time, they seemed devoid of hope. She cursed the war, the Germans, Italians, Nazis, Fascists, everyone who took up arms – it was they who had caused all this horror and pain, and ruined countless lives. If no one was prepared to fight, then how would governments wage wars.

They moved slowly in single file. In the distance explosions could be heard, but no planes flew overhead.

Smoke rose towards the horizon, five maybe six kilometres away. Fino pushed the pram, with Zita playing a game on her fingers. He turned and saw Sassa holding two tiny hands that belonged to children who skipped and hopped next to her. They had seen and heard so much in these past few months that the sound of explosions did not frighten them in the slightest.

Eruptions continued to be heard in the far distance, but for those here on the road, it seemed the war had temporarily ceased. The Tuscan countryside had returned to its idyllic best; a welcoming breeze suddenly came from nowhere to help give relief. The children continued to complain that they were thirsty, and the younger ones wanted to be picked up, complaining that their little legs ached. The adults found themselves hot and tired from balancing children on hips. The sweat coated their skin, shining in the sun and soaking into their clothes. The children continued to cry and the exhausted adults began to shout and argue.

Then the planes returned, flying in formation, and the procession of adults and children halted to stare skyward. The planes continued north, while up ahead, Amedeo turned to face Fino. The sound of an engine could be heard coming from up ahead. Fino shrugged his shoulders and Amedeo remained still, holding the daughter of his apprentice, Beppe. He looked into the girl's face and smiled.

A single German lorry suddenly came at speed around the bend, the driver's eyes focused on the sky, only to be filled with horror moments later at what appeared in front of him. Brakes squealed, sparks flew from beneath the vehicle, and the smell of burning rubber filled nostrils. Amedeo stood rooted to the spot as time slowed. In a split second, he threw the child to one side before he and the lorry became one. His eyes met the driver's briefly before the lorry left the road and struck a mine.

The explosion sent everyone to the ground. Pieces of metal and canvas went hurtling skyward and a thick, black column of smoke rose into the sky. Most lay flat on the ground for a moment, before rising slowly to their feet, one by one. A second explosion sent them tumbling back to the ground again. Fino fell sideways, and he lost his grip on the pram's handle. He watched in horror as it began to roll. Zita stared back at him in silence. Fear had not entered the child's head.

Gina was first to her feet and chased the pram, which had now picked up speed. Her fingers wrapped themselves around the handle but the pram continued. One more fatal revolution of its wheels took it off the road. The explosion came seconds later.

CHAPTER TWENTY-NINE

The deafening sound of boots on stone floors echoed around the church. Soldiers entered from all sides holding their rifles, all performed with typical German efficiency. They corralled the prisoners into a small area between the rows of pews, pushing and prodding with their rifles. The women and children cried out in panic, while the very young clung to the adults with fear on their faces.

Into the church marched three German officers, each immaculately dressed in field grey. Each wore knee-length boots, which almost sparkled, and their hands were clasped behind their backs, as if out on a Sunday stroll. They walked up the centre aisle like a trio of best men at a military wedding, inspecting the faces of those either side of them. They beckoned over one of the sergeants. The villagers looked on with unease, and the children, sensing the tense atmosphere, began to fidget. Over the church fell an eerie silence, until one soldier shattered it by screaming an order. Six soldiers went running towards him.

He stepped amongst the villagers, parting them like the red sea, stopping every few steps to study the faces of those around him. People looked away or down at the floor, no one wanted to make eye contact with the German. He suddenly reached across and took hold of a middle-aged man, gripping his coat while two of his men pushed him forward, knocking aside anyone in their way. They brought him to the front.

'Where are you taking him?' It was the shopkeeper, Alfonso, who spoke.

A rifle struck him full in the face and he tumbled backwards. His wife fell to her knees screaming his name. Blood stained his pristine white shirt.

'Alfonso … Alfonso …' she cried repeatedly until her husband acknowledged her.

The sergeant pointed his finger in the direction of Sonia. Franca sensed the danger and gripped her mother tighter. She clung to her neck as one of the soldiers tried to prise her mother away. Several of the villagers rushed forwards to help, but half a dozen rifles pointing in their direction stopped them.

'Stop,' Sonia shouted. She smiled at Franca and kissed her chubby cheeks. Then, wiping away her tears, she handed the girl to the woman next to her. 'I want no one else to get hurt, not for me, anyway … Look after her.' She walked away, unassisted, to join the middle-aged man, with Franca's screams ringing in her ears.

A woman collapsed when her twelve-year-old boy was taken. Villagers again swarmed around the mother and child, before the sergeant took out his pistol and held it against the mother's head. The boy reached out to his mother but she was pushed away. A soldier then took hold of his shoulders and guided him towards the other two.

This was too much for Mario, who stepped forward. 'Take me,' he shouted, 'and leave the boy with his mother.'

One of the German officers looked up and spoke in broken Italian. 'You wish to keep the boy company, old man?'

'He is just a child ... I will willingly go in his place.'

'I see ... Let me tell you this, old man ... When I was in Rome not so long ago, a child of his age ran from the crowd and threw a bomb at a group of German soldiers, killing them all.' He took off his glasses and began to clean them, looking Mario up and down. 'So, you see I am ... how do they say ...' He pondered for a moment. '... nipping in the bud ... You understand?' He smiled at Mario, then spoke to the sergeant in German. Mario was taken, as was the boy. Lorenzo dashed forward.

'No, old friend.' Mario had seen him. 'I've seen enough and this cruelty exhausts me ... Look after yourself, Lorenzo, you have been a good friend. Sorry I will not be able to fix your car when it breaks down next time.' The old man smiled before being pushed forward.

They pulled a pregnant woman out next; her husband was in the hills with the Partisans. She came willingly, with one hand on the bulge of her stomach as she looked back. 'God save Italy,' she screamed, before the butt of a rifle smashed between her shoulder blades.

All five were led from the church, watched in silence by those who remained. Suddenly, half a dozen soldiers rushed amongst the villagers, and dragged out two young girls. Both fought hard, screaming as they were dragged across the floor towards the priest's office. Their officers looked up, and one smiled, but all three turned and walked out of the church. The office doors were then closed, stifling both girls' screams.

~ ~ ~ ~

Vincenzo stood in the sunlight and placed the strap of his rifle onto his shoulder, allowing him to blend in with the other men scattered around the yard. He was confident that no one would recognise him; it was one of the advantages of remote living. He had seldom come to the village; he mainly found himself in places like Florence and Senna.

He placed a cigarette between his lips and walked up to the nearest man.

'Got a light?' he asked.

He felt the sweat soak into his clothes. The Fascist soldier stared at him, and Vincenzo wondered if he was trying to recall his face – but the man finally smiled.

'Sure.'

'Want one?'

'Grazie.'

The man hunted for his lighter. Finding it, he flipped the lid and ignited the petrol. Vincenzo placed his cigarette into the blue flame.

The man laughed. 'Can't control it ... found it on a dead Partisan.'

Vincenzo pulled away, sucking at the tobacco. 'Dangerous,' he added, controlling his temper.

'Yes ... but not as deadly as the Partisans in the hills.'

Vincenzo failed to answer after something caught his eye across the yard. What looked like a body lay in the sunshine. Around the head, a dark shadow had spread outwards. The man followed Vincenzo's gaze. 'Vito lost his temper.'

'Who is it?'

'The local priest,' the man replied, blowing out a cloud of smoke. 'Not a man to provoke.'

'I can see that ... Where is he now?'

'Vito or the priest?' The man smiled. 'This man is either in heaven or hell … And Vito …' he paused '… Only one place for him now.'

The man pointed to the large white building opposite them. Vincenzo sucked in another lungful of smoke.

~ ~ ~ ~

'I'll have it now.' Enzo's voice sounded weary. Standing in front of Vito's desk, he felt ill, his body ached and he was in desperate need of a drink. Life could only get better, he thought, and that was why he needed the balance of his money. He stared around the room, stripped bare of almost everything, including the paintings, which made the room look colourless. Vito opened his top drawer and allowed his hand to hover over the pistol and knife he kept inside but his fingers grabbed the small bundle of bank notes instead.

'Here, count it.' He threw it across the desk as if wanting to avoid touching the man.

'No need.' Enzo stuffed it into an inside pocket.

Vito could smell the man: he stank of sweat, cigarettes and cheap wine. He despised him. Yes, he had been a great help to him, and he almost had Isolina's cousin, but he was not a man he wanted by his side in a fight – he was just as likely to turn his gun on you. Vito could see the greed in Enzo's eyes. He was a man with no scruples, a man who would sell his own mother to the highest bidder.

'Where will you go?' Vito asked, closing the drawer.

'Switzerland.'

Vito shrugged his shoulders. They will find him there, no problem, he thought. He needed to get to South America like most of the Germans were doing, though, even that might not be far enough. He could never respect or like a man who betrayed his friends for money.

'What will you do there?'

'Who cares, as long as I get as far away as possible.'

Vito sat back in his chair. 'You will always be a marked man, you do know that, Enzo. No one will forget what you did.'

'It makes me the same as you.'

Vito controlled his anger. No, he thought, do not compare yourself with me. I am nothing like you. He smiled.

'Yes, except I have always been the enemy to those you fought with. It is people like you who they hate more. It is a hate that will stay with them for years, not months or weeks, Enzo. Sooner or later, they will catch up with you. You will be looking over your shoulder for the rest of your life, my friend. But, if what you have just put inside your pocket is worth all that, then who am I to question your actions – you were a great help to me.'

'Thank you.'

'And you have been rewarded.'

'Could have been more ... But I will accept this.'

Vito clenched his jaw. He wanted to reach into the drawer and blow the greedy bastard's brains out. But, like before, he forced a smile.

Enzo returned it.

'If you had done that to me, Enzo, I would have hunted you down like a dog.'

Enzo turned and walked towards the door, stopping to look out of the window, wondering if Vito had a man waiting outside to shoot him.

413

'If it's all right with you, I will go now.' He did not turn to look at Vito Sergi.

'Fine.'

Enzo blinked, rubbed the bristles on his chin, smelt his own stale body odour. It was then he noticed ...

Vito heard the door open and close again moments later. He did not look up from the piece of paper he was about to sign.

'Enzo, I hope you have not come back to ask for more.'

It was the long, drawn-out silence that made Vito look up. He gave the tall man in front of him a long, confused stare.

'Can I help you?'

Vincenzo almost smiled. He needed to finish this and go, but, instead, he found himself staring at the man. This was enough for Vito, who sensed something was wrong and slid open the drawer. Vincenzo removed the rifle from his shoulder and pointed it at him.

'Hold it,' he said, aiming the rifle at Vito's chest.

Vito froze and tried to gather his composure. His hand remained above the open drawer, but he was not going to be stupid. He looked into the man's eyes: this man is no killer, he thought. No, what he was doing did not come natural to him. This gave Vito a chance.

'Who are you?'

'The man who is going to kill you.'

'Then, do I not get a last wish? Do I not get to know who my assassin is and why I am going to die? Surely you can grant me that small concession?'

Vito Sergi spoke so calmly, it unnerved Vincenzo. It was he who held the rifle, yet he did not feel in control of the situation.

'I am Vincenzo Stolfi ... Does that mean anything to you?'

Vito smiled, placed the tips of his fingers together and sat back comfortably in his leather chair.

Does this man have ice running through his veins? thought Vincenzo. Sweat began to form on his top lip, and he moved his finger until it rested on the metal trigger – he only needed to squeeze it gently, and retribution for Lucia and his dead child, his brother and his mother, would be his.

It all happened so quickly. He saw the door behind Sergi, which was to be his escape. Almost at the same time, he heard the door behind him opening, then the sound of boots on the wooden floor, and men breathing heavily. He hesitated and turned, only to see three men advancing towards him. Vito Sergi seized the opportunity and leapt from his chair. The first man knocked Vincenzo off his feet while the other two leapt on top of him, forcing him to release his grip on the rifle. A fist smashed into the side of his head and he was overwhelmed by their numbers. A second blow and darkness descended.

A moment later, he felt himself being hauled to his knees.

'I thought I recognised him, I just could not think from when or where.'

He heard Enzo's voice while they bound his hands with rope.

'Your timing was perfect,' Vito Sergi replied. 'One of the Stolfi boys.'

Vincenzo opened his eyes but the room was a blur. He was being held down by his shoulders while Vito Sergi stood in front of him, staring down. He could not see the traitor, Enzo, but he could hear him. Sergi held something shiny in his hand.

Strangely, it was not fear Vincenzo felt, but anger – anger with himself. He had missed his chance, but for some strange reason, he smiled.

'What have you to smile about?' Sergi asked.

Vincenzo filled his mind with memories of the house, the fields, the mountains, the hillside, the rows of vines and, not least, the laughter. And now he thought of Lucia, the love of his life, mother to his unborn child.

'So, you came to kill me.' Vito Sergi's voice interrupted his thoughts. Vincenzo looked up. Sergi was speaking, but he heard nothing except the voice of his mother calling them all in to lunch. The smile on his face grew, and so did the annoyance on Vito's Sergi's face. He saw the knife in his hand, too. Vito Sergi stared into the young man's eyes before sliding the blade across his windpipe. Life flowed from Vincenzo, although he saw a light before the blackness took him.

~ ~ ~ ~

Father Remo walked slowly towards a group of officers. They ignored him and continued their conversation. The priest stood beside them in silence. This was one of the little games played by the conquerors; the priest was used to being patient. The youngest of the officers eventually looked in his direction, acknowledging his presence, before speaking in surprisingly good Italian.

'Yes, Father, may I be of help?'

Father Remo cleared his throat. 'Your general.'

'What of him?'

'The Partisans have agreed to release him. They will have someone drive him to the crossroads at four o'clock.' He explained the Partisans' terms.

The German turned to his colleagues and spoke to them. Each stared at the priest as he spoke. Moments later, one of the officers began to shout orders. The soldiers' response was swift, and the priest watched the trucks fill with troops.

Thirty metres away, Father Remo saw five civilians standing on the steps outside the church, surrounded by guards. He noticed that a young boy was being comforted by old Mario. Amongst them was also a pregnant woman. The priest felt his chest tighten and his heart beat a little quicker.

'What is this?' he asked.

'What does it look like?'

'I have told you: your general is being released.'

'I do not see him.' The German sarcastically looked in several directions. 'No, I do not see him.' He smiled and removed a silver cigarette case from his pocket.

'You cannot do this.'

'Oh, but I can.'

The priest looked towards the pitiful sight of the child, the old man and pregnant woman, before staring at the officer.

'Have you no shame?'

'Are you asking me a question?'

'I am asking a human being to show some compassion.'

The officer inhaled, looking at Father Remo.

'Leave these innocent people alone, they are no threat to you or your men. You're about to leave, why not just go now? Go and get your general and leave this village in peace, it has no part to play in this war.' The German continued to smoke in silence.

'If you do feel the need to have a hostage … take me.'

The German blew out a cloud of smoke. 'You would like to go in their place?' He looked towards the church.

'Yes.'

'I see.'

The German threw down his half-finished cigarette, took hold of the priest's arm and dragged him towards the church while the other officers began to laugh. Those outside the church watched them approach. The boy recognised Father Remo and almost found himself smiling. The German shoved the priest the final metre.

'The priest, here, has offered to stand in for you all.'

No one spoke for a moment.

'Not me,' Mario began. 'The boy, Gianni, Lalia, and Sonia, if you must, Father.'

Father Remo moved towards the boy, who fell into his embrace. 'There, child,' he whispered.

'Take him, Father.' Mario bent down and whispered into the boy's ear. 'Go with the Father.'

The priest looked at the German. 'Have you no children of your own, no brothers or sisters, no mother or father?'

The German said nothing; a faint smile came to his lips as he stared at the group.

'Somewhere in your heart there must be some kindness. There is good in everyone, all you need to do is search for it, allow a little …'

The German turned and walked away. A lorry reversed at that moment and stopped twenty metres away. The grey covers were pulled back to reveal two soldiers crouched behind a machine gun. Mario gripped the boy's shoulders, Father Remo began to pray and the pregnant woman fell to her knees. Sonia closed her eyes and the man began to cry.

The officer's arm fell and the machine gun exploded into life. In a matter of seconds, six lives were extinguished. The bodies lay motionless on the church steps. Above, the sun was beginning its descent behind the hill.

~ ~ ~ ~

Isolina brought the car to a stuttering halt, with the general seated in the back, his blindfold still in place. She stared at him for several seconds before getting out of the car. She breathed in the late afternoon air, certain that Father Remo had delivered the message by now. Now, all she could do was wait. She thought of removing the general from the car, and maybe removing the blindfold to allow him some dignity. She stared through the window; he cut an arrogant figure, and so she decided against it.

Six months ago, she would have shown a degree of sympathy, but the war had done something to her, which confused and disgusted her. She looked towards the surrounding hills and felt angry with everything and everyone. She knew Mason was keeping a watchful eye on her as Silvano had requested, but, right now, it was not her safety she thought about, but Sofia's.

Now was not the time to worry about Sofia's response to Silvano, although her mind had wondered there on several occasions. It was like putting the cart before the horse; her first priority was to get Sofia back safely, as well as Gino. After that she would cross the next bridge when she reached it. But, what if this did not go to plan? She smiled to herself – then none of it would matter. Again, her thoughts turned to Silvano. She had spent so long as a keeper of secrets, the truth had somehow become distorted with time. Who had walked away from whom? Who lied to who? Who loved who? The longer you kept a lie, the more you believe it to be the truth.

The noise of engines in the distance broke her chain of thought. Two cars led three trucks – she thought the instructions delivered via the priest had asked for one car to be sent. Her stomach somersaulted as she walked slowly back to the car. Had there been a change of plan? She gently lifted the general out and removed the blindfold, untied his hands and let his eyes become accustomed to the light. He finally saw the convoy in the distance and smiled. But she felt uneasy, as if the jailer was becoming the captive. The general flexed his fingers in an attempt to resume blood flow.

One of the staff cars reached them first. Two officers jumped from the rear doors almost before the car was stationary. They walked with purpose towards their general and raised their arms in salute: *Heil Hitler*. The general's reply was pitiful compared to their theatrical display. Isolina held back while they spoke. Right now, those in the village church should start to be released under the watchful eye of Silvano. They would all wait here until word reached them and the deal was completed. One of the soldiers handed the general a silver hip flask, which he lifted to his lips. The smile, when it came, looked sinister. He turned and beckoned Isolina over. She walked slowly towards the group. A second later, she was sent sprawling to the ground with the back of his hand.

The other two officers laughed, one shouted, and two very young German soldiers came running over. They lifted Isolina harshly by her arms. At that precise moment, mortars began falling across the hillside in a deafening barrage. Mounds of earth exploded skyward, and troops suddenly emptied from the trucks. The bombardment increased in its intensity along the ridge. The two young soldiers quickly escorted Isolina towards one of the empty trucks. They shouted to the driver before throwing Isolina into the back. Both soldiers joined her as the lorry sped away. Isolina held her cheek as she watched the hillside become a war zone.

~ ~ ~ ~

Mason, from his position high up on the ridge, had observed Isolina from the moment she had stepped from the car. He found it difficult to take his eyes off her: even from this distance her beauty intoxicated him. He could almost taste her, smell the aroma that escaped from her hair, feel the smoothness of her skin under his fingers. He laid the rifle down and pulled his notebook from his pocket. In the distance, he saw a cloud of dust rising into the air; it seemed they were on their way. He took one more look at her and replaced the pad. Now it was time for less pleasant pastimes.

Two staff cars led the way, followed by several trucks. Already, he had his doubts. They were supposed to come in one car. He hoped his fears were misplaced, although the soldier in him told him otherwise. He gripped the rifle and pulled the butt firmly into his shoulder. Two officers got out the staff car and saluted the general. He shifted his eyes from Isolina; he wanted to choose which one would get the warning shot. He chose the tallest; he would aim for his right shoulder. It would signal to them the insurance policy they had brought.

His eyes returned to Isolina at about the same moment she hit the ground. Uncertain of what was happening, he placed his eye along the rifle barrel. The first mortar exploded six metres to his right, forcing him to roll onto his back. More mortar fire rained down on the hillside, great clumps of earth flew into the air, and white smoke swept across the hillside. He heard shouts coming from the Partisans, but his eyes returned to where Isolina and the general had stood, just in time to see her being pushed into one of the trucks.

Mortar bombs fell on them from the sky, and hordes of German troops now appeared from all sides. He looked both ways, shaking his head. What fools he and Silvano had been, both blinded by a woman's beauty, he cursed. But, more importantly, he needed to get the hell out, and quick.

'Mason!'

He looked up the slope to where Ambra stood with her rifle strapped to her back.

'What?' he shouted.

'They are coming from both sides … we need to get to higher ground.'

Mason took one more look back down the hill.

'Forget about her,' Ambra screamed, 'we need to save ourselves … There are too many to hold back this low down.'

Ambra was right, and he began to climb to higher ground. The Germans would only go so far. Once the trees became dense, they would cease their pursuit. The Germans would fight but only on their terms. The noise of mortar was joined by the sound of gunfire. His boots slipped in the crumbling dry earth as he scrambled up the slope, his rifle strap slicing into the skin around his neck.

With the ground shaking all around and his body drenched in sweat, Mason gritted his teeth and climbed with more urgency. He could hear the blood pumping around his body, and he took fleeting glances back over his shoulder, making certain he kept a good distance between himself and his pursuers. He looked up to where safety waited. Ambra was gone. In her place stood two Partisans, who were standing their ground and firing back down the hill. Mason continued climbing but stopped at the sight of Ambra lying motionless twenty metres away. He quickened his pace to reach her. Breathing heavily, he placed a hand on her neck to feel her pulse. As he did, her eyes opened.

'Can you get up?' he asked.

His eyes travelled the length of her body, stopping where the blood was seeping through her trousers, soaking into the earth below. He looked at the injury, the wound was open, exposing white bone. He turned his head away sharply, biting his lip, and glanced down the hill. The mortars had done their job and had grown silent. His eyes returned to Ambra as the other two Partisans came and stood next to them.

'Slow them up,' he shouted.

Neither questioned the Englishman.

Ambra moved, but screamed in pain as she did so. Mason placed a hand on her shoulder.

'Ambra,' he whispered.

She opened her eyes and forced a smile.

'Ambra,' he whispered into her ear.

'Go.' She forced the word out through gritted teeth. 'Go,' she repeated.

'I can't just leave you.'

'Go.'

'I can't.' He turned and looked back down at the two Partisans, who were being outgunned, and he knew time was running out. He looked back into her eyes, eyes that had once been filled with passion, but now had life draining from them.

'You know what you must do, Englishman.'

He swallowed what moisture was still in his mouth.

'Do it … Do it now.'

Another look over his shoulder, just in time to see one of the men fall, clutching his chest. It had to be done now; he could not risk the lives of any more Partisans. He ordered the other to go on, then looked down at Ambra and stroked her forehead.

'Do it,' she mouthed the words.

He took out his handgun, placed the nozzle on her temple and pulled the trigger. The war stopped instantly. For a split second, he became a solid block of ice, without feeling, hollow, empty. The hillside became silent. He felt sweat form on his face and wiped it away, staining his head with her blood. Then he looked down and saw that her brains covered his shirt. He let out an almighty scream.

~ ~ ~ ~

Isolina stared at the two young soldiers opposite her; they swayed in rhythm with the lorry. She reached up and touched her cut lip. It stung. It had not gone as planned, but nevertheless, she was on her way to the village to join Sofia. In the distance, she could still hear gunfire and explosions. She saw smoke rising from the hillside and hoped Mason was safe.

The two soldiers sat watching her. They lit cigarettes and giggled like schoolboys; one removed a bottle of clear spirit and drank from it. The lorry moved at a slow pace, so the sound of war took its time to depart. The drink seemed to restore their confidence and one came and sat next to her. He leant across and tried to kiss her on the lips. She turned her head away, but he grabbed a handful of her hair and tugged her head back to face him.

The other now took the bottle. He clapped and stamped his feet while his mate tried to run his hand up Isolina's dress. She held her knees together but the cut on her lip reopened. With her free hand, she slapped the boy's face. A look of shock covered it and he said something to his mate. The laughter ceased. The older of the two moved the length of the vehicle and banged on the driver's panel. The vehicle slowly came to a halt.

They grabbed her arms, walked her to the back of the vehicle and pushed her off. She landed awkwardly, stumbled, but remained on her feet. One of the boy soldiers shouted towards the cab, before they began to walk towards a small wooded area. Suddenly, the realisation hit her: they were going to rape her, shoot her, or both. She became frightened, not for herself, but for Sofia. She could not leave her alone, not yet. She had done it once today and the guilt was still with her. She was just a child, her little girl.

The world spun and her knees gave way, but she was soon lifted back to her feet. She looked up to see the sun edging closer to the hills. They stopped at the first tree, where she was pressed hard up against the trunk and her wrists bound. She felt the roughness of the bark on her face, and her dress being lifted up. She now knew her fate.

An image of Sofia as a baby came to her. She took comfort in the knowledge that Silvano knew the truth about his daughter: Sofia would not be alone. She felt a hand cup her breast, and then laughter. One of them placed his mouth close to her ear and she smelt his foul breath. A hand ripped open her dress, exposing her breasts.

Suddenly, the sound of two gunshots echoed around the countryside. Isolina's body froze against the tree; a light evening breeze touched her naked skin. Finally, her legs gave way and she collapsed to her knees. Next, she felt her wrists being untied.

'Signora.'

Slowly, she regained her senses. Her back was resting against the tree and someone was pouring water into her mouth. She opened her eyes and stared at the two German uniforms in front of her; beyond them lay the bodies of the two boy soldiers. 'Signora, I have no Christmas tree today.'

She recognised them immediately.

'A favour returned, signora.'

'You owe me nothing.'

'Our lives.'

She smiled and touched the man's hand. 'But I need to ask one more favour of you.'

He gave her an inquisitive look. 'What would that be?'

'I need to get to the village.'

The German stared hard at her, but said nothing. He spoke to his friend whilst looking at Isolina.

'You do not want to go there, signora.'

'But I must … my daughter is there … I need to find her.'

Again, the older of the two translated what Isolina had said.

'Even we are not going back there. We are heading towards the advancing British army to surrender.'

'I need to find my daughter.'

He spoke once more to his friend.

'I know I ask a lot.' Isolina took hold of his arm. 'She is all I have.'

The soldier placed his hand over Isolina's. 'We, too, have family, signora. I have a daughter and two grandchildren. Karl, here, has a son and two daughters. We have not heard from them in more than a year and we want to return home and be reunited.'

Isolina stared at the man. 'I understand.' She reached across to his friend and placed her hand on his shoulder and smiled. 'Thank you, anyway, for what you did. I hope you make it and that you find your families, and they are well.'

She began to walk back towards the lorry.

'Stop,' the German said. 'We will take you.'

'But …what if…'

'Shh,' he placed a finger to his lips, 'we need to go now.'

'Tell me …'

The German turned to face her.

'… your names … please.'

'I am Jan.'

'Jan,' she repeated.

'And he is Karl.'

The other man smiled, but it was far from convincing.

'Grazie, Karl … Grazie, Jan.'

'You're welcome.'

Isolina reached the lorry and climbed into the back, and the one called Karl raised the tailgate. Moments later, the engine started up and they were moving. They sat opposite each other, silent, both deep in thought. Jan took out a cigarette and handed it to Isolina, before placing one between his own lips and lighting both. She looked again at Jan and smiled. She had never felt as guilty as she did at that moment.

CHAPTER THIRTY

Carlo Sergi gently touched the curls of Sofia's hair, allowing them to slip through his fingers before gathering more. He was perched on the edge of his desk when the front door opened. A man in a black shirt poked his head around it.

'Got the general, Carlo, we're moving out in about twenty minutes.'

Carlo acknowledged him with a nod of the head.

'I need to see him,' Sofia whispered.

'You will.' He reached out to touch her breast. The memory of doing so earlier left a burning sensation in his stomach, mixing with the brandy he had consumed. His thumb moved back and forth across her nipple, but the reaction he desired did not materialise. Sofia felt anger and shame in equal amounts – but Gino was her goal and she was so close now, nothing was going to stop her finding him, even if that meant being humiliated by Carlo.

'Now, Carlo!'

He sighed and stood before her. 'All right, follow me.'

A feeling of anticipation washed over her, an optimism she had not felt until now. They moved to the door, Sofia still holding the coat across her arms.

'Leave that,' Carlo said angrily.

She ignored him and continued to follow him down a long corridor. The walls either side were discoloured, with strange-looking stains that someone had tried to scrub clean. Sofia wondered if it was blood; it made her heart skip a beat. They passed two doors before Carlo halted outside a third. He took a key from his inside pocket and unlocked it.

The door squealed in protest as it swung back. He stepped aside and guided her in.

Without a window, the room was dark. She could just make out someone lying on a makeshift bed against the facing wall. Gino? Slowly, whoever it was, began to turn; Sofia sucked in the room's stale air and moved hurriedly towards him. His face was almost unrecognisable. Swollen, with deep cuts and bruises covering it entirely. His left eye remained completely closed while his top lip was swollen to twice its size. She dropped to one knee.

'Have you no water, Carlo?' She spoke as she clasped Gino's once beautiful face.

'For him? No.'

'Please, I beg you … Just a little.' She kissed his cheek. 'Gino … Gino, can you hear me?'

Carlo lit up a cigarette and felt his head begin to ache. He needed more brandy. He watched jealously as Sofia ran her fingers through the boy's hair. He wanted to pull her away and throw her to the floor, fuck her in front of him. But, most of all, he wished that Sofia wanted him as much as she wanted this boy.

A man shouted down the hallway that his father would be ready to go in twenty minutes.

'Yes … yes. I will not be long … Go.'

'But, Carlo …'

'I said GO!' His patience snapped. It was one thing he had in common with his father: his temper. The messenger did not hang around. They heard the door slam.

Carlo had had enough. He walked across the room and grabbed Sofia by the hair, dragging her away from Gino. He lifted her to her knees, before slipping off the braces that held up his trousers.

'Time for dinner.'

Gino slid across the floor and tried to lever himself up using Sofia's arm. Carlo pushed Sofia to one side and aimed a kick at the boy, connecting with his head. It was done with such force that it almost took it off his shoulders.

'No,' screamed Sofia, still on her knees.

Another kick crashed into Gino's face, and the spray of blood covered the nearest wall. The third kick made contact with the back of Gino's head. Carlo turned away from the lifeless figure. 'We have unfinished business ...'

Sofia stepped away to where her coat had fallen. She reached down and took hold of the handgun, the one that had spent so long hidden below the floorboards.

'Stay there, you *bastard* ... Gino ... Gino, can you hear me?'

Carlo smiled but held his ground. Gino moaned, but he did not move.

'Gino ... Gino ...' She raised her voice.

Then she heard another voice, one she instantly recognised: Luca. It came from the next room.

'Let Luca out, Carlo.'

Carlo remained where he stood.

'I mean it ... Go and open the door.'

'You won't shoot me, Sofia. You need guts to do that and you have none.'

Her outstretched arm began to shake, the gun was heavier than she thought. 'Put it to the test, Carlo, I dare you … Let us see who has guts.'

The smile slowly faded from his lips. The distance between them was too great: if he rushed her, chances were, she would get off at least one shot. It was not worth taking the risk. How far were they going to get anyway?

He walked out into the corridor and opened the other door. Luca emerged, looking almost as bad as Gino.

'Luca,' Sofia whispered.

'Sofia,' Luca smiled. 'Gino?'

'In here.' Sofia stepped aside to allow Luca in.

'Mother of God.' Luca looked up. 'He was just a boy, Carlo.'

'Then he should have stayed out of it, war is not for boys.'

Luca helped Gino to his feet and sat him on the makeshift bed. 'Gino, can you hear me? We have to move, we have to get out of here.'

'Yes.' The answer was barely audible.

'Here, take him … Give me the gun.' He looked at Carlo and smiled. 'I should shoot you now.'

'Do it then, Luca.'

'No, I will get out of here first.'

Sofia lifted Gino to his feet and they began to walk from the room. It was like carrying a drunk man: Gino swayed from side to side, using the wall to balance himself. He spoke but his words were slurred.

'That door leads to the courtyard, Sofia,' Luca whispered. 'Beyond, are the woods … We get to them and we can get away.'

'Are you mad?' Carlo said. 'You have no chance –'

'Shut up.' Luca turned to face Gino. 'Can you walk, Gino? It is not far.'

The boy mumbled an answer. Sofia looked from Gino to Luca, who smiled with as much reassurance as he could muster; but Gino looked like death. Outside, they heard the sound of activity, boots on the ground, voices, shouts and even laughter. Luca placed his hand on the door handle and held his breath.

~ ~ ~ ~

Silvano had worked his way around behind the village. He knew the plan had not worked, and the reason why. But they had got to the woods behind the church – there was still a chance to save some lives. The Germans were already moving out, taking little notice of what was happening behind their lines. Silvano looked through the binoculars, focusing not on the village but on the hills where Mason was. They had heard the mortar fire, but could not see anything except smoke rising into the sky. They were too far away to draw any conclusions. Tino came and stood next to him.

'What do you think?' he asked, handing them over.

'I have no idea,' he replied, bringing the binoculars to his eyes a second time. 'Just smoke and machine-gun fire.'

Silvano felt frustrated. 'You know the village better than I do, Tino, look down there.'

Silvano felt a feeling of helplessness creep over him. He could not stop worrying about Isolina, but he also knew he was responsible for those in the church, who now included his daughter. He looked back to the hills. Yes, he even felt responsible for Mason. The sound of engines starting up broke his train of thought.

'What is it?'

'Looks like they're moving out.' Tino passed the binoculars back to Silvano.

'They seem to be in a rush.'

'There are Vito Sergi's offices ...' Tino pointed. 'The church, the village square.'

The number of German soldiers had surprised Silvano; he had not expected this many, nor the heavy equipment they had with them. In the distance, the noise of battle continued unabated on the hillside.

'Let's get lower, Tino.' He ran his fingers through his hair. 'But tell the men to move slowly.'

~ ~ ~ ~

Lorenzo lowered his head and wept gently into his hands. Like those around him, he had heard the burst of machine-gun fire. A solid wall of silence had descended upon the church, and a giant reverberation of grief and shock now filled the interior, its energy sweeping up the centre aisle, exploding on the walls, rising and hitting the ceiling above. It came by way of screams, sobs and giant intakes of breath.

Lorenzo thought of his friend, Mario, and tried desperately to remember him in better times, working in his garage or sitting outside the bar on warm summer evenings. He looked down at the floor, feeling lost. A woman carrying a child came and sat opposite, but Lorenzo was not in the mood to talk. He wanted to tell the woman politely to leave him with his memories.

'What do you think is happening outside?' she asked.

'What?'

'The gunfire in the distance.'

'I have no idea.'

'Other than your friend … the pregnant woman … Did you know her?'

'I knew them all.'

'I only got here four days ago. I had to get away from the fighting on the coast.'

Lorenzo remained silent, desperately wanting to be left alone.

'What was your friend's name?' she asked.

He looked up, his face showing his annoyance. 'Mario,' he said, his answer harsh.

The woman stood. 'I'm sorry. I'm disturbing you at a sad time … I will go.'

Lorenzo reached up and caught her arm. 'Sit,' he whispered.

She did as he asked. 'I'm sorry. It's just … it's … I'm scared.'

'It is I who should be sorry. I am a selfish old man, and I apologise.' His hand moved to the sleeping child's face, his little finger traced the shape of her lips. 'What is her name?'

'Dona.'

'A sweet name … Hello, Dona,' he whispered as tears streamed down his cheeks.

~ ~ ~ ~

Luca peered through the crack in the door. Outside, everyone was rushing in one direction or another. He looked towards where the treeline began and measured the distance to there. He closed the door and leant his head back against the wall, trying to clear it.

'Let me think.'

Carlo's face lit up and his smile broadened. 'You have no chance ... and you know it. All you are doing is killing yourself and these –'

'Shut up, Carlo, or I will shoot you here and now.' Sweat coated Luca's face.

Gino moaned, placing his head against the cool brickwork.

'Are you all right, Gino?' Sofia began to panic; something was not right. 'Gino?'

Luca looked at the boy before his gaze met Carlo's smiling face. He clenched his jaw and ignored him. He took one more look into the yard, where a German troop lorry had just pulled in and was now parking directly outside. It just might be the piece of luck they needed. A German soldier jumped from the cab and Luca ducked back behind the door. The lorry would shield them until they almost reached the woods.

'When I say go, we move quickly.' He looked again at Gino, and it drained his confidence: there was a vacant look in his eyes. 'Are you ready?' he whispered.

'Does that include me?' Carlo grinned.

'Very much so ... or I will shoot you here and now.'

'First, you can't risk that ... Second, you're going to shoot me anyway, so why should I bother? The dilemma is yours, Luca.' The wide smile returned. 'You're as stupid now as you were at school.'

Luca stared back at him and gripped the gun tighter. He was right: shoot him now and there was no chance of escape. He tried to avoid eye contact with Gino. One more look outside.

'Sofia … you and Gino first … Be ready.' He placed Sofia in the doorway, but found himself looking into Gino's eyes. 'Keep hold of him, Sofia.'

She nodded. He wanted to tell her that if Gino fell, she was to leave him, but he said nothing.

Sofia kissed Gino before they emerged from the gloom of the building and into the warm sunshine. They had taken just three strides when she heard her name being called.

'Sofia.'

The girl turned to see her mother standing between two German soldiers. Isolina rushed forward; neither soldier tried to stop her.

'Sofia.' Isolina hugged her daughter.

The world stood still at that moment, and Carlo made his move. He grabbed the gun in Luca's hand and they began to struggle. The gun exploded as the two fought. Both for a moment lay still, and then Luca rolled onto his back, his white shirt stained in blood – but not his. Carlo Sergi lay groaning with both hands clasping a stomach wound.

Luca realised they had attracted the attention of those scattered about the yard. There was no time to lose, they needed to make their escape. The two German soldiers dived under the lorry; they had fulfilled their promise to Isolina.

'Go … Go …' shouted Luca, crouching on one knee and firing a shot that hit the first man who raised a rifle. How many more bullets were in this gun? He turned to see that all three had almost reached the trees. He released two more shots, making those around the yard dive for cover. The realisation that, by buying them time, he had made his own position hopeless suddenly hit him. He fired again, before looking down to see blood staining his trousers. He fired once more, but now the Fascists returned it twofold. It took a second for the pain to register in his shoulder.

He squeezed the trigger and prayed there was another bullet … Relief as it exploded, bringing down an advancing man. He glanced once more towards the trees, just in time to see Isolina, Gino and Sofia disappear inside the woods. Now, all around him, men moved in the shadows. He raised his gun but nothing happened, just the sound of an empty chamber. Luca prayed he had bought them the time needed as, seconds later, there was an explosion of gunfire. Luca was dead before he hit the ground.

The Fascists remained where they were, fearing there could be more Partisans. It was Vito Sergi himself who walked forward. He stopped when he reached the body of his son Carlo. He took a deep breath before walking across to where Luca lay. He stared down at the Partisan and the anger burst like a dam. He spat on the boy, before emptying his gun into his lifeless body.

'Don't just stand there,' he shouted at his men. 'Go and find those other bastards.'

Seconds later, at least a dozen men hurried towards the woods that Isolina, Gino and Sofia had just entered. Vito Sergi remained with his boy. He knelt, placing his fingers on the lids of his boy's open eyes to close them.

~ ~ ~ ~

Mason stood and ran to the nearest tree. Leaning against it, he was violently sick. Now he needed water, desperate to clear his mouth of the vile taste. Every time he closed his eyes, all he saw was Ambra's face pleading with him to shoot her. Suddenly, the bark of the tree exploded and he saw Germans advancing less than a hundred yards from him. He needed to make for higher ground.

He was on the move again, his lungs on fire, Ambra's face fixed in his mind, the nozzle of his gun resting on her temple. He knew he would always be able to draw her face, it would be stored in his memory for ever.

Bullets tore into the ground twenty yards to his right, making him throw himself to the ground, gripping his rifle. He crawled towards the stump of a fallen tree.

'Christ,' said an English voice. 'The bastards keep coming … We need to get higher.'

Mason just stared at the man, saying nothing.

'You all right, Mason?'

Mason continued to stare at the man, but the person he saw was Ambra.

'Mason … for Christ's sake, mate … *Mason …*'

Mason watched as the Englishman crouched and began to move towards him, his rifle slung across his back and bullets flying overhead. A second man began firing, trying to slow the Germans' advance, but Mason seemed disoriented.

The soldier had almost reached him when a bullet took off the top of his head. He fell with his eyes wide open, looking at the sky. The other man continued to fire round after round, glancing at Mason, uncertain of what was happening. Mason was staring down at the dead Englishman. If he had not seen the back of his head fly away, Mason would have thought he was just resting.

The other man looked at Mason in complete bewilderment. Mason turned and smiled at him. It was the man's signal to get the hell out of there. A quick glance back and he was gone. Mason took out his notepad and placed the pencil between his teeth, opened up the book on a fresh page and began to sketch the dead man. A shadow appeared across the page, growing larger by the second. He could see the silhouette of a gun and the outline of a helmet. He looked at the dead man's eyes, and replaced them with Ambra's.

~ ~ ~ ~

Isolina felt the thorns tear at her skin and saw thin, red lines of blood cover the surface.

'Come on,' she shouted. Behind her, Sofia struggled with Gino. Isolina stopped and went back to help. They leant the boy against a tree and tried to catch their breath. Isolina looked back through the trees and listened for any sound. Had they been followed? Of course they had. She looked at Sofia, then at Gino, and felt despair sweep over her, but she could not allow them to give up. Too many people had sacrificed themselves for them.

'Come on, Sofia.'

'We have to stop, Mamma … Gino.'

Isolina took a deep breath and placed a hand against the tree to steady herself. Sweat mixed with dirt poured down her face. Again, she looked beyond Sofia into the woods, certain she would see their pursuers – but none came. Sofia had allowed Gino to lie down, making Isolina angry. The girl knelt over him, desperately trying to make him talk to her, but all she got was mumbled responses to her questions.

'Mamma, I can't understand him.'

Isolina's eyes moved from her daughter to the trees below; she was torn between helping Gino and getting away. She bent down and placed her mouth close to the boy's ear. 'Where does it hurt, Gino?'

The boy looked up and Isolina stifled a gasp. Those eyes, those beautiful eyes were now ghost-like and lifeless.

'M-m-hhhd.'

Isolina closed her eyes.

'Mamma, *do* something.'

Do what? Thought Isolina. 'Gino, can you stand? Just a little further, then you can rest.'

'*Spleeep*,' he mumbled.

'No … not yet … Come on, stand.'

They lifted him to his feet but his legs had no life in them. Isolina was amazed that no one had come. Then she heard machine-gun fire and the sound of voices shouting, it was coming from the woods.

'Come on, let's move.'

~ ~ ~ ~

Enzo let the idiots continue the chase. He had had enough of this war. With a pocket full of cash, it was his turn to leave this war behind. He looked back. Vito Sergi remained on one knee, looking down at his dead son. 'Hope it was worth it,' he thought. He began to climb the slope. He would head for France or Spain, Spain being the most likely, as he spoke a little of the language. He would find a woman and buy her services for a few days. He watched the last of them disappear into the trees. '*Fools*,' he whispered, 'the war is lost and still they carry out orders. Why would you still do that?'

He moved in the opposite direction – he would go to a friend's house before setting off. His mind went over the year just gone, and at that moment he realised that everyone else was benefiting from the war except him. The Englishman had seen through him; he was not the fool he had made him out to be. The bigger fool was Silvano, who defended him to the end. He knew that, sooner or later, he would be found out, so that last big payoff from Vito was well timed.

Silvano stepped from behind a tree at about the same time as gunfire came from further inside the woods. Enzo had no time to remove the rifle from his shoulder. Instead, he looked down the barrel of Silvano's weapon.

'Drop the rifle, Enzo … slowly.'

He did as he was asked, and his lips formed a smile, as a refusal to show fear.

'Silvano,' he said with a hint of surprise in his voice.

'Why, Enzo?'

He extended his arms wide. 'Who knows … Maybe I just did not want to be a poor peasant anymore. Maybe I was sick and tired of being told what to do.'

'But, surely, once you believed.'

'Yes, at first … but the Fascists and then the Germans … they all seemed to be eating well and filling their pockets … and us … well, we starved, lived in caves and slept on hard damp dirty floors. There comes a time when what you believe in comes a poor second …'

'But this was about getting a better life.'

'You still believe that horseshit, Silvano? Yes, the Germans will be pushed out and the Fascists will go … But who will replace them, people like that fucking Mason … the

Yanks … No, Silvano, it will not change. I will still be poor and people will still be telling me what to do.'

'You make me feel sad, Enzo.'

The older Italian began to laugh. 'Do you think that it was just me? Look at our fellow Partisans … Going around the countryside stealing, robbing, and in some cases, raping … They did not give a shit about Mussolini, the Fascists or the fucking Germans, it was a way of getting some money and putting food into empty bellies … Yes, they would kill some Germans and Fascists, but that was not what it was all about. You listened too much to your English friend. You are not Robin fucking Hood and we are not your merry men.'

'He was right about you …'

'Yes … yes, he was … To his credit.'

Silvano without warning threw down his rifle and drew his knife. Enzo looked puzzled at first, but slowly a smile came to his face.

'You're a bigger fool than I took you for, Silvano.'

There was another burst of gunfire not far off. Enzo drew his knife and turned to look in that direction. 'Two battles to be fought.'

'Yes, Enzo … Two lots of filth to be washed away.'

'You are a fool … There is no honour in war.'

'Only greed, it seems.'

'Man cannot live on bread alone.'

With those words Enzo dived forward, burying his head in Silvano's stomach. Both fell backwards, Enzo landing on top. They struggled to hold onto each other's knife hand. One moment, Enzo straddled Silvano, the next, it was Silvano looking down. Enzo feinted one way but went the other.

Silvano felt the blade slice open the skin below his ribs. He looked down at the blood staining his shirt.

Silvano stepped back and touched the wound, feeling the blood warm his fingers. Enzo grunted and spat to the floor, beckoning him to come forward. Silvano suddenly dropped to his knees and Enzo froze, a look of surprise on his face, uncertain what was happening. Had his knife done real damage? A split second later Silvano rolled forward and brought his knife upwards. It entered Enzo's body below his ribcage, before Silvano forced the blade up to pierce the man's heart.

Silvano gripped the knife tightly and felt Enzo's life slip away. There was a chilling silence; a gentle breeze stirred Silvano's hair and the pain in his side intensified. He heard gunfire from beyond the trees again, took out a cigarette and steadied himself. His hand trembled as he held the match. He lit the cigarette and sucked in the tobacco. He stood and looked down at Enzo's body, staring into the man's eyes, trying to make sense of it all. He bent down to reclaim his rifle and winced with pain. He needed to head towards the gunfire, there was still much to do.

~ ~ ~ ~

The seamstress, Simona Piro, sat with her fifteen-year-old daughter, Lisa. The girl sat pale-faced and shaking with fear, unable to speak. At the slightest noise she would tighten her grip and begin to sob. She had been given a rosary to calm her, and now she slid it between her fingers. Alfonso's wife came across in a desperate attempt to comfort the mother and child. All around the church, people sat quietly, while outside, the sound of orders being bellowed in harsh German voices could be heard.

In the distance, the sounds of battle came from the hillside, making many look around with a curious expression. Above the altar, Christ looked sympathetically down on the two raped girls, who were being attended to. Lorenzo looked up and caught Irene staring at him. Her smile reminded him of another life, one before the war, before the Fascists, before the Germans – a life that now seemed gone forever. Maybe Mario was the lucky one: closing his eyes, never to open them again on the horror that now engulfed Tuscany.

The sound of glass shattering brought him out of his wistful state. First one window, then another. He watched as a hand grenade rolled across the stone floor; time seemed to decelerate. Irene had also seen it, as had Simona, who instinctively pulled her daughter closer. A young child laughed, and Lorenzo watched in horror as she chased it under the pew.

The explosions came one after the other, breaking the calm with a fury. A mixture of smoke, flames and screams filled the once tranquil church. Another two entered through the already broken windows and Lorenzo found himself diving between the pews. The warm breeze released by the explosions caressed his face as his skin rested against the cold stone floor. He stared down along the wooden pews towards the front of the church. His eyes met Simona's daughter's, but life had long since gone from them. Her mother lay motionless by her side.

A fire took hold at the far end of the church and thick black clouds of smoke began to fill the air. Those uninjured got slowly to their feet; dazed, they squinted through the gloom.

On realising the situation, they began to panic, trampling over the dead and dying in an effort to save themselves. Lorenzo got to his feet and touched his forehead. He felt the warm moisture, then saw blood glistening on his hand.

Three people ran to the unlocked main doors, where a burst of machine-gun fire cut all three down in a matter of seconds. Others tried climbing through the broken windows, only to be met with rifle fire. Lorenzo felt anger rise in him as he heard laughter coming from outside, and the words, 'Goodbye, traitors.' There were Italian voices amongst the shouts of the Germans. He closed his eyes; it filled him with revulsion: surely no Italian would be part of this act of barbarism, Fascist or not ... These people were also Italians.

Lorenzo began to choke, smoke filled his eyes and tears poured from them. He focused on the dead bodies of the shopkeeper and his wife in front of him. With bile in his throat, he crouched low and moved towards the main doors: burn or be shot was the only choice available to him. He looked up and saw the pained expression of Christ on the cross looking down at this hell on earth. He quickly made the sign of the cross before choking again, his throat on fire. He reached the partially open doors and looked back inside the church. What choice did he have? He stumbled into the fading light. A volley of gunfire reverberated around the square outside.

~ ~ ~ ~

They had reached a small clearing in the woods. Behind them, what seemed like a battle, continued to rage. Gino collapsed to the ground and Sofia fell to her knees next to him. Isolina remained concerned they had not put enough distance between themselves and those in pursuit. She stared back beyond the trees and saw black smoke rising above them, making its way into the darkening evening sky. It came from the village.

'Mamma, Mamma,' Sofia screamed. 'He's stopped breathing.'

Isolina averted her eyes from the smoke and dropped to her knees. She placed a finger on his wrist and found a weak pulse, but it gave her no reason for optimism. She looked up at Sofia without smiling and her daughter's bottom lip began to tremble. Isolina had that awful sense of being powerless, the worst feeling a mother could ever have.

'Gino.' Sofia buried her head into his chest, weeping.

Isolina laid a hand on her daughter's back, stifling her own cry. Gino lay silent on the grass, his beautiful face taking on a peaceful look at that moment. Remove the cuts and bruises and you could be forgiven for thinking he was asleep. Above them, planes were heading in the direction of the village, where the sound of explosions could be heard, but they were oblivious to that.

Sofia's tears fell onto Gino's face. Isolina reached up and began to play with her daughter's hair. The sound of crying filled the warm evening air. Isolina had forgotten about those pursuing them. Another minute passed before Isolina felt again for signs of life, although she knew his body would be unresponsive. She laid her head on her daughter's back, took hold of Sofia and held on tight. They remained motionless amid this beautiful setting, amongst the green fields, rolling hillsides and cypress trees, as swallows flew in the cloudless Tuscan sky, looking down on them. In the distance … the sound of war.

~ ~ ~ ~

They walked in complete silence. Fino pushed another pram, its wheels squeaking with every turn. He expected to see a child's face staring back up at him. Instead, there was just an empty space. Planes flew overhead, but he did not feel the need to look up. Somehow, it did not seem so important now. Sassa stared at her husband, who cut a pitiful figure. She wanted to catch him up and place her arms around his neck, kiss him. Instead, she walked with one small child balanced on her hip, while another held her hand. The horizon was blood red; below, the hillside was a black silhouette. Sassa remembered a time before the war: walking out of her French doors to watch the sun set over their land. She closed her eyes and swallowed a cry.

The view remained firmly fixed in her head: fields of sunflowers, row after row of vines, cypress trees tall and proud. The fields were a kaleidoscope of colour, deep greens, yellows, rustic reds and pastel beiges, set in a valley surrounded by towering groups of hills, all overlaid by an intense blue ceiling. Fino would choose that moment to come up behind her and gently place his hands around her waist. She would feel his warm breath on her neck, and, closing her eyes, she would breathe in the perfumed Tuscan air, before feeling his tender kiss.

The child she was holding smiled and Sassa kissed her forehead. But her memories continued to come unabated. She remembered the chestnut tree that sat next to a crystal-clear stream, and the gentle rhythmic sound it made as it tumbled over rocks and pebbles before forming hundreds of miniature waterfalls – but now, anxiety gripped her: what would they find on their return? Would it feel the same? Would it have that same calm ambience, that individual character that made it *their* home?

The group came to a sudden halt. In the distance advanced a motorcade with trucks and jeeps travelling in single file. Fino, as always, walked to the head of their party and waited. The first lorry stopped and a soldier leapt from the passenger side. He walked towards them, flattening his hair before placing a cap over it.

'Anyone speak English?'

'Yes,' Fino answered. 'A little.'

'Good for you, old boy.'

Fino stared at the man wearing a khaki shirt and shorts, before shaking his hand. He was the cleanest soldier he had seen in months – even his boots shone in the late-evening sun.

'Captain Murray, Coldstream Guards.' He looked over Fino's head to those behind. 'Been rough?'

'You could say.'

Sassa came up and stood next to her husband.

'My wife, she speaks good English.'

'How do you do.' He smiled and placed a finger under the child's chin. 'You're a cute one.'

The child pulled a face and began to cry.

'My wife always said I scared children … don't know why. I think it's the uniform.'

'I understand,' Fino said. 'Where should we go? The children have not eaten since early this morning, and they have hardly had any water to drink.'

'I see,' said the captain. 'It's still a good walk, but we have our main headquarters about four miles away.' The captain surveyed the faces of those in front of him. The walk would be too far.

'Maybe I can get you a lift.' He smiled turned and shouted. 'Sergeant, empty one of the lorries, turn it around and get it up here … Chop, chop.'

'Yes, sir!'

The man began bellowing orders. Fino felt overcome with tiredness. He wanted to smile and thank the man for his kindness, but instead, found himself grabbing his chest, which felt as if someone was squeezing it.

'FINO …' Sassa screamed, putting the child down. 'Not now, Fino … not now.'

'Send the medics up,' shouted the captain, helping to lower Fino to the ground. 'On the double.'

Fino lay on the ground with Sassa cradling his head. She placed her mouth close to his ear and whispered into it. 'Don't leave me now … not now.'

~ ~ ~ ~

Tino stared at Silvano as he emerged from the trees.

'Enzo?'

Silvano just nodded, and Tino smiled.

'What happened here?'

'Ran into a group of Fascists.'

'This far up?'

'Yes.'

'Why?'

Silvano winced in pain.

'You need to get that looked at.'

'Later.' He was desperate to locate Isolina and Sofia. He looked back down in the direction of the village, noticing the smoke rising, and was gripped by a burning anxiety. 'Why this far up?' Silvano murmured under his breath. 'They were this far up for a reason ...' He looked towards the hillside and down again at the village, sensing that something was not right. 'They were after something or someone ... Tino, send three men to see what's up there, if anything.'

Tino gave the order then stared back at him. 'Luca?'

'Who knows?'

Silvano looked back in the direction of the village.

'You know many there?' Silvano asked.

'Yes,' Tino replied.

It was five minutes before one of the men returned, breathless. 'You should come and see.'

They weaved through the trees and bushes before entering a clearing. Silvano saw two of his men looking down on three figures, one of which lay prostrate. Silvano's heart skipped a beat. He saw Isolina on her knees, and kneeling next to her, Sofia, her daughter – no, *his* daughter. So, who was lying on the ground?

'Thank God.' The words leapt from his mouth. Isolina said nothing, she just kept her eyes fixed on Gino, while Sofia continued to weep. Isolina looked up and caught Silvano's eye; she gently shook her head.

Silvano knelt. 'What happened?'

Before Isolina could answer, Sofia turned her head to face him, her face wet with tears, her eyes bloodshot.

'This is your fault ...' There was hate in her eyes. 'He was just a boy ... just a boy, and he wanted to be like you and fight the Germans ... and now he's dead ...'

'Sofia,' Silvano whispered her name.

'Why isn't it you lying here? Because it *should* be.'

'Sofia,' Isolina tried to interrupt.

'It should be you ... Why isn't it you!' Sofia became hysterical, screaming abuse at Silvano.

Isolina folded her arms around her daughter. 'Shhh,' she whispered, kissing Sofia's face. Slowly, Sofia began to calm, burying her head inside her mother's chest. Isolina looked into Silvano's eyes; Sofia's words had wounded him and he seemed helpless at this moment in time, like a child, lost. Part of her wanted to go and comfort him.

Silvano heaved a deep sigh. 'Tino, send three men to where Mason was. I need to know what happened there.' He watched them leave. 'Go and get the other car,' he ordered, 'and come and pick up Gino. Bring him to the village.'

'No, you bastard, don't you touch him ... None of you touch him ...'

'Sofia!' Isolina whispered.

Her daughter stood, pushing her mother aside, and walked across to where Silvano now stood. She stared into his eyes, silent, tears continuing to stream down her cheeks. It was then she slapped him.

'Sofia, no!' Isolina shouted.

'Do it!' Silvano shouted at the man who had stopped. 'Now!'

Sofia held her ground and continued to stare. Silvano never took his eyes off her.

'How can you *live* with yourself?'

'If you want someone to blame, then I am pleased to offer my services ...'

'Bastard.'

'Please, Sofia.' Isolina came and stood next to her daughter, her eyes drifting back and forth to Silvano. 'It is not Silvano's fault ...' She stepped in front of her daughter.

'Blame those who started this, not those that have tried to end it. Gino understood, that is why he wanted to be like these brave men. He had seen what the Fascists had done, and what the Germans were doing, and he wanted to do something about it …'

Sofia looked exhausted.

'Let us take Gino down to the village.'

'I want him home, Mamma …'

'Home?'

'I want to bury him under the chestnut tree in the meadow, so each morning when I wake, I can see him.'

Isolina smiled. 'Then that is what we will do.' She looked at Silvano.

'Yes,' he whispered. 'I will have that done.'

'Thank you,' said Isolina, holding on to her child. 'You're hurt,' she addressed Silvano … she had seen the blood on his shirt.

'It's nothing … leave it.' He began to walk away.

'Luca … Silvano …' she began as he walked away.

He stopped and turned to face her.

'… He did not make it either … I'm sorry. He died saving us … If it were not for him, we would not be here now.'

Silvano bit his lip. 'He was a good man.'

'Yes, but he was just a boy, too,' Isolina added.

'I will have someone stay with Gino and you both. We must go down to the village.'

'I'm coming.'

'Are you sure? We don't know what we are going to find, Isolina.'

'I'm a nurse – don't you remember, Silvano? Was it that long ago?'

'Okay, let's go.'

'I want to come too,' Sofia said. 'I want to see …'

No one said a word. Finally, they made their way down the hillside.

~ ~ ~ ~

They entered the village where Isolina had left it. The smell of destruction hung heavy in the air, congesting their nostrils and making their eyes water. Luca's bloody body remained where it had fallen. Isolina stood and stared at it, allowing the memory of what had happened here to subside. She kissed Sofia and told her to wait, before walking the twenty metres slowly towards the young man's motionless body. She placed a hand across her mouth and inhaled on reaching him. She had seen many dreadful injuries as a nurse, but Luca's face and body had been mutilated. Ten, twenty shots had been fired into him, many at close range. It seemed that, in death, someone had abused him further. She looked around and found a discarded jacket to hide his face, then knelt by his side and prayed. Remembering the boy made her smile. Sofia joined her and sobbed quietly on her shoulder. The others gathered around, hats were removed and eyes lowered to the floor. Silvano wondered what other horrors lay in wait.

'Keep your rifles at the ready,' he ordered.

They made their way towards the main street.

'Let's go to the church.'

The group headed past the square, past Alfonso's shop, past the bar where Vito Sergi and his henchmen drank, before, at last, they reached the church. Even from this distance, they knew. The windows had been blown out and part of the wall had crumbled in the heat, smoke still hung in the air. The roof continued to smoulder, and the sight of more bodies brought the group to a sudden halt.

Mario's face greeted Isolina. He looked at peace and she prayed that that was the case. A bloody Father Remo lay with his arms wrapped around a young boy. Isolina and Sofia dropped to their knees, unable to take in the scene before them. Silvano reached out and let his fingers touch Isolina's shoulder.

'Spread out and see if anyone is still alive.' Silvano moved towards the church door. The body of a man lay across the doorway, his torso punctured with bullets. They halted and took in the sight that greeted them; a sight that filled each man with revulsion. The dead lay everywhere, body parts were strewed across the floor, while blood smeared the walls. Even for these war-hardened men, the sight was too much. Several turned away and vomited.

Men, woman, children, a village, a community, entire generations, wiped out in a matter of minutes. Silvano picked his way slowly through the devastation; he knew none of these people, but he knew that they were Italians, and that none had wanted or brought on this senseless war. All anyone in this village had wanted was to be left in peace, to simply go about their life in this beautiful part of the country.

Isolina, with Sofia clinging to her arm, walked towards the entrance. Silvano looked up and shook his head. Isolina acknowledged him. Taking hold of Sofia, she turned around and went and sat on the steps. Not one person had survived this senseless slaughter, while Christ continued to look down. How easy it would be to blame him – but his hand was not in this. For over a thousand years, God or no God, the human race had behaved like barbarians. God cannot be held responsible for all of humanity's shortcomings, Silvano thought. He stared the length of the church, to where Isolina and Sofia sat with their backs to the horror.

Isolina felt numb as she held her daughter. She hoped the girl was strong enough to overcome this traumatic period of her life. The pain of losing Gino would take time to heal; the passing of a loved one at any age was difficult to deal with, but at fifteen, it must feel as if her own life was ending too. Sofia was angry: angry with herself, angry with Silvano, the war, the world. When would the recovery begin, if indeed it ever would? She had seen Silvano: the war had begun to unravel him. It showed on his face and she heard it in his words. The burden of responsibility had been a heavy load to carry and she had only added to that load by telling him about Sofia.

And Sofia's words had achieved their aim. She had seen the pain in Silvano's face, wounds that would fester if not dealt with. Isolina herself had remained silent, and that act made her feel ashamed. Had time made her that callous, that uncaring? She had lived with this secret, and now she had to live with its consequences. She stood, watching the two people she loved the most, knowing that her own foolishness and jealousy had, in some way, caused this division. But, no matter how hard it was, she was glad that both now knew the truth.

~ ~ ~ ~

His breathing was constant and gentle now, but his eyes remained closed. Sassa sat next to him with one hand on his chest, another on his forehead. Probably for the hundredth time she whispered her love for him.

'He is doing well,' a voice came from behind her.

Sassa turned to see a young doctor standing there. He reminded her of Simon.

'Yes … Thank you.'

'No need to thank me. It was lucky that it happened when it did.'

'*Luck* …' Sassa said softly.

'What?'

'Luck: we seem to have had very little lately.'

'I see … Do you live near here?'

'Not too far.'

'I think it is beautiful … Tuscany. I want to bring my wife here as soon as the war ends. I'm certain she will love it.' He smiled and stared out of the window towards the hills.

Sassa smiled. 'You seem too young to have a wife.'

He laughed. 'I'm twenty-seven. I married Sofi two years ago in London, just before I came overseas – we weren't sure how things were going to go …' His voice trailed off.

Sassa thought of Isolina at that moment: the doctor's wife's name reminded her of Sofia. She became filled with apprehension. What had happened to all those people they had left behind?

'When you bring her, I want you to come and stay with Fino and me. I would love to meet your wife and show her Tuscany.'

'That is very nice of you … Have you room?'

'We have plenty. There is always room for visitors and guests at our home,' Sassa smiled.

'Then I will look forward to it. Thank you, you're very kind.'

'Good.'

The doctor continued on his round and Sassa turned back to face Fino. Her smile faded momentarily as she looked into his exhausted face, thinking about their home and what they were going to find on their return. Tiredness, both mental and physical, made her feel her age, and she struggled to regain a positive outlook on life.

What if it felt different on her return? What if the memories of recent times contained too much grief? What if all those other wonderful memories became diluted by these recent painful images? Because they were deep-seated and potent. Other images flooded into her mind: Anna, her head shaven, smiling; Simon sipping brandy with Fino on the terrace; Isolina surround by the children. These were the images that brought a smile. But, far more sinister images were lodged in her mind. The burning lorry, Anna's rape, the sight of the dead, blood-stained faces and the distressing screams of children. She saw the haunting face of Simon as they led him away, and tears gathered as she recalled the day they buried Anna. Memories of that time would never erode; memories they would have to live with. The war had cast a giant shadow over their home. What if those dark clouds could not be lifted?

Fino opened his eyes at that moment and smiled.

'Hello,' he whispered.

'Hello.' She covered his hand.

'I was thinking …'

'Really.' She held back her tears.

'Yes, I can still manage that.'

'I don't doubt it.'

'When we get back home …'

Sassa felt a chill encase her.

'... let us contact that English gardener ... let's finish what was started, Sassa. Let's plant new trees, new flowerbeds. Let's fill it with wonderful colour.' His voice grew stronger as he spoke. 'Get me some paper, Sassa, I have an idea ... Come, move ...' He grinned at her as she got to her feet.

'Wait there, then.'

'Why, did you think I was going anywhere without you?'

'No.' She smiled, then turned away and allowed the tears to spill down her cheeks. 'Let me get your paper.'

'Sassa,' he called out as she reached the doorway.

'Yes, Fino.'

'I feel the best is yet to come, Sassa. After everything, after all of this, we have each other, we have our home, our garden, our fields and our hills ... We have more than most, Sassa, let us be grateful ... Many have nothing left to go back to; let's be thankful.'

Sassa's lips trembled as she listened to his words: they were like drops of rain watering the seeds of optimism. It was negligible, but yes, she thought, let's be thankful for what we have.

~ ~ ~ ~

British troops entered the village from both sides. Silvano watched them arrive as he sat with Tino, smoking by the side of the road. Isolina and Sofia had gone back to their home; he would join them later. As head of the resistance in this area, he needed to speak to someone in charge of the Allies, although, it seemed that no one wanted to speak with him.

'So, what do you think happened to him?' Tino asked.

Silvano shook his head and stamped on his finished cigarette. 'I wish I knew.' He held several pieces of folded paper.

'They looked for another body, after finding Ambra and Alfeo – but there was no sign of the Englishman.'

Silvano had been given Mason's sketchbook. It had been found on the hillside. He unfolded a loose sheet of paper, which revealed a charcoal drawing of Sofia. Her beautiful face stared back at him; the face of his daughter, his creation. Remembering how angry she was with him, the words she had used – the loathing in her eyes – he began to re-fold the sheet, ready to replace it in the book. As he did so, he noticed the face of Ambra, surrounded by his group of Partisans. When had Mason drawn this?

Another page revealed sketches of Isolina, some with her hair up, while others showed her curls resting on her shoulders. Mason had sketched her standing amongst the vines, and sitting on a wooden stool, her hair blowing in the breeze as she looked down upon the valley. Another saw her hair spread across a pillow, and he felt a stab of jealousy take hold. Had they been drawn from memory, or imagination? A British officer chose that moment to speak to him.

It was a full hour before Silvano could get away after answering the many questions fired at him about Mason. They seemed desperate to discover his fate.

He pulled up at Isolina's just as two of his men came from the fields carrying shovels.

'Is it done?'

They nodded.

'Are they still down there?'

'Yes … The girl is taking it very badly, Silvano.'

He looked down to where mother and daughter stood together under the large chestnut tree.

'Silvano.' The older man spoke.

'Yes.'

'I have heard the rumours ...' The man stopped to carefully consider his words. 'It is times like these that a father should be near.'

Silvano looked up and met his stare. 'But ... I don't think ...'

The man smiled. 'You have so much to learn, Silvano. Stop being a Partisan leader today, maybe tomorrow ... But today, be what you are, a father, and go and help ease her pain.'

'But I am the cause, am I not?'

'And the cure.'

With that, the two men walked to the waiting truck. Tino sat on the bonnet of the car smoking, saying nothing. The old man had said it all.

Silvano walked through the gap in the fence and came to an abrupt halt. He fought the urge to turn back and took several tentative steps forward. Isolina and Sofia stood facing each other down in the dip of the field. Neither looked in his direction, which pleased him. He felt a discomfort attach itself to him. As he began an apprehensive walk down the hill, he was reminded of the day he had paced the platform of Florence station. They chose this moment to look in his direction, and it was as if the train was about to leave again. He needed to make his choice all over again.

Isolina kissed Sofia's forehead and began walking towards him. He stood motionless, a sick feeling in his stomach, watching her approach. That imaginary train had begun to pull away … Isolina reached out a hand to him. He took hold of it.

'Go to her, Silvano.'

He looked over to where Sofia stood, alone.

'Go to her, now …'

'But –'

'I have told her … I have told her everything.'

'Everything?'

'No more lies, Silvano. They have cost us dearly. No more lies, no more secrets.'

'Is she …'

'Go and talk to her and find out.'

'Are you not …'

'No.' She shook her head. 'Time for you and your daughter to be together. I have had that privilege for fifteen years. Now it is your turn to get to know her.' She smiled.

He stared again in Sofia's direction.

'*Go*,' Isolina whispered. 'Let's not lose any more time, it is too precious … I will be waiting.' She allowed his fingers to slip from hers, glancing once more to where her daughter stood waiting. Then she continued her walk to the house.

On reaching the picket fence, she turned and watched as they came together. A smile reached her lips as conflicting emotions engulfed her: sadness that so much time had been lost; delight that it was still possible to make up that time.

Tino walked over and stood beside her. 'At least some good may come from all this misery.'

Isolina continued to observe the pair. 'Yes,' she whispered.

'Do you think Silvano will want me to wait?'

They watched as Silvano and Sofia suddenly embraced.

'Maybe not,' Tino answered his own question. 'Tell him I will drive here tomorrow morning.' He strolled away whistling.

Isolina watched. Her eyes filled with moisture that glistened in the last of the day's sunlight. She turned, wiping away the tears that had finally spilt over, and walked towards the house. A sudden gust of wind forced the barn doors together, and Isolina froze. It was then she thought of Mason.

THE END